W9-CEE-939

GOOD-BYE TO LONELY NIGHTS. GOOD-BYE TO MY WORLD OF FANTASY AND DREAMS . . .

Good-bye to my father's face of pity and to my own forlorn look in the mirror. A man, most handsome and elegant, had come calling and then had asked for my hand in marriage.

I hurried upstairs and sat before the dollhouse. I would live in a big house with servants. We would entertain with elaborate dinner parties. In time we would be envied by all.

"Just like I have envied you," I said to the porcelain family within the dollhouse.

I was to become Olivia Foxworth, Mrs. Malcolm Neal Foxworth. My life would no longer be colored gray. No, from now on it would be blue—blue as the sun-filled skies of a cloudless day. Blue as Malcolm's eyes.

Like any woman stupidly believing in love, I never realized that the blue sky I saw was not the soft, nurturing sky of spring, but the cold, chilling, lonely sky of winter . . .

V.C. Andrews® Books

Flowers in the Attic
Petals on the Wind
If There Be Thorns
My Sweet Audrina
Seeds of Yesterday
Heaven
Dark Angel
Garden of Shadows
Fallen Hearts
Gates of Paradise
Web of Dreams
Dawn
Secrets of the Morning
Twilight's Child
Midnight Whispers
Darkest Hour
Ruby
Pearl in the Mist
All That Glitters
Hidden Jewel
Tarnished Gold
Melody

Published by POCKET BOOKS

For orders other than by individual consumers, Pocket Books grants a discount on the purchase of **10 or more** copies of single titles for special markets or premium use. For further details, please write to the Vice-President of Special Markets, Pocket Books, 1633 Broadway, New York, NY 10019-6785 8th Floor.

For information on how individual consumers can place orders, please write to Mail Order Department, Simon & Schuster, Inc., 200 Old Tappan Road, Old Tappan, NJ 07675.

V.C. Andrews®

Garden of Shadows

POCKET BOOKS
New York London Toronto Sydney Tokyo Singapore

The sale of this book without its cover is unauthorized. If you purchased this book without a cover, you should be aware that it was reported to the publisher as "unsold and destroyed." Neither the author nor the publisher has received payment for the sale of this "stripped book."

Following the death of Virginia Andrews, the Andrews family worked with a carefully selected writer to organize and complete Virginia Andrews' stories and to create additional novels, of which this is one, inspired by her storytelling genius.

This book is a work of fiction. Names, characters, places and incidents are either the product of the author's imagination or are used fictitiously. Any resemblance to actual events or locales or persons, living or dead, is entirely coincidental.

An *Original* Publication of POCKET BOOKS

POCKET BOOKS, a division of Simon & Schuster Inc.
1230 Avenue of the Americas, New York, NY 10020

Copyright © 1987 by Vanda Productions, Ltd.
Cover art copyright © 1987 Steve Huston

All rights reserved, including the right to reproduce this book or portions thereof in any form whatsoever. For information address Pocket Books, 1230 Avenue of the Americas, New York, NY 10020

ISBN: 0-671-72942-X

First Pocket Books printing November 1987

20 19 18

POCKET and colophon are registered trademarks of Simon & Schuster Inc.

Virginia Andrews is a registered trademark of the Virginia C. Andrews Trust.

Printed in the U.S.A.

Prologue

ADDENDUM TO THE LAST WILL AND TESTAMENT OF OLIVIA WINFIELD FOXWORTH. TO BE OPENED TWENTY YEARS AFTER MY DEATH.

I have been forced to leave this record. Had others not decided to tell my story for their own gain, the secrets of the Foxworths would have been buried in my grave with me. Cruelty comes in many forms—ignorance is one of them. Because of ignorance, I have been judged. Now I have gone to Him, the only judge whose verdict matters, and accepted His pronouncement on my soul. Those of you who remain below will here come to know the true story. And knowing the truth, judge me if you dare.

Olivia Winfield Foxworth

PART I

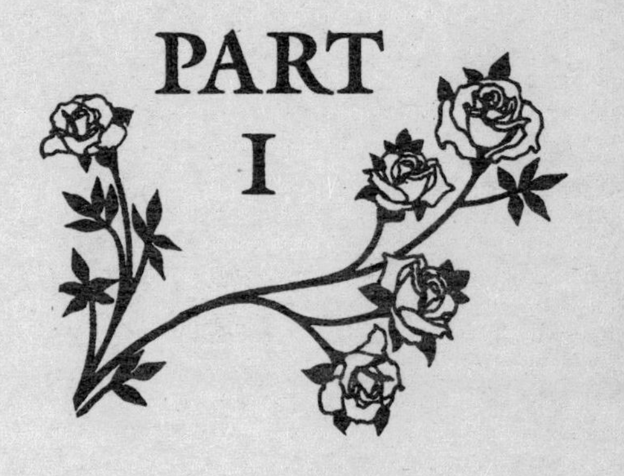

1

The First Bud of Spring

WHEN I WAS A LITTLE GIRL, MY FATHER BOUGHT ME A priceless handcrafted dollhouse. It was a magical miniature world, with beautiful tiny porcelain dolls, furniture, even paintings and chandeliers and rugs all made to scale. But the house was enclosed in a glass case and I was never allowed to touch the family inside—indeed, I was not even permitted to touch the glass case, for fear of leaving smudges. Dainty things had always been at peril in my large hands, and the dollhouse was for me to admire but never to touch.

I kept it on an oak table under the sash of stained-glass windows in my bedroom. The sun coming through the tinted windows always spread a soft, rainbow-colored sky over the tiny universe and put the light of happiness into the faces of the miniature family. Even the servants in the kitchen, the butler dressed in white livery who stood near the entrance door, and the nanny in the nursery all wore looks of contentment.

That was as it should be, as it should always be—as I

fervently hoped and prayed it would be for me someday. That miniature world was without shadows; for, even on overcast days, when clouds hung their gloom outside, the tinted-glass windows magically turned the gray light into rainbows.

The real world, my own world, seemed always to be gray, without rainbows. Gray for my eyes, which I had always been told were too stern, gray for my hopes, gray for the old maid no one wanted in the deck of cards. At twenty-four, I was an old maid, already a spinster. It seemed I intimidated eligible young men with my height and intelligence. It seemed that the rainbow world of love and marriage and babies would always be as closed off to me as that dollhouse I so admired. For it was only in make-believe that my hopes took wing.

In my fantasies I was pretty, lighthearted, charming, like the other young women I had met but never befriended. Mine was a lonely life, filled mostly with books and dreams. And though I did not talk about it, I clung to the small hope my dear mother had given me just before she died.

"Life is very much like a garden, Olivia. And people are like tiny seeds, nurtured by love and friendship and caring. And if enough time and care are spent, they bloom into gorgeous flowers. And sometimes, even an old, neglected plant left in a yard gone to seed will unexpectedly burst into blossom. These are the most precious, the most cherished blossoms of all. You will be that sort of flower, Olivia. It may take time, but your flowering will come."

How I missed my optimistic mother. I was sixteen when she died—just when I most needed to have those woman-to-woman talks with her that would tell me how to win a man's heart, how to be like her: respectable, competent, yet a woman in every way. My mother was forever involved in one thing or another, and in everything she was competent and in charge. She threaded her way through each crisis, and when one ended, there was always another to replace it. My father seemed content that she was busy. It mattered not with what.

He often said that just because women weren't involved in serious business, that didn't mean they should be idle. They had their "womanly" things to do.

Yet, when it came to me, he encouraged me to go to business school. It seemed right and proper that I would become his private accountant, that he would give me a place in his den, a manly room with one wall covered with firearms and another with pictures from his hunting and fishing expeditions, a room that always had the odor of cigar smoke and whiskey, its dark brown rug the most worn-looking of any rug in the house. He set aside a portion of his large black oakwood desk for me to work meticulously on his accounts, his business expenses, his employees' wages, and even his household expenses. Working with my father, I often felt more like the son he had always longed for—but never got—than the daughter I was. Oh, I did want to please, but it seemed I would never be just what anyone wanted.

He used to say I would be a great help to any husband, and I used to believe that was why he was so determined I would get a business education and have that experience. He didn't come out and say it in so many words, but I could hear them anyway—a woman six feet tall needed something more to capture a man's love.

Yes, I was six feet tall; I had shot up as a teenager, much to my dismay, to giant proportions. I was the beanstalk in Jack's garden. I was the giant. There was nothing dainty or fragile about me.

I had my mother's auburn hair, but my shoulders were too wide and my bosom large. I often stood before my mirror and wished my arms shorter. My gray eyes were too long and catlike and my nose was too sharp. My lips were thin, my complexion pale and gray. Gray, gray, gray. How I longed to be pretty and bright. But when I sat before my vanilla marble vanity table trying to blush and to flutter my eyelashes—look flirtatious—I managed only to look a fool. I didn't want to look empty-headed and silly, yet I couldn't help but sit before the glass-encased dollhouse and study the pretty, delicate porcelain face of the tiny wife. How I wished it were my face. Maybe then this would be my world.

But it was not.

And so I left my hope encased with the porcelain figures and went about my way.

If my father had really expected to make me more attractive to a man by providing me with an education and practical business experience, he must have been sorely disappointed in the result. Gentlemen came and went, all coming because of his manipulations, I discovered; and still I was yet to be courted and loved. I was always afraid that my money, my father's money, money I would inherit, would bring a man to the door pretending to be in love with me. I think my father feared the same thing, because he came to me one day and said, "I have written into my will that whatever money you receive shall be only yours and yours to do with what you like. No husband will ever expect to take control of your fortune simply by marrying you."

He made his announcement and left before I could even respond. Then he screened any candidates for my romance carefully, exposing me only to the highest class of gentleman, men of some fortune themselves. I had yet to meet one I didn't tower over, or one who wouldn't scowl at the things I said. It seemed I'd die a spinster.

But my father wouldn't have it so.

"There's a young man coming to dinner tonight," he began one Friday morning late in April, "who I must say is one of the most impressive I've met. I want you to wear that blue dress you had made for yourself last Easter."

"Oh, Father." It was on the tip of my tongue to say, "Why bother," but he anticipated my reaction.

"Don't argue about it, and for heaven's sake don't start in on the woman suffrage movement when we're at the table."

My eyes flamed. He knew how I hated to be bridled like one of his horses.

"A man no sooner shows some interest in you than you challenge the most treasured of manly privileges. It never fails. The blue dress," he repeated, and pivoted and left before I could offer an argument.

It seemed pointless to me to go through the rituals at my vanity table. I shampooed my hair vigorously and then sat down to brush it a hundred times, softening it and pinning it back neatly but not too harsh with the ivory combs my father had given me for Christmas the previous year.

My father didn't know or even seem to recognize that

I had commissioned the "blue dress" because I wanted a dress that looked like the dresses women wore in fashion photographs. The bodice was low enough to expose some of the fullness of my bosom, and the tight waist gave me a suggestion of an "hourglass" figure. It was made of silk, and the material was exceptionally soft and had a sheen to it like nothing else I owned. The sleeves were cut just above the elbow. I thought that made my arms look shorter.

I put on my mother's blue sapphire pendant, which I thought made my neck look slimmer. There was a blush in my cheeks but I couldn't say if it was there because of my healthy body or because of my nervousness. I was nervous. I'd been through enough of those evenings before—watching the man's face fall as he rose to greet me and I towered over him.

I was merely rehearsing for another failure.

By the time I went downstairs, my father's guest had arrived. They were together in the den. I heard my father's loud laughter, and then I heard the gentleman's voice, low but deeply resonant, the voice of a man with some confidence. I pressed my palms against my hips to dry off the wetness and proceeded to the doorway of the den.

The moment I appeared, Malcolm Neal Foxworth stood up and my heart skipped a beat. He was at least six foot two and easily the most handsome young man who had ever come to our house.

"Malcolm," my father said, "I'm proud to present my lovely daughter."

He took my hand and said, "Charmed, Miss Winfield."

I was looking directly into his sky-blue eyes. And he was gazing just as forthrightly into mine. I'd never believed in schoolgirl romantic notions such as love at first sight, but I felt his gaze slide right over my heart and lodge in the pit of my stomach.

He had flaxen blond hair, a little longer in the back than most men wore, but the strands were brushed neatly and looked heavenly light. He had a strong Roman nose and a thin straight mouth. Broad-shouldered, slim-hipped, he had an almost athletic air about him. And I could tell by the way he was gazing at me, with almost a wry smile of amusement, that he was quite accustomed to women falling into a flutter about him. Well, I thought, I mustn't give him something more to be amused at Olivia Winfield. Of course, such a man would hardly give me the time of day, and I would have to get through another evening of Father's doomed matchmaking. I shook his hand firmly, smiled back, and quickly looked away.

After we were introduced, my father explained that Malcolm had come to New London from Yale, where he had attended a class reunion. He was interested in investing in the shipbuilding industry because he believed that with the Great War over, the markets for exporting would develop. From what I learned of his background that night, I understood that he already owned a number of cloth factories, had commanding interest in a few banks, and owned some lumber mills in Virginia. He was in business with his father, but his father, even though he was only fifty-five, was distracted. I didn't learn until later what that meant.

At dinner I tried to be the polite, quiet observer that my father wanted me to be, the way my mother used to be. Margaret and Philip, our servants, served an elegant dinner of beef Wellington, a menu my father had chosen himself. He did so only on special occasions. I thought my father was being quite obvious when he said, "Olivia's a college graduate, you know. She has a business degree and handles a major portion of my bookkeeping."

"Really?" Malcolm seemed genuinely impressed. His cerulean blue eyes brightened even more with interest and I felt he was taking a second, more serious look at me. "Do you enjoy the work, Miss Winfield?"

I shot a glance at my father, who sat back in his high-backed light-maple chair and nodded as if prompting my responses. I did so want this Malcolm Foxworth to like me, but I was determined to be who I was.

"It's better to fill your time with sensible and productive things," I said. "Even for a woman."

My father's smile faded, but Malcolm's widened. "I totally agree," he said. He didn't turn back to my father. "I find most so-called beautiful women vapid and rather silly. It's as if their good looks are enough to see them through life. I prefer intelligent women who know how to think for themselves, women who can be real assets to their husbands."

My father cleared his throat. "Yes, yes," he said, and turned the conversation back to the shipping industry. He had it from good sources that the merchant marine fleet, built for the war effort, would soon be offered to private owners. His topic took Malcolm's attention for most of the dinner, but nevertheless, I felt Malcolm's eyes on me and at times, when I looked up at him, he was smiling at me.

Never had I sat with one of my father's guests and been so enraptured. Never had I felt as welcome at the table. Malcolm was polite to my father, but it was clear to me that he wanted to talk more to me.

To me!

The handsomest man ever to come to our house was interested in me? But he could have a hundred beautiful girls to adore him forever. Why should he be interested in a Plain Jane such as I? But oh how I wanted to believe I wasn't imagining all those side glances, those times he asked me to pass him things he could have easily gotten himself, the way he tried to bring me into the conversation. Perhaps, just for a few hours I could allow my slight bud of hope to blossom. Just for tonight! Tomorrow I'd let it gray again.

After dinner Malcolm and my father adjourned to the den to smoke their cigars and talk more about the investments Malcolm wanted to make. With them my hopes, so briefly flowered, so quickly withered. Of course Malcolm wasn't interested in me—he was interested in business with my father. They would be in there for the rest of the evening. I might as well retire to my room to read that new novel that was attracting attention, Edith Wharton's *Age of Innocence*. But I decided instead to bring the book down to the sitting room and read by the Tiffany lamp, happy to see Malcolm just to say good-bye.

It was very quiet on our street that time of evening, but I looked up to see a couple walking arm in arm. It was the way the husband and wife in my glass-encased doll world would walk if they could escape their imprisonment, I thought. I watched them until they disappeared around the corner. How I wished I could someday walk with a man like that—a man like Malcolm. But it was not to be. It seemed God was deaf to my hopes and prayers for love. I sighed. As I turned back to my book, I realized all I could know of love and life would be from books.

Then I spied Malcolm in the doorway. Why, he had been watching me! He stood so straight and still, his shoulders drawn back, his head high. There was a calculating look in his eyes, as if he were sizing me up unawares, but I didn't know what to make of it.

"Oh!" My surprise brought heat to my cheeks. My heart began to thump so loudly, I thought he might even hear it across the room.

"It is a lovely evening," he said. "Could I interest you in a walk?"

For a moment I just stared. He wanted to take me out walking!

"Yes," I said. I could see he liked the way I came to a quick decision. I didn't try to flutter my eyelashes or act uncertain to tease him with my answer. I wanted to go for a walk and I wanted very much to go for a walk with *him*. If I had a hope that what appeared to be his interest in me would flower, I was going to be just who I was. "I'll just run up and get my coat." I was glad for a reason to go off and catch my breath.

Malcolm was waiting at the front door when I returned. Philip had gotten him his overcoat and stood beside him waiting to open the door. I wondered where my father was and if this was something he might have arranged. But even though I knew Malcolm only a short while, I believed he was not a man to do something he didn't want to do.

When Philip opened the front door, I caught a look of satisfaction in his eyes. He approved of this gentleman.

Malcolm took my arm and escorted me down the six front steps. Both of us were quiet as we proceeded down the walkway until we reached the front gate. Malcolm opened the gate and stepped back to permit me to pass through first. It was a cool April evening, with just a hint of spring in the air. The trees by the gate still reached into the sky with bare gray arms, but their arms were softened by hundreds of tiny buds about to spring to life. Yet winter's chill still hung in the air, still hung in me. For a crazy moment I wished to turn to Malcolm and bury myself in his arms, something I'd certainly never done with a man, not even my father. I determinedly walked ahead and pointed toward the river.

"If we go to the end of the street here," I said, "and turn right, we have a beautiful view of the Thames River."

"Fine," he said.

It was always a fantasy of mine to walk along the banks of the river on a spring evening with a man who was falling in love with me. I was a blur of emotion—so many hopes and fears, confusion, frightening feelings moving through my body, I felt dizzy. But I couldn't let Malcolm see my agitation, so I kept my bearing straight, my head high as we walked. The lights of the ships moved up and down with their cargo. On a night as dark as that one was, the lights on the water in the distance looked like fireflies caught in cobwebs.

"Rather beautiful view," he said.

"Yes."

"How is it," he said, "that your father hasn't married you off yet? I won't insult your intelligence and tell you that you're beautiful; but you are extremely attractive and it's quite apparent that you have an extraordinary mind. How is it no man has captured you yet?"

"How is it you haven't taken a wife?" I responded.

He laughed. "Answer a question with a question. Well, Miss Winfield," he said, "if you must know, I find most women today tedious with their effort to be beguiling. A man who is serious about his life, who is determined to build something significant of himself and his family, must, it seems to me, avoid this type."

"And this is the only kind of woman you've known?" I asked. I couldn't see precisely, of course, but I felt he blushed. "Haven't you searched for others?"

"No. I've been too occupied with my business."

We paused, and he looked out at the ships.

"If I may be a little forward," he went on, "I feel you and I share some things in common. From what your father tells me and from what I can observe, you are a serious-minded person, pragmatic and diligent. You appreciate the business world already, and therefore you are already head and shoulders above most women in this country today."

"Because of the way most men have treated them," I said quickly. I nearly bit my lip. I wasn't going to express my controversial opinions, but the words just seemed to form on my lips by themselves.

"I don't know. Maybe," he said quickly. "The point is, it's true. And you know," he said, taking my elbow gently and turning me so we would walk on, "we have other things in common as well. We both lost our mothers at an early age. Your father explained your circumstances," he added quickly, "so I hope you don't feel I'm intruding."

"No. You lost your mother at an early age?"

"Five." His voice grew somber and faraway.

"Oh, how hard it must have been."

"Sometimes," he said, "the harder things are, the better we become. Or should I say, the tougher." Indeed, he did sound tough when he said that, so cold that I feared to ask him more.

We walked on that night. I listened to him talk about his various enterprises. We had a little discussion about the upcoming presidential elections and he was surprised at how informed I was about the candidates vying for the Republican and Democratic nominations.

I was sorry when we reached my house so soon, but then I thought, at least I had my walk with a handsome young man. I thought it would be left at that.

But at the doorway he asked if he could call again.

"I feel as if I have dominated the evening with my conversation," he said. "I'd like to be more of a listener next time."

Was I hearing right? A man wanted to hear *me* talk, wanted to know *my* thoughts?

"You could call tomorrow," I said. I suppose I sounded as eager as a schoolgirl. He didn't smile or laugh.

"Fine," he said. "There's a good seafood restaurant where I am staying. Perhaps we could have dinner."

Dinner? An actual date. Of course, I agreed. I wanted to watch him get into his car and drive off, but I couldn't do anything so obvious. When I reentered the house, my father was standing in the den doorway.

"Interesting young man," he said. "Something of a business genius, I'd say. And good-looking, too, eh?"

"Yes, Father," I said.

He chuckled.

"He's coming to call tomorrow and we're going to dinner."

His smile faded. His face took on that look of serious hope I had seen before.

"Really? Well, what do you know? What do you know?"

"I don't know what to tell you, Father."

I couldn't contain myself anymore. I had to excuse myself and go upstairs. For a while I simply sat in my room staring at myself in the mirror. What had I done differently? My hair was the same.

I pulled my shoulders back. I had a tendency to turn them in because they were so wide. I knew it was bad posture and Malcolm had such good posture, such confident posture. He didn't seem to see my inadequacies and imperfections, and it was so good not having to look down at a man.

And he had told me I was very attractive, implied that I was desirable to men. Maybe I had underestimated myself all those years. Maybe I had unnecessarily accepted a dreadful fate?

Of course, I tried chastising myself, warning myself. A man who's been to dinner has asked you out. It doesn't have to mean he has romantic inclinations. Maybe he's just lonely here.

No, I thought, we'll have dinner, talk some more, and he will be gone. Perhaps, some distant day, on some occasion, like Christmas, I'll receive a card from him, on which he will write, "Belated thanks for your fine conversation. Happiest of holidays. Malcolm."

My heart fluttered in fear. I went out to the glass-enclosed dollhouse and looked for the hope I left encased there. Then I went to sleep dreaming about the porcelain figures. I was one of them. I was the happy wife—and Malcolm, he was the handsome husband.

Our dinner date was elegant. I tried not to overdress, but everything I picked out to wear looked so plain. It was my own fault for not caring enough about my wardrobe. In the end I chose the gown I had worn to a wedding reception last year. Perhaps it would bring me good luck, I thought.

Malcolm said I looked nice, but the conversation at dinner quickly turned to more mundane things. He wanted to know all about the work I did for my father and he made me elaborate in detail. I was afraid the conversation would prove boring, but he showed such interest that I went on and on. Apparently, he was quite impressed with my knowledge of my father's affairs.

"Tell me," he asked when we returned to my house, "what do you do to entertain yourself?" At last the conversation was to be more personal; at last there was interest in me.

"I read a great deal. I listen to music. I take walks. My one sport is horseback riding."

"Oh, really. I own a number of horses, and Foxworth Hall, my home, is situated on grounds that would fascinate any explorer of nature."

"It sounds wonderful," I said.

He saw me to the door and, once again, I thought this would be the end. But he surprised me.

"I suppose you know I will be joining you and your father to attend church tomorrow."

"No," I said. "I didn't know."

"Well, I look forward to it," he added. "I must thank you for a most enjoyable evening."

"I enjoyed it too," I said, and waited. Was this the moment when the man was supposed to kiss the woman? How I regretted not having a close girlfriend in whom I could confide and with whom I could discuss the affairs between men and women, but all the girls I had known in school were married and gone.

Was I supposed to do something to encourage him? Lean toward him, pause dramatically, smile in some way? I felt so lost, standing before the door, waiting.

"Until the morning, then," he said, tipped his hat, and went down the steps to his car.

I opened the door and rushed into the house, feeling both excited and disappointed. My father was in the sitting room, reading the paper, pretending to be interested in other things; but I knew he was waiting to hear about my date. I made up my mind I would not give him a review. It made me feel more like someone auditioning and I didn't like all these expectations.

What could I tell him anyway? Malcolm took me out to dinner. We talked a great deal. Rather, I talked a great deal and he listened. Maybe he thought I was a chatterbox after all, even though my conversation was about things in which he showed some interest. I'm sure I talked so much because I was so nervous. In a way I was grateful for his questions about business. That was a subject on which I could expand.

I could have talked about books, of course, or horses, but it wasn't until just now that I learned he had any interests in anything other than making money.

So what would I tell my father? The dinner was wonderful. I tried not to eat too much, even though I could have eaten more. I tried to look dainty and feminine and even refused to order dessert. It was he who insisted.

"Did you have a good time?" my father asked quickly. He saw I would just go right up to my room.

"Yes, but why didn't you tell me you had invited him to join us for church?"

"Oh, didn't I?"

"Father, despite your expertise in business, you're

not a good liar," I said. He roared. I even laughed a bit myself.

Why should I be mad anyway? I thought. I knew what he was doing and I wanted him to do it.

"I'm going to sleep," I said, thinking about how early I would get up the next morning. I had to take extra pains with my appearance for church.

Before I fell asleep that night, I reviewed every moment of my date with Malcolm, condemning myself for this, congratulating myself for that. And when I recalled our moments at the door, I imagined that he did kiss me.

Never was I as nervous about going to church as I was that morning. I couldn't eat a thing at breakfast. I rushed about, not quite confident about my dress, not sure about my hair. When the time finally came to leave and Malcolm had arrived, my heart was beating so rapidly, I thought I would go into a faint and collapse on the stairway.

"Good morning, Olivia," he said, and looked quite satisfied with my appearance. I didn't even realize until we were all in the car and on the way to church that he had called me "Olivia" and not "Miss Winfield."

It was a lovely, warm spring day, really the first warm Sunday of the year. All the young ladies were dressed in their new spring dresses with veiled hats and parasols. And the families all looked so fresh, with the children scampering about in the sun, waiting to go in to the service. As we stepped from the car, it seemed all those gathered turned to look at me. Me, Olivia Winfield, arriving at church on a fine Sunday morning with my father and a strikingly handsome young man. Yes, I wanted to scream, yes, it's me! See? But of course I would never stoop to such guttersnipe behavior. I stood straighter, taller, and held my chin high as we walked directly from the car and into the dark, musky church. Most had stayed outdoors to enjoy the sun, so we had our choice of pews, and Malcolm led us directly to the very front seats. We sat silently as we waited for the sermon to begin. Never had I had such difficulty following the sermon; never did I feel so self-conscious about the sound of my voice when we stood to sing the hymns. Yet Malcolm sang out clearly and loudly, and recited the Lord's Prayer at the end in a deep, strong voice. Then he turned to me and took my arm to escort me out. How proud I felt walking down the aisle with him.

Of course, I saw the way other members of the congregation were watching us and wondering who was the handsome young man accompanying the Winfields and standing beside Olivia Winfield?

We left a stream of chatter behind us and I knew that Malcolm's appearance would be the subject of parlor talk all day.

That afternoon we went horseback riding. It was the first time I had gone horseback riding alone with a man and I found his company invigorating. He rode like an experienced English huntsman. He seemed to enjoy the way I could keep up with him.

He came to Sunday dinner and we took another walk along the river. For the first part of the walk I found him more quiet than ever and I anticipated the announcement of his departure. Perhaps he would promise to write. Actually, I was hoping for that promise, even if he didn't hold to it. At least I would have something to look forward to. I would cherish every one of his letters, should there be more than one.

"Look here, Miss Winfield," he suddenly began. I didn't like his reverting back to calling me Miss Winfield. I thought that was a dark omen. But it wasn't. "I don't see the point in two people who have so much in common, two sensible people, that is, delaying and unnecessarily prolonging a relationship just to arrive at the point they both agree would be best."

"Point?"

"I'm speaking of marriage," he said. "One of the most holy sacraments, something that must never be taken lightly. Marriage is more than the logical result of a romance; it's a contractual union, teamwork. A man has to know that his wife is part of the effort, someone on whom he can depend. Contrary to what some men think, my father included, a man must have a woman who has strength. I'm impressed with you, Miss Winfield. I would like your permission to ask your father for your hand in marriage."

For a moment I could not speak. Malcolm Neal Foxworth, six feet two inches tall, as handsome a man as there could be, a man of intelligence, wealth, and looks, wanted to marry me? And we were standing on the bank of the river with the stars above us more brilliant than ever. Had I wandered into one of my own dreams?

"Well . . . ," I said. I brought my hand to my throat and looked at him. I was at a loss for words. I didn't know how to phrase my response.

"I realize this seems rather sudden, but I'm a man with a destiny who has the good fortune to realize almost immediately what is valuable and what is not. My instincts have always proven reliable. I am confident that this proposal will be a good one for both of us. If you can place your trust in that . . ."

"Yes, Malcolm. I can," I said quickly, perhaps too quickly.

"Good. Thank you," he said.

I waited. This was surely the moment for us to kiss. We should consummate our faith in each other under the stars. But maybe I was being childishly romantic. Malcolm was the kind to do things properly, correctly. I had to have faith in that too.

"Then, if you will, let us return to your home so that I can speak to your father," he said. He did take my arm and draw me closer to him. As we walked back to my father's house, I thought about the couple I had seen strolling on the street that first night he came to dinner. My dream had come true. For the first time in my life, I felt truly happy.

My father waited in his den as if he had anticipated the news. Things were moving so quickly. On more than one occasion, I had brought myself to the double doors that separated my father's den from the sitting room and listened in on conversations. I resented being left out of some of the conversations anyway. They had to do with family affairs or business affairs that could affect me.

Nothing would affect me more than the conversation that was about to ensue. I stood quietly to the side and listened, eager to hear Malcolm express his love for me.

"As I told you the first night, Mr. Winfield," he began, "I am quite taken with your daughter. It is rare to find a woman with her poise and dignity, a woman who can appreciate the pursuit of economic success and grow gracefully with it."

"I am proud of Olivia's achievements," my father said. "She is as brilliant an accountant and bookkeeper as any man I know," he added. My father's compliments always had a way of making me feel less desirable.

"Yes. She's a woman with a steady, strong temperament. I have always wanted a wife who would let me pursue my life as I will, and would not cling to me helplessly like a choking vine. I want to be confident that when I come home, she won't be sulky or moody, or even vindictive as so many flimsy women can be. I like the fact that she is not concerned with superficial things, that she doesn't dote on her own coiffure, that she doesn't giggle and flirt. In short, I like her maturity. I compliment you, sir. You have brought up a fine, responsible woman."

"Well, I—"

"And I can think of no other way to express that compliment better than to ask for your permission to marry her."

"Does Olivia . . . ?"

"Know that I have come in here to make this proposal? She has given me permission to do so. Knowing she is a woman of strong mind, I thought it best to ask her first. I hope you understand."

"Oh, I understand that." My father cleared his throat. "Well, Mr. Foxworth," he said. He felt it necessary to refer to him as Mr. Foxworth during this conversation. "I'm sure you understand as well that my daughter will come into a sizable fortune. I want you to know beforehand that her money will be her own. It is specifically stated in my will that no one but she will have access to those funds."

There was what I thought to be a long silence.

"That's as it should be," Malcolm finally said. "I don't know what your plans might be for a wedding," he added quickly, "but I would favor a small church ceremony as quickly as possible. I need to return soon to Virginia."

"If Olivia wants that," my father said. He knew that I would.

"Fine. Then I have your permission, sir?"

"You understand what I have said about her money?"

"Yes, sir, I do."

"You have my permission," my father said. "And we'll shake on it."

I released the air that I held in my lungs and stepped quickly away from the double doors.

A man, most handsome and elegant, had come calling and then had asked for my hand in marriage. I had heard it all and it had all happened so quickly, I had to catch my breath and keep telling myself it wasn't a dream.

I hurried upstairs and sat before the dollhouse. I would live in a big house with servants and there would be people coming and going. We would entertain with elaborate dinner parties and I would be an asset to my husband who was, as my father had said, something of a business genius. In time we would be envied by all.

"Just like I have envied you," I said to the porcelain family within the glass.

I looked about me.

Good-bye to lonely nights. Good-bye to this world of fantasy and dreams.

Good-bye to my father's face of pity and to my own forlorn look in the mirror. There was a new face to know—and so much to learn about Malcolm Neal Foxworth—and a lifetime to learn it in. I was to become Olivia Foxworth, Mrs. Malcolm Neal Foxworth. All my mother had predicted had come true.

I was blooming. I felt myself opening out toward Malcolm like a tightly closed bud bursting into blossom. And when his blue, blue eyes looked into my gray ones, I knew the sun had come and melted the fog away. My life would no longer be colored gray. No, from now on it would be blue—blue as the sun-filled skies of a cloudless day. Blue as Malcolm's eyes. In the flush of being swept away by love, like any foolish schoolgirl I forgot all I knew about caution and looking beyond appearances to see the truth. I forgot that never once when Malcolm proposed to me and then made his proposal to my father had he mentioned the word "love." Like a foolish schoolgirl I believed I would lie beneath the blue sky of Malcolm's eyes, and my tiny little blossom would grow into a sturdy, long-lasting bloom. Like any woman stupidly believing in love, I never realized that the blue sky I saw was not the warm, soft, nurturing sky of spring, but the cold, chilling, lonely sky of winter.

2

My Wedding

THERE WERE SO MANY PLANS TO BE MADE AND SO LITTLE time to plan. We decided to have the wedding two weeks hence. "I've been away quite a long time," Malcolm explained, "and I have many pressing business concerns. You don't mind a bit, do you, Olivia? After all, we shall have our whole lives from now on to be together, and we shall have a honeymoon later, after you're all settled in at Foxworth Hall. Do you agree?"

How could I not agree? The size of my wedding, the abruptness of it, did not lessen my excitement. I kept telling myself I was lucky to have this one. Besides, I was never comfortable being on display in front of people. And I really had no friends to celebrate with. Father invited my mother's younger sister and her child, John Amos, our only living close relatives. "Poor relations," my father always called them. John Amos's father had died several years before. His mother was a dark drab thing, seemingly still in mourning after all these years. And John Amos, at eighteen, seemed already old. He was a hard, pious young man who always quoted the Bible. But I agreed with Father that it was only appropriate that we invite them. Malcolm brought no one. His father had recently begun traveling and intended to visit many countries and travel for a number of years. Malcolm had no brothers or sisters and apparently no close relations he cared to invite or, as he explained, who could come on such short notice. I knew what people would think about that—he didn't want his family to see what he was marrying until it was too late. They might talk him out of it.

He did promise to hold a reception at Foxworth Hall soon after we arrived.

"You'll meet anyone of consequence there," he said.

The next two weeks for me were filled with arrangements and fears. I decided I would wear my mother's wedding gown. After all, why spend so much money on a dress you would wear only once? But, of course, the gown was much, much too short for me and Miss Fairchild, the dressmaker, had to be called in to lengthen it. It was a simple dress of pearly silk, not full of frippery, lace, and doodads, but stately, beautiful, elegant, just the sort of dress Malcolm would appreciate, I thought. The dressmaker frowned as I stood on a bench; the dress reached only my mid-calves. "My dear Miss Olivia," she sighed, looking up at me from where she knelt on the floor, "I'm going to have to be a genius to hide this hem. Are you certain you don't want a new dress?"

Oh, I knew what she was thinking. Who's marrying this tall, gangly Olivia Winfield, and why does she insist on squeezing herself into her dainty mother's dress like one of Cinderella's stepsisters trying to get into the glass slipper? And perhaps I was. But I needed to be close to my mother on my wedding day, as close as I could get. And I felt protected in her dress, protected by the generations of women who had married men and borne them children before me. For I knew and understood so little of any of this. And I wanted to be beautiful on my wedding day, no matter how much pity and mockery I saw in the dressmaker's eyes. "Miss Fairchild, I must wear Mother's wedding dress for scores of sentimental reasons I'm sure it is not necessary to explain to you. Now, can you lengthen this dress or shall I have to call in someone else?" I put coldness in my voice and superior social standing in my posture and Miss Fairchild was back in her place. She did the rest of her work in silence, as I gazed in the mirror. Who was that woman gazing back at me—a bride in a white dress. A bride about to be taken by a man and made his own. And what would it feel like, to walk down the aisle. Oh, I knew my heart would stampede like wild horses. I'd try to smile, to make my face as sweet as the bride atop the wedding cake, as sweet as the faces of the young wives I saw in the society columns in the newspapers.

How could they look so sweet and innocent? Surely, they didn't go through their whole life looking like that. Was it something they learned or something that came naturally? If it was something learned, maybe there was hope for me. Maybe I could learn it too.

But still I'd be as shy as ever, knowing what people were thinking—she's so tall and her arms are so long. That beautiful head of hair is wasted atop that plain face. Even if I smiled back at them and they smiled and nodded at me, I knew they would be turning to one another immediately afterward, quiet laughter around their eyes. How foolish she looks. Those shoulders in such a dainty wedding dress. Those big feet. Look how she towers over everyone but Malcolm.

And Malcolm, so handsome and stately standing beside such an ugly duckling. Oh, people would have so much fun making jokes about the eagle and his pigeon, one bird magnificent, beautiful, and proud; the other plain, awkward, drab.

As I stood before the mirror and Miss Fairchild busied herself about my body with needles and pins and basting threads, I was happy that my wedding would be attended only by Aunt Margaret and John Amos, my father, Malcolm, and myself. No one would be there to make my worst fears come true, and I hoped that now my chance had come, my brightest rainbow dreams would be mine to claim.

On my wedding day it rained. I had to run into the church with my white dress covered by a gray raincloak. But, disappointing as it was, I would not let the weather dampen my excitement. We had a simple church service in the Congregational Church. As I started down the aisle, I hid my fears and nervousness behind a mask of solemnity. Wearing this face, I was able to look directly at Malcolm as I walked down the aisle to meet him. He stood waiting at the altar, his posture stiff, his face more solemn than mine. That disappointed me. I was hoping when he saw me in my mother's wedding dress, something of the magic would occur again and his would light with pleasure, anticipating our love. I searched his eyes. Was he hiding his true feelings behind the same mask I was? When he looked at me, he seemed to be looking right through me. Perhaps he thought it would be sinful to show desire and affection in church.

Malcolm pronounced his wedding vows so emphatically that I thought he sounded more like the minister than the minister did. I couldn't keep my heart from thumping. I feared my voice would tremble when I pronounced the vows, but my voice did not betray me as I vowed to love, honor, and obey Malcolm Foxworth till death us did part. And as I pronounced these words, I meant them with all my heart and all my soul. In the eyes of God I meant them and in the eyes of God I never broke them my entire life. For whatever I did for Malcolm, I did to please God.

When we had completed our vows and exchanged our rings, I turned to Malcolm expectantly. This was my moment. Gently he lifted the veil from my face. I held my breath. There was a deep silence in the church; the world seemed to be holding its breath as he leaned toward me, his lips approaching mine.

But Malcolm's wedding kiss was hard and perfunctory. I expected so much more. After all, it was our first kiss. Something should have happened that I would remember for the rest of my life. Instead, I barely felt his taut lips on mine before they were gone. It was more like a stamp of certification.

He shook hands with the minister; he shook hands with my father. My father hugged me quickly. I suppose I should have kissed him, but I was very self-conscious about the way John Amos was looking at us. I saw it in his face—he was as disappointed in Malcolm's kiss as I was.

My father looked pleased, but terribly thoughtful as

we all left the church together. There was something in his look that I had never seen before, as I caught him gazing up at Malcolm from time to time. It was as though he saw something new, something he had just realized. For a moment, only a moment, that frightened me; but when I looked his way, happiness washed the darkness from his eyes and he smiled softly the way he sometimes smiled at my mother when she did something that pleased him a great deal or when she looked especially beautiful.

Did I finally look beautiful, even if just for today? Did my eyes sparkle with new life? I hoped this was true. I hoped Malcolm felt it too. My father suggested we all adjourn quickly to our home, where he had planned a small reception. Of course, how large could a reception be, with only a bride and groom, a father, a grieving aunt, and a boy of eighteen. But reception it was as Father brought out a bottle of vintage champagne. "Olivia, my dear and only daughter, and Malcolm, my distinguished new son-in-law. May you live in happiness and harmony forever." Why did a tear squeeze from his eye as he raised his glass toward us? And why did Malcolm look at Father rather than at me as he drank his champagne? Suddenly I felt lost, not knowing what to do, so I turned up my glass and over the rim saw my cousin, John Amos, scowling at Malcolm. Then he walked over to me.

"You look beautiful today, Cousin Olivia. I want you to remember, you are my only family, and whenever you need me, I will be there for you. For God planned families always to stick together, always to help one another, always to keep his sacred trust of love." I didn't know how to respond. Why, I barely knew this young man. And what a thing to say on my wedding day. What in heaven's name could John Amos, the poor relation, ever hope to do for me, who was headed for a life of Southern gentility filled with wealth and ambition? What, indeed, did he know, even then, that it took me too long to discover?

Malcolm had booked passage for us on the train leaving at three that day. We were going right to Foxworth Hall. He said he had no time for a prolonged honeymoon and saw no practical sense in it anyway. My heart sank in disappointment when he told me that, yet at the same time I felt relieved. I'd heard enough stories about men and their wedding nights, about a woman's duty to her husband, that I had no wish to prolong my ordeal of initiation. Frankly, I was terrified at the idea of conjugal relations, and somehow, knowing we'd be traveling through the night, safe on a cozy train with people all around us, set my mind at ease.

"For you, coming to Foxworth will be romantic adventure enough, Olivia. Trust me," he said as if my face had turned to glass and he could read my thoughts within.

I didn't complain. The description he had given me of Foxworth Hall made it sound like a fairy tale castle so grand and fascinating it would make my dollhouse dream of beauty seem ant-sized.

At precisely two-fifteen Malcolm announced that it was time for us to get started. The car was brought around and my trunks were loaded.

"You know," my father told Malcolm as we left the house, "I'll have to do my dandiest to find an accountant as good as Olivia."

"Your loss is my gain, sir," Malcolm replied. "I

assure you, her talents will not go unused at Foxworth Hall."

I felt as if they were talking about some slave who had been exchanged.

"Perhaps my wages will be improved," I said. I half meant it to be a joke, but Malcolm didn't laugh.

"Of course," he said.

My father kissed me on the cheek and looked sad when he said, "You take good care of Malcolm, now, Olivia, and don't give him any trouble. Now Malcolm's word is law." Somehow that frightened me, especially when John Amos popped up, grabbed my hand, and said, "The Lord bless you and keep you." I didn't know how to respond, so I just thanked him, pulled my hand away, and got in the car.

As we drove away, I looked back at the Victorian house that had been more than a home to me. It had been the home of my dreams and my fantasies; it had been the place from which I had looked out at the world and wondered what would be in store for me. I had felt safe there, secure in my ways and in my room. I was leaving my glass-encased dollhouse, with its tinted windows and rainbow magic, but I would no longer need it to dream on. No, now I would live in the real world, a world I could never have imagined existed in that precious dollhouse world that had formed my hopes and dreams.

I took Malcolm's arm and moved closer to him. He looked at me and smiled. Surely, I thought, now that we were alone, he would be more demonstrative of his love and affection.

"Tell me again about Foxworth Hall," I said, as if I were asking him to tell me a bedtime story about another magical world. At the mention of his home, he straightened up.

"It's over one hundred and fifty years old," he said. "There's history in it everywhere. Sometimes I feel as if I am in a museum; sometimes I feel as if I am in a church. It's the wealthiest home in our area of Virginia. But I want it to be the wealthiest in the country, maybe even the world. I want it to be known as the Foxworth castle," he added, his eyes becoming coldly determined. He went on and on, describing the rooms and the grounds, his family's business and his expectations for them. As he talked on, I felt as if I were descending deeper and deeper into his ambitions. It frightened me. I hadn't realized how monomaniacal he could be. His whole body and soul fixed itself on his goals and I sensed that nothing, not even our marriage, was more important to him.

Somewhere in one of my books I read that a woman likes to feel that there is nothing more important to her man than she, that all he does, he does with her in mind.

"That is truly love; that is truly oneness" was the quote I couldn't forget. Married people should feel they are part of each other and should always be aware of each other's needs and feelings.

As the car turned off our street and I glanced at the Thames River crowded with ships moving up and down in their slow, careful, but determined way, I wondered if I would ever have that feeling with Malcolm.

I realized it wasn't something a woman should wonder on her wedding day.

We dined on the train. I had been too nervous to eat a thing all day, and suddenly I felt famished.

"I'm so hungry," I told him.

"You've got to order carefully on these trains," he told me. "The prices are ridiculous."

"Surely we can make an exception in our economy tonight," I said. "People of our means . . ."

"Precisely why we must always be economical. Good business sense takes training, practice. That was what attracted me to your father. He never lets his money get in the way of good business sense. Only the so-called nouveau riche are wasteful. You can spot them anywhere. They are obscene."

I saw how intense he was about this belief, so I didn't pursue it any further. I let him order for both of us, even though I was disappointed in his choices and left the table still hungry.

Malcolm got into discussions with other men on the train. There was a heated debate about the so-called "Red Menace" engendered by the United States Attorney General, A. Malcolm Palmer. Five members of the New York State legislature had been expelled for being members of the Socialist Party.

It was on the tip of my tongue to say how horrible an injustice that was, but Malcolm vehemently expressed his approval, so I kept my thoughts to myself, something I would have to do more and more and I didn't like it. I pressed my lips together, fearful that the words would fly out like birds from a cage when the door was carelessly left open.

After a while I ignored the discussions and fell asleep against the window. I had wound down from physical and emotional exhaustion. Darkness had enveloped us and aside from some lights in the distance here and there, there wasn't much to keep me interested in the scenery. I awoke to find Malcolm asleep beside me.

In repose, his face took on a younger, almost childish look. With his lids closed, the intensity of his blue eyes was shielded. His cheeks softened and his relaxed jaw lost its firm, tense lines. I thought . . . rather, I hoped, that this was the face he would turn to me in love, the face he would bring to me when he knew I was truly his wife, his mate, his beloved. I stared at him, fascinated with the way his bottom lip puffed out. There were so many little things to learn about each other, I thought. Do two people ever learn all there is about each other? It was something I would have liked to ask my mother.

I turned away and looked at the other passengers. The whole car was asleep. Fatigue had come silently down the aisle and touched each of them with fingers made of smoke and then slipped out under the car door to become one again with the night. The way the train wove around turns and shook from side to side made me feel as if I were inside some giant metallic snake. I felt carried along, almost against my will.

Occasionally, the train passed through a sleepy town or village. The lights in the houses were dim and the streets were empty. Then, in the distance, I saw the Blue Ridge Mountains looming like sleeping giants.

I was lulled into sleep again and awoke at the sound of Malcolm's voice.

"We're coming into the station," he said.

"Really?" I looked out the window but saw only trees and empty fields. Nevertheless, the train slowed down and came to a halt. Malcolm escorted me down the aisle to the doorway and we descended the steps. I stepped out onto the platform and looked at the small station that was merely a tin roof supported by four wooden posts.

The air was cool and fresh-smelling. The sky was clear and splattered with dazzling stars.

So vast and deep was the sky, it made me feel very small and insignificant. It was too big, and felt too close. Its beauty filled me with a strange sense of foreboding. I wished we had arrived in the morning and been greeted by the warm sunlight instead.

I didn't like the deadly quiet and emptiness around us. Somehow, from Malcolm's description of Foxworth Hall and its environs, I had expected lights and activity. There was no one to greet us but Malcolm's driver, Lucas. He looked like a man in his late fifties, with thinning gray hair and a narrow face. He had a slim build and stood at least two full inches shorter than I did. I saw from the way he moved that he had probably fallen asleep waiting for us at the station.

Malcolm introduced me formally. Lucas nodded, put on his cap, and hurried to fetch my trunks as Malcolm led me to the car. I watched Lucas load my trunks and then saw the train pull away slowly, sneaking off into the night like some silvery dark creature trying to make an unobtrusive escape.

"It's so desolate here," I said when Malcolm got in beside me. "How far away are we from population?"

"We are not far from homes. Charlottesville is an hour away and there's a small village nearby."

"I'm so tired," I said, wanting to lean my head against his shoulder. But he sat so stiffly, I hesitated.

"It's not far now."

"Welcome to Foxworth Hall, ma'am," Lucas said when he finally got behind the wheel.

"Thank you, Lucas."

"Yes, ma'am."

"Drive on," Malcolm commanded.

The road wound upward. As we drew closer to the hills, I noted how the trees paraded up and down between them, separating them into distinct sections.

"They act as windbreaks," Malcolm explained, "holding back the heavy drifts of snow."

A short while later I saw the cluster of large homes nestled on a steep hillside. And then, suddenly, Foxworth Hall appeared, jetting up against the night sky, filling it. I couldn't believe the size of the house. It sat high on the hillside, looking down at the other homes like a proud king surveying his minions. And this was to be my home—the castle of which I would be queen. Now I understood better Malcolm's driving ambition. No one brought up in such a regal and expensive home could think small or ever be satisfied with run-of-the-mill accomplishments. Yet, how lonely, how threatening, how accusing such a house could seem to someone timid or small. I shivered at the thought.

"You live here only with your father?" I asked as we drew closer. "It must have been lonely for you since he began his traveling."

Malcolm said nothing, just looked ahead, as if trying to see his mansion through my astonished eyes.

"How many rooms are in this house?"

"Somewhere between thirty and forty. Maybe one day, to pass the time, you'll make a count." He laughed at his own joke, but I couldn't put aside my awe.

"And servants?"

"My father had too many. Since he's been traveling, I have cut back somewhat. We have a cook, of course, and a gardener who complains constantly that he needs an assistant, a maid, and Lucas, who serves as butler and driver."

"Can that possibly be enough?"

"As I said, now there is you too, my dear."

"But I'm not coming here to be a servant, Malcolm," I said. He didn't reply for a few moments. Lucas pulled up in front of the house.

"Obviously, we don't use all the rooms, Olivia. At one time there were dozens of relatives ensconced within. Fortunately, the parasites have been removed." His face softened. "After you are settled in, you will evaluate our staff needs and do what is efficient and economical, I'm sure. The house is to be your responsibility. I don't have the time for it anymore, and I needed a woman like you who could manage it properly," he said. He made it sound as though he had gone shopping for a wife.

I said no more. I was terribly eager now to go in and see what such a mansion looked like, a mansion that was to be my home. It both thrilled and frightened me. I was sorry that we had come to it at night, for at night it had an ominous air about it. It was almost as if this house had a life of its own, as if it could make judgments about its inhabitants while they slept and cause those it did not like to suffer.

Also, I had learned something from my father about the places people lived. Their homes always reflected their personalities. He himself was evidence of that. Our home was quite simple, but genteel. There was warmth to it as well.

What would this house tell me about the man I had married? Did he dominate people as much as this house dominated its surroundings? Would I become lost within the vast structure, grow lonely as I wandered from room to room through the long hallways?

Lucas rushed up to open the large double entrance doors and then Malcolm led me into my new home. As he guided me through the grand entrance, with his hand resting on my back, my heart sank. I knew it was foolish but I had hoped he would carry me over the threshold into my new home, my new life. I wanted for just this one day to be one of those charming, delicate women men cherish and look after. But that was not to be.

A small figure emerged from the gloom, and my fantasy popped. "Welcome to Foxworth Hall, Mrs. Foxworth," a voice greeted me, and for a moment I couldn't respond. It was the first time anyone had called me Mrs. Foxworth. Malcolm quickly introduced Mrs. Steiner, the maid. She was a small woman, barely five feet four, and, as I towered above her, I flushed at my thoughts of being carried over the threshold. This woman, fiftyish though she was, would be a better candidate for such shenanigans. But she seemed kind as she smiled up at me. I looked to Malcolm but he was busily directing Lucas to carry in my trunks.

"I have your bed turned down and a small fire going, ma'am," she announced. "It's a bit chilly tonight."

"Yes." For a moment I was startled by the mention of bed. Why, it was almost morning! Was my wedding night to proceed now? Somehow I didn't feel ready yet, but I quickly hid my confusion. "I suppose Virginia mountain weather is something I'll have to get used to."

"It takes some getting used to," she said. "The days can be warm in late spring and summer, but the nights are cool. Come along now," she beckoned to me.

I hadn't moved from the entryway, but now the time had come to move forward and meet Foxworth Hall.

All the lights were dimmed, the candles burned low. I walked slowly, like a somnambulist lost in a dream, through the long entryway with its high ceiling. The walls were peppered with oil portraits of people I assumed were ancestors who had preceded me in Foxworth Hall. As I walked down the hall I gazed at them, one by one. The men looked austere, cold, haughty. So did the women. Their faces were pinched tight, their eyes saddened by some trouble. I looked in each of the portraits for some hint of Malcolm, some resemblance in the faces. Some of the men had his light hair and straight nose, and some of the women, especially the older ones, had his intense expression.

At the end of the front foyer, large enough to be used as a ballroom, I came to a pair of elegant staircases that wound up like ruffles on a queen's sleeves. The curving staircases met at a balcony on the second floor, and from there became a single staircase that rose another flight. The three giant crystal chandeliers hung from a gilt carved ceiling some forty feet above the floor and the floor was made of intricate mosaic tiles. The magnificence took my breath away. How drab and gawky I felt in this elegant room.

As Mrs. Steiner led me forward, I gazed at the marble busts, the crystal lamps, the antique tapestries that only the extremely wealthy could afford. Lucas hurried past us, lugging one of my trunks. I paused at the foot of the stairs, my mind numbed in a trance. I was to be the mistress of this magnificent mansion! Then Malcolm was beside me, laying a hand on my shoulder.

"Well, do you approve?" he asked.

"It's like a palace," I said.

"Yes," Malcolm said. "The seat of my empire. I expect you will manage it well," he added. He pulled off his gloves and looked about. "That's the library there," he said, gesturing to my right. I looked through the open doorway and caught a glimpse of walls lined with richly carved mahogany bookshelves filled with leather-bound volumes. "I have something of an office in the rear, where you can work on our accounts. The main hallways above," he said, turning my attention back to the staircases, "join at the rotunda. Our bedrooms are in the southern wing, with its warmer exposure. There are fourteen rooms of various sizes in the northern wing—plenty of room for guests."

"Yes. I believe that."

"But I tend to agree with Benjamin Franklin, who said fish and guests tend to smell after three days. Please keep that in mind."

I started to laugh, but I saw that he was serious.

"Come, you're tired. You can explore and explore tomorrow. I suspect you might find one of my older relatives still living in one of the rooms in the north wing."

"You don't mean that?"

"Of course not, but there was a time when that might have been possible. My father was often carefree about such things. Mrs. Steiner," he said, indicating she should continue leading me upstairs.

"This way, Mrs. Foxworth," she said, and I began to ascend the staircase on the right, running my hand over the rosewood balustrade as I walked up. Lucas came down the left staircase quickly to retrieve my remaining baggage. Malcolm walked beside me, just a step or two behind.

We reached the top of the stairs, and when we made the turn to the south wing, I confronted a suit of armor on a pedestal and I really felt I had entered a castle.

The southern wing was softly lit. Shadows draped the hallway like giant cobwebs. The first door on the right was closed. From the size of the door, however, I imagined the room was a large one. Malcolm must have caught my interest.

"The trophy room," he muttered, "my room," he added with a definite emphasis on "my," "in which I keep artifacts I have collected during my travels and hunts."

I was immediately curious about that room. Surely the things within it would tell me more about the man I had married.

We passed door after door until we reached a set of double doors on the right. The only doors we had passed which were painted white. I paused.

"No one goes into this room," Malcolm declared. "It was my mother's room." His voice was so cold and hard when he said that, and his eyes so far away, that I wondered what it was about his mother that bothered him so. He spat out the word "mother" almost as if it were poison. What kind of man could hate his mother so?

Of course, I wanted to know more, but Malcolm took my arm to lead me on quickly. Mrs. Steiner stopped before an opened doorway and stood to the side to allow me to enter.

The bedroom was large. An ornately carved cherry bed stood in its center. Its hand-carved posts were topped with a white canopy, and the bed was covered with a spread of quilted satin. There were two large white pillows with hand-crocheted pillowcases.

The bed itself was set between two large paneled windows that faced the south. The windows were draped in light blue pleated antique silk curtains. The room had a polished hardwood floor, but there was a thick light-gray wool rug beside the bed.

I looked at the dressing table on the left with its oval-framed mirror. There was a large dresser beside it, a tremendous closet beside that, and a blue cut-velvet chair facing the bed. There was another closet on the right and another, smaller dresser to the right of it. The fireplace, now aglow with a dancing fire, was opposite the bed.

Although the curtains, the bedding, and the rug suggested warmth and femininity, the room had a cold appearance. As I stood there, I had the distinct impression the room had been thrown together rather quickly. In such a glorious house, why would Malcolm want such a bedroom?

My question was answered immediately. This was not our bedroom.

This was my bedroom.

"You'll want to get right to sleep," he said. "It's been a hard day, with all our traveling. Sleep as late as you wish."

Malcolm leaned over and kissed me quickly on the cheek and then turned and left before I could say anything.

It occurred to me that Malcolm might just be very shy and made these remarks for Mrs. Steiner's benefit. He probably intended to come to my bed before or in the morning.

Mrs. Steiner remained with me a while longer, showing me the bathroom facilities, explaining the order of the house, how she handled the linens, when she cleaned the rooms, how the orders for meals were made.

"Of course, it's so late I can't give proper thought to all these things," I said, "but in the morning I'll go over it all again with you and decide what we'll continue and what we'll change." I think she was surprised by my firmness.

"Every Thursday the servants go to town. We do our own shopping then as well," she said, frightened that I would end that practice.

"Where do the servants sleep?" I asked.

"Servants' quarters are above the garage in the rear. Tomorrow you'll meet Olsen, the gardener. He'll want to show you the gardens in the rear. He's rather proud of them. Our cook is Mrs. Wilson. She's been with the Foxworths for nearly thirty years. She claims to be sixty-two, but I know she's closer to seventy," she added. She chatted on and on in her somewhat thick German accent while she unpacked my trunks and began to organize my wardrobe. Finally her words melded into one long, monotonous rhythm, so I could no longer follow. She saw she was losing my attention and excused herself.

"I hope you enjoy your first night's sleep at Foxworth," she said. Of course, it was practically morning.

I took out the blue dressing gown I had taken such pains to have made for my wedding night. It had a deep cut V-shaped neckline and it was truly the most revealing garment I had ever owned. I remembered when they had first come out with the V neck, it had been denounced from the pulpit as indecent exposure. Doctors said it was a danger to health and a blouse with a triangular opening in the front was dubbed a "pneumonia blouse." Women continued to wear it, though, and it had come to be popular. Up until now, I avoided anything that revealed so much of the bosom. Now I wondered if I should wear it.

Anticipating the possibility that Malcolm would come to me in the morning, I decided to do so. After I slipped into it, I let my hair down around my shoulders and contemplated myself before the dressing mirror. The glow of the fire put a tint on my skin and made it look as though the flame were burning within me.

Looking at myself like that made me think of an unlit candle, for that was what an unloved woman was, I thought. No matter how beautiful she was, if she did not have a man to love her, she would never burn brightly. My chance to light my candle had come. I longed to see the flame.

The desire lit my eyes. I ran the tips of my fingers down the strands of my hair and touched my shoulders. Standing there and thinking about Malcolm coming to my room finally to take me in his arms, I recalled love scenes I had read in books.

He would press his lips to my shoulders; he would hold my hand between his and gently stroke it. He would whisper his love for me and press me closely to him. My size that had always been my burden would arouse him. In his arms I would be a perfect fit, as graceful and soft as any woman could be, for that was the power of love—to turn the ugliest of ducklings into a swan.

I felt like a swan in this dressing gown. I had finally become a woman to be desired. The moment Malcolm came through that door, he would see it, and if there were any doubts in his mind about me, those doubts would be blown away like fall leaves in the wind. I longed for him to come through that door. I was ready for him to come through that door.

I put out the lights and slipped under the blanket. Fiery shadows danced on the ceiling; they looked like shapes that had emerged from the walls. The spirits of Malcolm's ancestors, asleep for years, had been nudged and awakened by my arrival. They performed a ritual of resurrection, excited with the prospect of a new mistress to haunt with the past. Rather than frighten me, the thought fascinated me, and I couldn't take my eyes off the dancing forms brought alive by the red glow of the fire.

From somewhere down the long, empty hallway, I heard a door close. Its echo reverberated, bouncing between the walls and threading its way through the darkness until it reached my doorway.

Then there was a deep, cold silence that pierced my heart, a heart so eager to be warmed and loved and cherished. I brought the blanket closer to my chin and inhaled the scent of newly washed sheets.

I listened hard for Malcolm's footsteps, but I never heard them. The fire weakened; the shapes grew smaller and retreated again into the walls. My eyelids grew heavier and heavier until I was unable to keep them open. Finally, I welcomed sleep. I told myself that when I awoke, Malcolm would be beside me and the bright new life I had anticipated would begin.

3

The Ugly Duckling and the Swan

SOMETHING BRIGHT TOUCHED MY EYES AND I AWOKE. IN my half dream I thought it was the light of love shining from Malcolm's eyes, but when I opened my eyes I realized it was merely the bright sun. Beside me the bed was cold and empty. Malcolm had not come to me during the night. Tears sprung unbidden to my eyes. I was a married woman; when would I lie beneath the light of love. All my dreams so newly flowered wilted as if from a winter wind. Who was my husband? Who was I now? I drifted toward the window and parted the satin curtains. Sunlight spilled into the room.

Just then I heard the gentle rapping of knuckles on my door.

"Who's there?" I called, trying to sound bright and cheerful. But it was no use. My voice trembled and shook.

"Good morning, Mrs. Foxworth. You slept well, I hope."

It was Mrs. Steiner. And before I could say anything

she had swung open the door and stood surveying me. A disapproving smile flitted over her lips.

"Has Mr. Foxworth risen?" I asked quickly.

"Oh, yes, ma'am. Some time ago. He's already left the house."

For a moment I simply stared at her. Left the house? I had to bite back the tears. Didn't he intend to spend my first day here with me? Had he stopped by my room, seen me asleep, and then gone on? Why didn't he finally wake me? Why didn't he come to me?

I felt like some invited guest, not like a newly married wife. Did the servants sense it too? Was that why Mrs. Steiner had that cold, disapproving look on her face?

"Did Mr. Foxworth leave any messages for me?" I asked, but I resented that I had to ask a servant for my husband's communication. The least he could have done was written some husbandly note and thoughtfully left it beside me on the bed. That would have given me some warmth. There was only chill in this room. The fire had died down along with my hopes and dreams. My heart felt like a cold ember. Last night it flamed with hope. Today it was coated with ashes. To my servants, I would show only strength and competence.

With a curt bow, Mrs. Steiner replied, "No, ma'am, he did not leave any messages. Would you want your breakfast brought up this morning?"

"No. I'll be dressed and down shortly."

"Very good." Mrs. Steiner went to start the fire.

"It's all right. I don't need it. I don't pamper myself in the morning."

"As you wish. Did you want anything special for breakfast, Mrs. Foxworth?"

"What did my husband have?"

"Mr. Foxworth always eats very lightly in the morning."

"As do I," I said.

Mrs. Steiner nodded and made a hasty retreat.

It wasn't true, of course. Some mornings, I woke up ravenous and devoured everything in sight. But I wasn't hungry this morning. Oh, no, I was devastated and determined to find a way to make things better, right away.

Something was terribly wrong. My father had always taught me that when something was terribly wrong, there was always a reason. And the reason was always hidden. If one wanted to know the truth, one had to search for it. "But Olivia," he had cautioned me, "when you search the shadows to find that truth, often you find things more horrible, more painful than you would have imagined." But I was a strong woman. I was brought up to be a strong woman. Malcolm Foxworth was my husband and I would find out why he was neglecting me on our wedding night. I couldn't let my disappointment get the better of my intelligence. I had waited so long for the morning kisses I dreamt would be mine. For the cuddling, the whispered words of love and affection. I, too, deserved these, and I wasn't going to give up this easily.

When I rose and saw myself in the revealing dressing gown that was to bring such pleasure to Malcolm, I felt terribly embarrassed, even though no one else was there. It was as though I had gotten into costume for a play that was never performed, that had never been intended to be performed. I felt foolish, foolish and angry. I took it off and got dressed quickly.

I'll never forget the first morning I came down those

stairs. I stood at the top and gazed out over the huge foyer and felt the vast emptiness within. It was going to be a challenge to make this into a home, a challenge I knew I could meet.

Yet, as I descended the stairway, I did feel like some queen. Mrs. Steiner had brought out Mrs. Wilson, the cook, and Olsen, the gardener, as well as Lucas to greet me. My servants waited below, anxious and intrigued with their new mistress. Surely, I made an impressive sight that morning. I imagined both Lucas and Mrs. Steiner had described me to the two others. However, none of them had expected Malcolm would bring home a bride so tall. With my hair still pinned up, my shoulders wide and straight, they must have thought some queen of the Amazon was descending from above. I saw both fear and interest in their eyes.

"Good morning," I began. "Don't expect that I will be rising at this late hour ever again. As Mrs. Steiner can tell you, we arrived in the middle of the night. Please make the introductions, Mrs. Steiner," I commanded. Malcolm should have been here to do this, I thought. I was sure they could see how disappointed I was about it.

"This is Mrs. Wilson, the cook."

"Welcome, Mrs. Foxworth," she said. Unlike Mrs. Steiner, Mrs. Wilson was a big-boned woman, at least five feet ten inches tall. Her hair was yellowish-gray and she had large, inquisitive hazel eyes. I thought there was a smile of understanding around her eyes and imagined she thought I was what she expected. From what Mrs. Steiner had told me, Mrs. Wilson had known Malcolm all his life and could anticipate what kind of a woman he would bring home for a wife.

"This is Olsen, the gardener," Mrs. Steiner said.

Olsen stepped forward, holding his hat in his hands. He was a bulky, thick-necked man, built like a bull. He had thick, heavy fingers and short but powerful arms. I thought I detected something simple, something child-like in his face. Although his features were large, there was a softness in his eyes. He looked like a terrified grade school boy about to be reprimanded by his teacher.

"G-g-g-g-good morning, Mrs. Foxworth," he said. There was a stutter in his speech, and he quickly looked down.

"Good morning." I turned back to Mrs. Steiner. "I will have some breakfast now. Then I will begin my survey of the house and the grounds. Return to your work, and I shall call you when I need you."

Sitting at the end of that long oak table large enough to accommodate twenty guests, I felt like a little girl in a high chair. This house overwhelmed even me. If I spoke too loudly, my voice reverberated, emphasizing the emptiness. If only Malcolm were beside me I would feel like a normal-size wife, neither a giant nor a child.

Mrs. Steiner excused herself immediately after serving the tray and went up to do the bedrooms. I didn't mind eating alone; I had done so so often, but this was the day after my wedding and, according to Malcolm, my honeymoon!

I looked about the large dining room. Although it was well lit, there was still something gloomy about it. Perhaps the wallpaper needed to be changed. Those curtains looked drab, even dusty. I knew that with my spit and polish, and my inner strength and determination, I could turn this barren house into a home.

Before I left the table, Mrs. Wilson came out of the kitchen to ask me if I had any special orders for dinner.

For a moment I was speechless. I really didn't know what Malcolm liked and didn't like.

"What do you usually serve on Wednesdays?" I asked.

"We have lamb on Wednesdays, but Mr. Foxworth said I should plan the menu with you from now on."

"Yes, but for the time being, please stay with the menu as it is. We'll make the appropriate changes as we go along," I said.

She nodded, that half smile around her eyes again. Could it be that she anticipated everything I would say? I wondered. I let myself relax. "Mrs. Wilson, I will come in later and you can tell me what you've been serving, what are Mr. Foxworth's favorite meals, what he likes when," I added. Whom was I fooling? She knew more about my husband than I did.

"Whatever you wish, Mrs. Foxworth," she said. Mrs. Steiner went back into the kitchen and I began my exploration of Foxworth Hall, truly feeling like someone about to visit a museum, the only difference being that everything about this house would tell me something more about the man I had just married. It would have been so much nicer to have Malcolm at my side, I thought, showing me the things he cherished, describing the history behind certain pieces of furniture or paintings.

I decided to begin with the library. It was an immense room, long, dark, and musty. Perhaps because three of the four walls were lined with books, it was as quiet as a graveyard within.

The ceiling was at least twenty feet high and the shelves of books almost met it. A slim portable stairway of wrought iron slid around a track curved to the second level of shelves, and there was a balcony above from which one could reach the books on the top level. Never had I seen so many books. Being an avid reader, it pleased me immensely. Of course, I had to consider that my responsibilities were now such that I would have less time for leisurely reading. A quick perusal of the shelves showed me volumes of history, biography, and classics. It was clear that Malcolm didn't stay conversant with the currently popular authors.

To the right of the entrance door was an enormous desk. I had never seen one that large. A tall leather swivel chair stood behind it. What surprised me most were the number of phones on the desk—six. Why would anyone need so many? How many conversations could he carry on at once? I imagined that he had to keep in contact with his various enterprises, like his cloth factories and such, and talk to lawyers and brokers, but six phones!

To the left of the desk was a row of tall narrow windows that looked out on a private garden—a beautiful, colorful, peaceful view. I saw Olsen weeding. He must have sensed me in the window looking out at him, for he turned my way, nodded, and went back on working, only faster.

When I turned back to the library, I noted a dark mahogany filing system made to look like fine furniture. Two long tan leather sofas were set out from the walls about three feet, providing plenty of room to move behind them. Chairs stood near the fireplace, and objets d'art were scattered on shelves.

Despite the size of the windows, there was little sunlight. Perhaps, however, some flowerpots could be placed near the windows, I mused. Surely they would warm up the room.

Then I saw the doorway at the end of the long

library. Was this where Malcolm wanted me to work, or did he intend for me to work in whatever room that door opened to? Naturally curious, I went to the door and opened it to confront a small room with a much smaller desk and chair in the center. There were files piled on one corner of the desk, pens and inkwells and tablets in the center. The walls were bare and the once oyster wallpaper had faded into a dull gray.

Had he set up this cold, distant place for me to work in? I wondered. I shivered and embraced myself. The room was like an afterthought, for some sort of storage, perhaps. It was a room in which to place a clerk or some secretarial servant, but a wife working on family affairs?

Of course I had to consider that Malcolm made his decision to marry rather rapidly. It had all happened so quickly, he probably didn't have time to warm up the room. That would be left to me. I would change the drab, dusty-looking drapes, fill the place with as many plants and flowers as I could, get some colorful paintings to put on the walls, have some shelving put up, and get a bright rug. There was so much to do. I was actually excited by the prospect.

And then, of course, I could envision myself working in here while Malcolm worked on his big deals in the library. We wouldn't be far away from each other. Perhaps that was why he wanted me in this back room. The thought cheered me.

I closed the door and retreated through the library to consider the next part of the house I should visit. My curiosity had been aroused the night before, when I had paused by the large white doors and Malcolm had said the room had once belonged to his mother. Eager to learn all that I could about him and his past as quickly as possible, I headed back upstairs to the south wing and the "secret room." When Malcolm said it was off limits to everyone, he surely couldn't have meant me.

I paused before the double doors set above two steps. Just as I started forward, I heard Mrs. Steiner close a door down the hall. She looked at me, and although we were some distance apart, I noticed a worried frown distort her brow.

I didn't like the way she made me feel, standing there and staring. It was as if I had been caught about to put my hand in the cookie jar. How dare a servant make me feel this way.

"Are you finished with your work?" I asked sharply.

"Not quite, Mrs. Foxworth."

"Then go on with it, by all means," I commanded. I stood staring at her until she turned and continued on to Malcolm's room. She did pause to look back at me, but when she saw I was still watching her, she hurried into the room.

I reached up and turned the knob on the door and stepped into what had been Malcolm's mother's room. The moment I did so, I gasped in awe. It wasn't like anything I would expect a room belonging to Malcolm's mother would be. Malcolm's mother slept here?

At the center of the room on a dais was . . . the best way to describe it is a swan bed. It had a sleek ivory head, turned in profile, and appeared ready to plunge its head under the ruffled underside of a lifted wing. The swan had one sleepy red ruby eye. Its wings curved gently to cup the head on an almost oval bed that obviously required custom-made sheets. The bed's architect had designed the wingtip feathers to act as fingers to hold back the delicate transparent draperies that were in all shades of pink and rose and violet and purple. At the foot of the big swan bed was an infant swan bed placed crossways.

There was a thick mauve carpet and a large rug of white fur near the bed. There were four-feet-high lamps of cut-crystal decorated with gold and silver. Two of them had black shades. In between the other two stretched a chaise longue upholstered in rose-colored velvet.

I have to admit here and now I was shocked. The walls were covered with opulent silk damask, colored a loud strawberry-pink, richer than the pale mauve of what had to be at least a four-inch carpet. I stepped up to the bed and fingered the soft furry coverlet.

What kind of a woman had Malcolm's mother been? Had she been a movie star? What would I feel like sleeping in such a bed? I wondered. I couldn't stop myself from lying on it, from feeling the soft, enticing sensuality of that bed. Was this what Malcolm wanted? Was this the bed he was conceived in? Perhaps I had misunderstood my handsome husband; perhaps what lurked in the shadows I was searching in him was a satin sheen, a sensuality I could never have dreamt or imagined.

"Who gave you permission to come in here!"

I sat up with a start. Malcolm was looming in the doorway. For a moment I thought that he was going to come toward me lovingly, but then I noticed a strange look burning in his eyes, distorting his handsome features. An icy cold chill ran down my spine. I held my breath and sat up quickly. I gasped as I brought my hand to my throat.

"Malcolm. I didn't hear you come in."

"What are you doing in here?"

"I'm . . . I'm doing what you told me to do. I'm learning about our house."

"This is not our house. This has nothing to do with our house." His voice was so cold, it seemed to be coming from the North Pole.

"I was only trying to please you, Malcolm. I only wanted to learn about you and I thought if I could know your mother, I could know you." It was all so confusing, so unreal; it made me dizzy and anxious. I felt as though I had walked into someone's dream of the past rather than the past as it was.

"My mother? If you think knowing my mother has anything to do with me, you are sadly deluded, Olivia. You want me to tell you about my mother. I'll tell you about my mother!"

I sank back onto the silk sheets. I felt so weak and confused as he loomed above me.

"My mother," he said bitterly, "she was so beautiful. So pretty and lively and loving. She was the world to me. I was so innocent then, so trusting, so unknowing. For then I did not know that ever since Eve, women have betrayed men. Especially women with beautiful faces and seductive bodies. Oh, she was deceptive, Olivia. For beneath her charming smiles and her cheerful love beat the heart of a harlot." He strode over to the closet and roughly pulled open the door. "Look at these dresses," he said as he pulled out a pale filmy frock and threw it on the floor. "Yes, my mother was a fashionable woman of the Gay Nineties." He pulled out brightly colored lace evening gowns and fine petticoats, a large fan of curved ostrich feathers, and hurled them all on the floor. "Yes, Olivia, she was the belle of every ball. This is where she refined her charms." He walked over to the golden dressing room in a recessed alcove. There were mirrors all around the vanity. As if in a trance, he picked up the silver-plated hairbrush and comb on the dressing table. "This room cost a fortune. My father gave in to her every whim. She was an undisciplined free spirit." He paused and then said, "Corinne," as if the mere pronouncing of her name would free her ghost from the sleeping walls. From the look in his eyes, I thought he saw her again, moving softly over the thick mauve carpet, the train of her dressing gown trailing behind her. I imagined that she must have been very beautiful.

"What did she die of?" I asked. He had never gone into detail about her during any of our conversations, even though I had told him about my mother's death. I just assumed that her death was so tragic and so sad for him that he could not talk about it.

"She didn't die of anything here," he said angrily. "Except maybe boredom. The boredom that comes with getting everything you want, the boredom that comes with pleasing your senses until you are stupefied."

"What do you mean, she didn't die here?" I asked. He turned from the mirrors and began toward the door as if to leave the room. "Malcolm, I can't be your wife and not know about your past, not know the things other people, strangers, will know."

"She ran off," he said, stopping with his back to me. Then he turned around. "She ran off with another man when I was barely five years old," he added, practically spitting out the words.

"Ran off?" The revelation left me trembling. He walked over and sat on the bed beside me.

"She did what she wanted, when she wanted, as she

wanted. Nothing mattered when it came to her own pleasure. My God, Olivia, you know the type," he said as his hands rested on my shoulders. "They are exactly what you are not—flimsy, narcissistic, flighty women. They flirt, they have no loyalty to any man, and they can't be trusted with anything," he added, and I reddened immediately.

Suddenly a new look came into his eyes. He blinked as if he had just convinced himself of something. When he looked at me again, there was a new expression on his face. He still had his hands on my shoulders, only his grip tightened and became close to painful. I started to pull back, but he held me even more firmly.

I couldn't turn away from him. The look in his eyes had become mesmerizing. After a moment he smiled, but smiled insanely, I thought. His fingers relaxed, but instead of lifting his hands from me, his fingers slipped down over my breasts. He pressed them against my bosom roughly.

"Yes, she left me," he whispered. "Left me only with the memory of her touch, of her kiss, of the sweet scent of her body," he added and inhaled, closing his eyes.

His fingers worked furiously, as if they had a mind of their own, and pulled the buttons of my blouse open. He brought his lips to my neck and whispered, "Left me forever in this room to see her, to feel her . . ."

He pulled my blouse back roughly. I was too terrified to speak. I even held my breath.

"Her name echoes throughout this mansion," he said. "Corinne," he said. "Corinne."

His hands were moving down my body, pulling at my skirt. I felt the garment tear loose and slip down. His hands felt like mad little creatures at my body, in and over the undergarments, pulling, tugging, stripping me roughly.

"Corinne," he said. "I hated her; I loved her. But you wanted to know about my mother. You wanted to know. My mother," he added disdainfully.

He sat back and unfastened his pants. I watched in amazement as he came at me, not as a loving husband, but as a madman, someone lost in his own twisted emotions, driven not by affection and desire, but by hate and passion.

I raised my hands and he pulled my arms apart, pressing them to the bed.

"My mother. You're not like my mother. You would never be like my mother. You would never leave the children we will make together, will you, Olivia? Will you?"

I shook my head and then I felt him press himself in between my legs, seizing me roughly. I wanted to love him, to make him happy, to caress him softly, but in this state, his face twisted, his eyes burning with rage, I could only close my own and fall back.

"Please, Malcolm," I whispered, "not like this. Please. I won't be like her; I'm not like her. I'll love you and I'll love our children."

He didn't hear me. When I opened my eyes, I saw he was lost in his anger and his lust. He came at me over and over again, thrusting into me viciously. I wanted to scream, but I was afraid of what it would do to him and I was embarrassed that my scream might be heard by one of the servants. I stifled my cries, biting down on my lip.

Finally, his anger poured into me. It felt so hot I thought it would scald me. He stopped his thrusts; he was satiated. He groaned and then buried his face in my bosom. I felt his body shudder and go limp.

There was one final "Corinne," and then he lifted himself from me, dressed quickly, and left the room.

So now I knew what lived in the shadows of Malcolm Neal Foxworth, haunting him. Now I know why he had chosen a woman like me. I was the opposite of his mother. She was the swan; I was the ugly duckling and he wanted it that way. The love I had longed for would never be mine.

Malcolm's love had already been taken and destroyed by the woman who haunted this room. There was none left for me.

4

The Ghosts of the Past

I WEPT ALONE IN BED THAT NIGHT. FOR EVEN THOUGH I thought I knew what Malcolm wanted, everything grew confused in my mind. His mother had left him when he was five years old. She had not died and she was more alive than ever in his mind. The shadows of the night ridiculed me. So you wanted to know, they whispered, now you know. My true education about my husband had begun. It was not my softness that Malcolm had wanted me for; it was my hardness. It was not that mysterious, graceful, womanly magic he had longed for, but a solid, trustworthy woman like myself. I would never be one of those thrilling spring flowers for Malcolm. No, I would be like a hardy lily that survived the frost, the tallest flower in the garden, sturdy, proud, and defiant of even the coldest winter wind. That is what Malcolm had seen in me. That is what I would be. With this determination I consoled myself and drifted off to a troubled sleep.

The next morning I awoke early and descended the staircase slowly. The beating of my heart made me so dizzy I had to take hold of the balustrade and pause. I closed my eyes, took a deep breath, and continued into the dining room. Malcolm was at the end of the table, eating his breakfast, as if nothing had happened between us.

"Good morning, Olivia," he said coldly. "A place for you has already been set."

All my fears had materialized. My place was at the opposite end of the long table. I tried to catch his eye as I sat down; I tried to read what he was feeling. But I couldn't penetrate his façade. All I could hope for was that Malcolm had lost himself in his mother's room yesterday, and that he, like I, was hoping it was something we could quickly consign to the past and go about building our future together—a future I knew would be practical and filled with material wealth, a future that would contain none of the frivolousness that had so perplexed me and had so hurt Malcolm.

I pressed my lips together and sat down.

"Olivia," Malcolm said, and I heard kindness in his voice. "It's time to celebrate our wedding. Tomorrow night will be our wedding party. Mrs. Steiner has made all the preparations and I have invited anyone who is anyone in the vicinity. I shall do you proud, my wife, as I expect you to flatter my own appearance."

I was thrilled. Obviously he, too, had decided to put yesterday's events behind us and start our wedding afresh with a celebration. "Oh, Malcolm, can I help?"

"That won't be necessary, Olivia. It's already all set for tomorrow night, and as I said, Mrs. Steiner has taken care of everything. My family has always been known for hosting the finest, most extravagant parties, and this time I intend to outdo myself. For as you know, Olivia, I have big plans, and of course you are part of them. Soon I will be the richest man in the county, then the richest man in the state, then, perhaps, the richest man in the entire United States. My parties always reflect my status in society."

I could barely eat. I wanted to make the best possible impression on Malcolm's friends and colleagues, but all I could think about was that I had nothing beautiful enough to wear. As Mrs. Steiner poured my coffee, I kept seeing my wardrobe floating before my eyes—the hanging gray dresses, the high button collars, the practical blouses. The moment my plate was whisked away, I ran to my room and hurriedly rummaged through my closet, so neatly hung by the servants the day before. I came upon the blue dress I had worn that night I had first met Malcolm. If it had impressed him then, surely it would impress everyone else now. I felt satisfied that the dress would reflect everything Malcolm wanted in a wife, a woman who was proud, conservative, well-bred, and, most of all, the match of Malcolm Foxworth.

That afternoon the house was abustle with party preparations. Since Malcolm had made it clear that my help was not necessary, I felt I should stay out of the way. It was sweet, actually, since the party was in my honor, that he insisted I have the day to myself. I hesitated to continue my explorations of Foxworth Hall, fearful now of what I might find lurking in the shadows. But I had already begun, and was it not better to know the whole truth than only part? Now I was determined more than ever to learn about the people who had lived here. As I walked down the hall of the northern wing, I counted fourteen rooms. Malcolm had told me that these were his father's rooms. These hallways were even darker, colder than the rest of the house. Finally I came to a door that was slightly ajar. I checked to make sure that no one was watching me and opened it to a good-sized bedroom, although to me it appeared cluttered with furniture. So far away from the main life of the house, it seemed to be a room for hiding people; for unlike the other rooms in the north wing, with the exception of his father's room, this one had its own adjoining bath. I could just imagine Malcolm condemning one of his more unpopular cousins to these quarters.

The furniture consisted of two double beds, a highboy, a large dresser, two overstuffed chairs, a dressing table with its own small chair between the two front windows that were covered with heavy, tapestried drapes, a mahogany table with four chairs, and another smaller table with a lamp. I was surprised that beneath all the ponderous dark furniture was a bright Oriental rug with gold fringes.

Had this room indeed served as some sort of hideaway, perhaps an escape for Corinne? It was most intriguing. I went farther into it and discovered another, smaller door at the far end of the closet. I opened it and broke the intricate cobwebs that spiders had spun undisturbed for some time. After the dust settled before me, I confronted a small stairway and realized that it must lead up to the attic.

I hesitated. Attics like this one had more than a sense of history to them. They had mystery. Faces in portraits were easy to read. No one cared if you saw some resemblances, and when I asked about the ancestors, only the facts, details, and tales Malcolm wished to tell me would be told.

Truly though, in an attic hidden behind a small door in a closet, there had to be buried family secrets better kept undiscovered. Did I want to continue? I listened to the house for a moment. From this position it was impossible to hear anyone or anything going on below.

The moment I took my first forward step and broke the wisp of cobweb drawn across the stairway by some guardian spider, I felt it was too late to turn back. A spell of silence had been broken. I was going up.

Never had I seen or imagined an attic as big as this one. Through the cloud of dusty particles that danced in the light coming through the four sets of dormer windows stretched across the front, I gazed down at the farthest walls. They were so distant, they seemed hazy, out of focus. The air was murky; it had the stale odor of things untouched for years, already in the early stages of decay.

The wide wooden planks of the floor creaked softly beneath my feet as I ventured forward slowly, each step tentative and careful. Some of the planks looked damp and possibly weakened to the point where they might split beneath my weight.

I heard some scampering to my right and caught sight of some field mice that had found their way into what must have been to them the heavens.

As I looked about, I realized there was enough stored in this attic to furnish a number of houses. The furniture was dark, massive, brooding. Those chairs and tables that were uncovered looked angry, betrayed. I could almost hear them ask, "Why leave us up here unused? Surely there is someplace for us below, if not in this house, then in another." Why had Malcolm and his father kept all this? Were they both hoarders? Were these pieces to be valuable antiques someday?

Everything of value had been draped with sheets on which dust had accumulated to turn the white cloth dingy gray. The shapes beneath the sheets looked like sleeping ghosts. I was afraid to touch one or nudge one for fear it would awaken and float right to the ceiling of the attic. I even stopped to listen, thinking I had heard whispering behind me, but when I turned around, there was nothing, no movement, no sound.

For a moment I wished there were voices, for they would be the voices of Malcolm's past and what they would say would prove most revealing. All of the secrets of Foxworth Hall had found sanctuary here. I was sure of it, and it was that certainty that moved me forward to look at the rows of leather-bound trunks with heavy brass locks and corners. They lined one entire wall and some still bore the labels from travel to faraway places. Perhaps one or two of these trunks had been used to carry Corinne's and Malcolm's father Garland's clothing when they went off on their honeymoon.

Against the farthest wall giant armoires stood in a silent row. They looked like sentinels. I opened the drawers of one of them and found both Union and Confederate uniforms. Because of the geographical position of this part of Virginia, it made sense to me that some of the Foxworth family would go their separate ways and even end up in battle against one another. I imagined Foxworth sons as stubborn and determined as Malcolm, hotheaded and angry, shouting oaths at one another as some joined the northern cause, some the southern. Surely those who saw the value and importance of industrialization and business went north. Malcolm would have gone north.

I put the uniforms back and looked at some old clothing like my mother used to wear. Here was a frilly chemise to be worn over pantaloons, with dozens of fancy petticoats over the wire hoops, all bedecked in ruffles, lace, embroidery, with flowing ribbons of velvet and satin. How could something so beautiful be hidden away and forgotten?

I put the garment back and moved across the floor to look at some of the old books left in stacks. There were dark ledgers with yellowing pages, the ends of which crumbled when I opened the covers. Beside them were dress forms, all shapes and sizes, and birdcages and stands to hold them. How wonderful! I thought. I should bring these cages back downstairs and bring back the music of birds. Surely that would enliven Foxworth Hall. I slapped my hands together to rid them of the dust and started back toward the stairway, when a picture left atop a dresser caught my eye.

I went to it and looked down at a pretty woman, perhaps no more than eighteen or nineteen. She wore a faint, enigmatic smile. She was ravishingly beautiful. Her bosom swelled out suggestively from a ruffled bodice. I was mesmerized by her smile, a smile that seemed to promise more and more right before my eyes. Suddenly it occurred to me who this was. I was looking at Malcolm's mother! This was Corinne Foxworth! There were clear resemblances in the eyes and in the mouth.

Could Malcolm have brought her picture up here to hide away with the rest of his past? But there was something even more unusual about this picture: it sparkled unlike anything else in the room. Everything else I had touched had a film of dust over it. Everything else left smudges on my fingers. This picture was clean, clear, freshly dusted and polished. It was just like her room. It seemed that everything that was Corinne's was kept spotless, shining, and cherished. Who in this house was preserving Corinne Foxworth so lovingly? It couldn't be Malcolm's father—he was in Europe. The servants? Or . . . was it Malcolm?

How many other things up here had once belonged to Malcolm's mother? I wondered. Surely they tormented him. He must have put them up here to keep them from his view and from stirring up his childhood memories, and yet, just like the swan room, drew him back.

I had come up here hoping to discover answers and had found more puzzles and more mystery. I put the picture down carefully and started toward the front stairway, when I discovered another, separate room to the attic, right off a second stairway. It looked like a school classroom because it had five desks facing a large desk up front. Blackboards lined three walls over low bookcases filled with faded and dusty old volumes.

I went to the desk and saw where names and dates were etched: Jonathan, age eleven, 1864 and Adelaide, age nine, 1879. There were two coal or wood stoves in the corners. It wasn't just a playroom; it had been a real classroom and could easily be restructured into one now. Was it traditional for the Foxworth children to receive their early education?

Wealthy, special, provided with a tutor, the Foxworth children were schooled in the attic of Foxworth Hall, far enough away from the adults so as not to be any bother. Why, they could even play up here on rainy days, I thought, noticing the small rocking horse. How many hours of his childhood had Malcolm spent up here?

I went over to one of the dormer windows and looked out at what would have been his view, but all I saw was a slate black roof fanning wide beneath the windows, blocking the view of the ground below. Beyond the roofs were treetops; beyond the treetops, enclosing mountains were shrouded by blue mists. It was not the kind of view that would distract children.

In a way, I thought, looking back down the vast attic, they were imprisoned here. I shuddered, remembering my mother shutting me in a closet because I had tracked in mud all over her bedroom carpet. Although the door wasn't locked, I was forbidden to open it. I was told if I did, I would be kept in longer, so although I was terrified of the terrible darkness and the small space around me, I sobbed silently and kept my fingers from the closet door.

The revived memory lingered like molasses on my fingers. I couldn't shake it off while I remained in the attic, so I hurried to the front stairway, which I noticed was far clearer than the rear stairway. There were no cobwebs here. I descended the steps and left the long, dark, and dusty room behind me, its secrets and its mysteries still intact.

I had barely scratched the surface of who the Foxworths really were and here I was, now one of them.

That evening, when Malcolm asked how I had spent my day, I didn't dare tell him about finding his mother's picture in the attic, but I did tell him I had found the room at the end of the north wing.

"There were some cousins who were an embarrassment to the Foxworths many years ago," he said, "and they were cloistered there for a time."

"It looked like a place for someone to hide from the world," I said. He grunted, not keen to tell me more about the cousins or why they were kept living there. When I told him I had wandered up to the attic and found the birdcages, which I wished to bring down, he became rather annoyed.

"My mother had them all over this place," he said. "At times it sounded like an aviary. Leave them where they are. Think of more dignified things to do when you re-decorate the house."

I was not about to argue any matter that concerned Malcolm's mother. We talked a bit about Charlottesville and he described his offices and why he was so busy. He blamed it on a number of slipshod practices and poor decisions his father had made just before beginning his travels and going into semi-retirement. But then he returned to a happier note.

"I made a rather good move in the stock market today. I bought one thousand shares at twenty-four and by late afternoon it was up to fifty. A brilliant move, if I do say so myself. Do you know much about the stock market, Olivia?"

"No, not really," I said. "I kept track of my father's investments, of course, but I couldn't advise him as to where to place his funds and where not to."

"Precisely why you ought to reconsider what you do with your own fortune, Olivia. In my hands it could be developed, increased, grow the way it is meant to grow."

"Must we talk about that tonight, Malcolm? There's so much for me to get used to."

His eyes clouded over, and he picked up his water

and drank the entire glass down. "Of course, dear. As a matter of fact, I have to be going now anyway. I have some business to attend to. But I shan't be late. I'll return just after you retire for the day," he said. Then, to be sure his meaning was clear, he added, "Olivia, don't bother to wait up for me."

5

My Wedding Party

THE GUESTS FOR THE RECEPTION BEGAN TO ARRIVE A LITTLE after one, fashionably late. Alone, with a few minutes to contemplate myself, I stood before the mirror and studied the image I presented. With my hair up in its usual manner, and the bodice of my blue dress somewhat tight and adding to the uplift in my bosom, and the fullness of the skirt, I thought I looked gargantuan. Because of the way the full-length mirror had been hung, I actually had to step back a few extra feet to see my entire body, from head to toe, in the glass.

Was there any style I could wear that would make me look dainty and lovable? I could have let my hair down, but I was always so self-conscious about that. It made me feel rather undressed.

I wondered if I was wrong to hope that this dress, the one that had attracted Malcolm, was dignified enough. Would Malcolm's friends and business acquaintances find me impressive? I closed my eyes and imagined myself standing beside him. Surely, this was something he himself had imagined before he took me as his bride.

He must have been happy with the picture that formed in his mind, because he married me and he wanted to introduce me to fine society here. I tried to convince myself I should be more confident, but I couldn't keep that small bird from fluttering its nervous wings inside my chest.

I pressed my hand against my breasts, took a deep breath, and started down the dual winding staircase to the foyer. Even though it was a bright day and we had more than the usual amount of sunlight pouring in the windows, Malcolm wanted to be sure that Foxworth Hall felt cheerful and gay, so he had ordered that all five tiers of the four crystal and gold chandeliers be fitted with candles and lit.

The room was brilliant, but my nervousness made my face feel so hot, it was as if I were descending into a pit of fire. I was breathing so quickly, I had to pause to catch my breath. My legs actually trembled and for a moment my feet felt glued to the steps of the winding staircase. I thought I would be unable to go any farther. I took a firm hold of the balustrade. My eyes filled with tears. The light from the lamps and the candles blurred, and the reflections that emerged from the giant crystal fountain spraying its pale amber fluid, and the silver receiving bowl at the center of the foyer, looked like threads forming a cobweb of light across the room. The mirrors reflected the light from the silver cups on trays, and sent it to be caught by the polished frames of chairs and sofas lining the walls.

Finally, I got hold of myself and continued down.

"This is to be a festive occasion," I overheard Malcolm commanding the servants. "Make people feel comfortable and relaxed. Watch for emptied glasses and plates. Get them up and out of the way quickly.

Circulate with the caviar, the small sandwiches, and petit fours continually. Guests should merely feel an inclination and then find you there beside them. But always, when you serve, smile, look pleasant, and be ready to be of some assistance. And carry napkins, do you hear? I don't want people looking about for a place to wipe their fingers."

Malcolm saw me descend the stairs. "Ah, Olivia, there you are," he said. I thought I saw a flicker of disappointment pass over his face. "Come with me; we'll greet all our guests at the entrance, just after Lucas announces them."

I laced my arm through Malcolm's, feeling nervous, tense, but doing my best not to show any of that. He looked remarkably cool and collected, as though he did this sort of thing every day. He looked handsome, in control, dashing. I hoped that on his arm, I would too.

The bell rang. The first guests had arrived! "Mr. and Mrs. Patterson," Lucas announced. Mr. Patterson was a short, rotund man with a pink flush blushing his cheeks. Mrs. Patterson, however, was dainty, thin, rimmed in lace, and wearing a dress that barely covered her knees! Her hair was worn down in ringlets, held into place by a daring bejeweled headband. Why, I didn't know people actually wore such costumes. I'd seen them only in fashion magazines.

"I'd like to present my wife," Malcolm said. And as I moved to greet Mrs. Patterson, I saw her eyes climb up to the summit of my head, then slink once again to my feet, then climb again, this time to Malcolm, where they rested on his blue eyes as a wry smile formed on her lips.

Mr. Patterson broke the tension by grasping my hand warmly and saying, "Olivia, welcome to Virginia. I hope Malcolm is showing you all the pleasures of our Virginia hospitality."

Mrs. Patterson, finally tearing her eyes from Malcolm's, merely looked at me and sighed, "Indeed."

The remainder of the guests followed in a steady stream, and soon the party was in full swing.

The men were correct and pleasant, but I was shocked to see that all the women wore sacklike dresses that ended just below or even above the knee and were either waistless or belted at hip level. The fine thin fabrics were all pale—creams, beiges, whites, and soft pastels. I thought they looked more like little girls than dignified women. Their large-scale accessories, huge artificial flowers of silk and velvet, and heavy ropes of beads, emphasized their diminutive size and added to their childish appearance.

Beside them, I was a veritable giant, Gulliver in Lilliput, the land of the tiny people. Every gesture, every move I made seemed exaggerated. There wasn't a woman I didn't look down on, and almost all the men were shorter than I was.

I must say the crowd was extraordinarily gay. Whatever inhibitions they possessed were immediately dropped as they moved from the punch bowls to the trays of food. The sound of chatter and laughter grew with every passing moment. By the time Malcolm thought it best we begin to circulate among our guests, the foyer roared with laughter and loud conversation. I had never been at such a gathering of exhilarated people.

My first reaction was to feel happy about it; it looked like my reception was off to a wonderful start, but as I began to circulate amongst the guests, my exuberant feelings fizzled, for I felt a chill in the air between me and these gay, lighthearted, and surprisingly whimsical people.

The women were drawn into small groups, some of them smoking cigarettes held in long ivory cigarette holders. All of them, I thought, looked very sophisticated and worldly. Whenever I joined a group of them, however, they ended their line of conversation and looked at me as though I were an intruder. They made me feel like an uninvited guest at my own party.

They asked how I liked living in Virginia, and especially, how I liked living in Foxworth Hall. I tried to give them intelligent answers, but most of them seemed impatient with my responses, as though they didn't really care about my opinion, or as though they didn't really expect me to make such an elaborate response.

Almost immediately after I finished speaking, they began to talk about the latest fashions. I had no idea what some of the things they were referring to were.

"Can you see yourself in one of those middy blouses?" Tamara Livingston asked me. Her husband owned and operated the biggest lumber mill in Charlottesville.

"I—I'm not sure what they are," I said.

The group stared at me and then they carried on as though I weren't standing there. As soon as I walked away, there were peals of laughter.

These women were so silly, I thought. All they talked about was clothing styles or ways to redecorate their homes. None of them said anything about politics or business and in none of my conversations did I hear mention of a book. As the reception went on, they looked sillier and sillier to me, laughing and giggling, flirting with their long eyelashes, their shoulders and hands.

I expected Malcolm would become outraged at the loss of decorum as time passed, but whenever I looked for him, he was standing among a group of these women, laughing, permitting them to put their hands on him, letting them rub up against him, petting him rather suggestively.

I was shocked. These were the kind of women he despised—vapid, frilly types without an ounce of self-respect. But there he was, rushing to bring a glass of punch to this one or that one or feeding a petit four to a woman who let him press the small cake through her lips. One even licked the crumbs off the tips of his fingers.

When I heard Amanda Biddens, the wife of one of Malcolm's business associates say, "I simply must see your library, Malcolm. I want to see where you sit and dream up all those schemes to make millions," I was appalled to see him take her arm and lead her through the heavy double doors. I felt as if I'd been publicly slapped in the face. My cheeks stung and tears sprang to my eyes. It took all of my strength not to follow them, but to remain dignified and in control, wandering about the party, giving the servants orders from time to time, eating and drinking very little myself. No one sought me out for any prolonged conversation. Some of the men asked me questions about my father's business, but when I began to give them detailed answers, they seemed bored.

Eventually, I began to hear things being said about me. Those in conversation didn't realize I was within earshot or simply didn't care.

One woman asked another why Malcolm Neal Foxworth, a man with such looks and wealth, would burden himself with someone so tall and plain, stern and Yankeeish as me.

"Knowing Malcolm," the other said, "it has to have something to do with business."

I could see from the way others were talking softly and looking at me that as the reception wore on, I had become the subject of ridiculing remarks. I even heard someone criticize my dress. She said I looked like I walked out of a museum.

"Maybe she's a statue brought to life," her companion replied.

"You call that 'brought to life'?"

They laughed and laughed. I looked hopefully for Malcolm. But he was nowhere to be found. From out of nowhere Mr. Patterson appeared, and took my arm. "Let's get that husband of yours to help me see Mrs. Patterson to the car. I'm afraid she's had a bit too much to drink."

Before I could stop him, Mr. Patterson had swung open the library doors. I was shocked to find Malcolm seated behind his desk, with Amanda Biddens draped across the mahogany top. He had a silly smile on his face. His hair was ruffled, his tie askew. "Olivia," he called, "come meet Amanda."

She propped her head on an elbow and looked up at me. "Don't you remember, Malc?" she cooed. "I've already been introduced to your bride."

I was practically shaking with rage and humiliation, but once again Mr. Patterson intervened. "Malcolm old man, I need some help with the little missus again," he said pointedly. Cheerfully, Malcolm rose, and without so much as a look my way, followed Mr. Patterson out the door. Through one of the windows, I could see them lifting Mrs. Patterson into the chauffeur-driven car, her entire leg exposed all the way up to her garter. Her foot was bare. Malcolm retrieved her shoes from the drive and tossed them into the backseat. Amanda, hovering beside me, said teasingly, "Your husband always was there for a damsel in distress. I'm glad to see marriage hasn't changed that."

I was glad when the reception began to wind down. Guests sought us out to say their good-byes and wish us good luck. Malcolm had to take a position beside me again. He reverted to his usual self and became more dignified. I knew that the women who promised to call on me would never do so, but I didn't care about it.

By the time the last couple left, I was exhausted, hurt, humiliated, but grateful it was over. I told Malcolm I was tired and I was going up to my room.

"It was rather a nice affair, don't you think?" he asked me.

"I didn't think much of the guests, especially the women," I responded. "Although I saw you did."

He looked at me with some surprise in his face as I pivoted and ascended the staircase. I felt defeated and let down. Malcolm should not have gone into the library with that lascivious woman, leaving me in that crowd of vipers. If this was what Virginia society was, I was glad they didn't take to me, I told myself.

And yet, I couldn't help thinking about the way some of those women moved about—the freedom they seemed to enjoy, the confidence they had in their own looks and desirableness, and the way the men in the party looked at them. No one looked at me that way—with eyes filled with admiration and longing.

My exhaustion wasn't as much physical as it was

mental and emotional. When I slipped under my blanket and lowered my head to the pillow, I felt like crying. The reception that I had hoped would give me the respect I longed for had done just the opposite. How could I show my face anywhere now after the way Malcolm had behaved at his own wedding party? I hugged my pillow in solace and fell into a tortured sleep. Demons in the guise of flappers haunted my dreams, so that I never slept for more than a few minutes, and my tears fell again and again until I broke out into sobs. Finally, I sobbed myself to welcome sleep.

Sometime before morning I heard the door creak open, and when I opened my eyes, I saw Malcolm Neal Foxworth, naked in the moonlight, his manliness looming over me. "I want a son," he said.

I shuddered and glared my eyes at him, but I didn't say a word.

"You must concentrate on what we are about to do, Olivia," he said as he climbed onto the bed. "That way we have a better chance of succeeding."

He peeled back my blanket and came at me. I was frightened by his intensity and determination. Once again, he gave me no tenderness or affection.

I turned into him, hoping for a kiss, listening for some soft words, but his face was stone serious, his sky-blue eyes curiously lifeless. It was as though he had turned them off and was seeing only what was behind them.

What did he see as he had his way with me? Did he envision Amanda Bidden? His mother? Someone else? Was he making love to some dream woman? In his mind did he hear the words of love? It wasn't fair.

I fell back against the pillow and turned my face away from his. My body shook and trembled. When I felt his seed emerging, I looked into his glassy eyes and thought I could almost hear him willing it to find its destination.

Afterward, he fell against me like an exhausted marathon runner, but I was grateful for the way he clung to my body. At least there was some warmth in that.

"Good," he muttered, "good," and backed off me. He put on his robe and gazed at himself in the mirror as if his image would now congratulate him. He saw something very pleasing in his own contented smile and smiled at me. "I hope, Olivia," he said, "that you are as fertile as I expected."

"You can't command nature, Malcolm. Nature is neither your servant, nor mine."

"I want a son," he repeated. "I married you because you are the serious type of woman who can be mistress of a great house, but also because you have a full body that can provide me with the children I require," he said. I stared at him, unable to respond. His eyes were hard; he was a stranger to me.

I knew that everything he said was true—a woman should be a good wife, a good mistress of her husband's house, sensible and reliable, someone on whom he could depend, and, of course, a good breeder of children; but all of this was missing something even more important, and that was love.

I would live in this big house and have everything a woman could want materially. People living below in small houses and with small incomes would be envious of me whenever I came down from the hill, but could anything grow strong and beautiful in Foxworth Hall if there wasn't love and affection to nourish it? I thought of all the shadows, all the damp and dark corners, the dimly lit hallways, the cold, closed rooms, that dusty, dingy attic filled with the dead past, and I shuddered.

"Malcolm, when you first looked at me, when you courted me, there must have been stronger feelings, feelings that—"

"Please," he said, "don't talk to me about feelings. I don't want to hear about bells ringing and the world turning rose-colored. My mother's letters are filled with such silly references."

"Letters?"

"She wrote to my father when they were courting."

"Where are her letters?"

"I burned them, turned them back to the smoke they were. I have a busy day tomorrow, Olivia," he said, obviously wanting to change the subject quickly. "Get a good night's sleep," he said. And with that, he left my bedroom.

In his wake he left a deep, deadly silence, like the silence that comes before a great storm. Even his footsteps echoing down the hallway sounded miles away. I embraced myself and sat up in my bed.

No wonder he clumped me with the servants when we first drove up to Foxworth Hall. In his mind I was hired on to perform a role, fulfill a specific set of functions, just the way a house servant would be hired. No wonder when he spoke about having a son it sounded like a command.

6
Fathers and Sons

MALCOLM HAD HIS WAY. OUR FIRST SON WAS BORN NINE months and two weeks from the date of the reception to introduce me to the fine Virginia society. We named him Malcolm, for his father, but we called him Mal so it would be easier to distinguish between them. By this time I knew without a doubt that Malcolm was a strong, forceful man who always got whatever he wanted. He was always a winner because he never entered a battle without first assuring himself that the odds were on his side. This was the way he conducted business; this was the way he conducted his life. I had no doubt that he would go a long way toward becoming one of the richest men in the world before he died.

After Mal was born, my hopes for love were born again for a short time. I thought that Mal's birth would bring Malcolm closer to me. Since I had come here, I had been treated more like a maid than like a wife. Malcolm worked all day, every day, returned late at night, hardly ever even sharing dinner with me. We never went anywhere, and the "society" whom I'd been introduced to at the reception seemed to have quickly forgotten my existence. Now that the son Malcolm so wanted had arrived, I thought he might want to have a closer family life, and would perhaps become more of a loving husband. I looked upon the birth of the baby as the coming of something wonderful for our marriage. Mal would be a bridge between his father and myself, drawing us toward each other in ways neither of us expected.

Like any other mother, I was thrilled at each coo, at each smile, at each new accomplishment of my wonderful, adorable son. And I waited for Malcolm's return each day with happy news of our son's progress.

"There's no question he recognizes you now, Malcolm!"

"Today he crawled for the first time!"

"Today he said his first word!"

"Mal began to walk today!"

Each announcement should have had us hugging and kissing, grateful that we had a healthy child. But Malcolm reacted to everything the baby did with a surprising indifference, as though he had expected no less. He took it all for granted and never showed a father's delight and happiness.

If anything, he was impatient with the baby's progress. He was intolerant of the growing process and didn't want to be around to watch the baby make his small but continuous movements forward. He hated it when I brought the baby to the dinner table and ordered me to feed Mal before our own meals. Rarely did he go into the baby's nursery.

Before little Mal was two years old, I was pregnant again, made so by another swift and loveless encounter. Malcolm was determined to have a big family; and now he wanted a daughter. This second pregnancy proved harder for me, I don't know why. I was sick in the mornings. Late in my pregnancy my doctor told me he wasn't happy about how it was going. His fears proved accurate, for during the seventh month I nearly had a miscarriage and then, just at the start of the eighth month, Joel Joseph was born prematurely.

From the start he was a small, fragile, sickly child, with pale thin hair and blue Foxworth eyes. Malcolm was upset that I hadn't given him a daughter, and angry that Joel was not a healthy child. I knew he blamed it on me, even though I did nothing to endanger the baby and followed all of the doctor's orders concerning nutrition.

He said, "The Foxworths are noted for being healthy and strong. Let it be your goal and responsibility to see that this baby of yours changes and becomes what I would expect my sons to be—strong, aggressive, assertive, manly in all ways."

One day after the Foxworth family doctor, Dr. Braxten, had come to see me, Malcolm came up to my room. The doctor told him he didn't believe I would be able to have any more children.

"That's impossible," Malcolm thundered. "I have not gotten a daughter yet!"

"Be reasonable now, Malcolm," Dr. Braxten calmed him.

Didn't Malcolm care at all about my health?

Neither the doctor nor I anticipated Malcolm's vehement reaction. His face became bright red and he bit down on his lip as if to keep himself from speaking. Then he stepped back, looking from me to the doctor and then to me again.

"What is this, something you two have concocted?"

"Pardon me, sir," Dr. Braxten said. He was a man in his late fifties, who was highly respected in his field. The doctor's face paled almost to the shade of his thatch of gray hair. His large fishlike eyes, magnified beneath those thick-lensed glasses, widened.

"Are you standing there and telling me I will never have another child? Never have a daughter?"

"Why, yes . . . I . . ."

"How dare you, sir? How dare you presume?"

"It's not a matter of presuming, Malcolm. This last pregnancy was quite difficult and—"

"I'll hear no more of this," he said, and turned to me with as hateful a face as I have ever seen him wear. "I won't hear of it, you understand?" Then he spun around like a marionette on strings and stormed out of my bedroom. Dr. Braxten was embarrassed for me, so I didn't prolong his stay any longer.

Of course, I was shocked by Malcolm's attitude, but by this time I had hardened myself against his tirades and terrible remarks. He didn't bring it up again, and I didn't discuss it with him. I wasn't sorry I couldn't bear him any more children. He wasn't a man who enjoyed the children he had.

He seemed to ignore Mal and to blame Joel for not being a daughter, the daughter I never realized he wanted so much. He was even more intolerant of the sound of Joel's crying and often spent days without seeing or speaking to either child. If he had been intolerant of Mal's growing process, he was an ogre about Joel's. God forbid the baby messed his diaper in his presence or spit up food while Malcolm was in the room.

Sometimes, I thought he was ashamed of his little family, as if having only two children was a blight on his manhood. It wasn't until Mal was nearly three years old that he took the four of us anywhere together.

We went to tour his fabric mills. All the while, whenever he pointed something out, he spoke to Mal as though his infant son would understand.

"This is all going to be yours someday, Mal," he said, speaking as though Joel wouldn't be alive after he died or as though Joel didn't matter. "I expect you will expand it, make it into something of a Foxworth empire."

We returned to Foxworth Hall on a bright spring day. The leaves were bursting out to say hello to the fresh April sunlight. My boys pointed at the robins eating fresh worms from the grass, and jumped and giggled like merry spring lambs. As I entered Foxworth Hall, Mrs. Steiner rushed out to meet me.

"Oh, Mrs. Foxworth, I'm so glad you're back. A telegram arrived from Connecticut for you this morning, and I'm sure it's something important."

My heart skipped. What could this mean? I tore open the envelope as Mrs. Steiner leaned nosily over my shoulder.

OLIVIA FOXWORTH STOP
WITH MY DEEPEST SYMPATHIES AND GREATEST RESPECTS I REGRET TO INFORM YOU THAT YOUR FATHER HAS BEEN TAKEN BY THE LORD TO HIS BOSOM STOP
FUNERAL HAS BEEN SET FOR APRIL SEVENTH

I crumpled the telegram to my breast, hollow now from grief. April 7 was tomorrow! Little Mal was pulling on my skirt. "Mommy, Mommy, what's wrong, why are you crying?"

Malcolm grabbed the crumpled telegram from my hand and read it. "Malcolm, I must go immediately, I must go on the next train!"

"What?" he said sternly. "What do you plan to do with the boys?"

"Malcolm, I'll leave them with you. Mrs. Steiner is here to help, so is Mrs. Stuart."

"But I would have to be in charge. Olivia, a woman's place is with her children."

"He's my father, Malcolm, my only father. I must be there for his funeral."

Malcolm and I argued the matter until it was too late. By the time Malcolm assented to let me go, the night train had already left, and the morning train I finally boarded arrived in New London five hours after my father's funeral had ended. I went home to find John Amos and Father's lawyer sitting in the parlor.

My eyes were red and swollen from the tears I shed on that long train ride—tears of sadness for my father, but I know they were also for me. Now I was alone in a different way than ever I had been before.

Both stood up as soon as they saw me, and John Amos came over and took my hand in his. He had become a man since I'd last seen him. A man now twenty-three years old, tall and stern and kind. My tears began again as he talked to me. "Olivia, I'm so glad to see you. I was surprised by your absence at the funeral, but I know you'd approve of it. I saw to it that your father was received by his maker in a most proper way. Now come sit down Olivia, you remember Mr. Teller, your father's lawyer—it seems your father added some rather odd clauses to his will that we'll need to straighten out."

Mr. Teller, too, took my hand and looked at me with

sympathy in his eyes and we all sat in the dark, gloomy room.

My mind was numb as all the details were explained. Father had left me his entire estate under the sole condition that only I manage the money. Oh—I know what he had done. He had made sure Malcolm Foxworth would never get his hands on my money. Oh, Father, how did you know the truth so long before I did! And why did you let me marry that man! My tears fell and I hid my head in my lap.

John Amos asked Mr. Teller to leave, telling him we'd make our decisions and let him know before I returned to Virginia.

What a comfort John Amos was to me! And during the two days I stayed in New London, I poured my heart out to him. By the time I left, John Amos knew more about me than anyone else in the world. And I knew, with his love of God and family, that I could trust him, always. It was a knowledge that grew in me as the years passed, and always, when things were hardest, I would turn to John Amos, writing him long letters and he would write me back with words of comfort from both himself and God—for he soon began studying theology at a New England seminary. He was my only family and he was wise and caring—so unlike Malcolm. But I returned to Virginia somehow strengthened—I had lost my father—but had gained a brother, an advisor, a spiritual counselor. "Now, Olivia," John said as he saw me off at the station, "return to your husband and boys, and may the Lord go with you. I am here whenever you need me."

Malcolm showed no regret at all at my father's death. The very day I returned he started in again about my fortune.

"Well, Olivia, you are now a rich woman, in your right. How do you intend to control your fortune now?"

I told him I had no plans, I was still mourning my father and was hardly interested in thinking about money right now.

Weeks passed with our barely speaking, except for Malcolm's almost daily inquiries about my plans for my father's estate. Then one day Malcolm appeared in the nursery to make an announcement that would change our lives completely. It was so rare to see him in the nursery that I greeted him warmly, hoping he had come because he had a father's sincere interest in his children. I was teaching Mal the alphabet, using blocks, and Joel was in his crib sucking on his bottle. The room was somewhat messy because children, especially three-year-old children, drop things everywhere. I usually had it cleaned and straightened by the end of the day.

"Is this a playpen or a pigpen?" Malcolm asked.

"If you were here more often, you would understand," I responded. He grunted. I sensed that he wasn't here to discuss the children.

"I have something to tell you," he said, "if you can tear yourself away from those blocks for a moment."

I rose from the floor, straightened my dress, and went to him.

"Well?"

"My father . . . Garland is returning. He will be here in a week."

"Oh."

I didn't really know what to say. All that I knew about Garland I knew from studying his portrait and listening to the odds and ends Malcolm offered from time to time. I knew he had been fifty-five when he left and I knew from his latest pictures that he was a handsome man who didn't look his age. The gray in his hair, what little there was of it, was nearly indistinguishable from the gold. He stood nearly as tall as Malcolm and in his heyday had been quite an athlete, sportsman, and, despite Malcolm's criticisms of his most recent decisions, businessman.

"However, he won't be returning to his room in the north wing. Instead, he will take the room next to yours in the south wing. You'll have to see that the suite is made livable, not that my father really knows the difference."

"I see."

"No, you don't see. The reason he wants a warmer room with an adjoining bath is because he is bringing his bride with him."

"Bride? You mean, your father has remarried after all these years?"

"Yes, bride." Malcolm turned away for a moment, then turned back. "I never told you, but he married before he left for Europe."

"What? Why didn't you tell me?"

"Oh, you'll see, Olivia. You'll understand soon enough," he said, raising his voice.

Joel started to cry. By now both our sons were sensitive to Malcolm's outbursts, and Joel, especially, had an inordinate fear of his own father. Mal was getting to be the same way.

"You're scaring the children," I said.

"I'll do worse than that if he isn't quiet when I speak. Quiet!" he demanded. Mal's face froze and he choked on his tears. Joel turned over and sobbed quietly in his crib.

"Just prepare yourself," Malcolm said, spitting out his words between his teeth and storming out of the nursery.

Prepare myself? I thought. What could he mean? Did he hate his father so much? Did he not want to share Foxworth Hall?

I didn't care about being the sole mistress of this house. There was to be another woman here, the wife of a fifty-five-year-old man. Surely, she would be an ally. I would look upon her, perhaps, as the mother who had died too soon for me. I could go to her for advice about Malcolm and myself. Surely, someone that much older would be wiser in the ways of men and women. I was happy at the prospect of Garland—his wife returning.

"Malcolm," I asked later at dinner, "will we have to leave Foxworth Hall? Do you want a home of your own?"

"Move out?"

"Well, I thought . . ."

"Are you insane? Where would we go? Buy or build a new home and leave all this? I'll take care of my father; his bride is your problem and your responsibility. You maintain control of this house and keep it a respectable, properly run home. Don't tell me you're afraid of her," he added with a sneer.

"Of course not. I just thought since your father is the older man that . . ."

"My father is older, but not wiser," Malcolm said. "He is more than ever dependent upon me. While he was off gallivanting through Europe with his new wife, I was expanding our business empire and seizing hold of all the controls. Our board of directors have practically forgotten what he looks like, and I've added some new blood since he went away. It would take him a year to understand all of the new developments.

"No," he added more thoughtfully, "don't feel you have to be subordinate to his wife. Remember the kind of woman who impresses my father."

His face drawn and sad, Malcolm walked off, the shadow of his mother's memory over him.

I said nothing more about it. I directed the maids to straighten and clean the suite next to mine and then put off thinking about the arrival of Malcolm's father and his bride.

Perhaps I shouldn't have, but nothing I could have done, nothing Malcolm could have done, would have prepared me for the first shock of their arrival, or prepared Malcolm for an even greater one.

[illegible] blood once he saw it. It would take him a year to understand all of the more devious ones.

"No," he said, more thoughtfully. "I don't feel you have to be subordinate to his wife. Remember the kind of woman who impressed my father."

His face drawn and sad, Malcolm walked off, the shadow of his mother's cruelty over him.

I said nothing more about it. I directed the workers to Malcolm and then [illegible] and then put off thinking about the arrival of Malcolm's father and his bride.

Perhaps I should have [illegible], but nothing I could have [illegible], nothing Malcolm could have said, could have prepared me for the [illegible] of their arrival or prepared Malcolm for it, for that matter.

PART II

7

Malcolm's Stepmother

MALCOLM SAT WITH THE NEWSPAPER BEFORE HIM, BUT I knew he wasn't reading it. My stomach felt as if I had swallowed a dozen butterflies. We were both awaiting the arrival of Garland and Alicia. Malcolm had left his offices early to be here when they arrived. He snapped the paper viciously and eyed the grandfather clock. They were more than a half hour late.

"Knowing my father," he said finally, "he might very well be arriving at four in the morning rather than four in the afternoon. Important details like that always escape him."

"He would know the difference between night and day, Malcolm," I said.

"Oh, would he? I can remember my mother sitting in this very room waiting for him to pick her up for an afternoon affair and he not coming at all because he wrote it down incorrectly in his calendar."

"You can remember? You were only five when she left."

"I can remember," he insisted. "I would sit with her and she would complain to me. She respected my intelligence, you see. She never spoke down to me the way mothers often speak down to their children. After a while, if he didn't show up when he was supposed to, she would go off by herself. It was his fault, don't you see?"

"He was occupied too much with his business," I said, hoping to make a point about him, but Malcolm either didn't hear me or didn't see the relationship to himself.

"Yes, yes, but he was often careless with business meetings too. He just doesn't have the concentration. He gets bored too easily. I can't tell you how many deals we lost because of him and how many I saved."

"Was your mother involved with the business?"

"What?" He looked at me as though I had just made the most ridiculous statement. "Hardly. She thought the stock market was a place to buy and sell stockings."

"Oh, come now. You exaggerate."

"Do I? She had no concept of what a dollar was. Why, when she went shopping, she never asked about the price; she never cared. She bought things without knowing how much she had spent and my father . . . my father never chastised her for it, never put her on a budget. Hopefully," he added, "things will be different with this wife."

"Where did your father meet your mother?" I asked.

"He saw her crossing a street in Charlottesville, stopped his carriage, and began a conversation with her. Without even knowing her family background! She invited him to her home that night. Wouldn't that tell you something? How impulsive a person she was?

Would you have ever done such a thing? Well?" he asked when I hesitated.

I tried to imagine it. It was romantic—a handsome young man stops his carriage to start a conversation with a young woman, a total stranger, and their conversation is so good that she is moved to invite him to her home.

"She didn't know of him?"

"No. She was visiting an aunt in Charlottesville. She wasn't from this area and never heard of the Foxworths."

"I suppose he was impressive."

"You would have invited him to your home?"

"No, not right away," I said, but something within me wanted to say I would, wished such a thing to have happened to me, but I knew what Malcolm was driving at, what was right and proper.

"See what I am saying? He should have been able to perceive the kind of woman she was immediately."

"How long did they court?"

He smirked.

"Not long enough," he said.

"But Malcolm, you and I must have had an even shorter courting period."

"It wasn't the same thing. I knew what kind of woman you were; I didn't need endless examples to demonstrate and support my view. He was blinded from the beginning and rushed right into a proposal. He once confessed to me that he suspected her aunt had brought her to Charlottesville for the sole purpose of meeting a distinguished gentleman. The guile of women! It wouldn't have surprised me to learn that she had planned crossing that street at just that time, knowing he was coming. He said she smiled up at him so warmly, he had to stop the carriage."

"I can't believe that."

"I do. Women like that are always conniving. They look so simple, so unassuming, so sweet, but they're plotting, believe me. And some men, men like my father, always fall for that type."

"Is that what his new bride is like?" He didn't respond. "Well, is she?"

"I can't see why not," he said, and folded his paper noisily.

I was about to respond, when Lucas came to announce that their car had driven up.

"Go help with the trunks and luggage," I said. I stood up, but Malcolm sat staring. "Well?"

He shook his head to shake away a thought and followed me to the front door as Garland and a young woman who could have been his daughter stepped out of their car. He held her in such a way that I suddenly realized that this child woman was his bride! My entire being was shaken. Why hadn't Malcolm told me? I turned to stare at him accusingly, but the face I saw was hardly recognizable as Malcolm's, so contorted was it with shock.

"My God," Malcolm said, "she's pregnant!" I knew what his concerns were—another heir. His face was bright purple and he clenched his hands into fists. "She's pregnant!" he repeated as if to confirm it for himself.

Indeed she was. The otherwise delicate, slender, and fresh-looking young lady with bright chestnut hair looked to me to be in her final months. Garland saw us in the doorway and waved vigorously, taking Alicia by the elbow to lead her on.

He didn't look as though he had aged much since he had begun his journey. I had photographs with which to judge. If anything, taking such a prolonged trip and marrying so beautiful a young woman had made him look younger. I saw a great many physical resemblances between him and Malcolm, of course, but there was a lightness to Garland's step and a warmth in his smile that Malcolm lacked.

Garland was nearly the same height and had the same broad shoulders. He looked fit, vigorous, energetic. It didn't surprise me that such a young girl would be attracted to him. He looked rather dapper in his light sport jacket and tan trousers.

And his wife was positively radiant. She moved lightly, gracefully, toward us for an introduction.

She had large blue eyes and one of those peaches-and-cream complexions usually found only in magazines. She had a soft, gentle mouth and a small, slightly turned-up nose. I was immediately envious of her delicate, feminine features. Her hands were so small and her neck so smooth and graceful. In many ways she reminded me of Corinne, Malcolm's mother, and I understood why Garland Foxworth would have pursued her and taken her for his second wife. When he had first seen her, he probably envisioned Corinne the way she was when he had first set his eyes on her crossing that street in Charlottesville.

I turned quickly to Malcolm to see his reaction to her. His eyes grew small, his gaze intense. Although he had prepared himself to be stern and coldly formal when they arrived, I saw his face softening. What kind of a woman had he expected? I wondered. Or was she what he had expected and that was why he looked so affected.

"Malcolm, you look absolutely . . . older," his father said, and laughed. "Alicia, this is your stepson. Malcolm, your stepmother, Alicia."

Malcolm looked at his father. I saw the cold sneer come into his face.

"Mother? Welcome, Mother," he said, and extended his hand. Alicia smiled and took it but let go almost immediately and turned to me, as did Garland.

"This," Malcolm said, pronouncing his words sharply, slowly, "is Mrs. Foxworth, Mrs. Malcolm Neal Foxworth. Olivia," he said.

"Well, well. How do you do, Olivia," Garland said. Coldness filled my chest. I could tell from the look on Garland's face that Malcolm had never written him to tell him he had gotten married. Which meant, he didn't even know he had two grandchildren!

"Why didn't you tell me?" Alicia asked Garland. She had such an innocent, simple way about her. Garland, knowing his son well, would rather have ignored this embarrassing moment. I could sense that. Later on, in private, he might discuss it with him and voice his unhappiness about such a surprise. "Garland?"

"Simply because I didn't know, my love," he said, staring at Malcolm. I could see that self-satisfied expression around Malcolm's eyes, the expression he usually took on when he had gotten the better of someone. "How long have you two been married?"

"Well over three years," Malcolm said.

"We have two children," I said, impatient with the way Malcolm was stalling them in front of the house and rationing the news. "Both boys."

"Both boys? Well, what do you know! Alicia, you're a grandmother before you are a mother. Boys!"

Alicia smiled warmly as Garland embraced her, pressing her to him with such force, I thought he might endanger the pregnancy. She was so fragile-looking.

"Well, let's get on with this homecoming," Garland said, moving forward. Malcolm stepped aside and I accompanied them into the house. "I see there have been some changes made," Garland said. He was referring to some of the things I had done to warm up the foyer—the addition of some new, brighter landscapes and pictures of other country-type scenes, and some colorful rugs. "All good things," he added for my benefit, winking as he said so.

I couldn't help but like him. He was so bright and happy. There was a positive energy around him that was contagious. Alicia beamed.

"It's everything you promised it would be," she said, and she kissed him on the cheek, but the kiss was so much more affectionate than the kisses Malcolm gave me that I was envious. It was nearly passionate.

"Your suite is in the south wing, next to Olivia's," Malcolm said, sounding more like the manager of a hotel than a son welcoming his father and his father's new bride home. "It's the one you requested."

"Good. Well, let us get settled in and then I want to see my grandsons, eh, Alicia?"

"Oh, yes, I can't wait."

"And dinner. We're both absolutely famished. The food on these trains leaves much to be desired. Have you done much traveling, Olivia?" he asked me. "Or is Malcolm keeping you a prisoner in Foxworth Hall?"

"Well, I haven't really done much traveling, no, but we traveled on the train right after we were married."

"She's from New London, Connecticut," Malcolm

said. "Her maiden name is Winfield. Her father was in the shipping industry—unfortunately he passed away recently—"

"Oh, a Yankee, eh?" Garland said. "Alicia's from Richmond, Virginia, so let's not have the war between the states," he added, and laughed vigorously. Malcolm, standing behind me, scowled, but Alicia smiled at me.

"You'll find no fight in me," she said, squeezing my hand. I must say I was taken with her warmth and her gregarious ways. She was as uninhibited as a four-year-old. Although I told myself it was just a lack of good breeding, I couldn't help being fascinated by her openness. True she was only nineteen, but she had traveled most of Europe and been with a very sophisticated man. She should have had a rapid maturing, yet she didn't seem affected by the traveling or by the realization that she was a very wealthy woman and the wife of a distinguished man.

"Ah, Mrs. Wilson and Mrs. Steiner," Garland said, seeing them standing to the side. Mary Stuart stood behind them shyly.

"Welcome home, Mr. Foxworth," Mrs. Wilson said warmly.

"Welcome home," Mrs. Steiner said. He took both their hands and kissed each. They were obviously embarrassed by such a greeting.

"I've become the Continental," he said, "traveling through Europe. You two better be on the lookout for me." The two giggled like schoolgirls. I thought it was absolutely uncouth to behave like that with the servants, but I did see how much more they admired him than they admired Malcolm. He looked at Mary Stuart, the maid hired after he had left. "Hello there," he said.

She nodded and he looked about. "Are these all the servants?"

"Olsen is in the gardens, working," I said. "You may resume your duties," I told the maids, and they quickly left. Garland lowered his chin to his chest and peered at Malcolm.

"Are we pressed to economize?" he asked.

"Of course not," Malcolm said. "We're just practicing good economic behavior. What you do at home carries over to what you do in business."

"I see. Well, with the addition of another child and the two of us, we'll have to look into additional help, eh, Alicia?" he said.

"Whatever you say, my darling."

I saw Malcolm grimace as if in pain.

"Onward and upward," Garland announced, and led his bride up the dual staircase, pointing things out to her as she giggled and exclaimed her admiration. Malcolm and I remained below, looking up at them. I felt as if a wild but warm wind had come crashing through the front doors of Foxworth Hall, awakening things that had been asleep for two centuries. It was all quite breathtaking.

"Now you see how ridiculous he is," Malcolm muttered. "Can you understand why I feel the way I do about him?"

"Why didn't you ever write him about our marriage or about the birth of the children?" I demanded.

"I didn't think it necessary," he said.

"Not necessary?"

"No, not necessary. And as for her . . . remember, you were here first and you are older. You treat her like a child, and never give the servants the chance to take any orders but yours," he commanded.

"But what if it's something Garland wants?" I asked.

He didn't respond. He muttered something unintelligible under his breath and went back to the salon, supposedly to finish reading his paper before dinner.

I went up to the boys to dress them for their first meeting with their grandfather and their step-grandmother.

Garland couldn't understand why Malcolm would not permit the boys to sit with us at the dinner table. At first Malcolm did not want to discuss it, but Garland's insistence finally brought a response.

"Because, Father, what they do is not pleasing to the appetite."

"Ridiculous. That's the way children are. It's the way you were," he said. Malcolm's face became bloodred, but his lips whitened so much, they were nearly indistinguishable from his teeth. "He was," Garland told Alicia. "He was enough to tire out any woman. He was always asking endless questions. His mother couldn't tell him to do anything without his questioning why. Sometimes I would come home and find her in an absolute dither because of him. I remember her rushing through the house and Malcolm trailing after her, wanting to know this or that. She was in flight from him. He exhausted her," he repeated.

"And sent her packing?" Malcolm asked through his teeth. "We had twice the number of servants then, including a full-time nanny."

"All needed because of him," Garland responded, refusing to be goaded into an argument. Alicia smiled softly and Malcolm's face relaxed.

Garland had insisted that his and Alicia's settings be placed together on the left side of the table. Malcolm was going to give up the head of the table to him, but Garland wouldn't hear of it.

"We're still on our honeymoon," he said, "and besides, we could never sit as far apart as you two sit, could we, Alicia?"

"Oh, no. Everywhere we went in Europe, Garland insisted we be placed right beside each other. He was an absolute tyrant when it came to that."

"I imagine he was," Malcolm said, but in a much softer tone of voice.

"Your father never stopped entertaining me and whoever was with us. We often joined other American tourists," she explained. She had a soft, melodic voice, like dark honey. "And he was always embarrassing me," she added, turning to me. Her smile was friendly, sincere. I nodded and smiled. Malcolm was staring at her as if she were some new species, when indeed I thought she was a great deal like some of the younger women who had come to my reception.

"But tell them the truth, Alicia. You loved every minute of it," Garland said.

"Of course I did. I was with you," she said. They kissed on the lips, actually kissed each other right there at the dinner table as if we weren't present, as if the servants weren't moving in and out. When I looked at Malcolm, expecting his expression of disdain, I saw a look of envy on his face. I thought there was even a smile around his eyes. It faded when he turned to me.

"We're going to have to tell you it all, you know," Garland said, more to me than to Malcolm. "We'll bore you to death day in and day out with the endless details and pictures, but that's what you get for marrying Garland Foxworth's son," he added, and laughed.

"You don't have to listen to any of it if you don't wish to," Alicia interjected.

"But we do want to listen," Malcolm said to her. "If you'll be the one who tells it. That is, if my father will let you tell it without interrupting continually."

"I won't speak unless need be," Garland said. "That's a promise," he added, raising his right hand.

"Don't believe him," Alicia said. Malcolm smiled. Actually, he almost laughed. As the dinner continued I saw Malcolm soften more and more until he was keeping up a continuous flow of conversation with Alicia. Their exchange didn't include me. It was as if I were sitting at a separate table, eating by myself. The girl was like a talking travelogue, and Malcolm, who had done some traveling himself, seemed entranced. Garland ate voraciously.

"Your children are adorable," Alicia told Malcolm. "I can see the Foxworth blood in them."

"Mal shows it more," Malcolm said.

"That's only because Joel is still so young. Oh, I can't wait for our baby to be born!" she said, clapping her hands. She bounced on the seat. I was quite astonished at her dinner etiquette. She talked with food in her mouth; she fluttered about like a bird in her seat, and she drank the dinner wine as though it were water. Malcolm was being extraordinarily tolerant this evening. I imagined it was because this was our first dinner together.

"Just how far along are you in your pregnancy?" Malcolm asked.

"I'm just at the start of the eighth month."

"No time to waste," Garland said. "Not at my age," he added with a laugh.

"You don't waste any time, any time at all," Alicia

said. They looked at each other so passionately, it actually brought a flush to my cheeks. They kissed again. In fact, they punctuated almost every sentence they spoke to each other with a kiss.

Malcolm seemed to move from moments of annoyance to moments of genuine pleasure. When Alicia turned her full attention to him, he was entranced. Once, she reached across the table and touched his wrist. I saw him blush, but he didn't move his hand away.

It was Garland's idea that we all take coffee on the veranda.

"Alfresco," he said, making a grand gesture. He put a napkin on his arm like a waiter and stood up, holding his other arm out for Alicia.

"We had such a good time in Italy," Alicia said. When Malcolm rose, Alicia put one arm in the crook of his and the other in Garland's. I was amazed at how Malcolm permitted it. With her between them, they started for the veranda.

By the time I joined them outside, they were all laughing at Alicia's description of a ride in a gondola in Venice. She was standing up and imitating Garland.

" 'Sit down please, sir,' the gondolier pleaded," she said, lowering her voice dramatically. "But your father had had a great deal of wine and he thought he could walk a tightrope. 'No problem,' he said, 'I'll be the navigator.' The other passengers were in a state of shock. The gondolier pleaded again and then the gondola began to rock." She rocked back and forth on her heels. "And then, what do you think?" she said. "Garland . . ." She laughed and Garland laughed at the memory. "Garland fell over the side," she said, and then fell toward Malcolm, who reached up quickly to keep her from falling into his lap. Garland roared, but Malcolm blushed when he saw me standing in the doorway.

"The coffee will be out in a moment," I announced.

"Everyone was trying to fish him out of the canal," Alicia went on, ignoring my arrival. "But he refused their assistance, claiming he was all right. It was absolute bedlam until he was finally pulled into the gondola." She ended by sitting on Garland's lap and putting her arm around his neck. They kissed again.

"She tells it so wonderfully," Garland said. "So," he said, turning to me, "you'll have to sit down one day and tell me all the details about your wedding, how my son won your heart, what lies he told you to do so. . . ."

There was more laughter, which set Alicia onto another story about Garland in Europe. Before our evening ended, I decided to call it Tales of Garland Foxworth by Alicia Foxworth. Never had I seen or even read about a woman as devoted to a man as Alicia was to Garland. She took note of every little thing he had done. She practically worshipped the ground he walked upon.

Our evening with them ended when they confessed to being tired from all their traveling. Alicia put her head on Garland's shoulder and he embraced her around her waist. Then the two of them, looking more like newlyweds in their twenties than a fifty-eight-year-old man and a nineteen-year-old pregnant girl, walked into the house and made their way up the staircase.

Malcolm and I had said little after they left us. The light and the excitement had left the veranda along with Alicia.

"She's rather pretty," I said.

"Is she?"

"Like a little bird flitting about your father, don't you think?"

"I'm tired," he said. "All that chatter has given me a headache." He left to go to his chambers.

I took my time going up. When I did climb the stairs, I checked on the boys first. They were fast asleep. Their grandfather had entertained them and I must say I thought Mal took to him rather quickly. I imagined that Garland would be a much better father than Malcolm had been so far. Garland, at least, seemed to like children.

When I passed their suite, I heard them still awake. They were talking and giggling like two teenagers. I hesitated, drinking in some vicarious pleasure from their soft, happy talk.

It was the way Malcolm and I should be, I thought. It was the way I had dreamt we would be. Behind the door Garland held Alicia in his arms. He pressed his beautiful young bride to him and made her feel wanted and alive. I imagined his hand on her stomach to feel the life within. Never once did Malcolm show any interest in doing that. During the final months of my pregnancies, when I carried low and heavy, he avoided me.

Why didn't Alicia's features widen and thicken the way mine had? If you looked at her from the bosom up, you wouldn't even know she was pregnant. It didn't seem fair that these slim, dainty girls never lost their feminine charm.

I walked on. My envy made me sad, not angry. My bedroom was right beside theirs, and the wall by my dressing table was thinner than my other walls. If I stood by it and pressed my ear to it, I could hear them almost as well as if I were in their room.

"She's exactly what I thought Malcolm would marry," Garland said.

"She's so tall," Alicia said. "I feel sorry for her being so tall."

"I feel sorry for her being married to Malcolm," he said.

"Oh, Garland."

"But he never understood women. He never really had a girlfriend, you know."

"Poor soul."

"Poor? That's one thing he's not, nor are you, my darling," he said. There was a silence that I knew was filled with a kiss.

"I was rich the first day you came into our house," she told him. And then they were quiet.

I went into my own bed, alone, wondering how I would compete with such a beautiful and innocent creature. Every time she spoke it would emphasize my silence; every time she laughed, it would emphasize my sadness; and every time Malcolm looked at her, it would remind me of all the times he avoided looking at me. Her smallness made my size greater.

I hated her, or at least I wanted to hate her.

And yet, how difficult it was to harden my heart against her simply because she had everything I wanted for myself.

Alicia appeared the next morning with the same energy and bubbly demeanor. If anything, she seemed to open to the day the way a beautiful yellow gardenia might greet the sunlight. Never was our breakfast as lively. Garland said they had slept like babies.

"Which proves how important it is for a man to return home," he said. "To our home," he added, looking at Alicia. Her rich chestnut hair was pinned up, rather like mine, but hers was glossy and revealed her small ears and soft white neck. I could tell that Malcolm was fascinated with her. I imagined that like me, he had expected them to be somewhat subdued—the early morning hour, their journey catching up with them. But they looked totally revived. Garland must have been right about the importance of home.

He insisted on accompanying Malcolm to the offices and getting right back into the swing of things.

"I know I have a great deal to catch up on. Malcolm never was one to let grass grow under his feet," he added, explaining to Alicia. "My son might be many things, but one thing he is for sure and that is a financial genius."

"That's what he kept saying about you, Malcolm," Alicia said. "When I asked him how he could stay away from his business so long, he said he had full confidence in your abilities."

I waited for Malcolm's caustic response, but he seemed speechless. He shrugged with an uncharacteristic modesty.

"We should be going," he said to his father.

Garland's good-bye to Alicia was so long and passionate, I was actually embarrassed for her. She didn't seem to mind it. However, she saw the expression on my face and, as soon as he left, she turned to me to explain that it was the first time they would be separated since they had embarked on the European journey together. Malcolm's good-bye to me had been as quick and perfunctory as usual—a slight peck on the cheek and some words about serving dinner at the usual time.

"You must tell me how hard it has been for you to be mistress of such a large house," Alicia said, and then quickly added, "Oh, not because I intend to take over. It's just that I find it . . . so overwhelming."

I stared at her for a moment. I thought she was sincere, but I couldn't help having Malcolm's suspicions. Who knew what things would be like in a week? In a month?

"I have everything pretty well organized," I said. "The servants have their duties well outlined and my day is well planned."

"Oh, I'm sure it is. I don't want to do anything to disturb the order of things. You'll just have to tell me whenever I do."

"I will," I said with definite assurance, but she either didn't hear or refused to hear any threat in my reply.

"I don't want to step on anyone's toes," she said. "All I want out of life is to make my husband happy. Garland is so wonderful. He has been so wonderful to me and my family, I can never do enough for him."

"What did he do for you and your family?" I asked innocently.

"Garland was one of my father's oldest, best friends. Since grade school days actually. My father injured his back in a horseback riding accident when he was younger and that kept him from gaining the kind of employment he needed to support his family. But Garland came along and set him up in his own accountant's office, for a sitting job was all he could handle.

Then Garland began sending people to him. Without his help, I doubt we could have survived."

I had my own thoughts about altruism, believing the charity was not given without some thoughts of profit in the future. Had Garland Foxworth had his eyes on this lovely girl from the very beginning?

"How old were you at the time Garland began coming to your house?"

"Oh, I remember him coming when I was about five or six. When I was twelve, he bought me this beautiful gold bracelet. See, I still wear it," she said, holding out her wrist.

"Twelve?"

"Yes. By the time I was fourteen, we were taking walks together. I would chatter away, holding his arm, and he would listen with a wonderful smile on his face. He made me feel so good. It got so I looked forward to his coming more than I looked forward to anything else. He kissed me while I was still fourteen," she whispered.

"What? You were only fourteen?"

"Yes, and it wasn't a peck on the cheek," she added, her eyes twinkling. My face must have been a window-pane. She had to see my utter astonishment. "We knew then, don't you see."

"No, I don't see how a man of his age and a girl of fourteen would know then."

"It was love," she said, unabashed. "True, unrelenting love. He began to come to my house more and more frequently. We would go for carriage rides through the park, stopping for hours to watch the birds. We talked so much, but I couldn't tell you about what . . . our conversation was like one long melody.

The sounds linger in my mind, not the words," she said, smiling to herself. I tried to envision such happiness, but I had no idea what she meant by a melody of words.

"I loved the horsedrawn sleighrides whenever the Virginia winter brought pounds and pounds of snow," she continued. "We would bundle up in thick blankets, clutching our hands beneath them, and ride into the wind, our faces red from the cold, but our hearts warm with our love. You can't imagine how wonderful that was," she said.

"No," I said sadly, "I can't."

"In the summer there were those wonderful concerts in the park. I would pack a picnic lunch for us and we would go off to listen to the music. Afterward we would go boating and I would sing to him. He loves me to sing to him, even though I don't have a singer's voice."

"But didn't you ever think about his age?"

"No. I thought of him as a wonderful older, but most gentle man. He was always so full of spirit and happiness that age never came into it."

"But how did you have the nerve to marry a man so much older? I don't mean to sound coarse, but he'll be dead before you reach middle age. Didn't your parents object?"

"My father died a month before Garland proposed. My mother was shocked at first, and at first she was against it. She said the same thing you said, but I wouldn't be dissuaded, and she adored Garland, you see. Soon she began to realize that I really did love him and that the years didn't matter."

"To be honest, my dear, I'm quite surprised you decided on having children, considering Garland's age."

"Oh, Garland would have it no other way. He said,

'Alicia, when I'm with you, I'm only in my thirties.' And he looks like a man in his thirties, doesn't he? Doesn't he?" she demanded when I hesitated.

"Yes, he looks younger than he is, but . . ."

"That's all that matters . . . what we think," she said. She was positively mesmerized by her romance. Reality, hard, cold facts would never be permitted to destroy her rose-colored world. She lived in the world of my glass-encased dollhouse. Of course, I pitied her for that, realizing reality would have its way eventually; but I also envied her for her happiness.

"Let me go with you. I'd love to watch you with your children. They're adorable. And I'm sure I could probably learn things from what you do," she added.

"I'm hardly an expert at rearing children," I said, but I saw how disappointed she would be if I turned her down, so I let her accompany me.

The children did like her, especially Joel. She brought a smile to his face and he enjoyed being held by her. In a way she got down to their level far better than I ever could. Before long she was playing with Mal's toys with him and Joel was quietly watching the two of them.

"Feel free to do anything you want," she said. "I don't mind staying with them."

"You've got to be more careful at your stage of pregnancy," I told her, and then I thought, wouldn't Malcolm love to see her have a miscarriage.

The thought lingered in my mind, clinging to my thoughts like a burr caught on my skirt. I couldn't shake it off, and the more I envisioned her having a miscarriage, the happier it made me feel.

I couldn't help being afraid of the child she would have, but not for the same reasons as Malcolm. I didn't have his greed about money, knowing we had and would always have more than we would ever need. I feared that her child would be far more beautiful than my children. After all, Garland was the father and he was just as handsome, if not more so, than Malcolm; and she was so much more beautiful than I could ever hope to be.

So I fantasized her starting down the spiral staircase tripping and falling down the steps, the accident resulting in an immediate miscarriage. She was too trusting to see these images in my face whenever I looked at her.

All day long, whenever she saw me, she was filled with questions—questions about Foxworth Hall, questions about the children, questions about the servants, and questions about Malcolm.

"What is he really like?" she wanted to know. "Garland can exaggerate so."

"It's better that you find out for yourself," I replied. "Never ask a wife what her husband is like—you won't get an honest answer."

"Oh. How right you are," she said. It seemed I could do nothing to upset her. "You are wise, Olivia. I'm so lucky to have you here."

I stared at her. She meant it, the foolish girl. Was there no suspicion in her? Was she satisfied being treated like another child in this house?

I expected, as time wore on, that she and Garland would cool down, that some of the gloom of Foxworth Hall would get to her, that as her pregnancy moved into the ninth month, she would be burdened and irritable. But none of that happened. Our meals were just as boisterous as that first day Garland and Alicia arrived.

Every evening Alicia insisted that Garland tell her about his business day in detail.

"You must never think I'll be bored by it," she said, "because it's *your* work and whatever involves you, involves me."

Such gibberish, I thought. She will never understand the details of business.

"Well, today I went over Malcolm's investment in two hotels in Chicago. He has an idea about catering to businessmen, making the rates more attractive for them."

"What do you call it, Malcolm?"

"Call it?"

"The special rates?"

"Business rates," he said dryly.

"Why, of course. How silly of me to ask. It's such a delightful idea," she said. Delightful? I thought. I waited for Malcolm to explode, but his tolerance grew every day.

A number of times I was tempted to tell him about my fantasizing Alicia's miscarriage. I wanted to see how he would greet such a possibility, but the closest I came to saying it was when I told him I thought she was far too active and wild for a woman in her ninth month.

"She's running up and down the stairs, holding her stomach as though she had a balloon under her dress. Sometimes she's outside with Olsen talking to him about flowers, and occasionally I see her digging alongside him. I saw her lift a large potted plant yesterday. I wanted to warn her, but I didn't. She insists on carrying Joel up to the nursery, and if I merely mention something, she's up after it, no matter how heavy or bulky it might be."

"It's none of your affair," he told me, and walked away before I could discuss it any further. Perhaps he was unable to see the possibility or perhaps he had been so charmed by her innocent beauty, he was blind to his own interests.

One day, two weeks into her ninth month, Alicia asked me about the attic.

"It's rather an interesting place," I said. I began to describe it and then stopped. "But really, it's something you'll have to see for yourself," I said. I thought about her walking up those shaky little steps and wandering through the huge attic, things strewn about, presenting the possibility of her tripping and falling.

"I was tempted to go through those double doors and go up the stairs."

"Oh, there's another way up," I said. "A secret way."

"Really?" She was intrigued. "Where?"

"It's through a doorway in a closet in the room at the end of the north wing."

"My goodness, a doorway in a closet. Do you want to go up with me?"

"I've been there," I said. "I'll show you the way and you can amuse yourself going through the old things."

"Oh, I'd love it," she said, so I led her down the north wing to the end room. She was fascinated by the room. "It's like a hideaway," she said.

"Yes."

"This house is so exciting, so mysterious. I must ask Garland about this room."

"Do that," I said. "And tell me what he says," I added.

I showed her the closet doorway.

"Now you must be careful," I said when she looked

back at me. "There's a cord just above the first step. Pull it and it will light the stairway."

She did, but it didn't turn on the bulb. I had unscrewed it earlier.

"Must be blown," I said. "Forget about it."

"No, that's all right. I can see fine."

"Remember," I said. "I told you not to go."

"Don't be an old fuddy-duddy, Olivia. It's nothing."

"Go on, then," I said. "I'll be down in the front salon, reading."

She started up and I closed the door behind her. I heard her gasp and then laugh. My heart was pounding in my chest. The dark, the darkness, those creaky steps and floorboards—all presented a terrible danger to a woman close to her delivery date. What a trusting young fool she was, I thought, and turned away. If anything happened to her, I would be too far away to be of any help. I had warned her. No one could blame me.

I rushed out of the room and down the north wing. I settled myself in the salon and began reading, just as I told her I would. It was difficult for me to concentrate on anything. Every once in a while I looked up at the ceiling and imagined her tripping and falling, perhaps banging her head against one of those trunks or armoires, and lying there in the throes of a miscarriage.

Afterward, when I told Malcolm how it had happened, he would thank me. Not in so many words, perhaps; but the thanks would be there. And maybe she wouldn't go flitting through this house bringing smiles to everyone's face. Maybe the miscarriage would affect her beauty, and darkness would cloak her eyes. Despair would wash the radiant colors from her face forever. Her voice would change and deepen, losing its melodious tones. Malcolm would no longer be enchanted by her chatter and wheedling charms. When we all sat around the dinner table and she spoke, it would be as if we had no ears to hear.

I didn't realize how much time had passed, but when Garland and Malcolm arrived home, she was still not down. Of course, Garland inquired about her.

"Oh, dear," I said. "I've been sitting here entranced with this book. She went up to the attic a while ago."

"The attic? Whatever for?"

"To explore. She was bored."

"The attic?" Garland repeated. His face turned dark. "She shouldn't be up there."

"I told her that, but she positively insisted. She called me an old fuddy-duddy for warning her against it and went up anyway."

He rushed out and up the winding staircase. Malcolm stood in the doorway watching him and then turned to me. Never did I see such a cold look in his eyes. It was an odd look, a mixture of fear and anger, I thought. It was as if he had just discovered something about me that he had never before realized.

"Perhaps you should go along with him and see if anything happened," I said. Suddenly a wry smile came to his face and he turned and left me.

Not long afterward I heard Garland's voice and I went out to the foyer.

"Is everything all right?" I asked. He was hurrying on toward the south wing.

"What? Oh, yes. Can you imagine? I found her standing before the dusty mirror, trying on Corinne's old dresses. I must say, she did them justice."

Malcolm appeared behind me as though he had been waiting in the wings. I could see that he was boiling with rage, and yet . . . yet . . . I saw that faraway look in his eye, a look, that if I didn't know better, I would have called love.

Two weeks later, almost to the day, Alicia gave birth. Dr. Braxten was there to deliver the child. Malcolm and I waited in the foyer. Garland came to the rotunda and shouted down to us.

"It's a boy! A boy! And Alicia is just fine! Why, she's ready to go dancing."

"That's wonderful," I said. He clasped his hands together and raised them in the air before returning to their suite. Malcolm said nothing, but when I turned to him, I saw the rage in his face.

"I was praying if a child had to be born, it would be a girl," he said.

"What difference does it make now? Come, let's see the child."

He hesitated, so I started up without him. The new baby, when I first saw him cradled in his mother's arms, did take my breath away. He had my sons' blond hair and blue eyes, but this infant radiated a quiet and a beautiful peace such as I had never seen in a child. He looked directly at everyone with clear, understanding eyes—and I knew newborns just didn't do that.

"Isn't he beautiful?" whispered Alicia, snuggling him protectively closer against her side. "I'm going to name him Christopher Garland for his father."

Garland stood by, looking as proud as any young papa. At that moment I thought he did look twenty years younger. Were they a magical couple? Could they turn back time? Had they found the Fountain of Youth, or was this what true love could do for people? Never was I as envious and as jealous of anyone as I was of

Alicia that moment. She had everything—beauty, a loving and adoring husband, and now a beautiful child.

"Congratulations, Father," Malcolm said, appearing in the doorway.

"Thank you, Malcolm. Come on in and take a closer look at your stepbrother."

Malcolm stood beside me and looked down at Alicia and the child.

"Good-looking. A true Foxworth," he said.

"You betcha," Garland said. "We'll be handing the cigars out tomorrow, eh, son?"

"Yes, we will," he said. "You did it, Father."

"Oh, I don't know if he did it alone," Alicia said. It even made me laugh. Malcolm's face reddened.

"Well, I meant . . . I . . . of course, congratulations, Alicia," he said, and knelt down to brush a kiss across her cheek. From the way he closed his eyes, I knew he wanted that kiss to last longer.

What a hypocrite he could be, I thought. I knew he hated that baby, and yet he could mouth all the right words, and do all the correct things.

He stood up quickly and backed away from the bed.

"Well, I'd better let you rest," he said. He and I left the room. Garland had hired a nurse for the first few weeks, something Malcolm had not thought of doing for me. We joined Dr. Braxten in the hallway, preparing to leave.

"So, Malcolm," he said, "you can be proud of your father, eh?"

"Yes," Malcolm said dryly.

"Looks like I was wrong," Dr. Braxten added.

"Pardon?"

"There was to be another Foxworth born in Foxworth Hall after all, eh?" he said.

For a moment Malcolm didn't respond. His lips whitened and he looked toward me.

"Yes, Doctor," he said, "you were wrong."

He followed the doctor down the staircase. Their footsteps sounded like thunder, the thunder that comes to warn us of an impending storm.

8

Days of Passion

AFTER THE BIRTH OF CHRISTOPHER, GARLAND BEGAN TO spend a great deal more time at home. Malcolm claimed he was happy to have his father out of his hair at the office.

"He doesn't understand the intricacies of high finance and I have to spend too much time explaining things to him. He annoys everyone with his questions," he said. "It's better that he behaves more like a retired man. I wish he would officially retire," he added.

Garland never did anything intentionally to upset me, but it was upsetting for me to have him around so much because I was forced to witness his and Alicia's love.

He hovered about Alicia, watching her feed the baby, and then he took them both for walks or for short rides. Occasionally, they asked me to accompany them, but I always refused. The few times I caught my reflection and Alicia's in a mirror, I thought I looked more like her mother than the wife of her stepson. I found it ridiculous to think of her as a mother-in-law. I knew it would just be too uncomfortable for me to go anywhere with Garland and her, unless Malcolm were with us too. And then something more disturbing began to take place.

Less than two months after Christopher's birth, Garland and Alicia began going up to their suite in the middle of the afternoon. At first I didn't understand their eagerness to do so. They would come in from a walk looking somewhat flustered, always clinging so closely to each other, forever kissing and embracing. Sometimes they walked past me as though I weren't even there.

With his arm around her shoulders and her arm around his waist, they would practically run up the spiral staircase and disappear into their suite for most of the afternoon. The maids and Lucas would smile slyly at one another when they saw them gallivanting up the stairs. On a number of occasions I overheard them talking about Garland and his young bride. Once, I was just about to go into the kitchen, when I stopped at the partially opened doorway because I heard Mrs. Steiner talking to Mrs. Wilson.

"It's remarkable," Mrs. Steiner said, "how they are always at it. I can't get into that bedroom to clean!"

"In the beginning it was like that with the first Mrs. Foxworth too," Mrs. Wilson said.

"Such a contrast between the elder Mr. Foxworth and his bride and Malcolm Foxworth and Olivia," Mrs. Steiner said. "I can't recall them ever showing affection for each other so openly."

"Affection for each other?" Mrs. Wilson said.

"Olivia is so cold. Those gray eyes of hers are like two granite slivers. I'm so happy the boys have his eyes."

"Yes. Whenever Alicia is in a room, there is such light and happiness, even if Olivia is in the same room. Alicia's brightness is too strong for Olivia's cloudy face," Mrs. Wilson said. "I wish she were the real mistress of Foxworth Hall, as she should be. She is just too sweet to exert her authority."

"It would be as different as night and day, wouldn't it? One has a constant smile on her face, and the other has only a scowl, no matter how hard I work. She told Mary to dust after me in the foyer yesterday."

"When a woman is unhappy in love, she takes it out on whoever is around," Mrs. Wilson said.

"Which is why I wish Alicia were the true mistress of Foxworth Hall."

I stepped away from the door, my heart beating so hard and my rage so strong, I was afraid what I would do if I heard any more. Was Alicia conniving to win over the servants? She would never criticize any of them. She was making me out to be the ogre. And their obscene passion for each other was something the servants admired? Where was decency? Where was self-respect? How could they be so loving and hot-blooded anyway? I wondered. Was it real or just a show?

One day, intrigued with their passion and energy, I followed them up the spiral staircase. I went into my room and placed my ear to the wall by my dressing table. What I heard brought the blood to my cheeks.

Their kisses were one thing, but the sounds of Garland's moaning in passionate ecstasy and Alicia's little cries were overwhelming. I heard them in their bed and I knew exactly when Alicia was experiencing the climax of her lovemaking, or should I say the climaxes, for she cried out loudly each time, and each time Garland said things like, "Oh, my love, my love. It's good, is it not? I'm far from an old man."

Sometimes they would grow very quiet afterward and I would think they were both asleep, but soon I would hear her pleas for more and their passion would begin again. Then I would lie in my own bed and try to imagine what it would be like if Malcolm made love to me the way his father made love to his bride. Never did I feel the need to cry out the way she did and never did Malcolm say the things to me that Garland said to her when she was in his embrace.

Their lovemaking, whether it be night or day, was soon something to which I looked forward. Listening to them, imagining them in bed together, I could find far more excitement than I could in reading my novels.

One day I listened to them talking in the dining room and understood that they were going for a walk for the express purpose of making love by the lake. Just thinking about such a thing made my heart flutter. My face flushed so, I had to go and dab cold water on my cheeks. Looking out of a window, I saw them start off toward the path that led to the lake. Garland carried little Christopher in his cradle. I watched them disappear around a corner and then I followed them.

I felt guilty about it, but I couldn't turn myself back. It was one thing to listen through the walls, but to actually see them making love was too great a temptation. They were too far ahead of me to know I was following.

There was a clearing near the dock where we kept a canoe. By the time I was close enough to spy on them, they had spread their blanket out and they were lying upon it. The baby was asleep.

Alicia's figure had returned rapidly after she gave

birth. It was impossible to look at her and know she was already a mother. She looked younger and more vibrant than ever. Her bosom was still high and her waist was so tiny. She had the perfect hourglass figure.

Her hair spilled down around her shoulders. She sat in her blouse and skirt and embraced her knees as she looked out at the lake. Garland sat beside her, leaning back on his hands. They were like that for the longest time, and I began to feel very silly and guilty about spying on them. I continually looked behind me to be sure Olsen or some other servant wasn't close enough to see what I was doing.

Suddenly Garland turned to Alicia and kissed her on the neck. She dropped her head back and closed her eyes as though that single kiss was a key opening the doorway to her ecstasy. I pressed my fingers against my own neck and watched in fascination as Garland brought his lips to the bodice of her blouse, untying the string that held it together.

He peeled the garments off her so gently and gracefully, it was as if they melted away. When they were both naked and in each other's embrace, the soothing words between them, spoken too low for me to understand, sounded like a soft religious chant, the cadences were so regular and continuous. I watched them go from great passion to gentle caressing, the words turning to laughter.

When I had seen enough, I turned to go back to the house and found myself so short of breath and weak, I was afraid to take a step. I heard the baby's cry and their laughter, and I took deep breaths to get control of myself. Finally I was able to walk back to Foxworth Hall.

I went directly upstairs to my bedroom and lay there

for over an hour staring up at the ceiling, recalling vividly the love scene I had just witnessed. How much I had been cheated! How much of what should be every woman's was not mine and would never be mine! I felt as if fate were pulling me through a knothole, dragging me to a destiny I never wanted to accept.

Someday, perhaps, my portrait would be painted in dark oils and hung on the walls of Foxworth Hall. With gray eyes and pale lips pressed together so tightly they looked sewn shut, I would regard my descendants. My great-grandchildren would look up at me and conclude that I was a very unhappy woman, a woman haunted by the other austere faces of Foxworth Hall, a woman pained by her own existence. And they would know.

While I was still in my room, I heard Garland and Alicia return from the lake. They were laughing, their voices high and gay. They both sounded so young, I felt as if I were the stepmother and Malcolm was Garland's father.

That night after dinner, Garland and Malcolm had a long meeting in the trophy room. Alicia and I were sitting in the salon, tending the three children. Mal was showing Joel and Christopher his toys, explaining each to each as though they could understand. There must have been some strong filial feeling among them, because the infants were quiet, entranced, attentive.

Alicia and I were crocheting. She was better at it than I anticipated she would be. Apparently, she had learned a great deal from her mother before she married Garland. Alicia smiled at the children and smiled at me.

"It's going to be wonderful for them all to grow up together," she said. "They'll marry beautiful, brilliant women and raise their families here at Foxworth Hall."

"Maybe their wives won't get along," I said. I couldn't stand her childish fantasies. Just because life was all roses for her didn't mean it would be that way for everyone.

"Oh, but they will. I'm not saying they won't have small differences. Everyone does, but they'll be Foxworths and their children will continue the traditions."

"We're not royalty," I said. "Neither you nor I are queens." She looked at me a moment and then smiled as though she had to humor me. I couldn't believe the audacity that came from such a simple mind. I was about to let her know how I felt about her smiling, when finally Garland and Malcolm emerged from their tête-à-tête and they came down to join us.

I could see from the expression on Malcolm's face that their discussions had been intense, and I could also sense that he wanted to tell me something; so I gathered Mal and Joel together, saying that I had to take them up, and left the room. Malcolm followed me to the nursery, something he rarely did. He watched me put the children to sleep.

"What is it?" I asked finally.

"We discussed his will. He's drawing up a new one, of course."

"Of course. You expected he would."

"I am to get the house and the business in the event of his death; however, Alicia and Christopher can live here as long as they want. Alicia is to get three million dollars in stocks from our various investments, and Christopher two million, held in trust. I will serve as administrator of their income, investing it as I see fit. He's more dependent on me than I had thought."

"All that should make you happy," I said.

"My father recognizes my financial abilities, something you should also consider."

I stared at him. "I'm not doing so badly with my own investments," I said.

"You're making a fraction of what you should."

"Nevertheless, it is I who am making it."

"Stubborn foolishness. Is that a Winfield trait?"

"I would have thought it a Foxworth trait. You continually tell me how foolish your father is, and who could be more entrenched in his own ideas than you?"

Malcolm's face reddened, but he didn't pivot and leave the room as I had expected he would.

"I wanted you to know these details," he said, "because I want you to tell me if you sense or learn that my father has any intention of changing them. Alicia tells you everything, apparently. I'm sure she'll be telling you about this. I suspect she's not going to be all that happy with the arrangements and she'll be using her charms to get him to give her more."

"You want me to be your spy, spy on your father and his wife?"

"Don't you?" he asked sharply.

My face whitened. He smiled, a cold, wry smile that left a layer of ice over my heart. He didn't wait for my response.

"It's in your own interest to do what I ask, and in the interest of the boys," he said, and left the room without so much as a glance at the children. Never, since they were born, did Malcolm ever kiss the boys good night.

I looked down at them. They were both already asleep. How good it was that they were still too young to understand their father's words. But what lay ahead for them when they were older and they would have to deal with what he wanted for them and demanded of them?

I sat there wishing they could remain babies forever.

Alicia wanted to move into the Swan Room and Garland decided they should. She had always been fascinated by the room and the furniture and often asked questions about it. I saw how nervous Malcolm became whenever she brought up the room in conversation, but I never thought she would want to move into the room that had belonged to Garland's first wife. A second wife shouldn't want to revive her husband's memories of his first wife, but either she was incapable of understanding this, or she didn't care.

In any case, one evening at dinner Garland announced that Alicia was moving their things into the Swan Room.

"And the small swan cradle is so perfect for Christopher," she said.

Malcolm stopped eating.

"That room belonged to my mother," he said as if no one knew.

"And it still does," Garland said. "Your new mother," he added, embracing Alicia.

"I hardly can think of someone so much younger than myself as my mother," Malcolm snapped, but neither Garland nor Alicia seemed to care.

"I don't want to change a single thing," she said. "Everything has been kept so clean and polished anyway. It all looks brand new."

"No one's ever slept in that room since . . . since my mother deserted me!" Malcolm exclaimed.

"Well, it shouldn't be kept like a museum," Alicia

said, and laughed. She didn't mean it to be a cruel remark, I know; but it cut into Malcolm like a blade through the heart. He actually winced in pain.

"A museum. I like that. A museum," Garland said. He joined her laughter.

Afterward, Malcolm ranted and raved about the disgusting way his father gave in to every whim and wish of Alicia's.

"He's spoiling her just the way he spoiled my mother," he told me.

"How could you know?" I asked. "You were so young."

"I was a precocious child; I saw, I knew. There wasn't a dress she saw and wanted that she didn't get. She had enough jewelry to open her own shop. He thought that by buying her endless things, he could keep her happy. I understood a great deal more than other children my age."

"I believe that," I said. "Your father is forever telling me how hard it was for your mother to handle you. You were too smart, he says. She couldn't discipline you because you were always finding ways to get around her punishments or prohibitions. You knew she didn't have the patience or tolerance for endless discussions. He thinks she ran away from you."

"He says that?" He clenched his teeth. "It was he who couldn't handle my mother. Do you think she would have run off with another man if he had been the firm, strong husband he should have been? Why, she even had her own personal funds," he added, "so that she could afford to pick up and go wherever and whenever she wanted." He stopped abruptly and left the room as if he had said too much.

Could this be why he wanted complete control of my

funds as well as his own? I wondered. Did he harbor the same fears in relation to me, afraid that I might leave him and go and do what I wanted whenever I wanted . . . something that would be an embarrassment to him, but even more than that, something that would be a reminder of what his mother was and what his mother had done to his father?

It didn't matter what he thought about my money, nor did it matter what he thought about what Alicia wished. The next day Alicia's things were moved into the Swan Room and the doors were opened. Whenever Malcolm and I walked past it together, he would speed up as though he could be burned by the light spilling from the room into the hallway. He wouldn't look into it. He would act as though it no longer existed. At least, that was what I thought, until one day he made a remark that left me wondering.

"It's disgusting what goes on in that room now," he said, and I understood that he either came upon the room when they were making love or he put his ear to the wall in the trophy room and listened in. Could he have done that? Would he have done that? Curiosity took me to the trophy room one day when he was at work and they were in the Swan Room.

Early in our marriage Malcolm had made it clear to me that the trophy room was to be his private sanctuary, a man's room in every sense of the word. No matter when I walked past it or looked into it, it reeked of cigar smoke. By now the odor was embedded in the walls, I thought. In some ways it reminded me of my father's study, but there were many differences. My father had one stuffed deer head with antlers given to him as a gift from a very satisfied customer. Malcolm's and Garland's trophy room was just that—a room filled with animal trophies.

There was a tiger head and an elephant head with its trunk uplifted. Garland's father had killed them both on safari. Garland had shot a grizzly bear, an antelope, and a mountain lion on hunting trips in western America. Malcolm had just begun his own collection. Two years ago he killed a brown bear. Now he talked about going on an African safari, as soon as business permitted him to take that much time off. Garland kept telling him he could go, that he would watch after things while he was away; but Malcolm wouldn't hear of it.

On the far wall there was a stone fireplace at least twenty feet long. There were windows on either side, draped with black velvet curtains. The mantel was covered with artifacts from various hunting expeditions. Against one wall was a dark brown leather couch and matching settee. Facing it were two rockers and one black leather chair with a small table beside it. Ashtrays were everywhere.

I closed the doors softly behind me and made my way to the wall on the left. On the other side of that wall Garland and Alicia lay in the swan bed. But when I put my ear to the wall, as I often did now in my own suite, I could barely hear their voices. This wall was too thick. Disappointed that my suspicions weren't proving true, I turned away when I saw a picture of Garland when he was much younger, dressed in his safari outfit, one foot on the carcass of a tiger. The picture was tilted. I moved it, intending to straighten it, and I discovered the hole in the wall.

It wasn't very large, but it had obviously been dug out neatly with some sharp instrument. I brought my eye to it and saw Garland and Alicia naked in the swan bed. I gasped and pulled myself back, looking about the trophy room, terrified that I would be discovered.

How long had this hole been here? Did Malcolm dig it out as soon as Alicia moved into the Swan Room? Or had this hole been here for years and years, perhaps dug out by a five-year-old boy?

I left the picture frame the way I had found it and slipped out of the trophy room, now feeling more like a burglar who had robbed the room of some great secret. I would never reveal to Malcolm what I had learned, I thought. I was sure he would deny knowledge of it, but what would be far worse would be my own embarrassment in letting him know that I knew he was more interested in his father's and Alicia's lovemaking than he was in our own.

Was he so taken with his father's bride? Did spying on them titillate him the way it had titillated me? My questions were answered one hot summer day.

Alicia and I had finished feeding the children. It was one of those rare days when Garland went to the offices. Christopher was now a year and a half old. Joel was two and a half and Mal five. It was Malcolm's decision that a tutor would be brought here to give both Mal and Joel their primary education. The classroom in the attic that had been Malcolm's classroom and his ancestors before him would now be theirs. For this purpose he hired an elderly gentleman, Mr. Chillingworth, a retired Sunday-school teacher. Mal hated him and I found him quite cold and much too firm in his manner with a five-year-old, but Malcolm thought he was perfect.

"Discipline is what they will need during these early years. It's when they will form their study habits for the rest of their lives. Simon Chillingworth is perfect for the task. He was my Sunday-school teacher," he said.

Nevertheless, every time Mr. Chillingworth arrived to tutor Mal, Mal resisted, sometimes clinging to my skirt and begging me to keep him downstairs. But Malcolm was intractable. The only thing I could do to ease Mal's fear was to permit Joel to go up with him, even though Joel was too young for lessons. Malcolm approved of Joel's attendance because he thought the little boy would learn something just by being present.

Mr. Chillingworth arrived after lunch for his three and a half hours tutorial session and Mal and Joel went up with him. I felt sorry for them up there in the hot attic on this particularly warm summer day, and offered the north salon, the coolest one, to Mr. Chillingworth. But he wouldn't hear of it.

"There's a sufficient breeze from the dormer windows," he claimed, "and I want the use of the blackboards and desks. The children must learn to cope with discomfort anyway. It makes us stronger Christians."

I dressed the boys as lightly as I could and shook my head in pity. Alicia was practically in tears for them. She vowed to say something to Malcolm that night, but I forbade her.

"I don't need you to speak for me," I said. "And I'm not in total disagreement with Malcolm," I added. It was a lie, but the idea of Alicia getting Malcolm to do something I had wanted him to do was infuriating.

"Very well," she said, "but the poor boys."

She took Christopher up for a nap and returned shortly after, still complaining about the heat and the stuffiness in the house. I retreated to the cool salon to do some reading, but she was too restless and too flushed to relax.

"Olivia," she asked, "don't you ever want to bathe in the lake?"

"Bathe in the lake? No. I don't even have a bathing suit," I said, and turned back to my book.

"We could go for a quick cool dip without suits," she said.

"Without suits? Hardly," I said, "and besides, I don't have any inclinations to do so."

"Oh. Too bad. Well," she said, "I think I might just do it."

"I don't want to hear about it," I said. "It's not something a lady should do," I added.

"Fiddlesticks," she said. "Garland and I have done it often."

I know I blanched, for I had spied on them once when they had. She didn't seem to notice my guilt. Instead, she left to get some towels and head for the lake.

As soon as I heard the front door close, I peered out the window to see her hurrying off toward the lake. Before she disappeared from view, however, Malcolm drove up. I was surprised to see him home so early, but I knew he wasn't above checking on Mal's tutorial. I saw him looking at the disappearing Alicia.

Then, to my surprise, instead of coming directly into the house, he followed in her direction. The hot summer breeze fluttered the lace curtains; insects trying to escape the direct sunlight beat their frail bodies against the screens. For a moment I was unable to move.

Then I rushed out of the salon and out the front door. I moved quickly but stealthily, the way I had when I wanted to spy on Alicia and Garland. What was Malcolm intending to do? Why had he followed her?

Before I reached the lake, I heard her voice and crouched down behind a large bush to peek out at them.

Alicia was already undressed and in the water. Malcolm stood on the bank, his jacket and shirt off.

"Don't come any closer," she warned, crossing her arms over her breasts and keeping herself down in the water. "Just go on back to the house, Malcolm."

He laughed.

"Perhaps I should take your clothes back with me," he said, teasing her with a movement toward her garments.

"Don't you dare touch anything! Go away!"

"Come now, Alicia, surely you don't enjoy being alone here."

"I'm only here for a short dip to cool off. Garland will be home any moment."

"No, he's doing business in Charlottesville. Actually, he won't be home for quite a while."

"Get away," she repeated, but he didn't move.

"I'd like to cool off, too, and it's more fun to have company."

"Go and get your own wife then, and stop pursuing me."

"But you can't possibly be satisfied with that old man."

"Garland is not an old man," she protested. "In many ways he's twenty years younger than you are. He knows how to laugh and enjoy himself. You know nothing about anything but making money. Why, you don't even treat your own wife properly," she said.

Malcolm stared down at her, but he didn't continue to undress. Her words had bitten him.

"You're just a child," he said slowly, his anger

building. "You married my father because he's rich, and you expect him to die any day, leaving you a fortune—but it won't happen that way. I promise you."

"Get away from here," she insisted.

"I don't think that's what you really want," he said, his voice softening. He dropped his trousers and she moved farther back.

"Go away!"

"I told you; I'm hot too."

He slipped off his shorts. Now, naked, he started into the water toward her.

"You don't want to scream," he said. "We don't want the servants here. Garland might not understand."

"You devil," she said. She swam to the right and he went after her.

"You are so beautiful, Alicia," he said. "So very beautiful. You should have been my wife, not his."

She didn't wait for him to reach her. She kicked up and swam toward the shore. He started in pursuit, but when she reached the shore, she turned on him.

"Leave me alone!" she screamed. Her loudness froze him in the water. "Leave me alone from now on, Malcolm, or you will force me to tell Garland how you keep trying to seduce me."

What was she saying? This wasn't the first time he had tried something like this?

"I've protected him from knowing what you try to do, just to give this family some peace—but no longer! I hate and despise you, Malcolm Foxworth. You're not half the man your father is, not half!" she yelled. She emerged from the lake and scooped up her clothing and her towel, wrapping it about her quickly, and then headed for the bushes, fortunately not close to me.

I watched Malcolm. He stared after her a moment and then he started out.

"My mother didn't believe that," he muttered, just loud enough for me to hear. "She ran off easily enough with some man not worth a cent."

He went to his clothing instead of pursuing her. She was nearly dressed and on her way back to the house anyway. I crouched lower in the bushes. I was disconsolate, so alone and betrayed, over and over. Slowly, slowly, I sank to the ground and began to cry silently. Where was security, truth, and honesty? Malcolm used me to fit his purposes and pursued me for my money, money he still hoped to control. There wasn't the slightest bit of love between us.

After he dressed, he began to make his cautious way back to the house, ever careful of his expensive clothes amongst the briars. He talked to himself as he went by me.

"She'll pay for this day of insult, and pay dearly," he mumbled. "The damned little conniving slut can't possibly love an old man like my father. She's playing her game. From now on, I'll play mine more subtly."

From that day on, whenever Garland was out of sight, Malcolm treated Alicia with disgust, disdain, and rudeness that bordered on cruelty. At times I was moved to take her defense, to confront him with the scene I had witnessed at the lake, but I never did.

Despite the way she had rejected Malcolm, I was angry at her for being so beautiful and tempting. I let the fire burn between them—Malcolm's fire of passion and anger, a fire that burned and singed her.

Garland was either blinded with love or too skeptical of anything Alicia told him about Malcolm, for as far as I knew, he never confronted Malcolm. Something was happening to him anyway, I thought, as time went by. He and Alicia were still passionate and loving with each other, but Garland seemed to be aging quickly. I noticed him taking longer naps by himself. His usually voracious appetite diminished. During their second winter at Foxworth Hall, he had a long, disabling cold that nearly became pneumonia.

Throughout it all, Alicia continually turned to me for guidance. I knew she was trying to reach out, to get me to help her, especially with her relationship to Malcolm; but I remained distant, cold, and disinterested. What I wanted to happen was beginning to happen. The cheeriness went out of her voice. She wasn't as bubbly and energetic. She stopped going out with her young girlfriends and spent more time alone, waiting for Garland to come home or to wake from a long nap, avoiding Malcolm in any way she could. She kept herself busy with Christopher, who was now nearly two and a half. In fact, she spent a good deal of time with the children. She was the one who started Mal on the piano, much to Malcolm's displeasure. Both Joel and Mal showed a natural talent for music, but Malcolm had the idea that musicians were weak, effeminate men who made little money.

I began to think that it was her way of getting back at him—teaching the boys something about music. I let that go on because the boys enjoyed it so much and because it annoyed Malcolm so much.

For a time I was like someone in the audience observing the unhappiness, taking pleasure in some of it, even though it did little to relieve my own sorrows.

I did not understand that my selfish pleasure permitted something else to grow. Without realizing it, I had opened Foxworth Hall to more demons of the heart and of the mind. They took their places in the shadows and waited for their opportunity to act.

It wouldn't be long before the opportunity came and the demons would bring with them more misery than I had ever imagined could live in the cold, empty rooms of Foxworth Hall.

9

Days Colored Black

THE MONTHS PASSED, EACH MUCH LIKE THE ONE BEFORE it, filled with tensions I thought were the result of Malcolm's attitude toward Alicia. His belligerence showed in his sharp, often biting comments and in the way he often ignored her. He was more irritable about many things, especially Mal's love of music. One afternoon he came home early and found Mal at the piano with Alicia at his side, teaching him the scales. I was crocheting a sweater for Joel and enjoying the way Mal was intuitively able to pick the right notes. There was no question that he had talent which, if properly nurtured, might grow into real musicianship.

Malcolm heard the piano and came to the salon, the rage already burning in his eyes. I looked up from my needlework just as he came charging through the doorway. He slammed the piano shut with such violence, he almost caught poor Mal's hands beneath the lid. I think he wanted to do that to end Mal's piano playing forever. Alicia gasped and embraced Mal as the two of them looked up at the towering Malcolm.

"What did I say about catering to these musical whims?"

"But, Malcolm, the boy is talented. He's a prodigy. Look at what he can do at his age. Let us show you," Alicia pleaded.

"I don't care what he can do on a piano. Will that make him competent in business? Will that enable him to walk in my footsteps? You are turning him into a soft, effeminate man. Get him off that piano bench," he said, but Alicia didn't release her embrace of him. "Mal, stand up," he commanded.

Mal moved away from Alicia and stood up, his lips trembling. He was afraid to cry, knowing how that would anger Malcolm even more. Usually, he sobbed silently, taking deep breaths and heaving up his shoulders. Joel, who sat on the floor playing with Christopher, looked up with the same terror in his eyes. The two boys shared their fear of their father. Whenever one was yelled at, the other would respond as if it were he. Christopher, on the other hand, simply looked interested in the sudden activity and noise. Alicia turned to me, hoping I would come to her aid.

"What are you doing?" I asked.

"The boy must learn never to disobey me. I told him to spend his spare time on his school lessons, not on the piano."

"He's not disobeying you," I said, "if his mother and his grandmother permit him to do it."

"He's disobeying me!" he repeated. "He knows what I said about it." He reached forward and took Mal by the back of his neck, nearly lifting the terrified child off the ground, and dragged him out of the salon to the library for a whipping. Almost immediately, Joel began to cry. Christopher looked confused.

"Malcolm, don't!" Alicia screamed after them.

"Concern yourself with your own offspring," he said, spitting his words back at her, "and leave my boys to me."

Alicia buried her face in her hands and then looked up at me. Joel had come running to my chair to embrace my leg.

"How can you permit him to do such things?" she asked.

"I can hardly prohibit him from expressing his opinion about his own children, especially in his own house."

"But you're the mother; you should have something to say, shouldn't you?"

"Are you trying to engender an argument between my husband and myself?" I responded. I knew she wasn't, but I wanted her to think I believed it.

"Of course not, Olivia. Oh, dear," she said, "I feel responsible. I've been encouraging him and you've permitted it," she added as though just realizing it. "You shouldn't have if you knew it was going to come to this. Malcolm is so cruel. Aren't you afraid for little Mal?"

"He will be all right," I told her. "If he wants something enough, even his father won't stop him. He's more like me when it comes to that. Try to ignore Malcolm. Stay away from him," I added, filling my words with another meaning. "The house is big enough."

"I feel so sorry for him, though." She was crying. She got up and left the room.

I didn't call her back to comfort her; I was happy that there were strong differences between her and Malcolm. As long as there were such differences, I had no fear that she would ever respond to his amorous approaches.

Then things changed again.

On the occasion of Christopher's third birthday, Garland and Alicia held a party and invited a number of neighboring couples who had children Christopher's, Mal's, and Joel's age. The foyer of Foxworth Hall sounded like a school yard. There were children all about. Alicia arranged for games and hung colorful paper streamers and balloons. Mrs. Wilson made a huge birthday cake decorated with all sorts of bright little animals.

Malcolm went to work in the morning, but Garland remained home to help with the party, something Malcolm thought was a ridiculous thing for him to do.

"He's ludicrous when it comes to Christopher," Malcolm told me that morning after breakfast. Garland and Alicia had left the table to prepare for the party. "He acts like a man in his dotage. You would think it was his first child."

"Perhaps he is proud of not only having been able to have a child, but having one so handsome and bright," I said. Malcolm's eyes narrowed, and for the first time I understood that he was jealous of Garland's attention to Christopher. "Didn't your father give you the same kind of attention?"

"Hardly. It was the other way around. I had to practically beg him to take me along on his business trips. After my mother left, he was so weak, he even tried to blame me for driving her away. I'll never forgive him for that. My mother loved me more than anything, and it was his own inadequacies that forced her to abandon me. Don't you understand, every time he looks into my blue eyes, he sees Corinne. He knows he could never make her love him the way she loved me. Oh, she must have hated him . . . otherwise she never would have left me. I'll never forgive him for losing her."

For the first time in years, I actually felt sympathy for my husband, and I reached out to touch his trembling hand. "But he spent more time with you when you were older, didn't he?" I asked, hoping to calm his agitation.

"Not until I was much older and I could relieve him of some of his business responsibilities. I was sent to one private school after another until college, anything to keep me out of his sight. When I was away from home, he never wrote or answered any of my letters. One Christmas vacation I returned home from boarding school and found a house full of servants, but my father gone on one of his safaris. It never occurred to him to take me along. I had no friends to speak of, so I spent the entire holiday vacation wandering about Foxworth Hall, listening to the echo of my own footsteps."

"Malcolm," I said, seeing he was in the mood to talk about his past, something he rarely liked to do, "I've always meant to ask you. After your mother left, did she ever write to you? Did you ever hear from her?"

"Not a word, not a card, nothing. When I was young, I used to think my father was hiding her letters to me and I would stay alone up in my room for hours writing her endless letters that were never mailed. I would plead for her to come back to me. I was only five years old! I needed her! I couldn't comprehend what possessed her to turn her back on her loving son. If I could talk to her right now, that's all I'd want to know."

"What good would that do you now?" I asked.

"You wouldn't understand," he said, and left me rather than continue the conversation.

I was surprised to see him return home on the day of Christopher's birthday party in time to attend the festivities. It wasn't beyond him to ignore the boy's special day, even though it would hurt his father. What surprised me was the way he looked at Alicia when he set eyes on her in the foyer, where she was entertaining the neighboring children.

She was wearing one of those sack dresses that made women look more like boys, although she didn't wear any flattener to keep her breasts from poking up against the flimsy material. She had her hair up and she wore two strings of enormous pearls. At a party, with people around her, she grew radiant and alive again. She looked as she had when she first arrived at Foxworth Hall. Even Garland seemed regenerated; the tired, worn expression he had been wearing lifted like a mask.

Alicia's laughter echoed through the large room. The children were delighted with her warmth and gaiety. They trailed after her, vying for her attention. Our two boys were at the forefront, chanting her name.

Malcolm stood like a statue watching her. I expected to see that characteristic sneer, that hateful look in his eyes, but instead, I saw his face soften and his lips relax. He looked like one of the children, enamored of her.

Something wild and frightening burgeoned in my heart. He was looking at her with the kind of longing only a man in love had for a woman. What I thought had died had not. It had been hibernating, sleeping like some giant bear, waiting for spring. Alicia's beauty was that spring. It tempted him, awoke the strong feelings in him, and beckoned him in pursuit once again.

I heard it in the way he addressed her when they spoke. I saw it in his eyes, eyes that would not move from her as she went about the foyer, conducting the party. He was satisfied sitting in a chair, sipping tea, and observing Alicia all afternoon.

Long after the party ended and the guests were gone, Malcolm remained in the foyer watching Alicia supervise the cleanup. Garland, tired from the activity, retreated to his bedroom to rest. I saw to bathing the children and preparing them for bed.

Alicia announced she was retiring to the Swan Room to relax with a good book.

"Wasn't it a wonderful little party?" she asked me.

"The children enjoyed it," I admitted. "One wonders, though, if a three-year-old can appreciate such festivity."

"Oh, Olivia, sometimes you sound just like Malcolm," she sighed. I was sorry he wasn't close enough to hear that.

I watched her go up the spiral staircase and then I went to gather my needlework and take it up to my bedroom. I didn't rush right upstairs. The servants had some questions about some of the glassware and Mrs. Wilson wanted to discuss the menu for the coming week.

What happened next was later told to me by Alicia, but she was in such a hysterical state at the time, it was difficult to understand all of it.

I was halfway up the staircase when I heard her scream. That was followed by a loud crash against the wall of the Swan Room. I hurried up the remaining steps and rushed down the hallway to her doorway in time to see Garland crumple on the floor, clutching his chest. He was in a nightdress; apparently he had been woken from his sleep, and had come running barefoot to the Swan Room.

Alicia was sprawled over the bed, her nightgown torn from the right shoulder to the waist, her breasts exposed. Malcolm stood over his father's collapsed body, his hands clenched into fists, his face beet-red, his eyes bulging. There was a long scratch down the right side of his face.

"What's happened?" I screamed.

"Quick, call for the doctor," Malcolm commanded, gathering some control of himself when he set eyes on me. I looked at Alicia, who was now crying hysterically and trying to cover herself with the torn shred of her nightgown. Garland wasn't moving, so I rushed to the nearest phone, the one in the trophy room, and called Dr. Braxten.

By the time he arrived, Malcolm had dragged Garland's body back into his own bedroom and placed him on his bed. Alicia, wearing a robe over her torn nightgown, was at Garland's side, sobbing and holding his limp hand.

"What happened?" Dr. Braxten asked, rushing to the bed. Malcolm looked first at me, then at Alicia before replying.

"He had an attack of some sort and yelled out. By the time I arrived, he was like this," he explained.

The doctor placed his stethoscope on Garland's chest and listened for a heartbeat. Then he checked his eyes and his pulse.

"Must have been a heart attack," he said softly. "I'm sorry. There's nothing left for me to do."

Alicia wailed and threw her body over Garland's.

"No! No! No!" she screamed. "It can't be. We just celebrated our son's birthday. Please, no. Please. *Garland, wake up! Show them you're not dead! Garland! Garland!*" Her sobbing was so intense, it shook the bed.

Malcolm turned and fled. He didn't look at me on the way out.

"I'll contact the undertaker," Dr. Braxten said softly. He looked back at Alicia. "It's best they get here as soon as possible."

"Of course," I said.

"He did come to see me a few weeks ago," Dr. Braxten explained, "and I told him I wasn't happy with his heart then, but he made me swear not to tell anyone, especially Alicia. He was that kind of a man."

"Yes," I said, understanding Garland's motives. He never wanted to admit his age. He did everything possible to make life rosy for Alicia.

"Will she be all right? I can give her something to help her sleep," he said. I went to her, hesitating to put my hands on her. Finally, I touched her shoulder.

"Alicia, the doctor wants to know if you want him to give you something to help you sleep."

She shook her head and then raised herself slowly from Garland's body. She wore a dazed look and gazed about the room as if she were in a dream. The doctor moved to her.

"It will be better for you if you go back to your own bed," he said. "Sleep is the only cure for such great sorrow."

She nodded and permitted him to help her to her feet. As he walked her to the door, she looked back at

Garland's corpse and began to cry hysterically again. I followed them out and closed the door behind me.

Malcolm was nowhere about. He had retreated to some room in the house, but I wasn't interested in locating him at the moment. I went with the doctor and Alicia to the Swan Room. Alicia permitted him to put her into her bed like a child.

"You should stay with her for a while," he told me.

"Of course I will," I said. I felt quite dazed by the events myself, but I was never one to lose control and dignity. It pleased me that the doctor sensed my ability to handle affairs in the midst of a crisis. Alicia was, after all, more like a child.

"I'll go call the undertaker," he whispered. "Call me if you need me."

"Thank you, Dr. Braxten."

"I'm sorry," he said. "He was a fine . . . I'm sorry," he added, and left.

I looked down at Alicia. She had turned her face into the pillow and was sobbing softly. I went to the doorway and closed the door, locking it behind me. I didn't want us to be disturbed for a while. Then I returned to the swan bed and sat down beside her.

"Alicia," I said. "I must know what happened here before I came upon the terrible scene. What was Malcolm doing in your room?" Her sobbing intensified. "Alicia, you must tell me. You have no one else now," I added, thinking that was a good point to bring up at this moment. It struck home, for her sobbing lessened and she began to turn to me. She pressed her hands against her face as if to stop the tears, and then brought the blanket to her face.

"It was horrible, horrible," she began.

"What was?"

"I was just lying here, reading, feeling so good about the party and how happy everyone was. Garland . . ." She started to cry again. "He was so proud, so happy."

"What happened here?" I asked, pursuing.

"I didn't lock my door. Sometimes . . . sometimes Garland comes to me in the middle of the night," she said. "When I heard it open, I assumed it was Garland, but it was Malcolm," she said, looking at the door quickly, her face twisting as though the entire scene were being reenacted before her very eyes.

"What did he want?"

"He wanted—" She stopped as if telling me were the most indecent thing she could do. "He wanted me," she said, her anger growing. "He came to my bed. I told him he shouldn't be in here. He laughed and said not to worry. Garland was asleep. He said terrible things to me. He told me Garland was too old to satisfy me now, that now I would need him more than ever and it was all right since he was Garland's son."

"What did you do?"

"I told him to get out or I would call Garland, but he wouldn't leave the room. I sat up, preparing to scream if he came any closer. He must have realized that, because he rushed onto the bed and put his hand over my mouth, pressing me back to the pillow and . . . fondling me roughly. I tried to fight him off and he ripped my nightgown. During the struggle I knocked over that small night-table lamp and I managed a scream. Garland heard it and came to the doorway in time to see Malcolm trying to smother me with his body."

"I thought as much," I said.

"Garland rushed to the bed and pulled Malcolm off. They began to wrestle, Garland cursed him, and Malcolm said all sorts of terrible things about Garland's first wife, this room, his manhood. They fell to the floor and continued struggling, but neither struck the other with his fist.

"Finally, Malcolm broke free of Garland's hold and crawled toward the doorway, but Garland was in such a rage, he wouldn't permit him to escape. He took hold of him again and they threw each other about until Garland screamed. He slipped out of Malcolm's arms and fell to the floor where he . . . he, oh, God. Is it true? Is Garland dead?"

"It's true," I said.

"Garland. Garland, my Garland." She fell back against her pillow and began to sob again. I knew she would cry herself into an exhaustion and fall asleep. There was nothing more I could do for her. I left her there and went out to seek Malcolm.

I found him in the trophy room and imagined he had been watching us through his peephole the entire time. He was seated in a leather chair, staring at the doorway, his face silkily white and his eyes wide and wild like the eyes of a man looking at his own death. His hands clutched the arms of the chair so hard, I could see the veins popping below his knuckles. He seemed to be holding on for dear life.

"What have you done?" I asked him.

"Leave me alone."

"Do you know what will happen when people hear of this?"

"No one will hear of anything. It wasn't my fault. He was a sick man anyway. The doctor will testify to that.

Now, get out and leave me be," he said, speaking through his clenched teeth.

"You're a hateful person, Malcolm. You'll never be a happy man after this."

"It was her fault," he said. "Not mine."

"Her fault?" I almost laughed.

"Get out," he repeated. I shook my head.

"I pity you." At that moment I really did pity him. No matter what kind of face he put on, I knew he would suffer guilt that would haunt him for the rest of his life. It would change him in other ways later, but for the present it would work like a knife, cutting into his heart. It was obvious that he was trying to ease his own pain by blaming it all on Alicia. In his twisted mind she was responsible because she resisted him and called for Garland's help. In his twisted mind the woman was always responsible, never the man.

Sometime later he would tell me that Alicia tempted him, tormented him. That was why she got what she deserved. He would blame it on the type of woman she was. He hated her and he loved her the way he hated and loved his mother.

I left him in that dark room, sitting in the shadows.

It was a large funeral, despite Malcolm's hope that it wouldn't be. People came from all over, some traveling great distances—business acquaintances, old friends, relatives, and many who were curious about the death of one of the area's richest men.

Malcolm wanted his father's body cremated, followed by a small, short ceremony, but Garland had anticipated his son's indifference. He had left specific instructions with the minister, in writing; and when Reverend Masterson produced the document, Malcolm could do nothing about it. The elaborate funeral would be held, the money spent.

The only fortunate thing, from his point of view, was Alicia's condition right before, during, and after the funeral. She was on heavy tranquilizers and moved about like a sleepwalker in a nightmare, her face ashen, her eyes vacant, hearing no one, seeing no one, saying nothing. Her mother, quite a sick woman herself at this point, was unable to make the journey. As I had told her the night Garland died, she had no one but me.

I saw that she was dressed properly, that she took some nourishment, and that Christopher was well taken care of. I guided her through the ceremony, remained at her side, sometimes literally holding her up. I could see the way people were watching us, how they remarked on my concern for her to one another, how they were impressed by the way I took care of her.

Mrs. Whipple, a middle-aged woman who had served as Garland's personal secretary for many years, told me: "Garland would be so grateful to you for the way you are helping Alicia. He was so fond of her, so fond."

"I'm doing only what is right," I told her. "No one need thank me."

"Of course," she said.

The mourners came to comfort Alicia, but she looked through every one of them. Garland's death had turned them all into strangers. In a sense all those she knew through or because of him died with him. She had already begun her transition into another world, a world without Garland, without his laughter and love, a world filled with echoes and memories. Perhaps I clung to her so tightly because I understood the world she was about to enter better than she ever would. It was almost as though I were welcoming her to it, understanding that she would be joining me, and from now on, we would both suffer the same loneliness.

During the month that followed, Alicia was practically an invalid. Still under great mental strain and taking medication, she often had to be reminded to do simple things for herself, like come down to breakfast or dinner. She herself chose darker, more simple dresses to wear. Her complexion remained pale. Her broken heart had come up and darkened her eyes until they looked as vacant as the artificial eyes of some of the animals stuffed and mounted in the trophy room. The only thing that brought any light to her face was Christopher. If it weren't for him, she would probably never have come out of her room.

During the days of mourning, Malcolm behaved as if Alicia were no longer there. Whenever he did see her, he looked through her, beyond her. He never spoke to her and she never said a word to him. He never asked me anything about her either. I knew it was his way of avoiding his own guilt. Perhaps he hoped she would languish and die and his responsibility for what had occurred would never be revealed.

Of course, she had made it easy for him to do all this, walking about like a ghost, dressed in either black, dark gray, or dark blue, with no makeup, her hair pinned back sternly, and she always avoided his eyes.

Our dinners, the ones she attended, were like funeral feasts. She ate slowly, mechanically. Malcolm sat looking forward, sometimes asking me a question, sometimes making a comment. There was never any long conversation—just questions and answers. Even though she ate, her fingers trembled when she took the fork into them. She cut her meat slowly, laboriously, as though the knife were terribly dull. Alicia didn't even realize when the dinner had ended. Malcolm would get up suddenly and leave the table, and she would look up, surprised. It was as if she had just realized she was sitting there.

She would look down at Garland's seat pathetically. The absence of a setting pained her every time she sat at the dinner table. I was sure that was why she resisted attending.

And when she did look at Malcolm, I saw her look of confusion. I imagined she was trying to put all of the events into some perspective, organize them in a way that would permit her to deal with them. He looked as calm and collected as ever. She couldn't see any change in him. Maybe it had all been a dream. Maybe Garland was coming down to dinner any moment. Once, I thought she even sat there waiting for him. I had to tell her to begin eating.

Malcolm didn't permit her eerie presence at these meals to disturb him. His appetite was good. Nothing weakened him. If he were haunted by any dreams, I never knew. He seemed satisfied with the way things were, especially the way things were between him and Alicia.

But her attitude was wearing on my nerves, and sending all three of the boys into a funk.

Finally one day I went in to have a stern talk with her. I thought it was time. I was hoping that once she recovered from Garland's death, she would think about leaving Foxworth Hall. I thought that she herself would want to start someplace new, once the financial situation was clear. She was young enough to find a new husband, especially with the kind of wealth she enjoyed. What man wouldn't want a beautiful, rich woman with a beautiful child?

"None of us is happy about what happened," I said, "but you still have responsibilities. You are still Mrs. Garland Christopher Foxworth, and as his wife you should overcome your grief and begin to take care of your son properly." She wanted to start to cry, but I wouldn't permit it, even though I pitied her sitting there on her bed, looking as fragile as a baby robin. Despair had washed all the color from her face.

"What kind of an example are you setting for Christopher? For Mal and for Joel?" I continued. "They all see what you are and what you are doing. Your attitude is turning this house into a morgue."

"Oh, Olivia, I can't get it through my head that Garland is really gone." She pressed her hands together and began to turn them as though she were wringing out invisible wet clothes.

"He is gone, and it shouldn't be such a surprise. Some time ago, I had a discussion with you about your marriage, and I pointed out that he would die long before you. You didn't seem to care."

"I cared. I just didn't believe it would happen."

"I tried to warn you about living in a dream world. Now you are living in reality, just as I have had to from the first day I walked into this house."

She looked up at me sharply. That she understood.

"You're so much stronger than I am, Olivia. You're not afraid of anything; you're not afraid of being alone."

"Life makes you strong. If you don't let it make you strong, it will kill you. Is that what you want? Do you want to leave your son?"

"No!"

"Then shake off this self-pity and be a mother to your child."

She nodded slowly.

"I know you're right. I am indebted to you in so many ways. I knew from the first day I came here that you were a wise and intelligent woman. Malcolm never intimidates you, no matter what he does."

"Get dressed, come down to dinner, and end this wallowing in grief," I commanded.

Perhaps I should have permitted her to remain forever in mourning. Perhaps I should have encouraged it. My little talk was too effective. When she came down to dinner that night, she began a rather quick recovery. Grief, no matter how you cater to its gloom, has a way of dissipating. She appeared at the table that night as someone who had just awoken from a long sleep. She had rouged her cheeks, and painted her lips, put on a bright blue dress and wore one of the diamond necklaces Garland had bought her. I had forgotten how beautiful and charming she could be. I should never have forgotten that. The moment she stepped into the dining room, I realized I had resurrected more than Alicia's beauty. Malcolm's eyes widened; his undertaker face disappeared. Not only did he look at her intently again, but before the dinner ended, he spoke directly to her. He put on his haughty manner like a hat as he explained some of the details of Garland's estate and how he planned to invest her money.

"It will be a while yet before I have things straightened out," he said, "but soon I will sit down with you and explain your financial situation."

"Thank you," she said.

"Why is it taking so long?" I asked. "It didn't take this long after my father died."

"Things were not quite as complex. My father insisted on some intricate clauses that the probate lawyers have to work out. Our money is invested in diverse areas. Your father was a businessman, not an investor. His fortune should have been doubled by now," he added for my benefit.

"It's all right, Olivia," Alicia said. "I'm sure it won't be much longer."

Malcolm was very pleased by her comment. It was almost as though she had come to his defense. If she wants to be the fool, I thought, let her.

Her recovery continued. She looked after Christopher completely and, as before, devoted most of the time to all the children. She went out to shop for some new clothing for herself and for Christopher and she grew stronger, brighter, even prettier every day.

I saw the way Malcolm watched her recovery. Although they said only what was necessary to each other, I was surprised at how civil she was to him. Surely she blamed him for everything, I thought. Surely she despised him. How could she even look at him? Was there no anger and hate in her? Was she so innocent and pure that vengeance could find no home in her bosom? Her tolerance, her softness, her returning happiness infuriated me. I had even hoped to see her plot against Malcolm; perhaps enlist me in some plan to force him to give her more money, for that was the one thing that would have hurt Malcolm the most—expanding on the settlement.

But she was entirely trusting and patient. Didn't she understand how dangerous it was to be kind to a man like Malcolm? When I could tolerate it no longer, I confronted her and was astonished at her thinking.

"Malcolm must be suffering too," she said. "It was his father. He has to live with it."

"Look how well he is living with it," I said. "Has it slowed him down even a little? He's at his business just as vigorously as before. He's even happier because Garland isn't around to question anything he does!"

"Perhaps it's just an act."

"An act! Do you know that he didn't want to spend half as much as was spent on Garland's funeral? Do you know he still complains about that?"

She smiled like some nun refusing to admit to violence and cruelty in the world God created. Everything had a reason, a purpose, and would be explained in the hereafter. She was incapable of facing or admitting the existence of evil in the hearts of men.

"I understand his motives. He couldn't face the funeral; he wanted to keep it small so it would be easier for him."

"You fool," I said. "He cared only about the cost, not the significance. Why don't you pressure him more to settle your estate? Who knows what he's doing to cheat you?"

"I wouldn't even know where to begin, Olivia. I was never very business-minded. He'll follow Garland's wishes, I'm sure," she said.

"Do you want to languish here forever, waiting? You're young, still very beautiful. Don't you envision a new life for yourself?"

"I don't know," she said, looking around. "I can't see myself leaving Foxworth Hall just yet. Garland's spirit is still here. Shouldn't his son grow up here?"

I sat back, frustrated with such simplicity, such innocent trust and faith.

"What about a new husband?" I said. "Do you think if you took a new husband, he could come here to live with you? Do you think Malcolm would tolerate that?"

"Oh, I don't want to think about a new husband." She smiled as though the idea were farfetched.

"You are making a mistake," I said. "You should be planning your future and the future of your son. No one else is going to do that for you, especially not Malcolm. Put the past away."

"There's a time for that. I don't think anyone would be in so great a rush."

"I would."

"No, you wouldn't."

"I assure you," I said, flushing with anger, "I would. And someday you'll wish you had listened to me." Someday was to come even sooner than I had expected.

10

Malcolm Has His Way

ALICIA NEVER FORGOT MY WORDS OF WARNING, EVEN though she pretended not to have heard them. She continued to move through the house like a grown child, her innocence and brightness lighting the dark shadows of Foxworth Hall. Whenever Malcolm spoke to her or whenever she was forced to speak to him, she looked like a young girl who had built up her courage to face the dentist. She listened to whatever she had to hear; she said what she had to say, and then she moved off, her smile and cheery voice returning as it would to one who had lived through the worst and now could go on.

The evenings were different though. After Christopher had eaten and she had finished dinner, and after she put her three-year-old son to sleep in the nursery, she would avoid any contact with Malcolm, and, after a while, even any contact with me. If she didn't leave the house for one reason or another, she would retreat to the Swan Room, supposedly to read and relax.

Often, when I put my ear to the wall in my room, I would hear her sobbing and talking as though Garland were there living beside her on the bed. I could almost believe that a love as passionate as theirs had been would enable them to reach across the abyss between life and death and join hands for some precious moments every night.

"Oh, Garland, Garland, I miss you so," she would cry. "How hard it is here without you and how much little Christopher misses you. Garland, my love."

I did feel sorry for her, for I understood why she was so reluctant to leave and why she hadn't pressured Malcolm to settle her estate and make leaving possible. As long as she was here, as long as she slept in the Swan Room, she kept Garland alive in her mind. Once she left Foxworth Hall, Garland would be left finally in his grave.

One dark night in midwinter I was awakened to the sound of her cries, only these were not cries of sorrow; these were cries of fear. Confused, I slipped out of my bed and put my ear to the wall. Her cries became muffled, almost inaudible. I put on my robe and went to the doorway of the Swan Room. I listened and then knocked softly.

"Alicia. Alicia, are you all right?"

There was no response, so I tried the handle, but the door was locked. I tapped again and waited. Still, there was only silence. Perhaps she was only having a dream, I thought and went back to sleep.

In the morning she was different, more the way she had been during her bereavement. She didn't come down to breakfast until after Malcolm had gone and she ate very little.

"Are you sick?" I asked her.

"No," she said, offering no other explanation. She continued to pick at her food and then put her fork down.

"You certainly look sick. And you've left practically everything on your plate."

"I'm not sick," she repeated. She looked at me with tear-filled eyes. I held my breath, expecting her to tell me some great secret, but she simply bit her lip and got up from the table.

"Alicia," I called. She did not turn around but returned to her room, where she remained for most of the day.

She was like that on and off over the next few weeks. Sometimes she would be talkative and full of energy and I would think she was herself again, and then she would become moody and quiet and withdrawn. She either couldn't or wouldn't explain why.

A week later I was again awoken by the sound of her cries. This time they were shrill but short. They stopped before I even decided to go to her door. In the morning she was dreary and tired, moving like one in a daze. Both Malcolm and I had finished our breakfast, so she ate alone. She spent the whole afternoon alone in the Swan Room. Finally, driven more by my curiosity than anything, I went up to her.

She was lying on her back, fully dressed, staring up at the ceiling. She didn't even hear me knock or open the door, nor did she hear me approach her.

"Alicia," I said. "Are you ill? Is this something that comes and goes?"

She looked at me as if she were accustomed to people simply appearing beside her in the room. There was no surprise in her face.

"Ill?"

"Again, you hardly ate today and you spent no time with Christopher. You've been up here for hours, apparently just lying here in your clothing."

"Yes," she said, "I'm ill." She turned away, eager for me to leave, but I was determined to know what was going on.

"What is wrong with you? Are you in pain? Do you wake up with pain every night?"

"Yes, I'm in pain."

"Where is this pain?"

"In my heart," she said.

"Oh." I shook my head and looked down at her. "I think it will be that way for you until you leave this house," I said. Her lips began to quiver and she brought her hands to her face. "Crying won't help; nothing will help but doing what I say. If you want to leave, I will pressure Malcolm into ending this deliberately prolonged settlement of your estate. Frankly, I think it would be better for everyone. You don't realize how depressing you can be and—"

"Oh, Olivia," she said, suddenly turning on me, taking her hands away from her face and looking more distraught than I had ever seen her look. "You are so intelligent, so strong. Don't you know what is happening? Surely you sense it."

I stared down at her, unable to speak for a moment. She bit her lower lip and shook her head as if she were trying to prevent herself from saying any more.

"What?" I asked. "Tell me."

"You knew. You always knew. You expected it. I saw it in your face, but I was afraid to say anything to you."

"Malcolm," I said. I looked about the Swan Room, instinctively understanding that it was this room, this magnificent bed, these sensual surroundings that were partly responsible. Why had she remained in here after Garland's death? "Tell me exactly what has happened."

She took a deep breath and wiped the tears from her cheeks.

"He has been coming to me at night and forcing himself on me," she confessed, speaking barely above a whisper.

I pressed my fingers into my own palms so hard that the nails cut my skin. Of course. In my heart I had known what she was going to tell me. I came in here and forced her to say it, partly to punish myself and partly, by forcing her to say it, to punish her. What had almost happened at the lake and what Garland had prevented with his death had finally happened. From the day I stood by Malcolm's side and first set eyes on her getting out of that car with Garland, I knew it was inevitable. I saw it in the way Malcolm had looked at her then and the way he looked at her whenever she moved through this house, her rich chestnut hair tumbling about her neck and shoulders, her eyes bright with life and energy.

"Why didn't you lock your door?"

"I did, but he had a key. He always had a key. He didn't have to use it until after Garland's death. I never told you this, but even before Garland died, he came in here one night. He knew I left the door open for Garland. I heard him. Of course I thought it was Garland at first, but when I looked up and saw it was Malcolm, I pretended to be fast asleep.

"He came to the side of my bed and he stood there staring down at me for the longest time. I thought if I moved, even in the slightest way, he would . . . he would attack me, so I remained as still as I could. I felt him touch my hair ever so gently and I heard him sigh. Then he turned and slipped out of the room as silently as he had come in."

"But you never told Garland?"

"No. I was afraid of what he would do, and as you see, I was right. It all came to tragedy. Oh, Olivia, Olivia."

"So you locked your door now and he came in. Why did you permit it this time? Garland was already dead."

"He told me he would hurt Christopher. He would find a way. It would be easy for him, he said. There was no one to stop him from doing anything anymore, he said. And he was violent at times."

I sat down beside her, my heart pounding. I recalled the first night he had come to me, how rough he had been. She had every reason to fear he would harm Christopher. Malcolm was capable of great violence in order to get what he wanted.

"How long has this been . . . has he been coming to you?"

"It's been on and off for over a month."

"A month?" I hadn't realized it had been going on that long. How could she have kept it to herself that long?

She sat up. "The first time he came, I thought it was a dream, a nightmare. It was late at night. He slipped in so silently, I never heard him until he was actually beside me in the bed. I turned and there he was, naked. He embraced me and pressed his mouth against mine before I could utter a word, a scream, and he held it there so long, I thought I would smother."

"What then?" I asked.

"He frightened me, not because I thought he would

hurt me so much, but because of the way he was acting, the things he was saying."

"What things?"

"He didn't call me Alicia when he stroked my body and kissed my breasts."

For a moment I thought I couldn't breathe. I pressed my palms against my chest and tried to swallow. In my heart I knew what she was going to say now, too, but I was terrified at hearing her say it.

"He called me Corinne. I thought he was having a dream, walking in his sleep, so I tried to reason with him, to tell him I was not Corinne, that he should wake and go back to his bedroom, but he didn't hear me. He pressed on, not roughly, but persistently, intently. It was no good trying to fight him off; he was too strong. When I finally tried to resist, he held my arms down, and every time I cried out, he pressed his mouth against mine so hard and roughly, I feared for my very life. I had to subdue my cries and let him have his way. It was awful, awful," she said, burying her face in her hands.

"What happened when it was over? Did he still call you Corinne?" She looked up and shook her head.

"When it was over and he had spent himself, he knew exactly where he was and who I was. That was when he told me never to speak about it or he would harm Christopher. I thought, I hoped and prayed, that would be it; but he came again and again. He was here last night," she added, and brought her hands to her face again.

"I came to your door once when I heard your cries. Didn't you hear me knock and call to you?"

"Yes, but he had his hand around my throat and he squeezed so hard, I couldn't breathe. Then he brought his face to mine and forbade me to utter a sound. I knew he would kill me if I did."

"Why didn't you come to me before this?"

"I told you. I was afraid for Christopher. Malcolm seems always to get whatever he wants one way or another. Even if you stopped it from happening, he would take his revenge, don't you see? I'm sorry, Olivia. I know I should have told you, but I was frightened. Please, forgive me for that."

I couldn't blame her for being afraid. There were times when I feared Malcolm myself.

For a few moments I sat there in silence, thinking about this room, thinking about what Malcolm had done. It was as if his mother's spirit still lived here, still tormented him. For him to come back to Alicia, even after the terrible and fatal scene with his father, was unbelievable. I knew Alicia felt safe because she didn't believe Malcolm could do that after being responsible for Garland's death.

"Does he always start off by calling you Corinne?"

"Yes."

"And he always ends by knowing you're Alicia?"

"Not always. Sometimes he leaves without calling me Alicia. He just gets up and walks out like he's asleep. One time, the third time, he made me do something terrible. He's insane."

"What did he make you do?"

"He took one of those old nightgowns out of the closet and made me put it on before he . . . before he got into the bed beside me. I had to walk about this room and sit at the dressing table. He put her brush into my hand and sat on the bed while I ran it through my hair. He even made me go into the bathroom and come out as though I were getting ready for bed. I felt just sick doing it, but I couldn't refuse him. He became even more enraged when I hesitated."

How horrible, I thought. How sick and how horrible. I spun around and looked at the wall between the Swan Room and the trophy room. Then I turned back to her angrily.

"You should have had all those dresses taken up to the attic when you first moved in here," I said. How could she ever have anticipated what Malcolm would make her do?

And yet, I couldn't help but think her responsible, she had been too trusting and innocent. I looked at her. She had been given all the warnings. I had practically pleaded with her to listen to me, but she was foolish and stubborn, insisting on holding on to a dead love.

Maybe she was lying to me; maybe she really enjoyed what Malcolm had done and was doing and now felt guilty about it. I knew Alicia was that kind of woman—the kind of woman who wore sex about her like a racy undergarment. "Have you done something to tempt him? Did you ever invite him to this room?"

"No; oh, no. You must never believe that, Olivia. I did nothing, nothing," she protested. "In fact, he once followed me to the lake when I went for a dip and tried to get me to make love to him. I ran from him and told him that if he didn't stop his advances, I would tell Garland."

"Why didn't you ever tell Garland before . . .?"

"I didn't want what finally happened to happen. Do you think I'm responsible for Garland's death, that if I had told him about Malcolm earlier, I might have prevented it? Do you, Olivia?"

"I don't know. Maybe. Maybe not. Maybe he would have died earlier." I looked at her suspiciously. "Why did you finally tell me this? If you're afraid of what Malcolm could do to Christopher?"

"Because I had to now."

"Why? What makes it any different now?"

"Oh, Olivia," she hesitated. "I'm in such trouble." She started to cry again.

"I can't help you if I don't know everything," I said. "All right, then. Why are you in so much trouble?"

"I am in trouble because . . ."

I felt all the shadows of Foxworth Hall gathering around me, to drown me in their darkness.

". . . because I'm pregnant with Malcolm's child."

I stood up and went to the window. I saw Olsen below trimming hedges and I thought, here I have all this—all this land, this beautiful house, two good-looking boys, wealth beyond imagination, and I was one of the most unhappy women in the world. It was unfair; it was a cruel joke. I wished that I would awaken and find that all of this—my marriage to Malcolm, the death of my father and of Garland, the rape of Alicia—was just a long terrible dream. I thought I might even welcome being back in my father's house with the prospects of being a spinster for the rest of my life.

"Please, don't hate me, Olivia," she begged. I did hate her; I couldn't help but hate her. I would always hate her and women like her.

I closed my eyes, straightened my back, and took hold of myself again. I vowed that nothing Malcolm Neal Foxworth did or would do would ever reduce me to the sniveling weakling Alicia now was. I turned to her slowly. She saw the resolve in my face and sat up in the bed.

"Does Malcolm know this?"

"Yes," she said. "I told him this morning."

"This morning? When this morning? He was with me this morning at breakfast and left before you came down."

"I didn't sleep all night. I wanted to tell him last night before he left my room, but he was like a man walking in his sleep again and he wouldn't respond." She looked down. "So I went to his room before he rose."

"You went to his room?" After all that had happened, that should not have seemed so important to me, but throughout all the years Malcolm and I had been married, I had never gone to his bedroom while he was there. "While he was still asleep?"

"Yes. I stood by his bed and waited for him to realize I was standing there. When he opened his eyes, he looked at me as though I were a ghost. It took him a few moments to realize it was me. At first he was angry I had come to his room, but I had to tell him what he had done, don't you see?" she said. "I blurted it out before he could say anything else."

"What did he say?" I asked, remembering how calm, how ordinary Malcolm's behavior had been at breakfast. But then again, I realized that it was his "poker face," his cool and controlled manner that enabled him to outsmart so many in the business world.

"First he smiled," Alicia said, "but so coldly, it gave me the chills. Then he said many terrible things, making it seem as if it were all my fault. I wanted to shout, to scream, to cry, but I was afraid to wake the house," she said. "He gave me an ultimatum. I don't know what to do," she added quickly. "I'm sure he would do what he said he would if I don't agree. I'm afraid, afraid for myself and for Christopher."

Now I understood that she had worked herself up to appeal to me for help. She had been lying here all day, trying to figure out a way to come to me. I had made it easier for her by coming to her.

"What was the ultimatum?"

"He wants me to remain here and have the child in secret. Then Christopher and I are to leave. We will get all the money Garland left to us. He explained that it has been invested in the stock market, but he will liquidate what we need to start somewhere new and then I will have full control of our funds."

"But why have the baby in secret? What difference does it make if you leave now and have the baby someplace else where no one knows you?"

She looked down. There was something more, something more terrible for her to add.

"He wants the baby," she said.

"What?"

"The child is to be his, yours." She spoke quickly. "He said if I didn't agree, he would accuse me of being a fortune hunter. He said that because I've become pregnant after Garland's death, he will be able to have his lawyers drag me through the courts and prove I am a woman of little virtue who married an elderly man to gain wealth, and after he died, I gave myself to Malcolm in order to blackmail him for even more wealth. He said he didn't care what kind of publicity it brought to the Foxworths. Publicity couldn't hurt him; it could hurt only me.

"He said he would drive me out of here penniless, and put me through a scandalous court trial. I would have a reputation and no one would want to be seen with me. The headlines and publicity would kill my mother, who, as you know, is already deathly ill.

"I wouldn't even know how to fight him. I have no lawyers, no contact with that sort of person. Garland took care of all that, and after he died, Malcolm has been handling my legal affairs. Here I would be, a widow with a three-year-old child, at the mercy of the cold world."

"He wants the child?" I repeated.

"Yes. He says he knows it will be a girl. I am to live in the north wing, secluded until after the birth. Then I will be free to leave with Christopher and my money intact." She wrung her hands and looked at me with plaintive eyes. "Oh, Olivia, what shall I do? You must help me decide! You must!"

I stared at her, and for a long moment, I felt helpless. Malcolm Neal Foxworth always got what he wanted, one way or another. He wanted a daughter. Now he had gotten one. In my mind I had no doubt Alicia's child would be a girl.

All this had been going on right before my eyes. I had sensed and suspected, but I had refused to permit myself to believe it, and now I had to swallow the bitter pill of truth. I couldn't close my door or look the other way. I was as much a part of it as she was because I had not prevented it. I was like a mother who had to take responsibility for the actions of her child who knew no better. Malcolm had used and abused her in the worst way a man could abuse a woman, and she had been helpless to protect herself.

Perhaps worst of all, she was now pregnant with the child that should have been mine. If a daughter was indeed to be born to the Foxworths, it should be my daughter, not hers.

I envied her, but I didn't respect her. In that moment I felt all sympathy for her slip away.

"Olivia," she repeated, "what should I do?"

"Do?" I said. "I think you've done enough." I looked at her and her eyes skipped guiltily away. She knew she shouldn't have let it get this far; she knew that now, but she was hoping I would come up with some sort of solution that would save her.

I looked at my own reflection in the mirror above the dressing table and saw that I had already taken on the hardness that was to characterize me for the rest of my life. I was looking at myself with flint-hard gray eyes. My lips, pressed tightly together, formed a thin, crooked knife slash, and my breasts looked like twin hills of concrete.

"Olivia?" Her voice was filled with pleading.

"There's nothing for you to do," I said, "but what Malcolm wants. Start to gather your things together. Plans and preparations must be made. Begin to tell people that you are intending to leave Foxworth Hall, so that when you go into hiding, no one will miss you."

"But what about Christopher? Someone's bound to see Christopher."

"Christopher won't be with you," I said, inventing the ideas as quickly as I spoke.

"What? What are you saying?"

"You will give it out that you are going on a prolonged trip, during which time Christopher will remain here. When you return, you will be leaving Foxworth Hall for good. This trip is to make preparations for your new life. No one need know the details, especially the servants. If anything, we will leave them with the suggestion you are finding a new husband," I added, satisfied with that touch. Her face was a study of shock and dismay.

"Shut away from my child? All these months? But

he's a little boy, just three years old. He's already lost his father. He needs his mother. I know that he is close to Mal and Joel and he'll enjoy their companionship, but . . ."

"They won't be permitted into the north wing," I went on, ignoring her objections. "You'll take the room at the end, the one that has the adjoining bath. The one," I added, "that you thought was so exciting because of the doorway in the closet that led up to the attic."

"But much of it is dusty and cluttered. It's no place for me to live."

"You'll make the best of it," I said. I had to make her see that she bore some guilt and responsibility for what was happening to her and her child.

"But what about the classes for Malcolm and Joel held at the far end? Mr. Chillingworth?"

"That will have to stop now, won't it?" I said, happy to have a reason to do so. "Obviously, Malcolm will have to agree to that. The boys will have to be sent to school. It will be better that they are away from the house anyway. There will be much less chance of their discovering anything."

"The maids, the servants," she said. She was grasping at anything to stave off her fate. I was amused by her frantic questions, her hope to find a reason why Malcolm's plan couldn't be carried out.

"The ones we now have will all be dismissed. They will leave thinking you are leaving, even thinking that I am pregnant," I added. I couldn't help but like the fact that they would think that. It was almost as if I really were pregnant.

"Even Mrs. Wilson?"

"All of them. Maybe not Olsen. Olsen is not in the

house that much and is somewhat slow-witted. I don't think it matters much about Olsen, and I rather like the way he handles the gardens."

"But a new maid will still have to come up to me, Olivia. She'll know."

"No maid will come up to you. I will come up to you."

"You?"

"I will bring you everything you need," I said. She would be entirely dependent on me for everything—her food, her clothing, her soap, even her toothbrush.

"The doctor," she chirped, thinking she had found a way out.

"We won't need the doctor. Later, we'll get a midwife. You're young, healthy. There'll be no problem."

"I'm afraid," she said.

"What alternative do you have?" With each sentence, I felt my power increasing, as my mind worked quickly to solve every detail. For the first time since I'd come to Foxworth Hall, I felt in control, in command. Yes, now I was true mistress. "You were right to think Malcolm would carry out his threats. And how would you feel having Malcolm's child to care for after all that he has done to you? You couldn't help but take out your frustration and pain on the poor thing," I said.

"I would never . . ."

"A penniless woman with two children to care for, rather than one?"

"I don't know if I can do what he wants." She looked down at her hands in her lap and then looked up at me, resignation settling in her expression. "Only if I know you are here to help me."

"I said what I would do, but I won't spend all my

time in the north wing baby-sitting you," I added. "You must not go into a dream world about this too."

She nodded, now resigned to her fate. Speaking to her like this made me feel even more powerful. I couldn't be as slim and as beautiful as she was, but finally, her beauty had proven to be a weakness and a fault. It had led her down a painful path, a path I would never choose for myself.

In a strange way I thought of her the way I used to think of the miniature dolls in the glass-encased house. I used to feel frustration because I couldn't move them about physically. I could only imagine their movements. But I could move her about. I could put a smile or a grimace on her face. I could make her laugh or cry. She was in my hands and as helpless as a little doll.

"I shall speak to Malcolm," I said. "And demand he explain everything and tell me everything, even the monetary details." She looked up hopefully. It was happening already. Her heart was beating in anticipation. I had sent the blood pounding through her veins with the utterance of a simple sentence.

"Maybe you'll change his mind. Maybe you'll get him to see it would be better if I just left now."

"Maybe. Only don't put too much faith in that. Malcolm has never changed his mind about anything."

"But he listens to you."

"When he wants to; only when he wants to, and only if it will suit his purpose."

"Without your cooperation, this can't work. You could refuse to go along with it."

"I could, but the alternative is not a good one for you, is it, my dear?" I said. If there was one thing I wouldn't tolerate now, it was her making my decisions for me. "He'll simply carry out his threats. You have to look at it another way now. Without me, you will leave this house penniless."

The smile of hope evaporated. I felt like a puppeteer. I had pulled a string and turned her back into a state of depression. From this day forward, she wouldn't go singing and skipping through Foxworth Hall unless I wanted her to. She wouldn't be bubbly and alive unless I wanted her to be.

She fell back on the bed and started to cry.

"I wouldn't do that either, Alicia. You must keep yourself strong and healthy. If you went through all this and something happened to the baby . . ."

"What?" She looked terrified, her eyes wide, her lips pulled tight.

"I don't know what Malcolm would do, but he would believe you hurt or killed the baby on purpose."

"I would never, could never do such a thing."

"Of course you wouldn't, but Malcolm would think you had. Don't you see? You will have to eat well and keep your spirits high."

"But Olivia, I will feel . . . imprisoned."

"Yes," I said. "I know. But we are all imprisoned in one way or another, Alicia. Ironically, your beauty has imprisoned you." I started away.

"But someday it will set me free," she said defiantly. I turned back to her, smiling.

"I hope so, my dear Alicia. But for now, you might as well consider it your lock and key. Who knows what Malcolm might do next time he looks at you? We know what he sees and we don't want him to have his way with you anymore. When you are secured in that room in the north wing, you'll be even more defenseless than you are now, won't you?" I thought aloud. The realization put more terror in her face.

"What should I do? I won't scar my face. I can't become fat and ugly overnight."

"No, you can't. But if I were you, I'd cut off my hair as soon as possible."

"My hair!" She brought both her hands to it quickly, as if it were already being cut. "I couldn't do that. Garland loved my hair. He would spend hours beside me running his fingers through it, stroking it, smelling it."

"But Garland is dead, Alicia. Besides, someday you can grow it back. Right?" She didn't reply. "Right?" I insisted on being answered. I would always insist on that.

"Yes," she said, nearly inaudible.

"After we give it out that you're leaving and you go into the north wing, I'll bring the scissors. I'll even cut it off for you."

She nodded slowly, but that was not enough.

"I said I would do it for you."

She looked up.

"Thank you, Olivia."

I smiled.

"I'll do what I can," I said. "But you must always understand that I am in a peculiar and uncomfortable position too."

"I know. I'm sorry for that. Believe me."

"I believe you," I said. "Take a nap now and later we'll talk more about what has to be done."

She lay back and I left the Swan Room, closing the door softly behind me. I went to the top of the spiral staircase and looked down at the foyer of the great house. I remembered the first morning I had stood up here and started down, how I had felt myself growing in stature with every step. I was to be the mistress of this mansion. So much had happened since that morning to threaten my authority and position, but ironically, as I began to descend now, I felt I had grown taller, stronger, wiser.

Mrs. Steiner, coming from Malcolm's bedroom, where she had straightened and cleaned, surprised me. She walked so softly, I almost suspected her of eavesdropping at the Swan Room door while Alicia revealed all to me.

"Is Mrs. Foxworth feeling ill?" she asked. It was always difficult for the servants to refer to Alicia as Mrs. Foxworth when they spoke to me. I knew they wanted to say "the young Mrs. Foxworth," or even to take the liberty to use her Christian name. I glared at her and she shrank back. "I mean, I want to know when I should go to do her room."

"You won't do her room today," I said.

"Very good, ma'am," she said. She started to go past me.

"She has a headache," I added, "but it's nothing serious."

Mrs. Steiner nodded. I watched her descend the stairs quickly, eager to make distance between us. She really won't mind being let go, I thought. Even though she has been here so long and we pay her well. Malcolm will see to it that she and the others get good severance pay. And afterward, I would tell him how many new servants I wanted. Of course, they would have strict orders to stay out of the north wing.

There would be many things he would have to do now. In many ways he would be taking orders from me. I was looking forward to his explanation of things later, for I would confront him with Alicia's confessions as soon as he returned home. I was sure he was choosing his own time and place to tell me how things were and how they would be. But I would upset his strategy, and I would do my best to get my pound of flesh.

All would be dependent upon me, even Malcolm, in ways he didn't understand or anticipate. I would be in firm control. It was little enough compensation for the things I didn't have, things I had always dreamt of having; but I was not lying to Alicia when I told her we were all imprisoned in one way or another. What I had decided after Alicia had told me about all that had happened between her and Malcolm was that I would accept my imprisonment, and in accepting it, I would become the master of my own prison house.

11

Malcolm's Way, My Way

ARROGANT AS EVER, MALCOLM SHOWED NO REMORSE, NO guilt, no shame. When he arrived home that night, I followed him into his private study, a study into which he retreated every evening before dinner, a study that was off limits to everyone in the house save Malcolm and the maid who cleaned it once a week. As I opened the wide oak door without knocking, Malcolm looked startled and angry. "What are you doing in here, Olivia?" he asked sternly.

I made my face like stone, and put the haughtiest sneer in my voice. "I'm here to talk about your new little baby," I said. Then I confronted him with Alicia's story. I spit every detail at him as I raged against his lust and audacity. The sky was shrouded by a spring storm, furious and dark, with angry bruised clouds hovering outside the windows beyond Malcolm's desk, threatening to come in and consume us. But the clouds were not as bruised and angry as I, and if anyone would consume today, it would be me.

"You're making far too much of this, Olivia," Malcolm said as he rearranged the pencils on his desk.

As I spoke, the desk lamp cast a glow over his face, darkening his eyes. The storm played havoc with the electric system, causing all the lights to blink. With the windows shut tight to keep out the fierce rain, which now pounded furiously against the windows, scratching at the glass, we seemed trapped together in his study. Malcolm continued to look down at the papers on his desk. He appeared calm and composed, even now. His brow was dry, his face smooth. He looked down at his papers, pretending that this whole situation was of little importance. I waited patiently as he sorted documents into two piles.

I knew why he was ignoring me. It was a battle of wills. I was determined not to whine, to scream, to act the role of the violated wife, even though that was the role in which he had cast me. Hysteria would only make me weak and cause me to lose control and dignity. Finally, he looked up at me.

"Olivia, I wanted another child, a daughter, and now I'm going to have one," he said calmly.

"What right do you have to assume that I would accept a child of such heinous sin into my home? Did you think you could carry this out without my cooperation?" I asked, my voice still low, my arms resting against the front of my body, my hands gently clasped. I did not allow my posture to reveal the tension building within me. I had learned from Malcolm how to put a shell of myself over myself.

"I should think you would be in favor of it," he said, a snide look on his face. He sat back in his chair loosely.

"Remember, Olivia, when we first contracted to be married, it was assumed that you would provide me with a large family, something I made clear that I required. I had and have definite ideas about what a Foxworth woman should be. You knew what I wanted, yet you failed me in this regard."

"That is an unfair statement. It hasn't been that I didn't want to have any more children," I said, moving forward, my hands on my hips.

"Nevertheless, my dear Olivia, the fact is that you didn't have any more children. Couldn't or wouldn't is not important," he said.

"So you went ahead and raped your father's wife?" I asked, smiling sarcastically.

He smiled, too, to show me he could not be intimidated. How I had come to hate that cold, calculating grin.

"You can believe it was that way if you want to."

"What do you mean, if I want to? I heard it all directly from Alicia," I said.

"What would you expect her to say? Olivia, you can be so blind sometimes. What do you think was going on here, even when my father was alive? Did you think a man that age could really keep the appetite of a girl like that satisfied? She was soon making eyes at me, finding ways to accidentally meet me alone in the house, tempting me with a turn of her shoulders, a glimpse of bare skin here, a glimpse of bare skin there. How many times did she find an excuse to come to me in the library here or even . . . to my room?" he said, raising his eyebrows.

"You're making all this up to justify what a horrible thing you have done."

"Am I?" He smirked.

"Yes. I know that she sought to drive you away from her, that you pursued her even when Garland was alive." He smiled again. I would wipe that confident smile off his face yet. My eyes drilled into his. "I witnessed it!"

"Oh? Exactly what did you witness?" I saw the worry around his eyes, the way his eyebrows turned in toward each other, the way his forehead creased.

"One afternoon at the lake. You followed her and tried to force yourself on her, but she refused you. I was in the bushes; I saw and I heard it all." I dropped each word as if it were a cold, hard stone to batter his composure.

"You fool." Anger came into his face and tightened his features into granite. "You thought by spying on me you would learn the truth. You learned only half of it. She was a tease, a temptress. Why do you suppose I came home early that afternoon and went to the lake? She left all sorts of hints that she would be there, swimming naked. She wanted me to come just so she could torment me. It was part of her pleasure.

"Later on," he continued, "she wasn't so eager to refuse."

"That's ridiculous. That day, before she went to the lake, she asked me to go along with her." I looked at him confidently; I had caught him red-handed in a lie.

"Knowing all along that you wouldn't. It was her way of being sure you wouldn't be around when I appeared. She didn't anticipate your snooping, however," he said thoughtfully.

"You're a liar!" I pounded my own thigh with my fist for emphasis. He winced, but he didn't give ground.

"Am I? Why do you think Garland's death lies on her mind so heavily? She was more responsible for it than you think. She wanted me in that room that night."

"Wanted you? Wanted you? I saw her nightgown ripped; I saw what you had done. You forced yourself on her!"

He maintained his cold, confident smile. "It was her way. She enjoyed it rough. The struggle helped to quiet her conscience when afterward she would give in wholeheartedly."

"You're mad!

"No, Olivia, hardly am I mad. It is you who are mad; you know and understand so little of the ways of men and women. So little because you are so little woman yourself, except, of course, in height."

Oh, he knew how to hurt me. How to try to blame me for his infidelity. But if sin and lust were true knowledge, I would rather remain ignorant. "I don't believe a word you say," I hissed.

"Believe what you want. You don't want to believe it, Olivia, because you don't want to face the fact that you are a disappointment in many ways as a wife. Besides not being able to provide me with any more children, you can't provide me with warm, affectionate love. It's not in your nature; it never was.

"I accepted that as long as I thought you could provide the other necessities. You do run the house well; you present a proper image to the community, but I can't think of one time that I walked past your bedroom and had the urge to enter it," he added.

I couldn't stand it a moment longer. "Yes, my nature may be as it is, but when you entered my bedroom, you never found a woman like your mother."

"You're despicable," he said.

"I am what I am, just as you are what you are," I

said, taking control. "Threats are of no significance anymore. The die is cast. Upstairs in that room that woman is pregnant with your child, a child that will be our child in the eyes of the world. This is how it will be: I will have command of everything, command of how every detail of this mockery shall be carried out," I said, savoring my power over him.

"Meaning?"

"Meaning? We'll follow your shoddy plan, but it is I who will carry it through. Alicia will hide in the north wing until the baby is born. And, yes, the word will be given out that she is leaving on an important family trip. Christopher will remain with me and you will treat him as though he were another of my sons. When we hold Alicia's staged departure, I want you present, Malcolm. Afterward, I'll dismiss all the servants, all except Olsen. You will provide each one of them with a year's salary as severance pay." I knew my gray eyes were cold, sharp, piercing him like darts.

"A year's salary!"

"No, two years' salary! I want them to leave very, very satisfied. After Alicia returns and is secretly hidden in the north wing, you'll hire some new servants to carry out the menial tasks. And you'll make sure that none of those servants ever goes into the north wing."

I watched him fuming.

"Furthermore, you are never to set foot in the north wing while she remains there. If you should do that, I will immediately end this charade and face whatever indignities result from the exposure. I mean that, Malcolm. Is that understood and agreed?" I glared at him intently. He knew he could not lie about this to my face now; he knew I would see it in his eyes.

"I have no interest in her other than to see that she gives birth to a healthy child."

"Is it agreed to then?" I persisted.

"Yes, yes." For the first time, I saw weakness in Malcolm. His shoulders drooped. His face looked haggard. I gloated in my newfound power, savoring every moment.

"Good," I said finally. "I will be in total charge of her. You will have nothing to do with her. I will inform you as to when we should seek the services of a midwife and you will contract with someone and bring her here."

"I was going to suggest that," he said.

"But you didn't, did you, Malcolm? I thought of everything myself," I said, delighted with myself and eager to continue revealing my intricate plan.

"After she gives birth to the baby, she is to leave immediately with her financial situation set up the way Garland wanted it to be. A deal is a deal," I said, making it sound as cold as it was. His snide smile formed again.

"To put that kind of wealth into the hands of a child . . ."

"A child who is to have your baby," I responded. His smile waned. "If she is old enough and capable enough to have your baby, she can have a portion of your fortune."

"Frankly, Olivia, I am taken with your motherly concern for her," he said, desperately trying to take power by hiding behind a shield of sarcasm. He hoped to slow me down by turning me against Alicia. But now it was I who wore the look of indifference and control.

"It's my concern for what she is and what you have turned her into," I said as matter-of-factly as I could.

"What is she?"

"A woman, something you don't highly regard."

"You're insane with your ideas," he said. He shook his head, but he knew I was right.

I stood arrogantly and confidently above him. He was slumping in his desk chair. The storm outside was beginning to lessen. I could even see some of the twilight filtering through the gray clouds, clouds as gray as Malcolm's face had become.

"Now for another thing," I said. "Classes for the boys in the attic will have to stop."

"Why? They'll be sufficiently far away from her and they'll be up there only part of the day," he said.

"We can't take the chance of Mr. Chillingworth discovering anything, and the boys must never know she is there. Can you imagine if Christopher discovered his mother locked away? Mal and Joel are to believe that the child to be born is their brother or sister. They must never discover Alicia waiting to give birth."

"It will be a girl," he said, "and it will be their sister."

"Half sister," I corrected. "But they will believe she is their full sister. I couldn't bear for my sons to know that their father produced a child with his own father's wife. There are sins and there are sins. Even your generous contributions to the church can't undo the evil significance of what you have done." I wagged a finger at him like a strict Sunday-school teacher.

He shook his head. I was beating him down; I could feel it and it made me feel stronger.

"What about their education?"

"They will be sent out to school, like other normal children. Dismiss Mr. Chillingworth tomorrow and make the arrangements for their public education," I said, stressing the word "public." He winced and glared at me with such hateful eyes, but the more hateful his look, the more satisfied I felt.

"Anything else?" he asked bitterly.

"You will transfer one million dollars into a trust fund for each of our sons until they reach the age of eighteen."

He nearly jumped out of his chair. "What? You're mad. Why would I do that?"

"So that they will have some control over their lives and not be totally under your thumb," I said, stating the obvious.

"I would never do that. It would be a foolhardy waste of money. What would boys that age know about handling such a fortune?"

"You will do it and it will be done immediately. Put your lawyers right on it and have the documents ready by the end of the week. They will be given to me for safekeeping," I said, waving the air like he often did to indicate I would tolerate no more discussion on the subject.

"A million dollars each?" He was facing the unavoidable fact that there was little he could do about it.

"Consider it . . . a fine," I said. He stared at me, with not so much a hateful look on his face as the look of a man who realized, perhaps for the first time, that his antagonist was formidable. I think that in his strange way, he even respected me at that moment, even though he hated everything I was demanding.

"Is there anything else?" he asked, fatigue and defeat in his voice.

"Not at the moment. We both have enough to do. I suggest we get started."

I'll never forget how I felt when I pivoted and started

out of the library. It was as though I were leaving him in my wake, in the shadow I now cast. For the first time, my tallness didn't bother me, for I felt I had fulfilled my height. I had rescued what could have been a very sad and tragic time for me and I had even benefited from it. Malcolm, who had always gotten his way and had always gained from whatever he did, had had to give. He was losing more than I was.

I stepped out into the foyer and looked up the spiral staircase toward the Swan Room, where Alicia waited to learn her sentence and her fate. It wasn't Malcolm who went up and told her; it was I. I was the one who started up the stairs; I was the one who carried the news and the orders. I was the one who would cause things to happen, people to move and to change. I was the one who would shift the shadows and the light in Foxworth Hall. I would close doors, open windows, put lights on and put lights off. I would decide when the sunlight could be permitted to enter and when the shades would be drawn. I would dole out happiness and pleasure, sadness and pain the way a maid served soup.

I opened the Swan Room door without knocking. These kinds of indignities were mine to impose now at will. Alicia, who had just taken a bath and washed her beautiful hair, quickly wrapped a towel around herself and reached for her robe.

"Sit down," I commanded her. She went to the bed and sat as obediently as any child. I hesitated as she looked up at me with her eyes wide, fear and anticipation in her face. I took my time, walked over to the window to stare out at the gray-white twilight sky. The rain had stopped and the clouds were moving quickly off to the east. The sight of such a rapidly changing sky filled me with more energy. I felt as though nature touched me with her power. Just like nature, I could change from one extreme to another almost instantly. I walked over to the dressing table and looked at her powders and perfumes.

The scents were all enticingly feminine. They filled the air with promises of love and affection. It was as if this were a magical dressing table. Any ugly duckling could sit down at it and moments later be turned into the most attractive and inviting woman, a woman who could break men's hearts by simply turning away or ending her smiles. Surely every time Malcolm inhaled these flowery scents, his mind raced with amorous thoughts and dreams. The scents lingered in the air, long after Alicia passed a room or descended the stairs. Malcolm, coming after her, would trail behind like some dog mesmerized by the aroma of promise. That would all have to come to an abrupt end. I spun around to confront her.

"When you move into the north wing," I began, "you can't take any of these things with you." It was my way of telling her it had all been decided as Malcolm wanted.

"Then I am to go into seclusion until the baby is born? You could not change his mind?" she asked, her voice dripping with defeat and resignation.

"No," I said. "It's the only way for you and for Christopher to leave with anything. You'll have to do it and do it as I described."

She brought her hands to her face, but she did not cry.

"You should continue to dry your hair," I said. "Before you catch cold. Getting sick now, even getting a cold, is the worst thing that could happen."

She nodded, looking like one in a trance. Her eyes

were vacant, her shoulders sagged. She looked down at her own small hands, held together in a clasp of prayer. A shawl of doom had been placed over her head, but I felt no need to offer any words of comfort or hope.

I started out of the room.

"Olivia," she cried. She stood up. "I'm afraid."

"After a while," I said, "you won't be. Believe me, I know." I left her looking small and alone, her face pale, her childlike beauty wrinkled with worry.

I waited impatiently to execute my plan. I had decided that Alicia's confinement would begin only after she began to show—around three months. That left me, and Alicia, time to prepare the boys for what was to happen. One morning in May, after I had told Alicia everything she must say, we entered the nursery.

The nursery was warm and sunny, the warmest, sunniest room in the house. Mal was on the floor, children's books all around him. Joel was on his knees, playing with his cars and trucks. Christopher was sitting, sucking his thumb, watching the two older boys. "We have something to tell you," I began. Alicia was hovering behind me, wringing her hands, trembling like a bird.

"What, Mommy, what?" Mal asked.

"Something very sad, I'm afraid."

The three of them moved closer together and all stared with wide eyes at Alicia, who was now on the verge of tears.

"May I tell them, Olivia," Alicia whispered.

"No," I said. "It is I who am in charge here."

Alicia sat down in the wicker rocking chair and all three boys ran to pile up on her lap. She put her arms around them and squeezed them to her breast as

Christopher rained kisses on her, and my boys joined in.

"Alicia is going to be leaving us."

They simply stared, not saying a word. They didn't seem to understand.

"Alicia is going to be leaving us," I repeated.

"I don't believe you," Joel shouted.

"Me too," Christopher said, staring wide-eyed at his now weeping mother.

"Why?" Mal asked, his little voice filled with pain. He was growing into an intelligent, sensitive little man. He was already years ahead of boys his age in reading and writing, and nearly a half a foot taller than other boys his age. He would be as tall as Malcolm.

"Why?" he asked again. "Is she mad at us?"

Christopher buried his head between her breasts as Alicia burst into sobs. Joel put his hands over his ears and said, "Alicia can't go, she gotta play piano with me today." Joel was still a small, frail child who suffered from allergies. A speck of dust could set him coughing and sneezing for hours, something Malcolm couldn't bear to witness.

Mal climbed off Alicia's lap and came over to where I stood, like a toy soldier looking up at his general. "*Why?*" he shouted at the top of his voice.

"You boys are too young to understand," I said, putting calm and compassion in my eyes and voice. "When you grow older, these things will make sense to you. If it were up to me, Alicia could stay here forever. But your father doesn't want her to."

Suddenly, Mal's little face crumpled up and tears poured down his cheeks.

"I hate him," he shouted. "I hate him! I hate him! He never lets us have anything we want!"

Joel was so hysterical by now. He was coughing uncontrollably, and Alicia began to stroke his back, desperately trying to calm him down, as her own son remained buried in her breast.

"Please, please," he choked, "can't we go with her?"

"No," I said sternly. "I'm your mother. And you belong here with me."

"But what about Christopher?" Mal asked.

"Christopher will stay here for a time, until Alicia gets settled in her new house," I explained. At the sound of his own name, Christopher suddenly looked up at me and just as quickly back at his mother. "Mommy," he cried, his little voice squeaking with terror. "I'm not coming with you?"

"No, my darling, no," Alicia cried. "But I'll be coming back for you soon. And then we'll be together always. It won't be for long, Christopher my darling, my boy. And you'll have Olivia to take care of you. And Mal and Joel to play with." Then she turned to my boys. "Please, please, remember that I love all of you, that I will always love you. In my heart I'll always be with you, watching you practice the piano, watching you make your beautiful artistic drawings, and when you go to sleep at night, I'll be kissing you in my dreams."

The next day I informed the servants of Alicia's coming departure. I could see the unhappiness in their faces when I told them. As I came down the stairwell, I overheard Mary Stuart and Mrs. Steiner talking in the dining room as they prepared the table for dinner. I stood just outside the doorway, listening.

"The light is going from this house," Mrs. Steiner said. "Believe me."

"I'm so sorry to see her go," Mary said. "She always has a smile for us, unlike the tall one."

So that's how they distinguish between us, I thought. "The tall one."

"If you ask me, the tall one got her way. She didn't want young Mrs. Foxworth here from the start and probably worked to get rid of her the day Garland Foxworth died. Can't blame her though, I suppose. I wouldn't want a beautiful young woman like that about for my husband to see day in and day out. Especially if I looked like her," Mrs. Steiner said, raising her voice for emphasis.

"That's for certain," Mary said. I was sure she was smiling when she said it. I could hear the smile in her voice.

Good riddance to you all, I thought, and decided that I would inform them sooner that their services were no longer required. I called them into the foyer one afternoon: Mary, Mrs. Steiner, Mrs. Wilson, and Lucas. I sat in one of the high-back chairs, my arms flat on the arms, my head against the back, my hair tightly woven up in a bun on the top of my head, looking more like a crown. They gathered around and faced me, both fear and curiosity in their eyes. I was like a queen about to address her subjects.

"As you know," I began, "Mrs. Garland Foxworth is leaving Foxworth Hall next month. She will be gone for some time, but her return here will only be long enough to get her son and then she will leave again. Permanently," I added. "I have given everything great thought and I have decided that we will no longer be needing your services."

Mrs. Wilson turned white. Mrs. Steiner nodded, her

eyes small, as if she had been expecting something like this. Lucas and Mary Stuart looked frightened.

"Our services? You mean you're letting us all go?" Mary asked incredulously.

"Yes. However, I have decided that all of you will receive two years' salary as severance pay," I added, making sure they understood it was my generosity that provided them with such a large settlement. "When do we leave?" Mrs. Steiner asked. She dressed her words in ice.

"You are to leave the same day Mrs. Garland Foxworth leaves."

The final preparation was to move Alicia out of the Swan Room and to store all her trinkets and wardrobe that she wouldn't be needing during her confinement. I supervised her packing, lording over her and approving and disapproving of every object, every garment she wished to take with her to the north wing.

"There is no need for you to take along your formal dresses," I said as I saw her press a frilly blue frock to her breast as she stood before the mirror. "You won't be going to any parties for a while and you won't be able to have your clothing cleaned and washed as regularly as you have it done now. I'm going to have to do whatever you can't wash for yourself in the sink and bathtub, so let's not take one item that's not necessary."

She looked down at her gowns sadly. I couldn't believe the array of clothing she possessed. The frivolity on which she had wasted Garland's money. Did she think she was a walking fashion magazine that had to change her entire wardrobe every season? It was profligate spending and vanity such as this that brought about what had happened to Alicia.

"But it makes me feel good to look good," Alicia said.

"You won't be able to fit in most of it soon anyway," I added.

"But I have no maternity clothes left, Olivia. I gave them all to charity after Christopher was born. What will I use for maternity clothes?"

"I'll give you some of mine."

"But yours are so . . . so big, Olivia."

"What difference does it make what you look like in that room, Alicia? Only I will see you. You're not dressing to draw the attention of men anymore, dear. All that matters is that you are warm and comfortable."

The image of her lost in my maternity dresses suddenly made me smile. Now she would know what it felt like not to see beauty looking back at her from the mirror. Now she, too, would be awkward and unappealing. And what was more fitting than that she wear my maternity clothing, I thought. After all, she was having what was going to be my child.

"Of course," I added, "I will be wearing maternity clothing also."

She looked up at me as if she were shocked. Could this not have occurred to her? Did she think I would move about the community as I was and then suddenly announce that I had given birth to a child? How simple and naive she could be! There was no conniving, no deceit in her, even when it was necessary for her survival.

"Oh," she said, finally understanding. She looked

back at her fine dresses and blouses and skirts. In the end I reduced everything she would take to the north wing to what would fit into one trunk and two suitcases.

Sadness reigned in Foxworth Hall the day Alicia made her false departure. It was a gray, rainy day, the sky crying along with the children. Although it was the first day of summer, a cold winter chill filled Foxworth Hall. We had to keep lights on and close windows tightly.

The servants, who had been packing their own things, stood in the downstairs as Alicia descended with me behind her, carrying her suitcase. I had never seen her look so small and gray, like a sad little mouse. I had insisted the children remain in the nursery. I did not want the histrionics of an overly emotional farewell. Christopher had been barely consolable for days, and my boys, too, were on a short tether. But I had insisted that Malcolm be present at this painful little charade. As we reached the bottom of the stairs, I handed Malcolm the suitcase and he grasped it awkwardly, annoyed, but afraid to cross me at this juncture. Alicia's eyes filled with tears as she came upon the farewell gathering, for she was truly bidding everyone good-bye. She looked about the great foyer like one who knew it would be some time before she would see it again. Her act was very convincing because it was only half an act. She would see it when she returned, but it would be only a short glimpse on her way up to the north wing.

She went to embrace Mrs. Steiner, but I grasped her arm and ushered her toward the awaiting car. "There is no time for sentiment," I said.

Suddenly, she felt limp in my arms. "Please, please let me say good-bye to Christopher one more time," she pleaded.

Malcolm whispered in my ear. "Must I stay and witness this hysteria?"

"Put her in the cab, Malcolm," I ordered.

Alicia had to be half carried, half dragged to the car. As soon as the suitcase was locked in the trunk, I rapped on the window and ordered the driver to be off. The tires spun in the wet mud and the car lurched to life. Behind me, I heard the front door fly open and the boys screaming "*Wait, wait*" as they hurtled down the steps, yanking themselves free of the servants' restraining arms. Mal led the pack, holding Joel by one hand and Christopher by the other, practically dragging them along. They chased the car for some time, screaming and crying.

"Get your sons, Malcolm," I ordered, "all of them."

12

The Prisoner and the Warden

THAT SAME NIGHT, AFTER ALL THE SERVANTS HAD LEFT, Alicia returned.

The cab drove up in the darkness. Clouds still hung over the sky, blocking out the moon and the stars. It was as if there were no light left in all the world.

Malcolm and I were waiting in a front salon, just the way we had been waiting for his father to arrive the day he had brought Alicia here. The boys had cried themselves to sleep, all three of them cuddled together against the loneliness of Alicia's departure. Truly, I wanted to comfort them, to be a mother to little Chris, to be a comfort to my own sons. I wanted them all to love me the way they loved Alicia. Oh, I knew I couldn't be lighthearted and gay as she was; I didn't know how to romp and jump and play silly rhyming games. But I loved them well, in my own way, and I would bring them up to be strong, moral young men. When they grew older, they would appreciate the values I had bequeathed them.

"What time is it?" Malcolm asked.

I pointed across the room, not saying a word. The house was quiet, still, except for the sound of the ticking grandfather clock and the evening winds winding their way in and out of the shutters, threading through the cracks between windows. Malcolm snapped his paper, folding it neatly to check the stock market columns.

We had been sitting there for two hours, drowning in our own silence. If either of us took a deep breath, the other would look up, surprised. In fact, Malcolm's only comment during the last half hour concerned one of his stocks that had appreciated ten points. I imagined he was making the comment to emphasize how much better he could do with my money than I was doing.

Then I saw the headlights of the cab tear an opening in the darkness and pull up in front of the house. Malcolm didn't move.

"She's back," I said. He grunted. "You'll take her trunk upstairs." He looked up, surprised. "Well, who did you think would do it? Lucas is gone, or did you forget we dismissed the servants today and there won't be a new driver until tomorrow."

I got up and went to the front door. Alicia emerged from the cab slowly, reluctantly, anticipating what awaited her in Foxworth Hall. I could see that she was exhausted from the traveling and the tension. The driver took her trunk and suitcases out.

"Leave them," I said to the driver quickly. It was impossible to remain outside long. "My husband will take them in."

Malcolm had appeared behind me on the steps. I took Alicia's smaller suitcase.

"How is my Christopher?" she asked the minute she stepped from the car. "Does he miss me?"

"Christopher is my responsibility now," I said curtly. "He's in bed, where he belongs." I took her arm and led her up the front stairs. "Go directly to the north wing," I told her, "and move as quietly as possible. You must not wake the boys."

She didn't respond. She walked like a condemned criminal, pausing only when she passed close to Malcolm, who was on his way to get her trunk and larger suitcase.

Stepping softly, we both floated like ghosts through the silent, dimly lit foyer. The loudest sound was the rustle of Alicia's dress when we turned the corner at the rotunda and headed quickly into the north wing, moving down hallways and passing the many empty, lonely rooms of Foxworth Hall. She paused at the doorway of the room at the end of the corridor. I came up behind her impatiently. Did she think she was the only one who was tense and upset?

"If you don't go in and go in quickly," I said, "this will become even more difficult for you."

She looked at me hatefully for the first time. Of course, it wouldn't be the last.

"I was thinking all the way to the station, on the train, and all the way back," she said. "Thinking that you might be enjoying all this." Her eyes narrowed.

"Enjoying this?" I stepped to the right, my shadow draping her in my darkness. She cowered back as if she could feel my weight on her. "Enjoying having to pretend that your baby is my baby? Enjoying the knowledge that my husband has been unfaithful to me, not once, but many times? Enjoying having to dismiss loyal and faithful servants who I have spent years training? Enjoying lying to my boys and to your son, watching him swallow his tears and unhappiness until he was exhausted and had to be put to bed?" My voice was thin, nearly hysterical.

Her eyes widened, and then her face crumpled, her lips quivering.

"I'm sorry," she said. "It's just that I'm . . ."

"We can't stand out here and talk with me holding this suitcase," I said. "Malcolm is coming up with the trunk."

"Yes, yes, I'm sorry," she repeated, opening the door.

I had left the lamp on the table between the two beds lit. It cast a weak yellowish glow over the ponderous dark furniture. My one donation to warmth and beauty was the red Oriental rug with gold fringe. It would help alleviate the dreariness in the room, which was large yet confining because of all the furniture crowded into it. I had found two paintings in the attic that I thought fit the circumstances and hung them on the walls that were papered in cream with white flocking. One had grotesque demons chasing naked people in underground caverns, and the other had unearthly monsters devouring pitiful souls in hell. Both paintings had bright red colors.

She went directly to the bed on the right and began to take off her coat. We both turned as Malcolm dropped the trunk to the right of the door. He looked at Alicia and then he looked at me. My glare was enough to hurry him.

"I'll get the other suitcase," he said. Although he was a strong man, the indignity of having to carry the luggage up the spiral staircase and down the hallways to this room wore on him. He was breathing hard and sweating.

"Hurry," I said, intensifying his indignation. He grunted and was gone.

"How will I eat up here?" Alicia asked.

"I will bring up your meals every day, after we have eaten ours. That way the servants won't be as suspicious."

"But the cook . . ."

"There will be no cook until you are gone. I will be the cook." She tilted her head and widened her eyes in surprise. "Don't look at me like that," I said. "I used to cook all the time for my father."

"I didn't mean to imply that you couldn't cook; I was just surprised that you wanted to do it." It occurred to me that all the time she had lived here, she never mentioned her own ability to cook. Her mother must have spoiled her, I thought, never giving her the opportunity to work in the kitchen and learn anything. And then Garland came along and put the icing on the cake. She didn't have to lift a finger to do anything for herself.

"There isn't much choice about it now, is there?" She looked away. "Is there?" I repeated.

"No, I suppose not."

"Of course, I won't be able to make special meals. This can't be one of those fancy restaurants you and Garland were always going to," I snapped. I went to the two front windows and closed the curtains more tightly.

"I didn't expect special meals," she retorted. It was beginning already—she was losing her softness, her gentle look, her warm coat of innocence.

"The meals will be nourishing, considering the condition you are in. That's what's most important, isn't it?" She nodded quickly.

"Oh, Olivia, what will I do here?" she asked, looking around. "I will positively be bored to death."

"I'll bring up your magazines. The servants won't know or care whether or not they are for me, and I will try to visit with you every opportunity I can get." she looked grateful for that.

"I would like a radio or a Victrola."

"Out of the question. Such noise, even in here, might be heard." I widened my eyes for emphasis, feeling as though I were talking to a child.

"But what if I took it upstairs, into the attic?" she pleaded.

I thought about it.

"Yes, I suppose that would be all right. I'll get you a radio and a Victrola. Your pile of records is still downstairs. No one would want to listen to them anyway." Neither Malcolm nor I liked the new jazz music she endlessly listened to, and it occurred to me that we should not have left them behind when I packed her things. Fortunately, none of the old servants noticed or cared.

"Thank you, Olivia," she said. She had already begun to understand that I could grant her little pleasures and little happiness and I could take it away as well.

I helped her start unpacking and putting clothing into the dresser. Malcolm returned with the larger suitcase. After he dropped it on the floor, he stood in the doorway looking in at us.

"That will be all, Malcolm," I said, dismissing him as I would dismiss any servant. His face blanched and he bit down on his lower lip. I saw the rage in his eyes and sensed the frustration he felt. He hesitated. "Did you want to say anything before you go? Something apologetic?"

"No. You seem to be saying everything that needs to be said," he added, pivoted, and stalked out of the room. I heard his footsteps pounding the hallway floor as he departed. When I turned back to Alicia, I saw she was staring at me. "He has already been quite clearly informed that he must stay away from you during your . . . your stay here," I said.

"Good," she said, a sincere look of relief on her face.

"However, I am not naive enough to believe what he tells me. I see the way he looks at you." She looked toward the doorway as though Malcolm were still standing there and she could verify my impressions.

"Surely he . . ."

"You must understand, my dear, that you are quite vulnerable alone in this room, far away from anyone else, the sounds muffled by the thickness in the walls. You can't shout out for help; you can't expose yourself. Where could you flee?" I held out my hands and turned from one wall to the next. "Up into the attic? That would be worse."

"But you would know if anything . . ."

"During the night, after I fall asleep, he could prowl these dark halls, moving over the floors barefooted, and if he came in here, you wouldn't shout and bring attention to yourself. Imagine if Christopher discovered you were hidden up here," I said.

"I'll keep the door locked," she said quickly.

"You kept a door locked before, my dear. Locking doors in Foxworth Hall does not keep Malcolm Neal Foxworth out."

"What do I do?" She looked frantic.

"As I told you when we discussed all this, you must change your appearance, make yourself unattractive to him, not remind him of anyone," I sneered. Alicia stared at me. I seized up her hair. "I'm sorry, but there is no other way."

"Are you sure? Are you sure?"

"I'm sure."

She began crying softly.

"Sit at the table," I commanded her. She stared at the chair as if she were about to step onto the gallows and then walked to it and sat down, her hands in her lap, her eyes flooded with tears.

I took the large scissors from my sweater pocket and stepped up behind her. First, I unpinned her hair, freeing the strands and stroking them down so they lay softly exposed. They did feel so silky and pleasing to the touch. I could imagine Malcolm stroking her hair for hours as he dreamt beside her. My hair, no matter what I did to it, never felt this good, and never once during our sexual relations—I could scarcely call them lovemaking—did he even touch my hair.

I grasped a section in my left fist and held it up tautly. She winced because of how roughly I tugged. Then I closed the blades of the scissors around her tresses and began to chop away, cutting her hair as close to her scalp as I could, deliberately cutting it unevenly so it would grow in awkwardly. As I cut away, the tears continued to flow down her cheeks, but she made no sound. I placed all the cut strands neatly in a silk shawl, wrapped them up, and tied a knot in it.

After I was finished, she pressed her palms against her scalp and uttered a single, mournful cry.

"You know it will grow back," I said, making my voice as sympathetic as I could. She turned and looked up at me with those hateful eyes again, but I smiled at her. The haircut had changed her appearance radically. She looked more like a boy now: the crown of her beauty had been removed. It was as if I had snuffed out the fire behind her eyes. "If Malcolm should look at you, he won't see the same things now, will he?"

She didn't respond. She simply stared at herself in the mirror. After a moment she spoke more to her image than to me.

"This is all like a bad dream," she said. "In the morning I will awaken and Garland will be beside me. It's all a dream." She spun around, her face dressed in a wild, insane smile. "Isn't it? Isn't it all a dream, Olivia?"

"I'm afraid not, my dear. You had better not sit there pretending. Tomorrow morning you will wake up in this room and you will have to face the reality of what is and what will be. Most of us have got to do that every day of our lives. The stronger you are, the less dependent you are on fantasy."

She nodded reluctantly, a look of total defeat on her face. I could almost read her thoughts. "Garland would not be happy it has all come to this, I know. Christopher and I were the light of his life. And to think, my son sleeps in the same house and must not know I am only a short distance from him. It's too cruel, too cruel."

Her tears began again.

"Nevertheless, it is what must be. I shall go now," I said. "I will be up here earlier than usual tomorrow only because the new servants aren't arriving until late in the morning." I picked up the bundle of her cut hair and started to leave.

"Olivia," she called.

"Yes, my dear?" I turned back to her.

"Please, can't I keep a lock; just one small lock of my hair?"

Benevolently, I handed her a bright chestnut curl.

"You don't hate me," she said, "do you?" I saw the fear in her eyes.

"Of course I don't hate you, Alicia. I hate only what you have become, as I am sure you hate yourself." Then I opened the door and stepped out. I closed it quietly behind me and turned the key in the lock, snapping it shut. The sound of her sobbing died away in the darkness of the hallway as I turned off the lights. The shadows held at bay rushed in, dropping a wall of blackness between Alicia and her sleeping child, who would wait for her in the world of light and life without.

I moved swiftly down the hall until I came to the rotunda. From the sounds below, I knew that Malcolm was still downstairs, probably in the library at his desk. I imagined him sitting there staring hatefully at the doorway, maybe in expectation of my arrival.

But I had no more interest in conversation with him tonight. All that had to be done was done. I was tired myself. I started for my bedroom, but stopped at the doorway of the trophy room. Something occurred to me, something I found deliciously vengeful and satisfying. I opened the door, snapped on the lights, and went to the desk behind which Malcolm often sat when he came up here to be by himself. I put the shawl filled with Alicia's cut hair at the center of the desk and untied the knot so that the pile of beautiful chestnut strands lay open and exposed.

Then I turned, went back to the door, looked back at the sight of her amputated hair on his desk, smiled to myself, and snapped off the lights. I stood there for a few moments listening to the sounds of the house. Tonight every creak seemed amplified. The wind wrapped itself around the great mansion, whirling madly, tying it in a chilled rope. It would take days of warm summer sunlight to defrost the icy wall over this house, I thought. And throughout that summer, Alicia would sit in a dark, stuffy room below the great attic, waiting for the birth of a child she had not wanted and would not be a mother to. It was truly a prison sentence and I was truly a warden.

I did not cherish the role, but Malcolm had cast me in it and I knew the only way to defeat him was to perform it far better than he ever could have expected. He would live to regret this night, I thought, to regret what he had done to me and what he would make me do to her.

I went to my bedroom quickly and rushed myself to sleep, which had become the only true escape from the madness of Foxworth Hall, something that was ironically true for both of us, Alicia and me.

The weeks passed as I had predicted they would pass for Alicia—painfully, slowly. Every day, the minute I entered the room, she begged me to bring her Christopher.

"If not here," she pleaded, "at least let him stand outside my window so I can peek at him, see him—I can't stand this any longer."

"Christopher has finally adjusted to your leaving. Why upset him now? If you really loved him, Alicia, you'd let things be."

"Let it be? I'm his mother. My heart is breaking. The days only seem to get longer. A week in here is like a year!"

In the mornings she complained about being nauseated. In the afternoons she wept for Christopher. She was always tired, and more often than not, I would find her lying in bed, staring up at the ceiling. Her once rosy cheeks paled, and even though I insisted she eat everything I brought to her, her face began to take on a gaunt look. After two months shut away in that room, dark circles formed around her eyes.

She usually kept a shawl over her head. After I had come in a dozen times and found her wearing it each time, I asked her why.

"Because I can't stand the sight of myself with my hair like this every time I pass in front of the mirror," she said.

"Why don't you just cover the mirror," I told her. I knew every woman had vanity, but I also knew that women like her had much, much more. Despite the fact that she had no cosmetics and her hair had been chopped away, I imagined that she still sat before the mirror pretending she was back in her beautiful bedroom suite preparing for an evening out with Garland, or planning what she was going to do with herself once her hair did grow back and she was free of this place.

Eventually, she took my suggestion and draped a sheet over the mirror. The dissipation of her beauty was a part of harsh reality that she would now rather avoid. However, when I walked in with her tray of food and I saw the sheet there, I didn't remark about it.

She looked up at me from her bed, her eyes bright with tears of boredom and anger. She no longer wore the shawl; there was no reason for it since the mirror was covered.

"I thought you had forgotten my dinner," she accused me. There was a new sharpness in her words. Her rage caused her to pronounce the consonants with exaggeration and her voice dropped in tone, almost sounding manly.

"Dinner? This is your lunch, Alicia," I said. The realization brought surprise and horror to her face.

"Only lunch?" She looked at the small clock housed in an ivory cathedral on the dresser. "Only lunch?" she repeated. She sat up slowly and looked at me with frightened, frozen blue eyes. I knew that she had come to see me as her jailer. Whenever she thought of something new to do, she had to ask my permission. Her life was no longer her own.

"How is my Christopher? Does he miss me terribly? Does he ask about me every day?" she inquired, hanging on my responses.

"Sometimes," I said. "The boys help to distract him."

She nodded, pathetically trying to conjure up his image in her mind. I thought of him myself, beautiful golden-haired Christopher, his face regaining its happy joy after the first few months of sadness at being separated from his mother. His eyes sparkled once again as I read him his favorite story every night before bed. Truly, I was beginning to think of him as one of my own. He and my two boys played so well together in the nursery. Mal and Joel adored him. He seemed to carry all the sunshine of his mother in her happier days. But that sunny joy wasn't seductive and lustful, it was bright and open, compassionate and innocent. He was more affectionate than either of my children. Sometimes I feared it was because both Mal and Joel had Malcolm's blood in them. Every morning he would run to me screaming, "I want hundreds of kisses. I want hundreds of hugs, o-weee-a!" Only yesterday, when I put him down for his nap, his beautiful blue eyes looked up at me and he asked, "Can I call you Mommy sometimes?" Of course I did not tell Alicia any of this. Instead, I kept the conversation always focused on her.

"You look unclean today, Alicia. You should take better care of yourself," I said, reprimanding her.

She turned abruptly on me, speaking through clenched teeth.

"I'm this way because I live from day to day in this . . . this closet."

"This is bigger than a closet."

"And the only sunlight I get to see is the sunlight that comes through the windows here and upstairs. Yesterday I sat in the rays until the sun moved on and left me in shadows. I feel like a flower hungry for the nourishment of the sun, a flower withering in a closet. Soon I will be dried and dead and you can press me into the pages of a book," she said, her voice a mixture of anger and self-pity.

"You won't be in here that much longer," I said. "It won't do you any good to sit and churn up your frustration day in and day out," I added in a matter-of-fact tone of voice. That only infuriated her more.

"Maybe I should go outside for a quick secret walk. You can take the boys away from the house and . . ."

"But, Alicia, the servants. How could I explain if they saw you? From where would I tell them you came? Who would I tell them you were? And if the boys heard about it . . . don't you see? What you are asking is impossible, just impossible." She nodded. "I do feel sorry for you," I said. "I hope you see that. Do you?" She looked up at me with scrutinizing eyes and then nodded. "No one is enjoying this, least of all me. Keep thinking about the future and you will survive the present," I advised. Suddenly a new idea came to her.

"Send all the servants away," she said, her face filled with the excitement of a new and, as she considered it, clever idea. "Give them a holiday, just for a weekend. That's all I would need, one or two days of fresh air. Please."

"You're speaking ridiculous thoughts. I would advise you to get a hold of yourself," I told her, gathering my own resolve. "You will only get yourself sick and maybe lose the baby. Now, feed yourself and the child within you," I added, and left the room before she could say another thing about it.

When I returned to bring her her dinner that night, she did seem changed. She had bathed and dressed herself in a pretty blue chemise. However, she was sitting on her bed as if she were in the back of a car and on a journey.

"Oh," she said when I came in, "here we are at the restaurant. What shall we have to eat?" She was pretending to be in a car with Christopher. I was amazed, but I said nothing.

She looked at me with expectation, hopeful that I would become part of the fantasy. I put the tray down on the table and watched as Alicia continued to create an imaginary situation for herself, getting up and approaching the table as if it were a table in a restaurant. She did look brighter, happier.

Alicia referred to me as she would refer to a waitress in a restaurant. Suddenly, I realized there was something strange about it all. She wasn't pretending just for the fun of it; she was actually experiencing this journey.

She rattled on and on as if I weren't there, or as if I were really some stranger. I didn't like it, but I didn't know what to do about it.

She dismissed me by saying, "You can take those now," referring to the dirty dinner dishes.

She began to feed her imaginary Christopher, telling him that after they left the restaurant, they would drive to the park, where they would see animals and go on the merry-go-round. I understood that the attic was to be envisioned as the park. She was wearing the nicest of all the dresses I had permitted her to bring. Her stomach was not quite swollen enough to prevent it, and she had torn a strip off a beige slip and tied it like a ribbon in her short strands of hair.

"Are you all right?" I asked her. She interrupted herself.

"Pardon me, Christopher," she said to the empty chair beside her. "The waitress wants to know something. What was it, waitress?" she asked, singing the question.

I pulled in the corners of my mouth and straightened my back. She was smiling madly. Did she think I was going along with this charade? I didn't repeat my question. Instead, I turned and carried the tray of dishes to the door.

"She said they are out of ice cream," Alicia told her imaginary son. "But don't worry. Perhaps we'll see an ice cream parlor at the park, and we'll never come back to this restaurant again, will we?"

I heard her laugh as I closed the door behind me. Madness, I thought, and for the first time since she had been brought back to Foxworth Hall, I couldn't wait for her to leave again.

* * *

The pretending continued. The room at the end of the north wing became Alicia's world of illusions. Sometimes when I entered, she and her imaginary son were in a car; sometimes they were on the ferry. A few times they were up in the attic. She was playing her Victrola and they had supposedly gone to see a puppet show. She made two hand puppets with her socks and used an armoire as the puppet stage.

Every time I entered, she called me something else. Either I was the waiter, the ticket taker at the puppet show, an engineer on a ferry boat . . . whatever; but never was I Olivia. I no longer saw any fear in her face when I arrived. She looked at me with a smile of anticipation on her face, waiting to see how I would react to her new inventions.

It went on and on like this, and then one day I came in and found that she had taken the sheet off the mirror. It no longer bothered her to look at herself and what she had become because she did not see that image. She saw whatever she imagined. With a brush in her hand she was standing in front of the mirror and stroking the air as if there were strands down around her shoulders.

The ironic thing about all this was that her complexion returned to its former peaches-and-cream richness. I knew that some women flourished during pregnancy. I had not been one of those women, but Alicia had remained quite beautiful during her pregnancy with Christopher. The same thing was true of this pregnancy, now aided by her illusions.

"What are you doing?" I asked her, and she turned away from the mirror. She hadn't heard me enter.

"Oh, Olivia. Garland said Venus herself couldn't

have more beautiful hair than mine. Can you imagine? Men can be so extravagant with their flattery. They don't know what it can do to a woman. I let him go on. Why not? Whom does it harm? Certainly not Venus." She laughed, but her laugh was as rich and as full as her laugh used to be when Garland was alive.

She is going mad, I thought. Being locked up and pregnant, she is being driven into insanity. But it wasn't my fault, I concluded. It was another sin for Malcolm to bear. Perhaps he had known this would happen; perhaps he had expected it. She would give birth to his baby and he would have the child. But she would be so unstable, he couldn't turn over the large fortune to her. In fact, she might have to be committed. He would have it all—the child, the money, and good riddance to Alicia. We would adopt Christopher.

Such a scenario enraged me. Once again Malcolm Neal Foxworth would get his way, defeating everyone, even me. I couldn't allow it.

"Alicia, Garland is dead. He couldn't have told you that now. You must stop this, stop all of this ridiculous pretending before it drives you insane. Do you hear me? Do you understand what I am saying?" She stood there, her smile unchanged. She heard only what she wanted to hear.

"There's nothing he won't buy for me, nothing he won't do for me," she said. "It's terrible, I know; but all I need do is mention something I see or want, and the next day, the very next day, he will have it delivered. I'm so spoiled, but I can't help it.

"Anyway," she went on, turning back to the mirror and brushing the air, "Garland says he likes to spoil me. He says it gives him pleasure to spoil me and I have no right to take that pleasure away from him. Isn't it wonderful?"

"I've brought you the maternity clothes, Alicia," I said. I thought that if I confronted her with that, I might be able to snap her back to reality quickly. I placed the pile of clothes on the bed. "Go through and sort them out. You can't wear those things any longer."

She didn't turn around.

"Alicia!"

"Last night Garland said, he said . . . Alicia, don't ask me for the moon or I will go mad trying to get it for you." She laughed. "Should I ask him for the moon, Olivia?"

"The maternity clothing, Alicia," I repeated. She continued to ignore me. Finally, I left the room, expecting she would confront the clothing herself and eventually realize what had to be done.

That evening, however, I lay there in my bed thinking about her insane ramblings. Of course, her pretending would have to be taking place in the present tense, I thought; but there was something about the way she referred to Garland that was more than just madness; it was eerie, as if he indeed had been visiting her nightly.

Suddenly a frightening thought occurred to me. What if Malcolm had disobeyed my orders and visited her? And what if she had looked at him and called him Garland? What if he were taking advantage of her madness and going to her in the middle of the night after I had gone to sleep? She would not realize that the man she embraced was not Garland but Malcolm. The possibility kept me from sleeping.

Sometime during the night I thought I heard footsteps in the hallway. By the time I looked out, Malcolm could have very well slipped around the corner in the hall and gone on to the north wing. I went back to my bed, put on my robe and slippers, and left my room very quietly. I was going to go to the north wing and merely open her door, but something better occurred to me. If he were in there, I would not want to give him the opportunity to get out of her bed. He could hear me coming down the hallway or move quickly before I had turned the key in the lock.

I went down to the front entrance to the attic instead. I put on the small light illuminating the stairway, closed the door softly behind me, confident that neither Malcolm nor any of the servants would hear me, and started up the stairway. My intention was to go through the attic and down the small stairway that opened into Alicia's room. I would watch them for a while in the bed and then I would confront them.

But when I was in the attic, vaguely lit by the small stairway light, the light suddenly went out and I was plunged into complete darkness. I hesitated, not sure whether I should go forward or retreat. Driven by my original intention, I went on, groping my way carefully through the attic.

I thought I remembered it well enough to make my way in the darkness. Then I heard loud scampering off to the right. Panic rose in my chest. I was sure it was rats, rats I could imagine running over my feet, causing me to fall, running over my face and body. Suddenly I felt as if I might faint. The scurrying seemed to whirl in my head. I had to get out of there!

I turned abruptly into a person standing there in the shadows! I barely subdued my scream, when I recognized an old dress form, but I had jumped back so abruptly that I tripped over a trunk and fell against a rack of old clothing, sending it toppling to the floor. Trying to regain my footing, I ran my hands over the floor. I touched something furry! A rat! My panic rose and I rushed forward on my hands and knees, knocking over a stack of old books. It was so hot, I could barely breathe.

I got to my feet, but I had lost my sense of direction. Everywhere I turned seemed to be a dead end. The darkness closed in around me, tightening its hold on me until I was unable to move to the right or to the left. Terror froze me. My feet felt leaden, my legs tied together. I willed myself to move, but I couldn't take a single step. I began to sob silently.

The rats went wild, rushing over furniture, in and out of trunks and armoires. The entire attic seemed to be alive with hideous beasts. I imagined the shadowy forms of Malcolm's ancestors scratching their way out of the walls, awakened by my turmoil. This was a house that tolerated no weakness or fear. When they smelled it on you, they sought to destroy you.

I turned to the nearest wall and began to feel my way down it in the direction of what I hoped was the front stairway. Frantically I bumped into old furniture and birdcages, and tripped over trunks. My hands clutched things that turned into pulsating, blood-warm creatures, even though somewhere I knew I was touching only articles of clothing or the arms of old chairs. Then my hair got caught by the tiny opened door of a birdcage and the cage came falling toward me. When I caught the pole in my hands, it felt like a long, dark snake. Everything here had become alive and sinister.

I don't know how long it took me to reach the stairway. It took all my control to calm myself so that I could continue on, but finally I recognized the top of the stairway and made my way down.

As soon as I opened the door and stepped back into the hallway, I felt so happy I wanted to cry. I rushed back down the corridor to the south wing and my bedroom. When I confronted myself in the mirror, I looked like a wild madwoman. My hair was disheveled, my robe streaked. There were streaks along my face as well, and my hands were black from the dust and dirt. I knew that never could I ever go back up and into that attic again. I would go through it many times in nightmares, but just the thought of opening the door and starting up the stairs threw me into a panic.

After I cleaned up, I returned to bed. For a long time I just lay there, grateful for the warmth and comfort of my room. Then I remembered my original purpose. Not long afterward, I was sure I heard footsteps in the hallway again. I rushed up and went to the door. It looked to me like Malcolm had just entered his own bedroom. I listened for the click of his door, but heard nothing.

I hadn't trapped and confronted him as I had hoped to do. I had trapped and confronted myself up in that old, terrifying attic filled with the twisted past of the Foxworths. It would forever taunt me now, I thought.

This house has a way of protecting its own. It cloaked Malcolm in silence as he stole through the hall. I was sure of it. The walls knew the truth, only they wouldn't speak to me.

I hesitated a moment and then closed the door and went back to my bed. I didn't fall asleep until morning and then I was abruptly awoken by Malcolm's loud, arrogant footsteps as he made his way down to breakfast.

When I joined him, I tried to read his face to see if there were any clues as to whether or not he had visited Alicia during the night. All this time he had kept to his word and not asked me a thing about her, pretending well that she was no longer here.

He sat at his end of the table looking at the morning paper, ignoring my arrival, as usual. After the maid poured my coffee, I spoke to him.

"Did you hear anything unusual last night?" I asked him.

He put his paper down, a quizzical look on his face.

"Unusual? What do you mean by unusual?" he asked as though it were a foreign word.

"Like the sound of someone walking through the north wing?" I said. He stared at me a moment and then with his inscrutable eyes he leaned forward so he could speak sotto voce.

"The door is locked, isn't it? She can't get out and about, can she?"

"Of course not. But that doesn't mean someone can't get in, does it?" I replied, my voice as low as his, but sharper in tone.

"Now what are you implying?" he asked, sitting back abruptly.

"Have you violated our agreement?" I demanded.

"I assure you, I do not need to spend my time sneaking about this house. I would hope you, too, had more to do than go skulking about watching for some . . . some violation, as you put it."

"I don't have to skulk about. There is only one place in this house that concerns me right now;" I said, feeling my face tighten. He looked away from my sharp gaze and shook his head.

"Has she told you something? Fabricated something?

A woman like that, stuck back in that room with no one would obviously daydream," he said, smiling with ridicule. His lips curled so sharply, he looked like a cat.

"How do you know if she daydreams?" I asked quickly.

"Please, Olivia, your childish efforts at being a detective are far more ludicrous than you can ever imagine. You will not find my fingerprints in the room." He picked up his paper and snapped it, making sure to show me his derisive smile before hiding behind the pages.

"I hope so," I said. If he was worried, he didn't show it. He went back to his reading, finished his breakfast as quickly as usual, and went off to work, leaving me to continue as caretaker of the madness his own madness had created.

13

Christmas Gift

As the green leaves of summer dried and shriveled and fell, and the trees stretched their lonely arms to the sky, becoming more and more barren, my own false pregnancy began to grow. All summer I had wandered the house, trying to collect pillows of different sizes and shapes to form my mock pregnancy. I found a pillow in the parlor and thought, "Yes, this is three-month size." I discovered a few more up in the north wing. But Foxworth Hall was such a dour and unadorned mansion that by month seven, when the baby was really beginning to show, I had to go to the Swan Room to find a pillow fluffy enough to be my baby at this time. Yes, I had agreed to keep up the charade that it was I that was due to give birth in December. How ironic it was that the baby was due on Christmas Day.

As soon as my "condition" became apparent, I knew it was time to explain the upcoming birth to the children. Mal and Joel, as I had insisted, had already been attending boarding school in Charleston since

September. Christopher had remained home with me. I missed my boys so much when they were gone and Christopher missed his mother so much that he and I became best friends, almost like a real mother and son. I doted over him morning, noon, and night. He was the only joy in my life during these strange, hard months. We used to play witch games, but Christopher always insisted I be a good witch. And indeed as the baby grew, I felt more and more that this child would be a gift from God, as I knew Christopher to be a gift from God. I decided the most appropriate time to tell the boys would be to announce it at Thanksgiving dinner, so Malcolm would be present to share the joyful tidings. We would have much to be thankful for on this Thanksgiving Day.

As we now had only two servants, I had been busy all morning helping prepare an extra-special feast. By midday, when it was time to sit down to eat, I was exhausted, feeling the "weight of my pregnancy" fully. As Malcolm carved the perfectly browned turkey, I held up my crystal goblet and rang my teaspoon against it. "Boys, boys, I have a very special announcement to make on this happy day. You may have noticed my figure has been changing of late. Well, here's the secret. Another child is to be born into our household, a very special child, who is due to come right near Christmastime. Truly God is giving us all a very special Christmas present this year."

Malcolm threw down the carving knife, his face reddened, and he looked at me with fury. "Olivia, this was my news to announce! How dare you try to play such a part in this!"

I narrowed my eyes at him and made my voice as cold as the November wind that blew away the dry leaves outside. "As we discussed, Malcolm, you will recall that I am to be in charge of all matters concerning the birth of our new child."

"Mother, is it going to be a girl or a boy?" Joel interrupted.

"Oh, don't be stupid," Mal chided, "nobody knows until it's born." Mal was becoming more and more like Malcolm. He loved being the smarter, wiser one, and often lorded his power over Joel. Christopher just burst into tears. "Please don't let anyone else come here, Olivia. I don't want a little baby taking up all of your time. I don't want to lose another mommy," he sobbed.

I comforted him, and said, "No one will ever replace you, Christopher, neither a little boy nor a little girl."

"It's going to be a girl," Malcolm thundered. He glared at me and resumed carving the turkey with a sort of vicious concentration aimed at me.

Malcolm's rage cast a pall of silence over our Thanksgiving meal. The boys seemed cowed, Christopher kept looking at me, silently pleading with his eyes for reassurance. Malcolm kept correcting both our boys in the way they held their knives and forks. Oh, couldn't he ever leave them alone! He accused Joel of cutting his meat like a sissy, and when Mal shot back, "But I thought you wanted a girl," Malcolm simply let out a snort of disgust, and went on eating his mashed potatoes.

I helped the maid clear the dishes. I could see her stealing glances at me, wondering why my news had not made for a more festive celebration. But I hardened my eyes; my sadness was not for maids to see. As soon as the boys were back in their room preparing for bed, and Malcolm, as usual, had some "business in town" to attend to, I prepared a picnic basket filled with Thanksgiving food to take up to Alicia. Usually, I brought her dinner before we ate. It was now eight o'clock. I knew she'd be famished.

As I ascended the stairs for what seemed like the millionth time, I rested the basket atop my pillowed ledge.

The first time Alicia had seen me with my built-up stomach she had laughed. Of course, she had to wear my maternity clothing and I thought if anyone was comical-looking, it was she.

She had made some clumsy attempts to pin up the hems, but most of the skirts dragged over the floor. The bodices hung down over her smaller bosom, and her arms looked lost in the sleeves. As with her previous pregnancy, she did not become bloated-looking. I thought she looked like a child in a grown woman's clothing. Her hair had grown back, but we had kept it trimmed so it reached only the base of her skull.

I opened the door and put a bright, cheerful smile on my face. "Thanksgiving feast, Alicia." Alicia ravenously attacked the basket, not even greeting me as she tore it out of my hands. She picked up the drumstick, bit into it, and sighed. Then, delicately, she scooped up the stuffing with her fingers and licked off every last crumb.

"Don't you find your appetite growing enormous now?" she asked. She sounded excited, like a schoolgirl comparing notes.

"Pardon?" I really didn't understand her question. She kept smiling in between bites. I had never seen her devour food in such a lustful manner.

"Your appetite," she repeated. "Isn't it absolutely huge? Sometimes I think I could eat all day and I'm tempted to go to the windows and shout for you to bring up more food. I would eat anything, any combination, any amounts, even things that weren't cooked. Last night I dreamt about steak and ice cream and cookies. Don't you have those urges?" she questioned, tilting her head and pressing her right forefinger into her cheek. She had been acting more normal lately and I wondered if her madness was returning.

"Hardly. Why should I?" I asked, not knowing whether to smile or to be angry.

She didn't answer. She laughed and went back to her food. Was she teasing me? Was it her way of taking some mad revenge on me?

"I eat no more or no less than I always do," I snapped, and left her. She was still laughing when I closed and locked the door behind me.

However, from that day on, every time I went to her to bring her things, she managed to make some sort of comment concerning my pregnancy as well as her own. She ignored anything I said to the contrary and acted as if I were the one who was going mad. Finally, I felt a need to spell everything out for her again.

"You realize why I am doing this, don't you?" I said one day after I had been in the room awhile. She was sitting by the window, endlessly knitting pink booties, receiving blankets, and buntings. She already had a pile large enough to outfit six infants, but on and on and on she knitted. The most peculiar thing was that she, too, seemed to be certain this child would be a girl, as if along with his seed, Malcolm had impregnated her with his obsession. The cold winter sun peered into the windows, making the room bright without making it truly warm. Of course, the layers of pillows strapped to my stomach always kept me warm. I patted my false stomach so she would understand exactly what I meant by "doing this." She looked up at me, her eyes dancing with glee.

"You are doing this," she said, "because Malcolm Neal Foxworth demands a large family, but mostly because he demands a daughter."

"But you are the one having the child, Alicia. All the real symptoms are yours, not mine."

The smile left her face. "Don't you wish you were pregnant with a child?" she asked with a sharp and biting tone.

"That is no longer the point now, is it?" I said, intending to intimidate her. If there was any one reason why I couldn't tolerate her weird questions, it was because they put me on the defensive, not her. I was the pure one; she was the one who had sinned. I was the one who would be rescuing her child from sin, and making it wholesome and pure.

Her expression didn't change. If anything, she became more aggressive.

"Yes, it is, Olivia. It is the point. You will have this child; you should feel it. Put your hand on your stomach and feel it moving within you. Feel it drawing on your strength. Eat for it, sleep for it, and pray for it as you would any child in your womb," she said with more determination and energy than she had said anything the entire time she was in this room. Her eyes were small, her mouth firm.

I backed away. I felt as if it were getting harder for me to breathe. "Why don't you open a window in here?"

She got up and walked to me. "It's life. Feel it." She took my hand into hers and put my palm on her stomach. For a moment we stood there looking into each other's eyes. She held mine to hers so intently, I did not look away, and then . . . I felt the movement in her stomach and it did feel as though I were feeling it in my own. I started to pull my hand back, but she held it to her. "No, feel it, want it, know it. It is yours," she said. "Yours."

"You're mad," I finally said, and successfully pulled away from her. "I'm doing this only to . . . to wash away your sin and Malcolm's and to convince people that the child is mine. And it will be mine. . . ." I backed up to the door, reached for the handle behind my back, and slipped out quickly, hurrying down the hall and away, pursued by that mad look in her eyes.

That night when I entered my bedroom and locked my door behind me I did not unfasten the pillows from my stomach. I lay there on my bed with my hands on my stomach thinking about the way Alicia had held my hand to her stomach. There was an electricity that still tingled in the tips of my fingers and the surface of my palm. As if the memory lingered in my hand, I felt the movement I had felt in Alicia, only I felt it in my false stomach. Was there a spirit I was touching within me? Had God indeed chosen this role for me and filled me with his spirit? Suddenly, it frightened me that I would feel such a thing and I jumped out of the bed and quickly removed the padding from myself.

After I fell asleep that night, however, I awoke to the strange sensation of movement in me again. It was a dream, I told myself, just a dream. But it took me a long time to fall asleep again. I even imagined I heard a baby's cry.

Mal and Joel stayed for the rest of the Thanksgiving weekend, and Monday morning I packed them off to school. During the next month, I waited with increasing eagerness for the birth of my child, while Christopher became more and more worried about it. He even became moody and cranky, so unlike his bright, sunny self. "You are the bad witch now, Olivia. And I'm going to eat your baby up."

The day we brought home the Christmas tree, Alicia's labor pains began. The boys had not yet returned for vacation, and Christopher and I were decorating the tree.

Just as I was hanging a Christmas ball on one of the high branches, I heard a distant scream. I dropped everything and ran to the north wing, leaving Christopher in the care of the maid.

"Alicia!" I called as I stormed into the room. "I could hear your screams in the rotunda. What do you think you are doing!"

"Olivia," she moaned, "please help me, the baby's coming."

Suddenly, Malcolm appeared behind me. "Olivia, now I shall take control. Go to your room immediately, you are about to give birth," he ordered me. His voice was so stern and certain, I obeyed him immediately, for the first time in months.

For twelve hours I lay in my room, screaming birth pain for the benefit of the two servants that remained and Christopher, while Alicia, muffled by Malcolm and the midwife he had called, silently labored in the north wing. At dawn the next day Malcolm appeared at my door carrying a squalling pink bunting. He walked over to my bed, and lay the baby beside me. "It's a girl," he announced with such pride and arrogance in his voice.

I unwrapped the bunting and peered at the most beautiful newborn I had ever seen. There was no redness to the baby's complexion. Why, it was as if she were indeed immaculately conceived and born without the anguish of the human birth process. This baby would be so easy to love, so beautiful and sweet, my heart went out to her. Oh, I would accept her as my own, and make her my own. And she would love me.

"It's the most beautiful baby in the world, isn't it? Dimpled hands and feet, golden wavy hair, the bluest of blue eyes . . . why, my mother must have looked like this when she was a baby," he cooed with a gentleness I had never before heard in his voice. "Corinne, my sweet beautiful daughter, Corinne!"

"Corinne!" I was shocked! "Surely, you wouldn't . . . how can you name that innocent baby after the mother whom you claim to hate?"

"You don't understand." He shook his head and waved his hand in front of his face as though he were clearing away cobwebs. "It will be my way to keep constantly aware of the deceitful, beguiling ways of beautiful women, or I may allow myself to believe and trust in her too much. As much as I love her already, every time my lips say 'Corinne,' I will be reminded of my betraying mother who promised to stay and love me until I was a man. I will never be so hurt again," he concluded, nodding with the same kind of certainty he had when he made his pronouncements about the business world.

His strange thinking sent a chill down my spine. How could he impose such character on this sweet angelic little baby? What was wrong with him? Would he never change? That moment I hated Malcolm with all my being, and I promised myself that I would try in every way I could to protect this child from his perversion. I would hold and cherish this child as one of my own. She may have inherited the Foxworth ancestry without my lineage to offset their madness, but I would raise her with my character and prevent her from becoming like Alicia or like the first Corinne.

"Leave my room, Malcolm," I ordered him coldly. "You are sick, and I do not ever want to hear you say such things about our daughter again."

Malcolm left, and I was happy to explore my new baby's perfect body, to introduce myself to her and assure her of my love and care. I counted her ten perfect dainty toes, her ten long, slender fingers. Yes, she would be everything I could never be, as well as everything I was. Through this special child, I would be able to live the life I'd never lived, for she would be loved by all who knew her. I rocked her to sleep in my arms, singing, "Hush little baby, don't say a word, Papa's gonna buy you a mockingbird." Then I drifted off beside her. It had been a long, hard day.

The winter sun was at its zenith when I pulled the curtains in my room the next day. Little Corinne, angel that she was, had slept six hours straight, unlike any newborn I had ever heard of before. The nurse came in to give her her bottle. "Let me do that," I insisted. I had no intention of keeping any nurse around for long. I wanted to raise this child myself. Then I remembered Christopher, I had to go and see him, and introduce him to Corinne. He must have felt very lonely and bewildered. Why, I had abandoned him at the Christmas tree without a word of explanation! Reluctantly I handed Corinne to the nurse and ran to find Christopher.

He wasn't in his bedroom. He wasn't in his nursery. With a mounting sense of dread I ran to the north wing.

I threw open the door. The room was empty, perfectly clean and still. Alicia and every trace of her ever having been there was gone.

"Christopher!" I yelled as I sped down the stairs. "Christopher! Where are you? Please, Christopher, come to your Olivia!" My voice echoed in the silent, empty halls. I sat down on the parlor sofa and cried as I hadn't cried ever in my life. Christopher was gone, without even saying good-bye. Alicia had reclaimed her son, and Malcolm had squired them off without so much as a faretheewell to me. I swore then and there that never, never would I let the same thing happen to Corinne.

The Christmas Mal and Joel came home to was a Christmas unlike any they had ever seen or even imagined. Malcolm planned the biggest, grandest, most extravagant Christmas party ever to be given at Foxworth Hall. He had even outspent Garland, whom he often accused of being extravagant. I was quick to learn that when it came to Corinne, Malcolm's usual frugality was forgotten. Efficiency and economy had nothing to do with what he was to consider her needs.

For one thing, the guest list was considerably expanded from the guest list for our previous Christmas parties. Close to five hundred people were invited, many who had only the slightest acquaintance with Malcolm. Almost anyone who owned property, had a business, or was a professional within a fifty-mile radius was invited. To stress the importance of Corinne, he designed a special Christmas party invitation. "Corinne Foxworth cordially invites you to her first Christmas party at Foxworth Hall" was lettered in gold at the top of the invitation.

He set up a bar in the foyer and ordered cases of expensive champagne. The bubbly liquid was fed into four enormous crystal fountains that sprayed it into great silver receiving bowls. Six waiters filled the stemmed goblets under the sparkling liquid and handed them out continuously to the arriving guests. Everywhere people turned, they were greeted by waiters and waitresses in black and white uniforms flowing in and out of the ballroom, bearing silver trays laden with dainty hors d'oeuvres—small pieces of bread smothered in caviar, pink chunks of salmon on crackers, the largest shrimps I had ever seen speared on golden toothpicks.

The other Christmas tree was replaced by one twenty-five feet high, bedecked with thousands of sparkling ornaments and lights. The star at the top of the tree was made of solid silver, and Malcolm surrounded the base with dozens and dozens of presents for Corinne wrapped in glittering holiday paper. I had to remind him to add the presents for Mal and Joel.

Malcolm tripled the number of extra servants for the occasion. Every five feet there was someone standing with a tray or someone to collect used glasses and dishes. A forty-foot table was set up against the far right wall and upon it were arrayed roasted turkeys, roasted hams, roast beefs, Cornish hens, chunks of salmon, dish after dish of caviar, platters of shrimp, and rows of lobster tails. Everything was dressed ostentatiously and placed on silver serving dishes. There were flowers on every available tabletop, and in some places tables were brought in to hold enormous poinsettias. He spared no expense.

He hired a ten-piece orchestra and had a temporary stage constructed for them in the left corner of the foyer. There was even a female singer who sang the most up-to-date music, something Malcolm rarely tolerated. He had planned this party out like a major business venture, not trusting me with any of the details.

It was as though we had ordered the weather for our Christmas party, for it was snowing gently and the big flakes added to the festive atmosphere. One of our neighbors below had harnessed a horse to a sleigh and brought some guests up the hill with the bells jingling, all of them wrapped in furs and singing holiday songs.

Butlers and maids took their coats and hats at the door and they were immediately directed to the champagne so they could toast the birth of Corinne with Malcolm, who drank more than I had ever seen him drink.

Malcolm had also ordered hundreds of red candles which flickered gaily in silver holders. All five tiers of the three gigantic crystal and gold chandeliers were lit too. The glittering lights created a web of dazzling beauty, stretched from the mirrors to the crystals to the jewels of the women.

It looked like a scene out of a movie about the kings and queens of Europe. The opulence created a sense of magic. One almost expected the arrival of Prince Charming with Cinderella on his arm.

The guests wore their richest clothing, their most expensive jewels and furs. The air was electric with their excitement, their animated chatter and laughter.

For the purpose of celebrating Corinne's birth, Malcolm had hired a professional photographer to take pictures of her in her crib or in his arms. The photographs were then blown up into enormous sizes and placed in gold frames, a half dozen of them held up by tripods in the entranceway so people who came to the party could first see Malcolm Foxworth's beautiful daughter. The photographer had caught the blue in her eyes and the richness of her golden hair. No one could walk past a photograph without remarking about her perfect complexion and dainty features.

In fact, Corinne's looks became something of a topic early on. Some people, like Beneatha Thomas and Colleen Demerest, were rather obvious with their thoughts, or, rather, their jealousy. When I stopped to talk to them and some of their friends, I discovered they had been analyzing one of Corinne's photographs in detail.

"I see so much of Malcolm in her," Beneatha said, "but not so much of you." I saw the way the other women smiled at one another and I recalled my first party with the Virginia society, how they had made me feel so awkward and foolish. I was determined to protect Corinne, and never let what had happened to me ever ever fall on her ears.

"I'm sure she will be strikingly beautiful and tall," Colleen said, stressing "tall." Some of the women turned away to hide their smirks and laughter, but I straightened into a firmer, taller posture, uninhibited. They didn't have daughters like Corinne. We would show them all.

Snidely, I said, "Yes, I can already tell she has my disposition. She doesn't cry and whine, so she won't be weak and dependent like so many women are today. I expect she will have my attention span and intellectual curiosity so that when she is our age, she will have more serious subjects to talk about." I left them standing there, speechless.

Other people made comments about Corinne's features, however. I overheard a number of comments about her blue eyes and golden hair, about how much she looked like a Foxworth. I was walking behind Dorothea Campden, whose husband was the president of a major textile factory Malcolm was negotiating to buy, and I heard her say that Corinne was proof that children often take after their grandparents more than they do their parents.

"And in this child's case, it's a blessing," she said. "At least on the mother's side."

Everyone in her group gasped when I stepped up to them immediately after the remark had been made.

"Blessing in what sense, Dorothea?" I asked. She was a small middle-aged woman who was in a constant battle with age, dyeing her hair, wearing clothing meant for younger women, seeking out skin creams with so-called miraculous formulas to wipe away wrinkles. I towered over her and she shrank back, her hand at her throat as if I had threatened to choke her.

"Well . . . I . . . I meant that she looks so much like Malcolm's mother."

"I didn't realize you were so old, Dorothea, that you would remember his mother."

"Well, yes, I do," she said, her eyes darting from one woman to the next. She was looking for someone to rescue her. How I enjoyed making them uncomfortable.

"Of course, babies change so as they grow older, don't they? Why, would anyone recognize any of you from your baby pictures?" I asked. Then I falsely raised my hand to cover my mouth, as if I'd made a terrible slip of the tongue. "Oh, I'm sorry, Dorothea. Did they have cameras when you were a child, Dorothea?"

"What? Why . . . of course, I . . ."

"Excuse me," I said. "I see the Murphys have just arrived," I added, and pivoted quickly to leave her stuttering.

"How rude," someone in her group said, and they closed around her like chickens around a wounded hen.

I circulated about, sometimes interrupting similar conversations, sometimes feeling that I had just appeared when derogatory things were being said about me. I rather enjoyed baiting and biting at these vapid women. Before long, when I looked about the ballroom it seemed to me that many of them were glaring at me hatefully. But I no longer cared. Now I had Corinne and I would be known as the mother of the most beautiful child in the state.

Somehow what I was doing got back to Malcolm and he grabbed my arm and dragged me into the library with him. I recalled again that first party and the way he went into the library arm in arm with that "flapper." It brought back my anger and pain. I was in no mood for any of his tantrums now.

"What is it that couldn't wait?" I demanded.

"It's you and what you're doing out there," he said, his eyes wide and a bit bloodshot. The champagne had gone to his head.

"Doing out there?" I knew to what he was referring, but I feigned ignorance and wore an expression of innocence.

"Insulting all those women, letting them know exactly how you feel about them, even insulting the wives of some very important business associates," he added as if I had uttered blasphemies in front of clergymen.

"As far as I am concerned," I began, "these so-called high society women are—"

"I don't care what you think," he snapped. "This

isn't your party to ruin. It's Corinne's. We're doing it for Corinne. We want to give *her* the good beginning, not you!"

"Corinne? Are you mad? She's my daughter, too, but she's only an infant. I don't want her growing up to be a frivolous spoiled thing like those women there—like your mother was. Besides, she doesn't even know what we are doing," I said. "And this expense for an infant . . . no matter how precious and wonderful she is . . . it's sinful."

"It is not sinful," he responded, pounding his right fist into his palm. I had never seen him so animated in an argument. "It's what she deserves."

"Deserves?" I started to laugh.

"You're jealous," he said, pointing at me. "You're jealous of an infant, jealous of Alicia for having such a beautiful baby, envious of her blue eyes and golden hair and magnificent complexion. Well, I won't have it, I tell you; I won't have it!" Both of his hands were now clenched into fists. I thought he was enraged and drunk enough to actually strike me, but I wouldn't permit him to intimidate me this way.

"No, Malcolm, it's you who are jealous. Jealous of me and my daughter."

"What?" The idea seemed to confuse him. He backed away as if I had been the one to strike him. "She's my daughter, not yours. She has none of your blood and none of you in her. And I'm glad of that." His look was hateful and mean, but I wouldn't let him hurt me now.

"Oh, no, Malcolm, you're wrong about that. You wanted me to be this child's mother. And I will be. And she does have me in her, she has had me in her from the moment I said I would participate in your little scheme. But now, Malcolm, it isn't simply your scheme, it's your life and mine, and our sons' and our daughter's. It's our family and I am now as much a Foxworth as you are." I walked past him and opened the library door.

"I am returning to the party," I said. "You can remain in here and continue this argument with yourself for all I care."

He collected himself and joined me, glaring at me threateningly from time to time. I ignored him. At twelve o'clock he had the nurse bring Corinne down. I had kept the boys up even though they were exhausted, and the five of us stood in front of the great Christmas tree for a family photograph.

Malcolm held Corinne, and the two boys stood on either side of me and held my hands. The lights flashed and the crowd of guests applauded. Malcolm was beaming with pride as he looked down at his daughter. She was awake, but she wasn't crying.

"She knows it's her party!" he announced, and gave me a piercing glance. The crowd laughed at his joviality.

"A toast," Matthew Allen, one of Malcolm's business associates announced. He was more like Malcolm's stooge, I thought. He raised his champagne glass and the waiters scurried about quickly offering glasses to the guests. "To the Foxworths," he said, "and especially to their beautiful new daughter, Corinne. Merry Merry Christmas and a Happy New Year."

"Hear, hear!" the audience chorused, and the glasses were emptied. The band struck up "Deck the Halls with Boughs of Holly" and Malcolm circulated through the crowd displaying his beautiful new daughter.

I gathered my boys to me.

"Father loves her more than he loves us," Mal said. He was so perceptive. It gave me hope.

"You must learn to live with that, Mal. Both of you must learn," I said. I hugged both my boys to my breast. I loved them dearly, and my love and protection were large enough for three children. No one would be left out of my affections. I kissed them both on their heads and hugged them again as the three of us watched Malcolm across the big room holding his golden daughter up into the air so she almost looked like a cherub that had flown from the Christmas tree. He held her there and smiled in jubilation.

14

Corinne

FROM THE NIGHT OF THE CHRISTMAS PARTY ON, MALCOLM never hesitated to show that his love of Corinne had no boundaries. The boys knew this, and it really hurt them and I tried and tried to compensate, to reassure them that all children were precious to their parents, that they would always be cherished by me and by Malcolm, too, even if it wasn't so easy for him to show his affection for his sons. I think the boys were actually happy to return to school after the New Year, so displaced did they feel by the fuss Malcolm continually made over Corinne. He was home most evenings now, where before he almost always went out. He endlessly crowed and crooned over Corinne, while, as usual, criticizing and overly disciplining Mal and Joel. My heart went out to them. They were good boys, sweet and loving, and I know they felt lost amid the attention Malcolm lavished on Corinne. After they left, I felt free to turn more of my attention to her too.

But Malcolm insisted that the nurse whom he had hired in the beginning remain. Every time I went to feed, or even to lift Corinne, that woman was hovering behind me, trying to take control, frowning disapprovingly at the way I handled my daughter. This really angered me.

One morning, while Mrs. Stratton was giving Corinne her bottle, I blew up. "I told you time and time again that I am to be the only one who feeds Corinne. How dare you disobey my orders."

"Ma'am," she countered snidely. "I was never told I was to follow your orders. On the contrary, Mr. Foxworth instructed me in detail exactly how he wanted every aspect of the baby's schedule to be executed."

"What?" I was flabbergasted. "I want you out of this house this afternoon. Services such as yours will no longer be necessary."

"I'm afraid there's some confusion, Mrs. Foxworth," Mrs. Stratton persisted. "When Mr. Foxworth hired me, our agreement was that the child would remain under my care indefinitely."

I was furious, but I didn't want my rage to infect my sweet innocent child, so I quickly turned and stormed out of the room. All that morning I paced the corridors of Foxworth Hall, filled with agitation and determined once again to take control of this situation from Malcolm.

That afternoon I had my second surprise: the decorators arrived. Again it was something Malcolm had contracted to do without my knowledge. They proceeded to the room adjacent to his and began planning out the construction of Corinne's personal nursery. It was Malcolm's decision that she not use the boys' nursery. New furniture had been ordered, and I saw from the intensity with which the decorators worked that Malcolm had demanded everything be completed post haste. Again, no expense was too great when it came to Corinne, and I was to have no input about the colors of the new wallpaper and rug or the style of the furniture. The decorators barely acknowledged my presence.

I sat fuming all day. I tried reaching Malcolm at his offices, but Malcolm rarely, if ever, spoke to me on the telephone. During Corinne's first few weeks, he did call once in a while to ask about her, but usually he spoke to Mrs. Stratton. If I ever did phone him, his secretaries told me he was in a meeting or away from his desk. It mattered not that I left a message for him to return my call. Whenever I asked him about it, he told me he was just so busy, he never got to call me back; so I stopped calling him.

I was waiting for him in the doorway of the library when he came home early that evening. He would have been home earlier, but he had gone to a shop specializing in infant wear and purchased five new sleeping outfits for Corinne. With the packages in his arms, his face lit with excitement, he entered Foxworth Hall intending to rush right up to the child.

I was amused by the way he spoke to her whenever he did go to her. It was as if he expected her to understand his words, his promises, his plans for her education and training. Sometimes, when I overheard him speaking to Corinne, I got a chilling feeling. It was as if he thought she was his mother who had been fed goblets of liquid from the mythical fountain of youth until she had been returned to this infant state. In his mind she was a baby, but she had a grown woman's comprehension of things said to her, especially things said to her by him.

"Malcolm!" I called as he passed by me on his way to

the spiral staircase. He often ran up those stairs like a boy of sixteen, drawn to the south wing by a love that was absolutely magnetic and overwhelming, driven by worship for his child.

"What do you want?" he demanded, impatient with my presence. During the last month he had ignored me anyway. Whenever he was home, he was with Corinne; and when she was sleeping, he was at his work. Sometimes, when he did look at me, he looked right through me, as if I weren't even there.

"I want to talk to you immediately," I said. "It cannot wait."

"What is it that cannot wait?" he asked, grimacing. He juggled the boxes in his arms. He hadn't even shaken the snow from his shoulders and back. The white flakes were melting on his golden hair, making the strands glitter under the lights. But he didn't seem to notice or care.

"Please step in here," I said, and backed up. I heard him groan in impatience, but he came in quickly. He put the packages down on his desk.

"Well? What is this new emergency?" He shook his head and brushed the melted droplets of snow off his shoulders.

"I want Mrs. Stratton let go. *Now*, Malcolm."

"Mrs. Stratton is a professional. A professional when it comes to taking care of infants. Corinne will have only the best."

"Am I not the best? I am her mother. I am also the mother of your sons!"

"It's different with boys," he said, looking at me as if I were an idiot who understood nothing.

"Why? How?" I demanded.

"It's just different!" He hated being contradicted. I

imagined that it was only here, in his own home, that he was ever contradicted. None of his employees and stooges would dare. It must have been a source of bitter irony to him that his wife challenged him the most. Malcolm's attitudes about women left little room for equal treatment and respect.

"It's wasteful extravagance," I said, shaking my head. "The woman will grow bored here if she's as professional as you say. Most of the time, I will be—"

"You will be doing nothing," he snapped. "Leave Corinne entirely to her. That's why I am paying her. She has my instructions; let her carry them out."

"What mistakes did I make with your sons?" I wasn't about to let him have his way. If he was going to make things difficult and unpleasant for me, I would do the same for him. He tried to ignore the question. "Malcolm, what mistakes?"

"Mistakes." He sneered. "Look at the boys."

"What's wrong with them?"

"What isn't wrong with them, you should ask. They're weak; they're lazy; they're not interested in the business world, a world that has provided them with all this," he said, making a wide gesture. "You've poisoned them so they can't stand being in my presence—"

"That's your own fault," I interrupted. "You terrorize them."

"Simply because I demand things of them," he continued. "I want them to be men, not mama's boys. Mal still sneaks around that piano when I'm not at home. Don't deny it," he added quickly. "And Joel . . . Joel is still as fragile and meek as a little girl."

"But all that has nothing to do with—"

"Enough!" He pounded his desk. "Enough," he said in a lower but much more threatening tone of voice.

"Mrs. Stratton will remain until I want to dismiss her. It's what I want; it's my money I'm spending. Don't interfere."

"Corinne is my child too!"

A wry smile twisted his lips. "Really, Olivia? Did you forget? She's my daughter. Did you forget? She's a complete Foxworth," he added, as if by sending away Alicia he had stripped Corinne of all of Alicia's heritage. In his deranged thinking, Corinne was solely his creation. "She deserves the best and the best is what she will have, from now on. You can't understand this," he added, shaking his head and looking at me as though I were someone to pity. "Your father treated you more like a son than a daughter. Anyway, it should not concern you. Go about your business and let Mrs. Stratton do her job. Look after the boys," he said. "They are certainly enough for you," he added bitterly. He picked up his packages again.

I did not know how to win this argument. I was temporarily silenced.

He started toward the library door.

"Wait," I called. "What about this new nursery you are creating for her?"

"What about it?"

"I must insist," I said, "that you inform me of these decisions before you make them. I won't be embarrassed like this again."

He turned and contemplated me as if I were some annoying insect that just wouldn't go away. He tucked in the right corner of his mouth and shook his head.

"When I agreed to go along with your plan about this child, it was under the terms that from now on I would be in charge of this household and things would be run the way I saw fit. You also agreed that the child would be mine, and indeed she is mine. It is only God, not you, who could take her away from me now." I paused long enough to catch my breath and bore my eyes into him like daggers. "I'll let you have your new nursery, Malcolm, but only on one condition. Mal and Joel will each be given a new room, too, one of their own, for them to use however they wish when they are home from school. And each of those rooms will have a grand piano in it."

"Very well," he said with a look of complete contempt and disgust on his face. "I don't care anymore how you raise your sons. They've already been sissied and ruined." He stalked from the room and I heard his feet pound the stairs as he ran up the steps to his daughter.

I, too, couldn't wait to get to Corinne's room every day. Every day Corinne grew more beautiful and my heart filled more and more with love for her. The first time her lips smiled, she was looking at me, and I knew she felt my love and care for her. When her silken golden hair was long enough, I tied pretty pink ribbons in it. She looked like a fairy tale princess child. Oh, now I understood the sort of love everyone always seemed to feel for those dainty, pretty girls I had watched in my youth. Their beauty seemed to pluck a special string in the heart, leaving a sound as lovely and resonant as an angel's harp.

During the summer when Corinne was almost three years old, Malcolm again did something without my approval. He replaced Mrs. Stratton with someone he imported from England.

Her name was Mrs. Worthington and she was a fifty-four-year-old spinster, who, according to Malcolm, had been governess to the children of the Duke and Duchess of Devon. I didn't like the woman from the start, and she didn't like me. Malcolm had obviously made it perfectly clear to her that I was of little or no consequence when it came to decisions pertaining to Corinne. She didn't pay any attention to me; she tried to take control of Corinne's life as if I were dead. She never asked me before she did anything with her. She set up a schedule for the child and followed it religiously.

For the first week Corinne rebelled and begged me to send Mrs. Worthington away. "I want to stay with you, Mommy," she cried tearfully. "I don't like that other lady."

"Corinne darling, you know I would rather it be only the two of us. But your father insists. Your father thinks it's important that you have a governess, and even if I don't agree, your father will not back down. The best thing for you to do is obey Mrs. Worthington."

Despite my dislike of Mrs. Worthington, I quickly began to admire her talents, and I did so want Corinne to have all those graces that could never be mine. Mrs. Worthington's program consisted of lessons in etiquette, elocution, and dance. Ironically, Corinne was to be taught how to play the piano as well.

She was a confident and somewhat arrogant woman, standing nearly five feet seven. Although her clothing was conservative and Victorian, she did have some very fine dresses, blouses, and skirts made from fine cottons, silk, and taffeta. I never saw her once without her hair neatly pinned. She rose very early in the morning and prepared herself each day as though she were going to have an audience with the queen.

She wore no makeup and spent all her personal time either in her room reading or taking solitary walks over the grounds of Foxworth Hall. Unless the weather was inclement, she walked daily as a form of exercise. She was very careful about how and what she ate and maintained a rather trim figure for a woman of her age.

Actually, I became something of a student of hers myself because she did nothing without turning it into a lesson for Corinne, whether it be holding her fork correctly, reaching for food correctly, walking with the proper posture, greeting people—whatever it was, she always turned to Corinne and made sure the child understood and appreciated her actions.

It was Malcolm's decision that Corinne, unlike the boys, who couldn't come to the dinner table to eat with us until they were at least five years old, should join us at meals, as a learning experience.

This was the source of one of many arguments Malcolm and I had about Corinne's upbringing. The first time Corinne was brought to the table with Mrs. Worthington, she was only three years old. The boys and I looked up in surprise as Mrs. Worthington appeared holding Corinne's hand. Malcolm beamed and patted the chair beside him. Corinne started to run to it, but Mrs. Worthington stopped her instantly.

"Corinne," she said, and the child hesitated. I was amazed at such obedience. Mrs. Worthington had been with us only a week, and despite Malcolm's feelings about Corinne, I had observed a willfulness in her already. She was like a baby bluebird, flitting from this thing to that without much concentration.

I thought her bright blue eyes were full of mischief. There was something impish about her beauty and the way she had learned early on to twist and turn Malcolm. He couldn't resist any of her demands. She needed only look toward something to have him go fetch it. Whenever he took her for rides, her arms would be filled with new toys or dolls when she returned. Sometimes, she was dressed in a brand new outfit or wore new shoes. She would come skipping into the house, her tiny laughter echoing through the foyer. Malcolm insisted her golden hair be brushed a hundred times each day and it did gleam with a richness that made her look angelic. It was kept down in long, flowing strands that reached below her shoulders. She never lost the rich complexion with which she had been born. If anything, she grew more beautiful and pleasing.

I was fascinated with her every movement, whether it be the way she flew through the house, birdlike, her little feet barely touching the carpets, or the way she brought food to her lips, touching them ever so gently, acting as though she knew she was some kind of little princess.

I thought she was very bright and understood immediately that her father wanted her to obey Mrs. Worthington, and that if she mastered whatever Mrs. Worthington set out for her to do, she would have even more control over Malcolm. He doted on her every movement, and if she did something the way Mrs. Worthington told her to do it in front of him, he beamed.

And so right from the start she was a perfect little pupil. She stopped and looked back at Mrs. Worthington, who stood solid and correct, her hands clasped before her, waiting for Corinne to return to the dining room doorway, which she did immediately.

"We walk to the table," she said, "like a lady should. And remember how you take your seat," she added.

Corinne straightened her little posture, lifting her head high with the characteristic Foxworth arrogance. The boys and I watched in fascination. Malcolm got up and pulled her chair out, something he had never done for me, not even during the first week of our marriage. Corinne turned quickly to Mrs. Worthington, who nodded, and Corinne said, "Thank you, Daddy."

It was as though the sky had opened and all the light and glory of the heavens poured down into this house. Malcolm was positively illuminated. He looked at Mrs. Worthington with an expression of gratitude and respect. Corinne took her seat at the table and her education had begun.

Afterward, when all the children were put to bed and Mrs. Worthington had retired, I went down to the library and interrupted Malcolm.

We were having a terrific summer thunderstorm. The raindrops pounded the windows and the thunder rattled the glass. Our lights flickered and the wind threaded in and out of shutters and through cracks in window casings, creating a symphony of discordant sounds. Behind Malcolm I saw the coal-black sky sizzle with lightning, but he, as always, remained indifferent to anything around him when he worked. My appearance did more to disturb him than did this terrific storm.

"What is it now?" he asked, looking up impatiently. His forehead creased with annoyance. Undaunted, I continued across the library to his desk.

"I understand what Mrs. Worthington is trying to do by bringing Corinne to the table to eat with us, but how can you permit it after forbidding the boys to eat with us until they were five years old? Don't think they don't see and understand this . . . this unnatural favoritism."

"Unnatural favoritism? What are you talking about? Must you oppose everything I do?" he asked. He sat back in his seat and feigned a look of reason and control to make me feel as though I were the one at fault. "How many times do I have to tell you? Girls must be brought up in a different manner. Socially, more is expected of them. Just because you weren't provided with these opportunities does not mean that Corinne won't be.

"Didn't I provide the boys with a private tutor?" he asked quickly, before I could respond. "Until you twisted things around so I had to dismiss him."

"I twisted . . ." I could barely get my words out, I was so angry. "It was your doing that ruined that for them, and I never approved of that man anyway."

"Precisely my point," he said, sitting up quickly. "You conspired against him until you found an opportunity to get rid of him. *You* denied the boys their special opportunity, not I," he insisted. "I told you once before and I am telling you again, when it comes to Corinne, whether it be her education or her clothing . . . whatever, I will make all the decisions. Now, stop interfering."

We had similar arguments when Mrs. Worthington began Corinne's musical education, but no matter how I pointed out the inconsistencies between his treatment of Corinne and his treatment of the boys, he refused to acknowledge them. He always managed to end the arguments by accusing me of jealousy.

To some extent he was right. As I watched Corinne grow into a beautiful young girl receiving all the benefits and opportunities Malcolm's huge fortune could provide, I couldn't help but compare myself to her when I was her age. Of course, I saw much of Alicia in her as time went by. I imagined Malcolm did, too, and whenever he looked at her, he couldn't help but think of his adoration of his father's bride.

When she reached ten, it pained him to have to send her off to private school because it meant she wouldn't be there in the house when he returned home from work. And truthfully, it pained me just as much. With Corinne gone, it was as if the sun had moved permanently behind the cloud of Foxworth Hall. I was lonelier than I'd ever been before. Malcolm spent hardly any time at home, except during school vacations. He was out "doing business" most every night. Oh, I knew what sort of business he was doing, I heard the tongues wagging in town, and although I really had no friends (how could I, when everyone knew what my own husband thought of me, and how he treated me?), I was ashamed of Malcolm and for Malcolm, and determined to protect my children from the worst in him.

Perhaps that is why I found so much comfort in God, the Bible, and, later, in the church. It was my one consolation, my companion, indeed, my salvation. It was my cousin John Amos who led me back to religion. His own mother had died, and he, like myself, was all that was left of his family. He came to visit, and encouraged me to pray with him, and as we sat quietly meditating in the guest parlor, I indeed felt filled by the holy spirit, as John Amos promised me I would. He insisted I start attending church more often, and before he returned up north, he left me with a stirring program of daily Bible readings. I had refused for so long to surrender my will to Malcolm that it was with relief and gratitude that I learned to surrender my will to God.

Malcolm grew annoyed with my devotions. He missed Corinne every bit as much as I did, but the only comfort he took was the visits he made to her at school. He never visited the boys at their boarding schools. I did visit them whenever I could, and they wrote me long letters describing their activities. Malcolm didn't know, of course, but Mal was taking an instrumental course and Joel was in the orchestra.

The boys also adored Corinne. They were just as fascinated with her beauty and charm as was Malcolm, but they couldn't help being jealous of her relationship with him. By now she was very spoiled, whereas the boys, even though they lived with great wealth, had grown up relatively unaffected. Malcolm never gave them things with the ease and full heart he gave things to Corinne. When they were teenagers, he insisted they work summers in one of his banks, serving as messengers and doing other menial tasks.

Still, despite all the reason they had, the boys never resented Corinne. They, too, spoiled her, were eager to do things for her and buy things for her. They took her sailing and horseback riding, and when Mal was old enough to drive, he drove her anywhere she wanted, anytime she wanted. Joel, especially, was at her beck and call whenever the three of them were home together. There was nothing he would refuse to do for her and she knew it and took advantage of it.

One Thanksgiving holiday, when they were all home from boarding school, I took the boys aside in a front salon and discussed it with them. Malcolm had taken Corinne to Charlottesville for a shopping spree because she told him all her clothing was out of date, and that was important to her even though she was only eleven years old.

I sat Mal and Joel on a settee and stood before them, not unlike one of their lecturers at school. We were having an early winter snowfall. It was a light one, however, with the sky remaining quite bright. It had the effect of putting everyone into the holiday mood, anticipating the coming of Christmas. The boys and Corinne had begun to decorate our tall Christmas tree, only Corinne spent most of her time sitting in one of our tall-back French provincial chairs dictating to them what she wanted where, and Joel scurried about like a slave, stretching and straining to get this ornament here and that ornament there.

"Mal," I began, "you will be eighteen on your next birthday, and as I told you boys years ago, each of you at eighteen will have access to a trust fund. It will provide each of you with a great deal of independence, but independence requires a well-developed sense of responsibility," I said, and paused to see how they were listening to me.

Mal, as usual, stared up intently, sitting as quietly and as still as a statue. He was so long-legged, he looked uncomfortable on that soft light-blue cushioned settee, but he didn't utter a word of complaint. Joel, on the other hand, fidgeted about, strumming the arm of the settee, running his hand through his thin gold hair, leaning forward then bouncing back.

"I know, Mother," Mal said. "Father has been talking to me about that very thing lately. We had a discussion right after I arrived yesterday, as a matter of fact," he said. He had Malcolm's strong, deep voice.

"Yesterday? What has he been telling you?" I asked.

"He's asked me to sign the money over to him so he can continue to invest it properly."

"What did you say?" I asked quickly. Joel stopped fidgeting and looked up, concern in his face. The boys were always very sensitive to my feelings.

"I told him I would discuss it with you," Mal said, and smiled wryly. How like Malcolm he looked, but oh, how like me he was. I smiled back at him and Joel smiled widely.

"Good. Good boy, Mal. You should never turn that money back to your father. He might just take it and spend it all on Corinne," I said. Joel started to laugh, but my look stopped him. "I don't mean to be facetious, boys. I've called you in here because I think you've got to stop pampering your sister. She's using you, taking advantage of you. And I don't think she appreciates the things you do for her. Your father has spoiled her so. I'm telling you this for Corinne's good as well as for your own. Your father won't listen to reason. He's blind when it comes to her, but you two can be of inestimable help if you won't be so eager to do anything she wants whenever she wants."

I started to pace before them.

"It's not too late to help her, but you can just imagine what kind of a woman she is going to turn out to be if this continues. She has no sense of money and its worth; she thinks everyone exists to be her servant, especially you two, and I don't like the way she takes advantage of you."

I peered over my shoulder to see how they were taking my little lecture. Both boys looked serious and thoughtful, although Joel did look more unhappy.

"I love your sister. Don't misunderstand me," I said. "But I wasn't kidding about your inheritances. Your father is capable of assigning everything to her, and don't for one moment think she is not a bit conniving. I know she wears that innocent, childish look, but behind those eyes, Corinne thinks like a Foxworth." I stopped and stared at them. Mal nodded and Joel sat back, his arms folded across his narrow chest. He still had difficulty gaining weight and looked thin and fragile.

"What should we do?" Joel asked. His voice was thinner, softer, more high-pitched and feminine. I often thought Joel would have made a much prettier little girl, although perhaps not as pretty as Corinne.

"Give more consideration to what she asks of you. Teach her some abstinence and patience. Help her become a better person," I added. Mal nodded and then Joel nodded. "As for your father and his demands on your trust funds, continue to tell him you're discussing it with me. Let him come to me," I said.

"Why did he give us these trust funds if he wants to take them back?" Mal asked.

"It was something he and I decided a long time ago, and there are some decisions that cannot be broken. The reasons are not important right now. Just understand that you're not as defenseless as you might sometimes feel, not as long as I am still mistress of Foxworth Hall," I added. Mal nodded thoughtfully, but Joel continued to look worried.

I was sadly aware of the fact that I could create two opposing camps in Foxworth Hall—Mal, Joel, and myself against Malcolm and Corinne. I knew it was distasteful to the boys and to me, so I didn't harp on it.

"Everything will get better in time," I concluded, smiling. Of course, I knew it wouldn't.

The holidays continued to be festive occasions for us. It meant the children would be home, and for Malcolm it meant his princess would arrive. Despite the way I felt about Malcolm's relationship with his daughter, and his hard relationship with his sons, I couldn't wait for her arrival either. She brought light and life to Foxworth Hall. By the time she was thirteen, she was quite the little lady and very popular with her peers. I could tell that all her girlfriends vied for her attention and favor. There was little that they valued more than an invitation to spend the night or to attend a holiday party at Foxworth Hall.

Our Christmas parties continued to be lavish affairs, only now with Corinne a little lady, Malcolm conducted each one the way he would conduct a debutante's ball. Every Christmas Eve Corinne was presented to our high society. The parents of all of Corinne's girlfriends and peers were invited. He always bought her an expensive new dress for the occasion. Her girlfriends knew what was expected of them. Everyone came formally dressed, fathers in tuxedos and mothers in gowns. There was always a great deal of glitter and glamour. Women and teenage girls wore expensive jewelry. People drove up in expensive cars, costly flowers grown in hothouses were everywhere, and the feast was as varied and as rich as it was at the Christmas Eve party when Malcolm had introduced the newborn Corinne.

Malcolm screened Corinne's friends carefully, inviting only those he believed were "good enough." Our guest list was pruned more vigorously every Christmas, until Corinne reached eighteen, for during that year, a great many things changed.

But until then, Malcolm's adoration of his beautiful daughter increased daily. He not only had photographs taken of her continually, he had her portrait painted, something he still hadn't done for me. The picture of Corinne was placed in his trophy room for his private viewing. In his eyes she was perfect.

One evening Malcolm and Corinne were alone at the dining table. The boys had not returned from their boarding schools yet. Corinne was home because Malcolm had made a special trip to get her. She was sitting like a little lady, a graduate of Mrs. Worthington's tutorship, describing events at her school. Malcolm was entranced, his chin on his hand, propped up on his elbow, a constant smile on his face. He was mesmerized by her sparkling blue eyes and her musical laughter. I watched them through a crack in the doorway. They seemed so far away from me, in more than actual distance. It was as though they were in their own private world. I envied them, envied the way Corinne held Malcolm's attention.

When she finished her story, she leaned forward, as if by instinct, and kissed him on the forehead. She did it so quickly and so unconsciously, it was a perfect heavenly act.

He caught her hand in his.

"You like your daddy?" He looked serious, as if he really weren't sure.

"Oh, yes, Daddy." She pulled her lips back gently to tease him with her smile.

"Then promise to stay with me forever and I promise that all this will be yours." He made a sweeping gesture with his hand and Corinne looked up at the high ceilings. She giggled. "I mean it," he said. "Everything I own will go to my princess. Will you stay with me forever?"

"Of course I will, Daddy," she said, and he kissed her on the cheek. "But will you do a favor for me now, Daddy?"

"Anything, princess, anything your little heart desires."

"Do you know that special room upstairs, Daddy?

The one that's always locked? I want that to be my room. Can it be mine? Oh, please say yes right now and I'll move all my things myself," she said, clapping her hands together. Her face was red with excitement.

"What room?" Malcolm asked. He looked up, a half smile on his face, not anticipating what she was about to say.

"The room with the swan bed. Oh, how beautiful it is."

Malcolm turned crimson, but his lips turned white.

"No, no," he said through clenched teeth. "You must not go into that room. It's not a room to be used."

"But why?" Her face crumpled with disappointment, something she was unaccustomed to. She clenched her hands into little fists and pounded them against her thighs. Corinne's hands always betrayed her emotions. Sometimes they seemed to be separate creatures, turning and twisting of their own will.

"It's a bad room, a tainted room," Malcolm said, not realizing that by saying such a thing he would make the room even more enticing for her.

"Why?" Corinne asked.

"Because the ghost of my father's second wife lives in there," Malcolm said, hoping such a statement would terrify her. Her eyes did get big and she pressed her hands against each other in prayer fashion. "And she was not a nice woman."

"Why wasn't she a nice woman?" she asked almost in a whisper.

"It's not important. There are some things you are too young to know," he said.

"But, Daddy, I'm a big girl now. We know there's no such thing as ghosts. I don't believe that room is haunted by a ghost. Let me move in there, and if you're worried that there's a ghost there, silly Daddy, I'll scare it away for you."

"I want this subject dropped now, Corinne. I want it dropped right now," he shouted.

"But I want that room," she insisted. "It's the prettiest room in the house; I want it to be mine." And she fled from Malcolm, tears streaming down her pretty cheeks.

From that time on, whenever Malcolm was gone for the day, I let Corinne visit the Swan Room. I found her interest in the room fascinating. She loved to sit at the long vanity table and pretend she was a grown woman, the mistress of Foxworth Hall preparing for an extravagant ball.

I knew what she was doing in there because I used the peephole behind the picture in Malcolm's trophy room. Of course, Corinne never knew I spied on her. She would sit at the vanity table, brushing her hair with Alicia's own brush. One time, after she had locked the door behind her, she stripped off her clothing and put on one of her real grandmother's nightgowns. She tied the lace strings of the bodice extra tight so the garment wouldn't slip off. I saw how much she enjoyed the feel of it, how she ran the palms of her hands down over her budding bosom and onto the small of her stomach. She closed her eyes and wore a look of ecstasy I thought far beyond what someone her age was capable of feeling. She paraded about like the princess Malcolm had turned her into and then crawled onto the swan bed. She actually fell asleep there, wearing the silver silk nightgown.

I studied her little chest lifting and falling and thought about Alicia making love with Garland in that bed. Perhaps Malcolm was right; perhaps there were ghosts in there; perhaps there was something evil drawing little Corinne to it.

I didn't stop her from sneaking in; I didn't prevent her from using some of Alicia's and some of Malcolm's mother's things. In my heart I worried that it was not the ghost of Alicia or Corinne that inhabited that room—it seemed to be the devil himself, come to corrupt any innocent young girl who lived there.

15

The Blackest Day

"MAMA, I'VE BECOME A WOMAN!"

I was out in the garden, cutting the last of the late summer chrysanthemums. My garden had thrived that year, I felt, because all the children were home with me for the summer and often we'd all work on it together, weeding and watering and working in fertilizer. This year my prize mums stood tall and proud—some of them over five feet high, in glorious colors of lavender, blood-red, and sun-yellow. Mal teased me to enter the county fair, "You'll be the queen of the mums, Mother, most certainly." Corinne had also pressed me to enter my flowers, but I demurred. I wanted the flowers from our garden saved for us, for our home, to make our lives bright, to mirror the happiness my children brought to the gloom of Foxworth Hall. Too soon it was September, and in a week the children would be off again, Joel and Corinne back to their respective boarding schools, Mal back to Yale, where he was beginning to realize all the ambitions Malcolm had driven into him since the day he was born. I had just snipped off the crowning glory of my deep purple mum, when I saw the excited Corinne running toward me, her golden-blond hair fanning out behind her like a shawl spun of sunlight.

"Mama, I've become a woman!"

"Darling, what are you talking about?"

"Mama, I'm in a womanly way!"

My heart stopped and I reeled around, shocked and trembling.

"Mama, I've got my . . ."

Her face was flushed, her big blue eyes filled with wonder and excitement, and she was shyly giggling. "Mama, I've got my period. Now I'm really a woman."

I reached down and took her hands in my own. I was flabbergasted. Corinne was only fourteen years old; she didn't even know the difference between being a woman and being in a womanly way. But she was so proud and excited to be a woman. How poignantly happy I felt for her. How different it was for me. Why, I hadn't gotten my period until I was sixteen years old, and by that time my mother was dead, and I had no one with whom to share the secret of my change.

"Mama, make me a garland for my hair to celebrate. In the olden days, didn't you used to do that to celebrate big events?"

Corinne began gathering the flowers I had cut, weaving the stems together, entwining blossoms of all colors to make a festive wreath. I watched her with a bittersweet mixture of envy and love. For when I was a girl, the only crown my womanhood brought me was a barren crown of thorns. Indeed, I had been ashamed of the coming of my menses, wanting to hide it from my father and the servants, so embarrassed and ashamed that someone would find out that that night I had gone to bed praying to God to let me stay a little girl. I hadn't wanted to be a woman, and for good reason, for even now what did it bring me in terms of love but my dearest children, all now about to embark on their own adult lives. And here was Corinne already the sort of woman I had never been and would never be.

Corinne went over and sat on the ship rock that decorated the center of our garden. "Aren't you going to tell me all about love now, Mama? Aren't I ready now? Oh, I have so many longings inside me, I feel like I could burst."

"Love, Corinne? You're only a child."

"But Mama, I'm so filled with questions. I'm so . . ." She bent her head over and swept up the hair, fastening bright forget-me-nots to her golden locks. "I'm so curious to know everything."

"Corinne—"

"When a man kisses you, Mama, do you just die inside?"

"Darling—"

"When he takes you in his arms"—she embraced herself, jumped up, and waltzed around the flowers—"do you feel like the ground is dancing with you? Mama, I must know! I'll just die if I have to spend the rest of my life in Foxworth Hall. I want marriage. I want love. I want to go dancing every night. I want to be taken on cruises to exotic lands where the women don't wear blouses and the men beat drums. Oh, I know Daddy would never approve, he wants me to be his little girl forever, but you know I can't be. You must have once wanted these things too, Mama. You must have wanted a man who swept you off your feet, who promised to love you forever and ever, who made the world shake and tremble every time he touched your hand. Did Daddy make you feel that way?"

"Your father—"

"He's so handsome, I bet, I just bet and"—Corinne threw her hands around my waist and began waltzing me around the garden—"I bet you were just wild about him."

I stopped the dance and sat down on the ship rock to catch my breath. Could Corinne see the pain in my eyes? Wild about him? Yes, I was wild—wild with a desperate hope for love. But what did I get instead? The consummation of our marriage that should have been warm and wonderful was literally a rape. He attacked me with his mother's name on his lips. That was my initiation to love. I never had Malcolm's love.

Corinne was staring at me with the strangest expression in her sky blue eyes, expectant, almost afraid.

"Mama," she said, "promise me someone will love me, some wonderful young man will win my heart. Promise."

Suddenly a dark cloud passed over her eyes, and she bent over, pained by a cramp.

"Womanhood brings pain along with its joys, and every month you'll be reminded of this. You know, Corinne, relations between a man and a woman are more complicated than you can ever imagine. It's not just flowers and rainbows, though we might wish with all our hearts it were. As the poets have always told us, love more resembles a rose, with harsh, hurting thorns beneath its bright, beautiful blossom. For some of us, the thorns are hardly noticeable, so sweet is the scent of the rose, but for others the rose is small, and shriveled almost before it's bloomed, and we are left with a bush of thorns, like tiny needles poking your heart—"

"But, Mama, the pain's already gone. I know you know everything about life, Mama, and I know you're trying to protect me. But I know something in my heart, and I just know it's true. I know I'm going to be one of those special lucky girls—I mean women—who have a special special love, pure and bright, an all-life-long true love. And I know that when it comes I'll be ready, and I'll do anything, anything, *anything* to claim it for my own. Oh, Mama, I can tell things aren't always fine between you and Daddy. But that doesn't mean it has to be that way for me, does it?"

I knew it would be different for her—as it had been for Alicia—and for the Corinne before her. How I envied her. How I dreamed for her.

"Does it, Mama? Won't it be different for me?"

I looked at her face, her full rose-petal mouth opened slightly in question. "Of course, Corinne, of course it will be different for you. For you have the gifts all women long for—beauty, sweetness, innocence, a loving heart—"

I hugged her to my breast to hide the tears that sprang to my eyes. Oh, how I wished she were really mine. But she *was* mine. My love had made her mine. At last my love had created something beautiful, and had been rewarded with the brightest flower in all Virginia.

"Come, dear, let's go inside. Have you taken care of your situation?"

"Oh, Mama, of course. Mrs. Tethering gave me the necessary, and of course you know, Mama, all the girls at school talk about nothing else. Oh, I'm so happy this happened just in time before I return to school. I may have left a girl, but I'll be returning a woman!"

Corinne practically skipped back into the house, and just as we climbed the front steps, Mal roared up the drive on a shining black motorcycle. We both stopped and stared, mouths agape. Malcolm had repeatedly forbidden Mal to have a motorcycle. It had been the source of bitter disputes between the two of them, Malcolm trying to force Mal to be pointed only toward the business world, Mal insisting on "sowing his wild oats." I tried to stay out of it, for truly, those machines frightened me and seemed so dangerous, but Mal wanted one so desperately, and, after all, he had come into the trust fund I'd forced Malcolm to set up for each of the boys when Corinne was born. And now Mal had gone and bought a motorcycle. Inwardly I smiled, satisfied in some way to know that Malcolm had not succeeded in breaking my son's spirit the way he had broken mine. Oh, I was proud of my son Mal, so bright and handsome, wise beyond his years, and fun-loving too. I was glad he had followed his wishes. He looked dashing as he drove up, and Corinne was practically jumping up and down in excitement to see her big brother on his motorcycle.

"Hey, Corinne. Want a ride?" He revved the motor. His manly young body was straddling the huge bike. He wore leather boots with metal taps and a beautiful flowing white silk scarf, like a pilot from the Great War.

"Oh, Mama, Mama, can I?"

"Corinne, you are a young woman. It's so dangerous. I forbid you—"

"Mother!" Mal said. "I'll just take her for a spin around the driveway. Don't be so old-fashioned."

"Can I? Oh, please, Mama?"

"Do you really think this is how a lady behaves?"

"Lucy McCarthy's brother has a motorcycle and he sometimes drives her to school and the McCarthys are really rich and prominent and Daddy even says so and—"

Mal revved his motor once again. A booming filled the driveway. I didn't want Malcolm to come out to see what the commotion was.

"Mother," Mal said, kicking the dust with his leather boot, "it's only around the driveway. I'll drop Corinne off at the gate and she can walk back. Besides, if you don't let me take her for a ride, I'm going to make you get on."

Both my children laughed and laughed, and I, frightened as I was, said, "Only around the driveway."

"Oh, thank you, thank you, Mama," Corinne squealed, and she climbed onto the huge bike, holding Mal tightly around his waist.

I had to admit that they looked dashing together. Corinne with her blond hair, blue eyes, delicate arms around her brother, and Mal, with his leather jacket, boots, and white scarf.

"Drive carefully," I shouted, but the loud machine had already pulled away, kicking up gravel and sand in its wake.

As I watched them disappear beyond the rim of the hill, I felt a cold presence on the back of my neck. "What was that?" the cold, angry voice of Malcolm demanded. I spun around to confront him. His anger had already built up to a combustible force, but was contained, revealing itself only in his blood-red complexion, his bulging, angry eyes, and his clenched fists held firmly against his thighs. He looked like an overheated stove about to explode.

"Did I see what I thought I saw?" he demanded.

"Malcolm, I long ago ceased to even try to imagine what you see," I retorted. Then I sat down on the rocker on the porch. He was so angry he looked like a parody of himself. I couldn't help but tickle his torment.

"What is it you thought you saw?" I asked.

"I saw," he thundered, "a moronic middle-aged woman let her precious young daughter climb onto a motorcycle with her idiot first son. A motorcycle I have forbidden time and time again! And, without a thought to her children's well-being and good breeding, I saw them climb onto that dangerous machine and roar off like hooligans down the driveway. Then I saw that same moronic middle-aged woman smile."

"I was smiling," I replied, lifting myself up to my full height and putting all my pride for my children in my voice, "because I was contemplating taking a ride myself."

"You are an even bigger fool than I thought you were, Olivia. You were fool enough when you blackmailed me into giving those boys trust funds that they would come into at the ridiculously young age of eighteen. See how much economic responsibility and wisdom they have? This is a young man I am supposed to turn over the leadership of a billion-dollar empire to? I warned you; I warned you. Let me handle the money; let me control the expenditures; but no, you had to . . . to blackmail me into giving them a small fortune to squander.

"And that's just what he has started to do . . . squander it. I insist, no, I demand that you order him to sell this . . . this thing immediately and attempt to recover most of the expenditure."

"I don't see how I can do that," I said, my voice calm. I knew the calmer and softer I spoke, the more enraged he became.

"What! Why not?"

"The money is his to do with what he likes. He cannot be checking with me every time he wants to spend some of it. It would take away from his independence, and his assuming independence is a very important thing at this stage in his life," I said. "You had it at his age."

"I had more sense at his age!" He glared at me. "You are enjoying this, aren't you? You think this is a way to take some sort of sick revenge on me, don't you?"

"Of course not," I said, even though what he said was true in a sense.

"This will weigh heavily on your conscience," he warned me, waving his right forefinger at me threateningly. "In the end you will regret not listening to me," he added with that Foxworth confidence I had come to hate. He looked away and stood there silently for a moment. I said nothing. Then he turned back to me. I could sense that he had been calming himself down enough to go on.

"So now you expect me to send my eldest son back to Yale on a goddamn motorcycle. You are undermining me, Olivia. You know the plans I have for Mal. I can't have him riding off like riffraff on some newfangled machine. And Joel—look what you've turned him into—a fairy musician, and I warned you! He'll end up useless, useless, I say."

"Alicia truly believed Joel was a prodigy," I reminded him tartly. "She called him a musical genius, and he is, Malcolm, if you were only sensitive enough to know that genius comes in many forms, not just in the form of making money."

His lips trembled with acrimony. His eyes positively glowed like hot coals, brightening as the fire behind them raged. The veins in his temples pressed out against his skin as he worked his jaw. He swallowed and stepped forward, his shoulders rising, his chest puffed out.

"You are using my sons to whip me. Don't deny it. You are swinging them about the way you would swing a whip against my naked back, extracting some horrible satisfaction from each stroke. But beware," he warned me. "Your vengeance will rebound upon you."

"Don't try to pass the guilt on to me," I responded quickly. The days of his intimidating me were long over. "I never encouraged the boys to disobey you. They are who they are because of you, because you never spent enough time with them to provide them with an example. How many times have I asked you, no, begged you to take more interest in them, to be more of a father to them?

"But no, you had your own hardened views of what a father-son relationship should be, punishing them because of the way you felt about your own father.

"Well, now you are reaping that harvest. You planted the seeds, not I. And if the crop isn't to your liking, it's your doing, not mine."

"My sons may be lost to me," he stormed. "But I still have my daughter. And she is mine, Olivia, *mine! Do you hear me?* And I will not permit her to ride around on dangerous motorcycles like some teenaged harlot. I will not let you turn her against me. I will not have you threaten her young life riding around on that *thing!*"

"Here she comes now, Malcolm. Don't ruin this day for her with your idiotic rage."

Corinne was running up the long driveway, waving to Malcolm and me. She was still so far in the distance, I thought her wild gestures were the result of her excitement. A dark cloud passed over the sun, and I could see only her fluttering white hands, like tiny doves, beckoning to me, and those bright blue eyes, like glowing sapphires, in her now pale face. Oh, had I known! Had I known what those beautiful blue eyes had just seen!

"Mama! Daddy! *Mama! Daddy!*"

I ran toward her. I knew at once something was terribly wrong. "Malcolm," I screamed. *"Malcolm, come at once!"*

Corinne suddenly froze, and fell to her knees, weeping.

"Corinne!" Malcolm screamed. "My darling, what's wrong? Are you hurt? Oh, my God!"

"Oh, Daddy, Daddy, it's Mal. It's Mal, he . . . oh God . . . oh God . . ." she sobbed.

"Are you okay, my precious," Malcolm moaned, holding her in his arms.

"What has happened to Mal! What has happened to my son!" I wailed.

"He . . . we . . . oh Lord, Mama, he told me to get off and then . . . and then he . . . he was going so fast . . . oh, Mama."

"Where is my son!"

"The bike just went roaring, Mama. It all happened so fast. Mal was speeding down the road and then . . ."

"Yes?" I didn't recognize my voice. It sounded like an animal's.

"And then the bike just seemed to take off, like he

was flying, and the next thing I knew he went over the cliff and . . . oh God, oh God . . . there was a horrible explosion and a huge cloud of smoke rose and I ran home to get Daddy."

I began running, running down the driveway, running down the road. "Mal, oh my son, my Mal!"

I could see the smoke rising in a large black cloud. A fire, like a burning sun, roared at the bottom of the cliff. I tried to run toward it, into it, but Malcolm's powerful arms stopped me.

"Stop, Olivia, you can't help him now." Malcolm's voice was cold and clipped. I clawed at his arms like a wild woman. I had to get to Mal.

"It's my son!" I screamed. "I must save him!" Malcolm was shaking me, shaking me as he stared at the black smoke that rose from the gulley. Then he looked up at the sky, the sky gone suddenly cold and distant. He dropped me to the ground as he reached for Corinne, who was weeping silently, watching the black smoke color the sky black. Color the day black, color all my days black from then on. Mal. My first son. My first love. Mal. I wanted to tear up the ground, tear at the earth until there was nothing left. Malcolm and Corinne stared at me, as if my grief were too much for them to bear. "I must go to him," I said, rising to my feet, but Corinne threw her arms about my waist, and Malcolm looked at me, his cold blue eyes burning ice into my soul. "It's too late, Olivia. You let your son go. Mal's dead."

"The Lord giveth, and the Lord taketh away."

On the day we buried Mal it seemed the whole world was mourning with us. The sky was dark and angry, distant thunder rolling, as if God were punctuating his sentence to remind us his wrath was all-powerful, and he could crush us antlike mortals here below with one exhalation. There were hundreds of mourners at the funeral—friends of Mal and Joel and Corinne, Malcolm's many business and social acquaintances. Only one mourner was there on my side—John Amos, my last living relative, who had taken a train down from Connecticut as soon as he got my telegram. We had kept up a letter correspondence over the years, and I had seen young John Amos progress into a full-fledged man of God, a one-horse preacher as we called them, a minister without a congregation. On this day he had a congregation, for he was delivering the funeral service for my beloved Mal.

The silent scream that had resounded in my head for three days was not calmed by John Amos's words.

"Our beloved Mal has gone to a better place. His true Father has called him in the bloom of youth, to his breast, and there this innocent soul shall rest in peace eternally. His Father has truly claimed him." Malcolm looked over at me, his cold blue eyes trying to pierce my black veil. We stood at the side of the grave, Corinne and Joel between us. Joel clung to my hand, Corinne to her father's. In the two long days since the horrible accident, Malcolm had not spoken a word to me, but I could see in his glare he was trying to blame me for Mal's death, silently telling me that if I hadn't disobeyed his orders and allowed the motorcycle, my dear son would be with me still. Oh, it was so unfair that Mal had been taken from me. I wanted to cut off my hair, my hands, my legs, I begged God to take me and give Mal back. The world was out of joint, and truly I did blame myself. Was Malcolm so all-powerful that he could enlist God's aid to punish those who defied him? I had stayed sequestered in my room, Corinne and Joel would come in to try to comfort me, but they were suffering, too, really suffering. But how could I comfort them? Mal was dead. Mal dead? My favorite, dead? In my mind's eye I saw him standing in the nursery looking up at me with those inquisitive eyes, his face serious, his posture erect.

"Will Father be taking us for a motor trip?" he asked. "He promised he would."

"I don't know, Mal. He makes promises and then forgets them."

"Why doesn't he write them down then?" he asked. Such a logical mind he had, even then. And now he was dead.

As the raindrops began to fall, and the thunder, growing closer, began to boom, my darling Mal was lowered into his grave, and one by one, Malcolm, myself, Joel, and Corinne picked up a handful of earth and threw it on his coffin. My veil hid my tears, but I was so weak I could barely walk. How I wanted to jump into that grave with him, to be covered with dirt, to have the world blocked out from me. But I had to go on, I had to stay strong, as John Amos had told me, for Corinne, for Joel. Malcolm had remained distant even from Corinne, and she was baffled, confused. Both of them wondered if his love had died along with Mal.

Joel was the most heartbroken. He said almost nothing, but remained constantly at my side tuned in to my every word, my every gesture, as if he thought that somehow I could change events and bring his brother back. They had been so close to each other despite the difference in ages and temperament. I knew that Joel depended upon and looked up to Mal. Mal was the buffer between him and his father, a father he was still quite terrified of. It was easy to see it; he said nothing to him during the entire period, gave him no comforting words or gestures.

Corinne was beside herself with grief, blaming herself as I blamed myself, wishing she could turn back the clock and bring Mal back again. It was John Amos, not Malcolm, who tried to comfort her, calm her guilt, soothe her grief. Of all the Foxworths, only Malcolm stood tall, dignified, and alone in his grief.

The next day, Malcolm returned to his business. John Amos stayed on, reading with us from the Bible, holding Corinne's hands as she cried, stroking her, acting like the loving father Malcolm had always been to her. John Amos had grown into a tall, lanky man with dark brown hair so thin he was actually balding prematurely. It added dignity and maturity to him. He had a minister's stern, pale face with pecan-brown eyes and a hard mouth, his lips so straight they looked drawn on by an artist. He seemed much older than his thirty-one years, and much much wiser.

From my letters, he knew how important my boys were to me, and he had some idea about my relationship, and Malcolm's, with Corinne. He knew exactly how I felt about Malcolm.

It seemed he understood me in some deep blood way; he understood that I was blaming myself, as Malcolm blamed me, and he would not let me shoulder the blame alone. "Olivia," he said, his warm, calm voice a balm to my spirit, "it is the Lord who calls us, the Lord who metes out His justice. He has taken away the son Malcolm could not appreciate; perhaps His message was for Malcolm, to learn to love what is his rather than trying to control it. For you see where control ends. Do not blame yourself, Olivia. God's plans are often mysterious, but they are always just."

Malcolm did not like John Amos, but that was of little consequence to me. In fact, Malcolm's not liking him confirmed his value and importance to me. It was why, after the funeral when John Amos took such a firm hold of things—helping me with the servants, preparing for the visiting mourners, comforting members of the family—I decided I wanted him to stay with us at Foxworth Hall. Already Corinne was due to go back to school. And I could tell she was ready to leave this dark, gloomy house of mourning. She loved Mal as much as any young girl loves her brother, but for one so full of life and love and hope, death's shadow does not linger as it does for those of us with fewer hopes and dreams before us. The day we saw Corinne off, I proposed to John Amos that he stay on. John seemed genuinely flattered by the idea. He wasn't happy with the work he was presently doing. I called him into the salon.

"I would like you to stay on," I began, "at Foxworth Hall and become something of an assistant to me. Officially, you will be considered our butler, but you and I will always know that you will be more to me," I said. Grief, so deeply felt, had a way of weakening me. I felt as if I had been cast in a new form and I wore my body like a suit of armor hiding a heart and will gone slack and impotent. Truly, I couldn't bear to live here any longer alone with Malcolm. I couldn't bear having to fight him and his megalomanic plans day after day. I needed an ally, someone to give me strength, to help me, to take my side. I needed John Amos. And he was a man of God, a godly, godfearing man who would deflect and thwart Malcolm's evil intentions. I would not let him drive another of my sons to death, nor would I let him take over Corinne's life as he planned to do.

"Please, John Amos, won't you stay? You are such a comfort to me. I feel you are truly my family—the only family I have left, and I need your strong Christian hand to guide me."

John nodded thoughtfully.

"I have always admired you, Olivia," he said, "admired you for your strength of purpose, your sense of determination; but most of all, for your faith in God and His ways. Even now, in your mourning, you do not blame God for being unmerciful. You are an inspiration. More women should want to be like you," he said, nodding as though he had just arrived at a significant conclusion.

I understood why Malcolm didn't like him. He had Malcolm's way of making statements with an air of certainty, but whereas Malcolm arrived at his conclusions from an arrogant faith in himself, John Amos arrived at his from a strong faith in God and God's will.

"Thank you, John. But contrary to what you think, I am a woman with weaknesses too. I will need someone beside me to help me with my children and to help me maintain this house in the proper manner and spirit," I added.

"I understand, and I can think of no greater purpose. Long ago, I understood that my calling lay in directions others were afraid or unwilling to take. The Lord has His way of soliciting His soldiers," he said, smiling.

"I think," I said, looking at him intently, "you saw today some of what I have been describing to you in my letters. You should understand why I sometimes feel alone here," I added.

"Yes. And you have more than my understanding. You have my sympathy and my dedication." Those brown eyes of his, although not bright and warm, grew quite fixed. He stepped forward. "I pledge to you, Olivia," he said, "that as long as I am here at your side, you shall never feel alone."

I smiled slightly and lifted my hand. He took it and in that handshake made a covenant with me and with God Almighty. It was the most reassuring thing that had happened to me in years.

When I brought the news to Malcolm, he had his characteristic reaction. He had retreated to the library. The pall of silence that had fallen over Foxworth Hall lingered like the heavy humid air right before a summer rain. The lights were dim, the sky outside starless and cloudy. Unmerciful winds clawed at the windows. To me it was like the grinding teeth of some vicious, vengeful beast.

Malcolm was standing with his back to the doorway, his hands clasped behind his back, looking up at the books on a high shelf. He didn't turn when I entered, even though I knew he had heard my footsteps. I waited a moment.

"I have made a decision," I said finally, "to hire my cousin, John Amos, to be our butler."

Malcolm spun around. The expression on his face was almost hideous, a mixture of grief and anger that distorted his features. Never had his mouth looked a twisted, his eyes as cold.

"What butler? We have a manservant." He made ordinary words sound like profanity.

"A man who serves as driver as well. It's not proper and it is a foolish economy, undignified for a family and a house as important as ours," I replied sternly.

"At this time you think about servants?" He seemed both amazed and upset.

"You didn't go to work today and receive business calls? You didn't give your subordinates orders to carry out? Your mind was solely on Mal?" I asked in the tone of accusation. He shook his head, but not to deny what I said, only to dramatize his disgust.

"I don't like this man. He's too . . . too sly-looking for my taste."

"Nevertheless, I have hired him. The running of the house has always been and will always be my responsibility. It's necessary for us to have a servant solely to perform the responsibilities of a butler, and John Amos has the background for such responsibility. He is a decent, religious man, who understands the needs of people of our class. He has agreed to take on the position and he will begin immediately."

"He will be your butler, not mine," Malcolm said defiantly.

"Suit yourself. In time I am sure you will grow to appreciate the man," I added calmly.

He turned his back on me and stared up at the books again.

"Joel is leaving in the morning," I said. He didn't turn around.

"That is good. He is better off returning to school and occupying himself with his studies than moping about here. He will only add to the depression," he said, and waved to the side as though he were dismissing me. I straightened my posture.

"He is not returning to school," I said. That turned Malcolm around again.

"What? Not returning to school? What do you mean? Where is he going?"

"Before Mal's death, he auditioned for an orchestra and they were impressed with his talents. They have offered him a position for their current tour of Europe. He will go directly to Switzerland."

Malcolm fumed.

"Tour! Orchestra! Switzerland!" he said, waving his arms with every word. "A Foxworth, a professional musician, earning coolie wages and traveling with a bunch of spineless . . . effeminate . . . artsy types . . . I won't hear of it! I won't hear of it, do you understand?"

"Nevertheless, it is what he wants," I said, again fanning his fury by speaking so calmly. "I will not force another of my sons to extremes to prove that he can live his own life rather than the one you dictate."

Malcolm's eyes narrowed, and he was silent for many moments. "Let him understand," he said, pronouncing each word with a hateful, vicious tone, "that if he leaves this house to begin such a venture, he will never be welcomed back to it."

"I understand that, Father."

We both spun around to see Joel in the library doorway. He was standing there with a suitcase in each hand. I did not know he had intended to leave that very night.

"I was coming down here to tell you this myself," he said.

"And I meant what I just said," Malcolm said, pointing his finger at him. "If you throw away your formal education to go tooting a horn throughout Europe, I'll write you out of my will."

For a long moment Joel and Malcolm contemplated each other. It was as though father and son saw each other for the first time and really understood who the other was. If Joel had any fears, his gentle face and soft blue eyes did not reveal them. If anything, he looked like a martyr forgiving the violent and hateful tyrant who was sentencing him to death. I saw a smile around his lips.

"You never understood me, Father; nor did you ever understand Mal," he said with no anger in his voice. "Neither of us were so driven by your pursuit of the almighty dollar."

"That's because you always had so many of them," Malcolm retorted. "If you were poor, you wouldn't be standing there so cocky and defiant."

"Maybe not," Joel said. "But I wasn't poor and I am what I am." He looked at me. "Good-bye, Mother. I shall miss you very much. Please walk with me to the door. There is a car waiting for me outside."

"You are going to permit this?" Malcolm asked.

When I looked at Joel, I saw so much of myself in his face. It was as if I were leaving, as if I were escaping, escaping the sorrow and the torment, escaping the cold shadows that seemed to reside permanently in Foxworth Hall.

"It is what he wants," I said softly, staring at him. "He is old enough to be able to make his own decision. He has a right to his own decision."

"This is madness and your doing," Malcolm said,

pointing the accusing finger at me. "It will add to your already heavy burden of guilt."

"What?" I took a few steps toward him, feeling my face burn with rage. "You stand there and try to place the guilt on my head? You, who have brought sin into this house, invited it in as though it were a welcomed guest? You have eaten beside it, walked beside it, and slept with it," I added. "You have brought the wrath of God down on the House of Foxworth, not I. If anyone stands bearing the guilt, it is you," I responded, pointing my accusing finger at him.

He looked at Joel and then turned away.

I went to Joel and the two of us walked out to the front doorway arm in arm. John Amos, already assuming some responsibility, had brought Joel's trunk to the car. He took the suitcases and carried them out as well.

Joel and I stood in the great doorway of Foxworth Hall and looked out at the car and the darkness that now surrounded us.

"I am sorry to leave you at this time of grief," he said, "but I fear if I don't go now, I will never go. Mal would have wanted me to go. I can almost see him standing there by the piano, smiling, cheering me on," Joel added, smiling at the image.

"Yes, I suppose he would," I said. I envisioned Mal as well, and the vision filled my heart with a heavy aching. It gave birth to a little gray bird of anxiety that fluttered wildly in the cage of my ribs, but I hid these feelings from him. "How I will miss you, Joel," I said, grasping his hands in mine and bringing them to my lips to kiss them. "You are my only son, my beloved Joel, it's only you now. Please go with God, and be happy."

"Thank you, Mother." He leaned forward and kissed

me on the cheek. I held him for a long moment and then he rushed down to the car. He waved once more and then got in.

John Amos and I stood watching the car go off into the cold autumn night, its taillights fading like two bright red stars dying away in the universe.

PART III

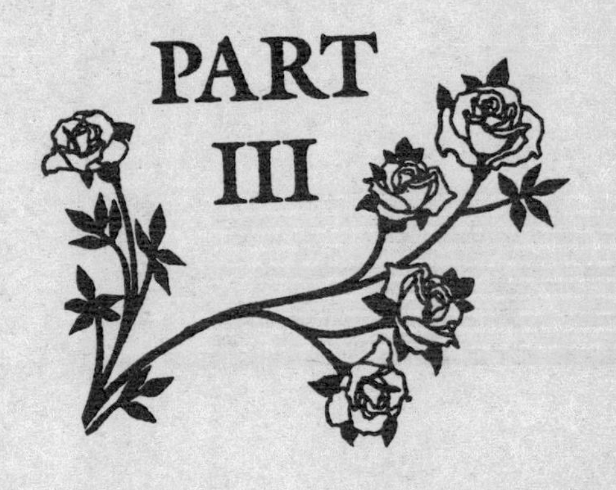

16

Shadows and Light

I GRIEVED. I GRIEVED FOR THE LOSS OF MY MAL; I GRIEVED for the bright happy summer when all my children had been around me, joyous and strong—a time that was to never come again. The only brightness in that long gloomy winter were occasional notes from Corinne, who barely seemed able to recover from Mal's death, and an occasional letter from my Joel. Joel, once a weak and frightened boy, a boy who finally stood up to his father, had found himself in Europe. *Signore Joel Foxworth,* read the Italian paper he sent. *The brilliant young pianist, Monsieur Foxworth,* the French papers said, *"a talent to watch in the future."* Pride bloomed again in my heart, pride that John Amos continued to warn me against: "Pride cometh always before the fall, Olivia, remember the words of God, let them be your guide." My pride, however, was not self-pride, but pride in the only son God had left me.

I loved to brandish the glowing reviews of Joel's musicianship in front of Malcolm's face. "You thought your son was a failure, Malcolm," I sneered. "But look how the world worships him!"

Then one day, the first day of spring, just as the world, and me with it, had begun to open its arms to life again, a telegram arrived. No good news had ever come my way in a telegram, and I sat and stared at the yellow envelope, trembling, afraid to open it. "Joel," I whispered involuntarily, for somehow, even before I opened it, I knew what was inside.

HERR MALCOLM FOXWORTH STOP
WITH DEEPEST REGRETS I AM TO INFORM YOU YOUR SON JOEL WAS LOST IN AN AVALANCHE STOP WE HAVE BEEN UNABLE TO RECOVER HIS BODY AND THOSE OF HIS FIVE COMPANIONS STOP MAY I EXTEND MY HEART-FELT SYMPATHIES

I crumpled the telegram in my hand, and stared out the window. I didn't cry or moan; for this son, my second son, I had no tears left to shed. They had flowed and flowed out of me for Mal, and now my heart was bone dry and barren. I grieved like a desert grieves; a desert that allows nothing to grow, a desert where the only passion is the blowing of sand, the shrouding of all that lives. Once again my world had turned utterly, irrevocably gray.

Malcolm, too, acted strangely. At first he refused to believe Joel was really dead. I showed him the crumpled telegram the moment he returned from a business trip. I said nothing. I just handed it to him to read as soon as he came through the front door.

"What kind of a thing is this?" he said. "Lost in an avalanche?" He handed the telegram back to me as though it were a business idea he was rejecting, and he walked away to busy himself with his paperwork in the library.

But when the official documentation arrived, a police report, neither he nor I could deny it to ourselves. Then I cried; then my heart tore; then I found the hidden well of my tears just under my parched soul. The memories rushed back over me, and all I could see throughout that big house were Joel and Mal sitting together or walking together, playing together and eating together. Sometimes a shadow would fall in such a way that I thought I saw their faces in the darkness. Sometimes I would secretly visit the nursery, and almost see the three of them, Christopher, Mal, and Joel, Mal acting as though he were their teacher and Joel and Christopher looking up at him with full attention. I would lift up their old toys and hold them to my breast, weeping uncontrollably.

Malcolm went into seclusion in the library. I was incapable of preparing for Joel's memorial myself, and if it weren't for John Amos, my beloved second son, my sensitive Joel, might not have had the proper service to welcome him into God's home. John Amos was such a help to me, he even traveled to Corinne's boarding school to deliver the tragic news to her in person and to bring her back to Foxworth Hall. On the morning of the memorial service, Corinne and I donned the same black dresses we'd worn for Mal's funeral, and drifted like two ghosts down the winding stairs to the rotunda. A black-veiled carriage, hired by John Amos, awaited us before the front door. John waited stoically by the door of the carriage.

"I'm afraid Malcolm will not be attending the service," he announced. "He asked me to escort you there."

I lifted my veil and looked around. The servants were waiting, all dressed in black, ready to attend the services and mourn the beautiful little boy they had watched grow into a man. But the boy's father was nowhere to be seen. I stormed into Malcolm's library. He was seated at his desk, but he had his back to it. He had turned the chair around and was facing the window behind him.

The sky was a pale gray and the air had turned rather cool for a March day. It was a day without promise of sun, a mirror of my life.

"How dare you not attend your son's service," I shouted. He didn't move or acknowledge my presence in any way. I suddenly became frightened for him. Was it pity I felt? Pity for a man who tried to destroy his sons' spirits? Pity for Malcolm Foxworth? He looked so small and lost surrounded by all his possessions, his hunting trophies, his business ledgers, his precious *objets d'art*, the ghosts of all the women he had seduced in his study. I leaned over him and gently touched his back. "Malcolm," I said quietly, "this is a service for our son, your son." He lifted his hand slowly and then dropped it back to the arm of the chair. "How can you not attend?"

"It's wrong," he finally said. His voice sounded strange to me, like an echo distant and hollow. "A funeral without a body. What are we burying?" he stammered.

"It is a service in honor of his memory, in honor of his soul, Malcolm," I said, coming farther around until I almost faced him. Still, he did not turn my way. He shook his head.

"What if they found him alive after we had such a

ceremony? I won't go through the mockery of it. I won't be part of it," he said, his voice still drained of energy, his face unchanged.

"But you saw the police report. You read the details. It was an official document," I said. What point did it serve to ignore reality now? Why, of all people, was Malcolm attempting to do it?

I believe he thought he could postpone reality, postpone the aching guilt. I believe he believed that if he attended the memorial service, there would no longer be any way of avoiding the truth.

"Go," he said. "Leave me be."

"Malcolm," I began, "if you—"

He spun around in his seat, his eyes bloodshot, his face so contorted with anger and pain, I hardly recognized him. I actually stepped back. It was as though he had been possessed by some dark creature, perhaps the devil himself.

"Go!" he ordered me. "Leave me be." Then he turned away.

I stood there looking at him for a long moment and then left him alone in the shadows, staring into his own thoughts.

Most of those who had attended Mal's funeral attended the service for Joel. No one came to me directly to ask where Malcolm was, but I heard the whispering around me and saw people questioning John Amos. Corinne stood by me, but she looked lost and forlorn without Malcolm to hold on to.

Malcolm kept himself shut up in the library for days afterward and, oddly enough, permitted only John Amos to bring him any food and drink. Whenever I went in to speak with him, I found him still sitting in shadows, staring out the window. He barely responded. Only later did John Amos tell me that Malcolm was going through a religious transformation.

One night toward the end of the week, I sat alone with John at the dinner table. Corinne had no appetite. She had gone to speak with Malcolm, hoping to cheer him up and blow away the clouds of gloom that hung above us in Foxworth Hall. She loved her brother so; but she was young, and the world was before her, and she wanted to begin living again.

Suddenly, she stormed out of Malcolm's study. "It's hopeless," she announced, "Daddy won't stop mourning! No one will! I love Joel and Mal, too, but I want to live, I want to be able to smile and laugh again. I must!"

John was reading a passage from the Psalms. We often sat together like this and read from the Bible. We would talk about the scriptures and John would find ways of relating it to our lives.

"Mama," Corinne pleaded. "Is it so wrong for me to want to live and be happy again? Is it so wrong for me to want to attend parties again, and dress in beautiful clothes again, and see my friends again?"

John Amos looked up from the Bible, but he didn't stop reading. Corinne stood there impatiently until he reached the end of a section and paused.

"I can't get Daddy to talk to me," she said. "He won't even come to the door." She looked from me to John Amos, who put the Bible on his lap and sat back. Sometimes, when he looked at her, he reminded me of a man studying a fine jewel, turning it over and over in his fingers to catch the way the light was reflected by it.

"Your father is in deep meditation at the moment," he said. "You really shouldn't disturb him."

"But how long will this deep meditation go on? He doesn't eat with us; he doesn't sleep in his room, and now he won't even talk to me," she protested.

"You of all people should feel sorry for him," I told her. I put on a stern face. "And appreciate what he's going through."

"I do. That's why I want him to come out, but he won't come to the door when I knock and call. I can't stand this . . . this horrible sadness."

"At this particularly sad time," John Amos began, "we shouldn't be thinking about our own discomfort. It is very selfish to do so. You should be thinking about your lost brother," he added softly but firmly.

"I have thought about him and thought about him. But he's dead and gone. There is nothing I can do anymore to bring him back!" she exclaimed, her eyes wide, her face filled with pent-up energy.

"You can pray for him," John said softly. I saw how his calm, pious tone added to her disappointment.

"But I have. How much can I pray?" She turned to me.

"You can pray until you stop thinking of yourself first and think of him. It doesn't surprise me that you are this way now. Your father has spoiled you and made you self-centered," I told her. She pouted. I knew how frustrated she was. Corinne could not tolerate refusal, and refusal was everywhere around her now.

"Join us in prayer," John said, gesturing toward her empty chair.

"I'm going to go back to Daddy to try to get him to talk to me," she said, and turned away quickly.

"Corinne!" I called.

"It's all right," John said. "Let her go for now. I will speak to her later." He turned back to the Bible.

I sat with John and prayed and studied the Bible and waited. The lights were low, memorial candles burning everywhere. Foxworth Hall had been turned into a tomb. Through the imposed silence, the slightest footsteps echoed. Gloom not only hung about the walls of Foxworth Hall, turning everything gray and dull; it hung from the trees, filling the world with cobwebs of sorrow. It rained on and off for days, the drops tapping on the windows and roof, hammering in the misery.

John Amos was a great comfort during these days. Dressed in black, his face pale and ascetic, he moved about the rooms with the grace and stillness of a monk. He commanded the other servants with a gesture, a look. No one raised his voice for fear of shattering the solemn air he created whenever he entered a room. He seemed to slide over the floor, ooze over the walls and around corners. Sometimes he simply materialized in a room. Even the maids who brought out my dishes and glasses struggled to maintain the greatest silence, watching him carefully out of the corners of their eyes to be sure his face showed no disapproval.

One night after I had eaten, John brought me my coffee. He put the coffee cup and saucer down before me as though they were made of air, and stepped back. I looked down the long table and thought about Malcolm still refusing to come out of his study.

"How long does he intend to remain in there?" I asked. I was beginning to feel Corinne's impatience.

"He has become Job," John Amos responded in a stentorian voice. He sounded like an Old Testament prophet predicting Malcolm's destiny. He didn't look directly at me when he spoke. It was as if he were speaking to a full congregation of devoted followers.

"Only now when he asks why hast God forsaken him, he knows the answer. The Lord has smitten his two sons, taken from him his male seed, his Foxworth lineage, something he cherished almost as much as life itself."

"You spoke to him directly about it?" I asked, fascinated by any change in Malcolm. I had always thought him molded so solidly in his form that the slightest change would crack and shatter him.

"We knelt beside each other on the floor of the library just an hour ago," John said. "I recited the prayers. I told him God was wrathful and angry and that all we could hope for was some respite from His vengeance. Knowing what I knew of his life, I talked about King David and his taking of Bathsheba, how David had turned his back on his God and how God brought down His vengeance on his house. Malcolm understood.

"He no longer blames you or the boys for what happened to them; he blames himself and he is trying to come to terms with that. He understands that he can do such a thing only by giving himself over to Jesus Christ our savior," John said, his eyes lifted toward heaven. "Let us pray for one another," he added. We both bowed our heads, he standing beside me, me sitting at the table.

"Oh, Lord, help us to understand Your ways and help us to help one another. Forgive us our weaknesses and permit us to grow stronger from our travail."

"Amen," I said.

The mood in the house did change when Malcolm finally emerged from his self-imposed exile. He was indeed different. He looked physically weaker and older, and in many ways he reminded me of Garland during his final year. He didn't stand as straight or walk with his usual self-confidence and arrogance. When he spoke to me or to the servants, his voice was lower and he often looked away, as though facing anyone straight on would expose his guilt.

His complexion never regained its healthy, virile look; his blue eyes dimmed like weakened light bulbs. He moved through Foxworth Hall like another shadow, robed in a funereal atmosphere, spending most of his time reading the Bible and talking with John Amos. Sometimes the three of us sat together and read the Good Book. John would do most of the reading and a good deal of the explaining.

I felt that God had sent John Amos to us, that John's letters to me and his arrival at Mal's funeral was all part of His overall plan for Malcolm and myself.

It was Corinne whom John saw as the greatest challenge. She was rebellious. She said, "If God is a kind God, He wouldn't ask us to give up all the pleasures the world has to offer us."

"Who said God was kind?" John Amos posed the question.

But Corinne would just giggle and shrug her shoulders. "I believe God made us to find happiness on earth," she would say, tossing her head. Sometimes she would even chuck John Amos under the chin and admonish him to cheer up. "God said let there be light."

I noticed that she could never enter a room without his watching her and speaking to her and getting her to speak to him. He seemed to dote on her in much the same manner Malcolm had.

He was not beyond bringing things up to her room to

her. But soon she was back at school and we were childless again.

"It is so good to have you with us," I told John, "at these, our greatest times of need. Even Malcolm has come to believe that and I am grateful."

"I am glad to be here, Olivia."

That summer Corinne blossomed into a truly beautiful young woman. She looked more and more like Alicia every day. The Foxworth traits she inherited only complimented the delicate features her mother possessed. Her hair grew more golden as the summer progressed, her eyes took on the deep blue of the midsummer sky, and her complexion was as soft as a summer cloud. It was as though some divinely inspired artist had fashioned her. Corinne knew how beautiful she was. I could see her confidence and her ego growing. She revealed it in her walk, the way she held her shoulders back and her head high. She knew the power that such beauty possessed too. I saw the way she looked at men, flirted with her eyes and her laugh, even turning her coquettish devices on John Amos. It was already important to her that when she walked into a room, all eyes be on her.

With midsummer beauty now in and out and around our house, I felt a sense of optimism and hope. Because of our new faith in God, Malcolm and I had settled into a more comfortable and cordial relationship. Our strengthened faith and commitment was our common ground.

And so when the letter from Alicia arrived, I felt it was part of God's great new design for us. I recognized the handwriting immediately. The letter was addressed to Malcolm, and when I looked at the return address, I felt excited. Gradually, through Corinne's development from a child into a woman, Alicia had been coming back to us. Now, when she was looking so much like her mother and Alicia was heavily on my mind, Alicia's letter had arrived. From the name she used, I quickly gathered that she had remarried.

I held the letter in my hand for a long moment, considering what Malcolm's reaction would be when he discovered I had opened and read it. But then I thought, after what had happened and after what I had done, anything pertaining to Alicia now was my affair as well as his. He had no right to privacy when it came to her. I opened the envelope and took out the scented pink stationery.

Dear Malcolm,

By the time you have received this letter, I shall be that much closer to the end of what has become a rather sad and disappointing existence. But be assured I am not attempting to encourage any sympathy for myself. I am beyond that and I have come to understand and accept the inevitability of my own impending death. Knowing your love of details, I will tell you that I have been diagnosed as suffering from breast cancer, a cancer that has spread too rapidly for there to be any medical rescue. No handsome young and brilliant doctor will sweep into my hospital room and work any magic. Death's grip is too tight. The Grim Reaper, as Garland used to say, has his hand firmly about my throat. But enough about me.

I remarried shortly after leaving Foxworth Hall to return to Richmond. I married a doctor, but a small-town general practitioner, whose patients often paid him in jars of fruit and pickles. Despite my money, we lived a rather simple life in his modest home. In fact, he didn't want to know about my money. It was always a source of pride for my new, devoted husband that he be the provider.

So I took your advice and left my fortune in the stock market, but unfortunately, not being very wise about these matters, I did not withdraw any of it in time to avoid the famous Black Monday. To put it simply, I lost all of my fortune in the Depression. Of course, my husband, being a man of simple tastes, did not mourn this loss.

Shortly after that he passed away from a chronic illness that suddenly intensified. Being the man that he was, he kept the seriousness of his illness a secret from me until it was no longer possible for him to do so.

However, all this has left me with another great deep and tragic disappointment—my inability to send Christopher to medical school.

Christopher has grown into a fine young man, as handsome as his father. He is very bright and at the top of his high school graduating class. All of his teachers encourage him to go on in the pursuit of his dream to become a physician.

Now, with my life coming to its tragic end, my fortune gone, my new husband no longer around to be of assistance, I have no one to turn to but to you. I beg of you, consider my request, if not for my sake or for Christopher's, then for Garland's.

Find a place in your heart for him. Take him in and send him to medical school. He will be an endless source of pride to you.

Of course, he knows nothing about Corinne or about the events that led up to my departure from Foxworth

Hall. He knows he is the son of Garland Foxworth and he has a stepbrother, but other than that, he knows very little about his family background. I will leave it up to you to tell him what you wish.

I know that Olivia will love Christopher and he will love her. I remember how wonderfully she treated him while I was up in the north wing. He is a polite and respectful young man who will bring only joy and happiness to you both.

Malcolm, I beg you from a dying bed, to find it in your heart to grant this wish. Put aside any bad feelings you might have for me and for the sadness we all experienced and think only of your father's son, a boy driven to become a doctor, and help him reach his goal.

I know God will bless you for it.

Hopefully yours,
Alicia

I put the letter down, and sighed. Memories of caring for little Christopher rushed back. Surely the return of this golden-haired child was God's way of forgiving us our sins. He had taken Mal and Joel and now he was giving us Christopher.

Even Alicia's tragic end was part of God's plan. From what she said in her letter, I couldn't help but believe Malcolm had invested her funds in poor stocks as a form of some revenge. He was obligated to rectify his wrong. I was determined to convince him. Before doing so, I discussed my thoughts with John Amos and he was in total agreement.

I waited for Malcolm in a front salon, prepared to discuss the matter. He returned home from his work somewhat earlier than usual, looking fatigued.

"Malcolm, I must speak with you," I said. Without

responding, he followed me into the salon and sat down on the blue velvet settee. I remained standing, Alicia's letter in my hand.

"A letter arrived today, a letter from Alicia," I said, and for the first time in weeks, his eyes brightened and his face filled with interest.

"From Alicia? What does she want?" For a moment his renewed energy and obvious excitement disturbed me. I made him wait. I walked to the chair across from him, contemplated sitting in it, and then turned back to him. He was practically on the edge of the settee. "Did she write to you?" he asked, his voice rising with anticipation.

"No. The letter was addressed to you. But as soon as I saw from whom it had come, I opened it. I have a right," I added quickly.

"What does she want?" he demanded.

"She is dying, dying of cancer; and she is bankrupt. I will give you the letter so you can read the details, but the most important issue is Christopher."

"Christopher? Why?"

"He is seventeen; he has graduated from high school, and he wants to be a doctor. Apparently, he has the capability to do so, but she no longer has the funds. She wants us to take him in and send him to medical school," I said, and thrust the letter at him. He took it greedily and perused its contents quickly, his face changing expression until it returned to his characteristic stern look.

"I feel sorry for her, but the boy should make his own way in the world," he said.

"I think not, and neither does John Amos. We both think this is God's will," I added quickly.

"God's will? How is this God's will? Are we to take

in every waif?" he asked, gesturing at the doorway as though tens of thousands of orphans waited for entry.

"I hardly think your father's son is a waif, Malcolm. And he is your stepbrother," I said, pressing my lips together tightly.

"Just because she squandered a fortune, a—"

"A fortune you invested for her and never advised her about properly," I said quickly. "Malcolm, whatever your motives were then no longer matter. We have been given an opportunity to rectify the mistakes of the past. It is we who will be squandering if we don't take up this chance to do what is right and good. You must make peace with your troubled soul, and by caring for your father's son, a promising young man now in terrible distress, you will have gone far toward doing so. Alicia is dying. We cannot turn our backs on her at this time," I said.

He stared up at me for a long moment and then looked at the letter again.

"What kind of a marriage did she make for herself after she left here if the man, a doctor, left nothing for Christopher?" he asked, looking down at the letter as though he could see and question Alicia through it.

"That is beside the point. Anyway, Christopher was not her new husband's son. He is not of his blood; he is of yours. We have more reason to provide for him. Malcolm," I repeated, "it is God's will."

After a moment he nodded slowly.

"Very well," he said, and sat back. "Send word and let it be so."

I left him in the salon, the letter clutched in his hand, his eyes locked in a vision of the past. I did not wish to question what it was he saw. Instead, I reported the decision to John and he saw to the correspondence and made the arrangements for Christopher's arrival.

Malcolm's only requirement was that I explain the situation to Corinne. I knew that he didn't trust himself to do so. I called her to my bedroom, something I rarely did, and sat her down to listen. She was intrigued from the moment I began. She looked up at me expectantly, her eyes burning with interest. I stood before her, my hands behind my back for a moment, phrasing my thoughts carefully before speaking.

"As you know, your father's father remarried when he was quite along in his years and he married a woman considerably younger than he was."

"Yes, Alicia," she said quickly, "and she slept in the Swan Room."

"Alicia and Garland, your grandfather, had one child, a son named Christopher. I know that Mal and Joel often spoke about him." She nodded slightly. "Your father never approved of Alicia, nor did he approve of his father's marriage. When your grandfather died, your father insisted Alicia leave Foxworth Hall with her son. She did so. She returned to her home in Richmond, where she eventually remarried a man who, unfortunately, suffered a serious illness and died as well."

"How dreadful," Corinne said.

"Yes. Even more dreadful, perhaps, she lost all her income in the terrible stock market crash and became quite poor. Now we have learned that Alicia herself is dying of cancer. Her son is seventeen and quite brilliant. She has written to us requesting that we take Christopher in and provide him with a college education so he can become a doctor. Your father and I have agreed and Christopher will be arriving here at Foxworth shortly. He will go on to Yale, your father's alma mater, but this will be his home until he graduates and sets up a practice."

She stared at me to be sure I had finished.

"How wonderful," she said finally. "And generous."

"It's God's will," I said. Corinne nodded quickly. "I expect you to act properly when he arrives. Make him feel at home. Remember that despite the fact that there are only three years between you, he is your half uncle and should be thought of in that manner."

"It will be good to have someone in the house to talk to," she said. "I mean someone who is not an adult yet," she added quickly.

I knew what she really meant—someone who spoke of things other than God and gloom. "Nevertheless, he is practically an adult. Don't distract him from his purpose." Then I smiled. "Christopher was such a wonderful boy. I'm sure he's grown into a delightful young man. I think the two of you will get along wonderfully," I kissed her on the forehead. I didn't blame her for her excitement. Foxworth Hall had become a large, empty house for her since the deaths of Mal and Joel. Christopher's arrival brought the promise of new light and life, not only for her, but for me as well. I couldn't help recalling the sweet child that he was, how polite and affectionate and thoughtful he was. Like Corinne, I was filled with happy anticipation.

Christopher arrived on a bright summer day, and it seemed as if the sun had followed him into the house. Alicia had passed away only a month before. John Amos had gone as our emissary and had handled the funeral arrangements, and after a proper mourning period, brought Christopher back with him.

I could remember Christopher only as a child alongside Mal and Joel, but the moment he entered Foxworth Hall, I saw that those handsome qualities he had inherited from Garland and those beautiful qualities he had inherited from Alicia had been developed and embellished. I saw something of Mal and something of Joel in him as well, and those characteristics endeared him to me.

He had grown into a tall, handsome man. When I saw him standing there in the sunlight, it was as if his golden hair were haloed by an aura of light. I sensed a gentle, beautiful temperament in him. He radiated an inner peace that warmed my heart.

He stood there wide-eyed, obviously not remembering much of Foxworth Hall. From what John Amos told me, I knew he came from a four-room cottage into this huge, grand house that dazzled him. He looked at Malcolm and me with such an expression of gratitude that I was actually embarrassed. He didn't understand that half of this entire estate, indeed, half of Malcolm's businesses, rightfully belonged to him.

Then I felt sorry for him, standing there, holding his two suitcases and gaping about. He wore shabby shoes and clothing that looked worn. I was about to direct John to take his things up to his room, when Corinne appeared on the staircase.

She had come running down the first half and then stopped abruptly in the middle. Christopher looked up at her. She had dressed in her prettiest light blue cotton dress. Her golden hair was washed and curled so that it gleamed richly.

I saw Christopher's eyes sparkle with surprise and interest. My heart skipped a beat. Would they sense who they were to each other? Was there something in their blood that would signal their relationship? They both had that thick, flaxen blond hair and those cerulean blue eyes and that peaches-and-cream complexion. I looked at Malcolm quickly to note his reaction to his stepbrother. I saw the pleasure in his face as he read his own and Alicia's lineage in Christopher's face. He obviously approved of the young man before him.

I hesitated no longer.

"Christopher, welcome," I said, stepping forward to him. "It is sadness and tragedy that brings you here, but hopefully you will find happiness and joy here with us in Foxworth Hall." I wanted to embrace him, as I had when he was a child. But I stopped myself. After all, he was now a grown man, and practically a stranger to me.

"Thank you. . . ." I could see he was struggling for a way to address me. I was, after all, in his mind, his sister-in-law. "Olivia," he finally said, and looked up at Corinne again.

"This is Corinne, our daughter. Corinne, come down and properly greet your uncle," I said, stressing the word "uncle." She brushed back a lock of her golden hair, rested her hand on her bosom, and drifted down the staircase with a radiant smile lighting her face.

"How do you do," Christopher said, and extended his hand. Corinne took it and then looked at me quickly. I nodded as she greeted him and quickly released her hold on his fingers. Then we all looked to Malcolm.

"Christopher," he began, "John Amos will take your things to your room and show you where you will reside. After you are finished unpacking, I would like you down in the library, where you and I will discuss your residence here and your college education," Malcolm said in a most formal, cool tone.

It didn't seem to discourage Christopher, however. He smiled that gentle, beautiful, trusting smile and thanked Malcolm. Then he allowed John Amos to lead him forward and up to his room in the north wing.

He paused at the center of the staircase as though just remembering something important, and turned back to look at Corinne, who stood there staring up at him. He smiled at her and continued on. Malcolm had already gone to the library.

I waited a moment and then turned to Corinne.

"Remember our discussion," I said, hiding my own nervousness behind a mask of sternness. "He is your uncle," I added, feeling the need to underline that deception strongly. "Don't forget that."

She looked at me with the oddest expression on her face.

"Why, of course I won't forget it. Look how much we look alike," she added in a happy voice, and hurried up the stairs after them.

17

Christopher Garland Foxworth

CHRISTOPHER BROUGHT A BURST OF LIGHT INTO OUR LIVES again. Corinne, John Amos, Malcolm, and I were drawn to him like moths, to the brightness of his golden hair, to his brilliant, radiant smile.

"Good morning, Olivia," he would say upon joining me for breakfast, "don't you look lovely this morning."

"Don't tease and flatter an old woman," I would insist.

"Tease and flatter?" he would say, and his blue eyes filled with the purest light, a blue light found in the freshest mountain lakes. "I meant it from the bottom of my heart." Then, with a boyish smile and a healthy appetite he would butter his blueberry pancakes and say, "Even as a little boy, Olivia, I remember you were the best cook. You always made cookies, the kind with raisins in them. You were always so kind to me."

My heart would fill with a joy I'd forgotten could exist in this earthly life.

With Malcolm, Christopher could discuss the most intricate of business plans. "I'm not sure investment in public railroads is going to be the thing of the future," Christopher would say. "I think it's time to look to the heavens, sir. I think aviation will be the transportation of the future."

"You mean to tell me that the common man will go flying around this great land of ours. I find that hard to believe, young man."

"It's already happening, sir. Why, look at how many companies are opening public stock options." And Christopher would open *The Wall Street Journal* and I would see their blond heads bow over the paper as they read over the stocks.

"Why, son, I believe you might be right," Malcolm would finally agree. "You have quite a business head on you. Are you sure you want to waste it on medicine?"

"Sir," Christopher would say, "I want to help people, like my stepfather did."

Even John Amos was impressed with the boy's understanding of the scriptures. Far into the night they would go over passages, and discuss various interpretations. Christopher always saw the Lord as forgiving, while John insisted that He was vengeful as well.

But it was Corinne who was most mesmerized by this beautiful young man. She sought every opportunity to be with him. Only when I walked into the room and saw them sitting together on the sofa, whispering and laughing, did Corinne remember to pull away, drop Christopher's hand, and heed my warning to treat him as she would treat an uncle. But it warmed me to see these two radiant children, children who brought such joy into gloomy Foxworth Hall, and I would fix them a pot of tea and bake them cookies, always remembering to put raisins in. I thought that Christopher had interminable patience when it came to Corinne's constant questions about his past, even when she asked him things that might bring back painful memories. He seemed incapable of losing his temper. He was full of forgiveness and understanding, warmth and sympathy.

At one dinner Corinne asked Christopher about Alicia. Malcolm was at his usual seat at the head of the table, and I was at mine at the other end. Corinne now sat directly across from Christopher, who sat in what had been Mal's seat. She had almost been late to dinner, taking so long deciding what to wear and how to fix her hair.

It was one of our warmest evenings of the summer, but Malcolm still wore his jacket and tie, as did Christopher. Malcolm would never admit to any discomfort. He maintained a cool, relaxed appearance, almost willing his body to behave. Although Christopher was uncomfortable, he did not say a word. There was absolutely no breeze outside, so nothing passed through our opened windows. All our ventilation came from the ceiling fans.

Corinne began by teasing Malcolm about his tightly knotted tie.

"Why don't the two of you loosen your ties and take off your jackets," she said. "I think it would be romantic." She rolled her eyes and sighed. I had told Malcolm that she was spending too much time reading the fashion magazines and following the lives of the movie stars. More and more she behaved as if Foxworth Hall were a Hollywood set.

"We are not performing on some stage," Malcolm retorted, recalling my complaints. I nodded in approval. "This is our dinner. I suggest you concern yourself with other matters than how the men in this house dress, Corinne."

"Daddy can be so stuffy," she said, smiling at Christopher, undaunted. He did not smile back, knowing well how Malcolm would have reacted. I knew she was showing off for Christopher. Although there was a look of pleasure in his eyes, he maintained his decorum. "Was it stuffy for you at dinner at your house, Chris?"

I raised my eyebrows. Chris? She caught my look of reprimand. You don't shorten the Christian names of people older than yourself, I had told her.

"My father wanted us to dress properly for dinner," he said. "I wouldn't say he was stuffy, nor would I say your father is either," Christopher replied diplomatically. Malcolm did not show his reaction, but I knew he was pleased.

"What about your mother? I know so little about her. She left with you shortly after I was born," Corinne asked. Whenever Alicia's name was mentioned, both Malcolm and I involuntarily stiffened. Oh, I worried so that somehow the truth would come out, that I would lose forever the love and affection of these two young people, who would never forgive us for the lie we had forced Corinne to live in. But it was for the best, I consoled myself, and there was no way they would ever guess; for indeed, who could ever guess such a deception?

"I don't think we should be talking about Christopher's mother over dinner," I said quickly. "It can't be very pleasant for him, considering the tragedy," I added.

Corinne blushed. "Oh, I'm sorry, I didn't—"

"It's all right. But Olivia is right," Christopher said. He quickly asked Malcolm a question about one of his mills and the subject was dropped, but the tension lingered in the air between Corinne and myself for the remainder of our meal. She hated how I had made her look cruel to Christopher, but it was the quickest way I could think of to end the topic. I was just as reluctant to discuss Alicia in front of Corinne as was Malcolm. Later I overheard Christopher assure her that she had not offended him. They were walking in the hallway toward the east patio. She did not know that I was close enough to hear their conversation.

"My mother can be very cold at times," she told him. "She is so exasperating," she added, fluttering her eyelashes. Christopher laughed.

"You must not judge your mother so harshly, Corinne," he told her. "What she said, she said only to protect me. She was concerned for my feelings," he added in a tone of voice that suggested a teacher-student relationship. I thought he was doing well in his effort to keep Corinne in her place, and I was proud of him for it.

The next morning Christopher came to me on that same east patio. I was enjoying the humid, overcast day because there was a comfortable breeze. As he walked toward me, I saw a look of seriousness furrow his brow, though he smiled and greeted me warmly. "Good morning, Olivia, may I sit down?" I put down my needlepoint as he sat beside me. I knew he had something on his mind, and for a moment I froze in fear, so afraid he would ask me endless questions about Alicia and why she had left here. I hated lying to Christopher, it seemed so unfair; yet what would he think of me, of Malcolm, of Alicia, even of himself if he knew the truth?

"You look like you have something on your mind, Christopher," I said warily. "What is it?"

"Olivia," Christopher began, a look of sweetness crossing his face. "I want you to know how grateful I am for what you and Malcolm are doing for me. It's so wonderful here. I feel as if I've found a second home—and so quickly after I lost my mother. And thank you for understanding that it's difficult for me to talk about her. Last night at dinner, I felt you understood me so well, and then, when I was thinking about it later, I realized why. For you've suffered a loss, perhaps even greater than mine. I know children expect their parents to die; but I can't imagine how horrible it is to lose both your sons." He reached over and took my hand.

"I have hesitated speaking about Mal and Joel because I know how painful it is for you. But I feel that we can share that pain. Oh, I remember Mal, so serious and so adult. I remember when I was here with them, and they treated me like a brother. And really, when my mom was away all those months, you were a mother to me, and I loved you so. I never forgot that. And now I have lost my mother and you have lost your sons. But we can have each other now, can't we? I mean, isn't it as if I have found a mother and you have found another son? Can we be like that, Olivia? I always wanted brothers and sisters and used to complain to Mom about that. But whenever I asked for one, she'd look so upset, and start twisting her fingers. I don't know why, she'd never explain to me. But I feel as if I've truly found a second family. And I adore Corinne, she sure is going to be a beautiful woman! You've raised her so well—she's so sweet and charming, and really fun to be with. You know, I really don't mind at all the way she seeks me out. It's very flattering. And nothing would honor me more than to be a real brother to Corinne, and if you'll let me, to be a son to you."

"Thank you, Christopher," I said. I felt the warmth and respect in his eyes. Oh, this young man touched me more than I could ever tell him. How strange it was, strange and odd that I'd lost my own two children but had been given Alicia's. And I vowed I would take care of them, and protect them. Even though they were almost adults, we truly were a family, the sort of family I'd dreamed of—beautiful, loving children with the world at their feet. "There is nothing I'd like more, Christopher, than for you to consider yourself my son. I'm honored, really I am."

Christopher smiled, his handsome face filled with love and interest.

"I wish my mother had never left Foxworth Hall. I wish I had thousands more memories of Mal and Joel. I wish that I had had the opportunity to know them as we all grew up, but I realize all that is in the past and there is no point to resurrect it. My mother told me so little about our life here. But we can make new memories now, can't we, Olivia?"

Christopher looked down and then up at me with those blue Foxworth eyes, his warmer, deeper, richer. "I'm going to make you so proud of me, Olivia."

His sweetness, his love, was so moving, it brought tears to my eyes. I had known so little love in my life, but I believed Christopher really did love me, love me as if I were his mother. A lump was lodged in my throat, and I could tell Christopher knew how sincerely he had moved me. I smiled and patted his soft hand.

"Christopher," I began, "if you achieve what you have set out to achieve, you will bring me the kind of pride and happiness only a mother can have for a son. I feel honored that you have these feelings now." I looked away quickly because my heart was beating fast and I felt my tears about to flow.

I couldn't help but think of Mal and Joel and the mother-son talks we used to have. All that had been taken away from me, and now, suddenly, some of it was returned. As if to comfort me, the warm breeze caressed my face and the long, billowy cloud that had covered the sun moved on. There was warmth all about me, but most important, there was warmth in my heart.

"I will do my best," Christopher said. He leaned forward to kiss me on the cheek. The warmth of his lips on my cheek remained after he got up. I swallowed my urge to cry and turned back to him only when he started away. I watched him go to the house and then I looked up and saw John Amos standing by a second story window, looking down at us. He had his hands behind his back and his body seemed to cast a deep, heavy shadow.

I began to notice how John Amos kept watching Christopher. He would appear out of nowhere, hovering in a doorway, emerging from a shadow. He seemed to be observing him, looking for something in Christopher. With his eyes like inquisitive, probing scalpels, he sought to slice out a hint, a sign, a clue. Whenever Malcolm and Christopher did have a conversation and John Amos was nearby, he scrutinized Christopher like a spy sent from some distant land filled with suspicion. For a while he said nothing about him, and then one day about a week after my conversation with Christopher on the patio, he came to the door of the front salon while I was reading.

"I must speak to you about Christopher," he said. I nodded and indicated he should come in. He did not sit down, so I knew that his thoughts troubled him. He stood for a long moment with his hands behind his back and then turned to me. "There is danger in paradise," he began.

"What troubles you, John?" I asked, impatient with him. I wasn't happy that he had come to me critical of Christopher. "What has he done?" I demanded.

"It's nothing that he has done specifically, but I am a cautious man and I want you to be cautious too. I worry that everyone has grown so attached to him so quickly. Even Malcolm appears to have lost his cautious eyes and careful ways. Only you, Olivia, have the insight to see what I am suggesting," he said, and brought his lower lip over his upper, his eyes small. He nodded his head slowly, as though confirming his own statements.

I considered what he had said.

"But there is nothing that you have observed . . ."

"I have seen him with Corinne. They spend a great deal of time together walking through the gardens, going on the swings, talking, laughing," he said as if those were sins.

"But they are innocent. She follows him about like an obedient puppy dog. You have observed no indiscretions, have you?" I asked quickly.

"No, and yet . . . as I said, I worry. Corinne is spending a great deal more time and placing a great deal more attention on her appearance. She sits before her vanity mirror and brushes her hair a hundred times before she will emerge from her room," he said quickly. I sat back.

"You watch her brush her hair? I don't understand," I said. He suddenly looked very flustered. His face reddened and his mouth opened and closed without a word. "Why do you watch her so closely?" I asked. "How do you watch her so closely?"

"Sometimes she leaves her door open a little and I . . . I do what I can to . . . to keep us aware of whatever troubles may be brewing, Olivia," he said quickly. "You know that is all I want to do."

I considered what he had said.

"Was there anything else you witnessed that you think I should know?" I asked, realizing that John had been doing more spying than I could imagine.

"Yes. I must confess I followed them about yesterday because I sensed something."

"What?" I demanded. I was becoming more and more angered at John Amos's suspicions about these beautiful, innocent young people. Was he trying to destroy the peace and happiness that we had at last built at Foxworth Hall? "What did you sense, John Amos?"

"I followed them to the lake. They were giggling and splashing each other in the water. I stood watching them play, and was greatly shocked when they emerged from the water. They were swimming in their underwear!! Olivia, it was obscene! You could see everything! It was lewd!"

I must say, I was quite shocked to hear this. I had raised Corinne to be a modest young woman, and I did not approve of her doing this. But, I excused them—after all, they were young, it was hot, humid summer weather. I'm sure their natural exuberance just got of the best of them. "John Amos," I said sternly. "I don't like your suspicious mind. After all, they are members of the same family, and in such situations, people often drop their proper modesty. I know both you and I were only children, but I have heard that siblings and cousins often feel very comfortable being so open and unabashed with one another. Let's not make a mountain out of a molehill."

The first summer with Christopher drew to an end. Christopher went off to Yale. Corinne, now in the tenth grade, was enrolled in the best girls' school in New England. I wanted her to be exposed to the old traditions of the eastern seaboard. I wanted her to learn about something other than Southern balls and Kentucky Derbies. I wanted her to study Latin, to study ancient Greece, to become more than those pretty, empty-headed mistresses who ran the estates around Virginia. And, a happy coincidence, her school was in Massachusetts, only an hour or so away from New Haven. I was really comforted to know that a member of the family was nearby, should Corinne need anything.

I was sorry to see them go. They left Foxworth Hall on the same day—they were taking the train up together—and Christopher had offered to see that Corinne was settled in her new school before he went on to Yale. It was so sweet to see how quickly they really had become to each other the brother and sister they truly were. Only they didn't know.

The big house felt empty without them, and our rather dull routine quickly took over again; Malcolm always at work, John Amos managing the servants and reading Bible lessons with me. But I was comforted by my children. Truly I did think of them as mine.

Just as he had promised, Christopher wrote to me every week. He wrote long, interesting letters, describing everything he was doing and how much he already missed Foxworth Hall and the happy days he had spent during the last half of the summer. And Corinne wrote sweet notes, describing her new school and her new friends. She did complain that there were no boys around, and I had to worry some, that she would become boy crazy and get herself into some sort of trouble, but I consoled myself that I had raised her well and properly. I had to trust the fruit of my own child-rearing. I did believe my tutelage could overcome whatever tendencies she had inherited from her mother.

We all looked forward to the holidays, when Christopher and Corinne would return. Thanksgiving was too short a holiday for them to come all the way to Virginia, but one of Christopher's professors invited both Corinne and Christopher to his home for dinner. I was consoled that at least they were together. We all waited eagerly for Christmas. And the two of them arrived together, looking flushed and happy, as bright and expectant as two small children waiting for Santa's arrival. Our Christmas party that year was spectacular.

Our Christmas tree was forty feet high and reached all the way to the top of the rotunda. Christopher and Corinne decorated it, spending almost two entire days with Christopher up on the ladder and Corinne handing him the bright, gay decorations. They even strung popcorn and cranberries—yards and yards of lively red and white garlands to drape around the tree like dancers dancing around the maypole. By the night of the party, Corinne was beside herself with excitement. Malcolm had bought her an extravagant red velvet gown, and she wore her blond hair piled on her head with ringlets cascading down. I had assented to her wearing some light makeup—mascara and lipstick. She was breathtaking, I have to admit it. She looked like a princess, a movie star, a queen.

Malcolm, Christopher, John Amos, and I, as well as the servants, all turned as she drifted down the stairway. Oh, we all felt so much pride; Malcolm was beaming fit to burst and I heard Christopher let out a sigh almost of wonder as Corinne reached us, gaily said, "Happy Christmas, Daddy," and threw her arms about Malcolm, and then, as she was hugging him, gave Christopher a sly wink. Only John Amos looked on with a tight expression. And suddenly it dawned on me, as I watched him watching her. Why, John Amos was jealous of Christopher! That was the spring of his suspicions. I took his arms and led him into the grand ballroom. "Come, John Amos, let's make certain all the preparations are perfect. Our guests will begin arriving any moment now."

Our party was a grand success. Corinne, quite the sophisticated young lady and well-schooled in etiquette, played the hostess more than I did. I saw how proud of her Malcolm was, how he sat back or stood to the side and watched her move about the great foyer greeting people, laughing with this one or that, saying the right things, charming older people as well as younger. I saw the smiles on their faces and the enchantment in their eyes when she greeted them. And I didn't even mind so much that they had never responded to me in such a way. I was not that type of woman. But my Corinne was, and reflected glory was certainly more sweet than no glory at all.

She had Christopher on her arm, introducing him as her long-lost uncle who was on his way to becoming a famous physician and telling them how proud of him she was. She was positively radiant as they flitted from this person to that, like a sparkling wind bringing Christmas joy to everything it touched.

Christopher was, as always, perfectly charming, complimenting the women, making them feel pretty and attractive. He had a kind word for everyone, and it always sounded sincere, never phony. He sought and found in each person he met their best quality, and then brought it to the fore. Everywhere I turned guests were talking about him and Corinne, how impressed they were with both of them.

I did overhear Mrs. Bromley tell a group of women that it was difficult for her to believe anyone as energetic and charming as Corinne could be a daughter of mine.

But this time I felt no need to cut in and answer her back as I had done at previous gatherings. I knew she spoke out of jealousy, and I felt proud. There wasn't a finer, more handsome young man or woman in the community. I had succeeded at last in my role as Malcolm's wife.

We had survived our disasters and tragedies, and like the great house, we now stood at the pinnacle of the community. We were people to be admired and envied.

As the band struck up the dance music, Christopher led Corinne out onto the dance floor. It was a waltz, and their dance was breathtaking. Christopher spun Corinne around the floor as if they were born dancing together. Everyone turned to watch, no one else wanted to dance, happier to watch this gorgeous couple glide across the floor like happy snowflakes in a friendly wind. Then Malcolm, tall and dignified, came and cut in. Corinne smiled at Christopher as he took his place in the circle about the dance floor to the applause of the guests, and Malcolm danced on with Corinne. But somehow he had broken the spell, both of them appeared stiff and slightly uncomfortable; it was as if Malcolm were trying to compete with Christopher and prove he was just as accomplished a dancer—but he wasn't. At that moment I really realized how old Malcolm had become. His youthful vigor was gone; dancing with Corinne, he looked like a foolish old man.

Christopher came up to me, smiling. "Dare I cut in, Olivia? Malcolm looks like he's tiring out."

I smiled and patted his hand. "You go right ahead, Christopher," I encouraged him.

Christopher walked out onto the floor, and as he tapped Malcolm's shoulder, and Corinne floated into his arms, the guests broke into another round of applause.

It was then I saw John Amos looking at me, looking at me as though he were some angry God trying to wreak vengeance on my happiness so lately found. He looked back at Christopher and Corinne dancing and raised an eyebrow in alarm and suspicion. "There are none so blind as those who refuse to see," he intoned. Why did he have to make beauty seem so sordid? Why did he resent Christopher so? Did he feel that since he was a member of the family he should have the benefits Christopher had gotten rather than being merely a butler? I pushed the thought away. This was the best Christmas party we had ever given, and I was having a wonderful time glorying in my children. I wasn't going to let John Amos's suspicions ruin my happiness.

During his second year at Yale, Christopher did more than simply establish himself as a promising student. His professors found his papers to be extraordinary. As a sophomore, he was already doing senior work. Credit limitations were waived for him; and Malcolm and I received his excited letter announcing that he would be graduating in three years instead of four. Medical school was just around the corner.

I was delighted to learn that he and Corinne kept in contact with each other. Christopher had even taken a ride or two to her boarding school to pay her a visit. Corinne must have been so proud to show off her handsome stepuncle to her girlfriends. I envisioned her sitting on the bed in her dormitory room, the other girls gathered about her to listen to her descriptions of Christopher and the Christmas parties and Foxworth Hall. I was sure she made them all envious, promising to introduce this one or that one to Christopher. When he arrived, she probably displayed him like a precious jewel.

John Amos, however, never let up his suspicions and jealousy of Christopher. "It's unnatural, Olivia; even siblings aren't that close at their age."

"Really, John," Malcolm would say, "can't you let Corinne alone." He remained enamored of her.

By the time she was seventeen, Corinne was a stunningly beautiful woman. Her golden hair never had more of a sheen or looked as soft. Her eyes were brighter and a deeper blue, the cerulean blue of Christopher's eyes. She had Alicia's slim, very feminine figure, with a graceful neck, small round shoulders, a firm, full bosom, a narrow waist, and small hips. Her legs were long, and she moved with a confident grace that would make angels envious.

Now twenty-one years old, Christopher, too, had filled out. His shoulders became wider and more muscular from his athletic activities at Yale. He was the champion rower on his scull team. He was at least an inch taller than when he had first arrived at Foxworth Hall, and I thought his maturity made him even more handsome. There was a great deal of Garland in him now. I heard him in his laugh and saw him in his happy strut.

It was heartwarming to watch them rush about the great house, going from one activity to the next. One afternoon they were off to sail on the little lake, another afternoon they were going out to hunt for wild flowers or spy on bees so Olsen could steal the honey. At dinner they chattered incessantly about their lives at school.

Malcolm looked from one to the other, doting, of course, on Corinne. Something was happening to the granite in his face. It was beginning to be chipped away until he no longer looked as though he carried a stone bust of a head on his shoulders. Occasionally, even he would burst out in laughter at the table when Corinne would describe some silly thing she had done or said.

Christopher was full of stories about her, too, loving to repeat things she'd said or done when he visited her at school. They were becoming so close that it finally began to concern me. One afternoon, when the two of them came back from sailing, I realized what was bothering me about their relationship.

Corinne's arm was laced through Christopher's, her hair bouncing gently on her shoulders as the two of them crossed the lawn toward the patio, where I sat looking off at the Blue Ridge Mountains.

They looked so much like brother and sister now that I was almost sure they sensed it. For a few moments I was plunged back into the memory of my own sons, and I imagined that if Mal or Joel were alive and walking with Corinne, either of them would look as wonderful. Such was the power of her beauty that any man standing in the reach of that beauty would be enhanced by it himself, the same way a woman's hands could be enhanced by jewels and her wrist and neck by bracelets and necklaces.

I heard their laughter first. Their voices, still a bit far off, were indistinct. When they drew close enough to see me, they stopped and looked at each other as though they had been caught doing something illicit. I felt myself tighten. A moment later they were walking toward me, moving faster and not standing so close to each other, even though Corinne still had her arm in his.

"Isn't this a magnificent day, Olivia?" Christopher said. "There was just enough breeze to move our little sailboat," he added. "I wish you would permit me to take you for a boat ride on a day like this."

Corinne looked at me with a teasing expression; she couldn't envision me in a sailboat.

"I have been on a sailboat many times," I said. "When I lived in New London, sailing was as common as walking."

"Really?" Christopher said. "I have been down to New London and it is a rather beautiful harbor."

"Yes," Corinne said. "It is."

"You have been to New London?" I asked her quickly. She looked at Christopher furtively and then nodded.

"I picked her up at school and took her for a ride one Saturday," he confessed. "We knew it was your birthplace and we wanted to see it."

"It's such a lovely place," Corinne said.

Then Corinne and Christopher looked into each

other's eyes in a way that excluded everything else in the world. And I felt a sharp pang of terror grip my heart. It was as if the two of them were living under a veil, a veil that let nothing and no one else into their secret world.

The next year sped by, and quickly enough it was summer again. This time Malcolm and I traveled to New England, first to attend Corinne's graduation from high school, then to attend Christopher's graduation from Yale. Christopher was the valedictorian of his class. People nearly wept at his moving address. He spoke eloquently about the idea that just when you think you've lost something—a hope, a dream, or someone you love—you can stick to your dreams and make them come true again. I knew in my heart he was talking about our family, with its bitter tragedies, the loss of Alicia for him, and then his finding a home at Foxworth Hall. When he stepped down from the podium, even Malcolm was moved, and we rushed toward him, our arms outstretched. Corinne ran up to him first and they embraced for a long while. Malcolm and I, growing a little impatient, waited for our turn to hug him. But when he finally took us in his arms, sweeping us both into his embrace, I cried tears that burned from happiness. Then all of us together touched his cap and as a family we threw it into the air. The sky was almost black with graduation caps spinning higher and higher. A cheer of thousands of young male voices filled the air.

We drove home in the graduation car Malcolm had given Corinne. It was a cream-colored convertible Cadillac. We took turns, sometimes Malcolm driving and me riding beside him in the front seat while Christopher and Corinne rode in back. Then Christopher would take a turn at the wheel, then Corinne. For children who'd just proudly graduated, both Christopher and Corinne were oddly subdued on the long two-day drive back to Virginia. We stopped for the night in Atlantic City, New Jersey, and Malcolm wanted to take us all out for a night on the town.

"Have I got some places to show you kids," Malcolm declared. "There's a ballroom here that has gold embedded in its tiles. Why, it even puts Foxworth Hall to shame!"

"Oh, Daddy, that's so sweet of you," Corinne sighed. "But I'm so exhausted. All this excitement with my graduation and Chris's has left me feeling like I could sleep for a year."

"Boy, I know what you mean," Christopher agreed. "That speech yesterday really took it out of me."

"Well, if you kids don't want to go out and celebrate, I guess we'll just have a quiet evening at the hotel."

"Oh, no, no, Daddy," Corinne insisted. "You ought to take Mother out. Why don't you pretend you're graduates and we'll stay home and wait up to make sure you get home at a decent hour. And boy, are you going to be in trouble if you're late," Corinne teased.

I understood their exhaustion and insisted that Malcolm take me on his tour. After all, didn't I deserve some celebration for the great job I'd done raising his child and his father's child? We left Christopher and Corinne in their respective rooms, dressed in our Sunday best, and went to the restaurant overlooking the ocean. It was filled with newlyweds and youngsters headed for senior proms. We felt rather uncomfortable and out of place surrounded by so many young people. We barely touched the expensive champagne that Malcolm had insisted we order.

"Let's have a toast, Olivia," he said, trying to add cheer to our rather silent meal. "Here's to our wonderful daughter, coming home again, to be with us forever."

I gave him a stern look. Did he really think Corinne would never leave him? He had to let her have her own life, meet some nice young man and marry and raise a family of her own. That's what every girl wanted, and I didn't want Malcolm to continue to make Corinne feel guilty about her quite normal dreams and desires.

"Let's toast to Corinne finding everything she wants from life and love," I corrected him.

We returned to Foxworth Hall late the next night. I let the children sleep as late as they wanted in the morning; after all, come fall, both of them would have to begin taking up adult responsibilities. Christopher was still waiting to hear where he would be accepted into medical school. He was on the waiting list at several Ivy League schools, and had already been accepted to his stepfather's alma mater in Georgia. Corinne had wanted to go to Bryn Mawr, but I had insisted that she apply to Vassar and Connecticut College for Women in my own hometown of New London. She had been accepted at both but had not yet decided which she most favored.

In the morning, after checking in with John Amos and the cook, I went to my room and sat down at my desk to go through the mail. There was a large manila envelope addressed to Christopher Foxworth, Jr., and the return address was Harvard Medical School! I was so excited to see that, and I knew I shouldn't open it, but I just had to know. I told myself I wanted to be able to help Christopher to cope with whatever news it contained, good or bad, but in my heart I knew the news would be good. How could any intelligent college turn Christopher down? My fingers trembled as I tore open the envelope.

> Dear Mr. Foxworth,
>
> It is with great pleasure that I inform you of your acceptance to Harvard Medical School. As Dean, I am happy—

I couldn't read any further. Tears of happiness filled my eyes and the letter blurred before me. Clutching it to my breast, I bolted up the stairs like a young woman and pounded on Christopher's door. He wasn't there. I tried Corinne's room next, thinking that she might know where he was. But she wasn't in her room either. Suddenly I heard a muffled noise. I couldn't imagine where it was coming from. I moved toward the sound. For a moment my heart beat so loudly, I could hear nothing else. The noise grew louder. It sounded like laughing, but very strange laughing, like laughter being muffled in a pillow. A light was on at the far end of the corridor and I began to creep toward it.

"Corinne," I heard a voice whisper, "what would I have done if I never found you? How would I have lived? You are my life. You are the sole reason for my existence. You are—"

"Shhh," Corinne said, "someone might hear."

"I don't care if they hear. I love you. I want the world to know it."

The light was pouring forth from under the double

doors to the Swan Room. Clutching Christopher's acceptance letter from Harvard, I nudged the door open an inch or two. Sprawled on the swan bed, half undressed, limbs entwined, clutching and clawing passionately at each other, were Corinne and Christopher. Her head was thrown back, her lips, blood-red, were slightly parted. Christopher was kissing her exposed breasts!

Without thinking, I almost slammed that door shut. My mind was dizzy with rage and terror. My heart beat in my chest like a wild bird before a fox. Christopher and Corinne! They were lovers! Lovers! My God, they were brother and sister! Oh, God, what had I done? What had we all done? I sunk to the floor, my head spinning, feeling as if all the life in me were being turned to poison. My mind searched frantically for what to do. Should I confront them? Should I tell them the truth? Would God strike them dead for what they had done?

Just then I felt a dark shadow fall over me. I looked up and there stood John Amos, looking down on me with a cold dismay.

"Olivia, what are you doing stooped on the floor like a beggar? What's happening here?" And then his beady eyes turned to the door to the Swan Room. I could hear a rustling inside. Quickly John Amos grasped the door and swung it open, and there, revealed in all their naked glory, were Christopher and Corinne on the swan bed. He was lying on top of her. They were entwined in the union that should exist only in marriage.

John Amos seemed to embody all the wrath of God, and as he stood there staring at them, he seemed to grow taller, darker. He seemed an avenging angel sent down from heaven. *"Sinners! Fornicators!"* he thundered. *"How dare you disgrace this house. You will bring the wrath of God down on you. This is incest, lustful unholy incest. May God damn your souls to everlasting hell!"*

I tried to stand up, to pull John Amos away from the doorway and close the door on their shame, but he ruthlessly pushed me away. "You stupid woman," he sneered, "I told you, I told you what was going on right under your nose, but you wouldn't listen.

"You have harbored the devil in your house, woman, do you hear me? You invited him in, and fed him, and cosseted him, and now he has come to claim your life."

18

The Wages of Sin

I WAS BEING PULLED DOWN INTO A WHIRLING MASS OF confusion and terror. I felt betrayed and so angry, hurt and bruised. And yet, there was so much love—oh, but it was a sinful, ungodly love. Who had caused this? Was it my fault? Or was it Malcolm and his lustful lineage coming to its final fruition? One moment I would be overcome with rage, the next I would be beside myself with pity for them. I knew I had to tell Malcolm. It took all my strength to rise to my feet and tell John Amos to go. Then, slowly, clinging to the doorway for support, I entered the Swan Room and in a voice so strange and faint, I barely recognized it as my own, I told Christopher and Corinne to be in Malcolm's library in fifteen minutes. Corinne was hiding her nakedness behind Christopher, who had draped himself in a sheet. Both of their eyes were already reddened by tears. Then I quietly shut the door behind me and, reeling slightly, went to find Malcolm.

"I want you to brace yourself," I said, opening the door of his library, "something . . . something terrible has happened."

"The children? Oh, God, not again!" Malcolm said, bolting upright.

"Your father's son has seduced our daughter!" I informed him.

Words cannot describe the torment that twisted Malcolm's face. As I watched him, I felt I was seeing a mirror of my own feelings, yet, as the rage and bitterness and hatred and love for his daughter all fought for dominance, one emotion showed itself stronger, and banished all the others. Rage. Rage as I had never seen before.

"Now, Malcolm," I warned, his lack of control helping me find my own. "We must remain calm. We must figure out what is best for us to do. There is too much at stake here, you know it and I know it. They are coming here, to the library, in a moment. Please, Malcolm, please find some strength within you so we can put a stop to this dreadful abomination."

Just then we both heard the door creak open and Christopher, his arm protectively around Corinne, entered the library. They had had only a few minutes to throw on their clothes, and some of their buttons were unfastened. Christopher was wearing socks without shoes. Behind them I saw John Amos looming at the top of the stairs, looking down at us with the face of doom. He seemed to grow larger with every passing silent moment, for he had known, he had always known; and I had refused to believe. I heard his prophetic words in my memory.

"There are none so blind as those who refuse to see."

And I knew the wrath of God had fallen hard and completely on the House of Foxworth. Every shadow, the ghost of every descendant, moaned in the wings.

All that was left was to hear the words. Malcolm stepped forward and slammed the doors behind them.

"Daddy," Corinne began, grasping hold of Christopher's hand as they moved toward Malcolm. "We are in love. We've been in love for a long time. We are going to be married." She looked at Christopher to gather her courage. He smiled that sweet, compassionate smile that had so charmed everyone at Foxworth Hall these past three years. "Christopher and I have been planning it almost from the day we first met, waiting until I reached eighteen. We were thinking of eloping; we didn't know if you would approve. But we'd love to have a church wedding, to bless the sanctity of our love."

Every word Corinne spoke drove the knife deeper and deeper into my heart. She had said everything I feared most. Malcolm looked as though he had heard nothing. He stared at Corinne in a strange way. It was as if he didn't see her, but instead saw Alicia, or, perhaps, even his own mother. Then his face took on the worst contortion I had ever seen. The rage that built in him swelled up his face, inflamed his cheeks, and hoisted his shoulders until he looked gigantic.

I walked forward quickly to join him.

"We hoped you would be happy for us," Corinne said, her voice beginning to quiver, "and give us your blessing. Of course, if you want to make us a big wedding and invite hundreds of guests and then have a big party here in Foxworth Hall, we would be thrilled. We want you to be as happy as we are," she added.

"Happy?" Malcolm said, pronouncing the word as if it were as the strangest one he'd ever heard. "Happy," he repeated, and then he followed it with a hollow, devilish laugh. Suddenly, he stepped forward, his right arm extended stiffly, forefinger out, pointing accusingly. "Happy? You two have committed a most heinous sin. How can anyone be happy? You know he is your uncle and he knows you are his niece. What you have done is incestuous. I will never give it my blessing and neither will God. You are making a mockery of the idea of marriage," he thundered, zigzagging with his finger in the air before him as though he were annulling their love then and there.

"It is not incestuous," Corinne said softly. "And our love is too pure and good for it to be sinful. These are not the laws of God, but the laws of man you quote. In many societies, marriage of cousins and close relatives is even expected. Why—"

"Incestuous!" Malcolm screamed, his arm still extended. His entire body shook with the effort and the blood rushed to his face. *"Sinful! Ungodly! Unholy!"* he shouted, pumping the air with his arm after each accusation. *"You have betrayed me, betrayed me!"*

"Please listen, Malcolm," Christopher began, "Corinne and I have felt this way about each other from the first day I set foot in Foxworth Hall. Surely, it was something meant to be."

"Judas!" Malcolm retorted, turning on him. "I gave you life; I gave you hope and opportunity. I spent money on you, placed my trust and faith in you. I opened my home to you and you have seduced my daughter."

"He didn't seduce me," Corinne said, quickly coming to Christopher's defense. She pulled him even closer to her. "What has happened between us I wanted as much as he did," she said. "In fact, it was I who followed him about; it was I who pursued him and begged him to look at me as he would look at any other woman. I filled his every possible free moment with my presence, with my chatter, with my laughter and my love. He was always the gentleman, always talking about what you and my mother wanted. I was afraid that you might not understand at first, so I waited until I was eighteen. I haven't betrayed you. I still love you and want to live here with Christopher. We will have our children here and—"

"Children?" Malcolm repeated as if stung by the concept. A cold chill ran up my spine.

"If you will just listen," Corinne said.

"There is nothing to listen to," Malcolm said. "You talk of having children. Your children will be born with horns, with humped backs, forked tails, hoofed feet; they will be deformed creatures," he pronounced, his eyes hateful. Both Corinne and Christopher retreated from his accusing words. Corinne took on a look of terror and clung harder to Christopher's arm.

"No," Corinne said, shaking her head. "That's not true; that won't happen."

"Beguiler," Malcolm said. "Delilah, deceitful, lustful creature, cunningly beautiful, evil thing," he continued, driving her back farther and farther with every pronouncement. "I want you both out of my house, out of my life, and out of my memory," he said. "Go from this house," he said, pointing to the door, "and never set foot in it again from this day forth. You are dead to me, as dead as . . ." Malcolm looked at me, and my eyes restrained him from saying anything more.

"You can't mean this," Corinne cried, the tears streaming down her cheeks, her chin quivering. Christopher looked to me for rescue, but I looked away. I felt almost as betrayed as Malcolm did. I had loved him as my own, and now he had betrayed me. Those happy years, when I believed in his devotion and love for me, it wasn't for me at all, but for Corinne. He was as trapped by beauty as Malcolm was. Oh, it was true, all men were alike. I returned his look with a stare so cold, I hoped it froze his heart. Then and there I wanted to destroy them with the truth, but the new coldness and clarity I felt told me that I would destroy only myself.

"I mean every word," Malcolm finally responded, his voice dry, cold, and as brittle and sharp as ice. "Go from this house and know that you are disinherited. Neither you nor your Judas shall receive one penny from me. I curse you; I curse you both and condemn you to a life of sin and horror."

"We shall not be cursed," Christopher stood tall as he defied Malcolm. "We shall go from your house but we shall not carry away your curse. We will leave your curses at the door." As he spoke, he looked more like Malcolm than Malcolm looked himself.

"These are not Malcolm's curses." I finally spoke up. "They are the curses God Himself will lay on you for what you have done. It is incestuous and you will breed only horror," I predicted. Christopher looked at me with great pain in his eyes. Now it was he who felt betrayed by me.

"Then we will go," Christopher said. He turned Corinne from us and the two of them walked to the front door. He looked back once, defiantly. Corinne, still crying, looked lost and frightened.

After a moment they were gone.

Malcolm's fury burst. He lifted his arms toward the ceiling and released a howl that emerged from the deepest recesses of his being. It was the howl of a beast in fatal agony, a howl that shook Foxworth Hall, echoing down the corridors and through the shadows, seemingly gaining volume and intensity as it traveled. Perhaps the ghosts of all his ancestors howled with him. For a moment there was a chorus of Malcolms crying their pain and torment.

The scream that had emerged suddenly died quickly. Malcolm turned toward me, his eyes bulging, and he grasped at the air, churning at it to bring oxygen to his face. He clutched his chest and his legs crumpled. As he fell to the floor, I heard John Amos behind me.

"God's wrath has come to this house today," he muttered. Then he joined me at Malcolm's side.

Malcolm was sprawled on his stomach, his right arm under his head. John turned him over and we saw the distortion in his mouth. The right side of his face was collapsed. The corner of his lips dipped, revealing his clenched teeth. His eyes were turned upward as though he were trying to see into his own head. He made an effort to speak, but nothing could be heard or understood.

"Call the physician," I shouted.

The doctor insisted Malcolm be taken to the hospital. I saw the resistance in his eyes; he shook his head and begged me silently to oppose the doctor's orders.

"Of course, Doctor," I said. "I want only what is best for my husband. Call for the ambulance." Later I would learn that the doctor told people I was one of the strongest women he had ever encountered in the midst of a terrible crisis.

The ambulance attendants came and took Malcolm, speeding him off to the hospital, where he remained for nearly a month in a private room with round-the-clock personal nurses. Every time John Amos and I visited him, he pleaded with us to take him home. At first he could plead only with his eyes, for he had experienced a stroke as well as a heart attack and the entire right side of his body was paralyzed.

By the time we brought him home, he had regained some of his muscle control and he could make distorted sounds that resembled words. Sometimes I thought I heard him calling Corinne.

The days dragged by monotonously. It was as though time itself had weakened and could barely move on from hour to hour. Malcolm remained confined to a wheelchair and could not go to his offices. All his work was brought to me. And I was thankful for every bit of it because while I had things to occupy my mind I did not wander through Foxworth Hall, torturing myself with memories, wondering how I could have made things end differently.

The house seemed like a giant tomb. Our footsteps echoed through the emptiness. The clang of dishes and utensils could be heard from the kitchen across the great foyer.

The servants traded information as each learned another tidbit, whispering, listening eagerly. None of them would ask anything about Corinne or Christopher directly, but I knew John Amos gave them just enough information to fan the embers of their curiosity.

Our dinners were mime shows. From the moment Malcolm was wheeled up to the table, not a word was spoken. He ate mechanically, his gaze ahead, looking through me, looking, I was sure, at the pictures he saw behind his eyes. His daydreams were like cobwebs, easily torn to shreds as he muddled through the memories, groping for some understanding of Corinne's betrayal.

For days he wouldn't mention her name, nor would

anyone in his presence. If he said anything, it was always prefaced with, "When this is over . . ." I could imagine his nightmares, the nightmares that shadowed his days. Corinne's hauntingly beautiful face had seized him and dragged him into endless dreams of loss and defeat. They lingered on the surface of his skin until he became a ghost himself.

John Amos and I would take out the Bible and lay it across Malcolm's chest, open to the pages we wanted to read. I had, like Malcolm before me, gone through a transformation with John Amos's help. I now knew I could trust his connection to God completely, for, not even knowing the secret about just who Corinne was, he had instinctively seen the truth, and tried to lead me to it before it was too late. But I, indeed, had been too blind to see. I was determined never to be blinded again. "Olivia," John Amos would comfort me, "the ways of the Lord are mysterious but always just. I know He will give you an opportunity to redeem the heinous sin of your daughter and her uncle."

His words froze my heart.

"The truth is always found in our Lord," he continued. "Get down on your knees, woman, and save your soul."

"I can't get down on my knees, for I haven't been honest with the Lord. You don't know the whole truth."

"Come, Olivia, confess everything."

I knelt beside him. "Oh, John, it's worse than you imagined." I felt the devil gripping my throat, but I forced the words through his evil fingers. "Christopher is not really Corinne's half uncle. He is her half brother."

"What! My God, woman, how could this happen!"

"You see, John Amos, Malcolm was in love with Alicia and he made her pregnant after Garland died, and he forced her to give Corinne to us. And then she went away. And no one ever knew I wasn't really Corinne's mother." I looked at the floor, my face filled with shame, too much shame to face John Amos.

"Rise up, woman," he commanded me. "For you know the depth of your sin—you have not so much sinned as been sinned against, and God has already sent down his sword to fell your husband. He shall do the same to his children, I assure you, He shall do the same. Now we must watch over Malcolm, Olivia, watch over his business dealings, take control of this heathen household and turn it to God again. Let us pray, Olivia. Our Father, who art in heaven . . ."

As though my confession brought hope back into Foxworth Hall, Malcolm's speech began improving. The doctor explained that although he might improve even more, he would never speak normally again. Because of the way his facial muscles had collapsed, he looked as though he wore a perpetual happy smile. In a strange, almost eerie way, that smile of distortion suggested the charm and handsomeness he had once enjoyed as a young man. It was as though a mask of his former self had been cast in ceramic and pressed onto his face forever.

When I felt charitable, I permitted him to be wheeled to his desk so he could look over the papers and the business dealings I had managed. At first I simply followed the regular order of things, studying Malcolm's work and making decisions in a like manner. But after a while, when I felt confident enough, I made decisions that were purely my own. I moved money around the stock market, changed procedures in some of the mills, bought and sold some real estate.

At first he was shocked by my independent activity. He demanded I return things to the way they had been, but I ignored those demands.

I had also provided a large annual salary for John Amos, transferring funds regularly to his personal accounts. Despite Malcolm's illness, it took him only moments to realize it. He held up the bank statement.

"Malcolm, you have to understand that things are not as they were. You should be grateful for what you have left considering all that you brought upon yourself. And you should be grateful that you have me and John Amos at your side. Could you imagine a woman like Alicia or even your daughter contending with all this? Would she be able to assume these business responsibilities? Would things be running as smoothly? Could she even set eyes on you in your deformed state?" I asked bitterly. "What she would do is run off with all your money; that's what," I added in a fury. I walked over to the desk and easily took the bank sheet out of his hands.

One day, almost two years after his stroke, Malcolm looked up from his wheelchair while I worked behind his desk. I had him wheeled into the library occasionally while I worked and read him some of the decisions I had made and some of the results. I knew he didn't want to be there, and he especially didn't want to hear of my actions; but it brought me some pleasure, so I had him wheeled in and excused his nurse.

This particular day, an early spring day, the sunlight

pouring through the window behind me and warming my back, I saw that Malcolm had a new expression on his face. It was a softer expression than usual. His eyes were gentle, the blue in them almost warm. I knew he was thinking of something that brought him good memories. I paused in my work and looked up expectantly.

"Olivia," he said. "I must know something; I must learn something. Please," he pleaded. "I know you have hard feelings for me, but be merciful enough to grant me this one request." I was reminded of the Malcolm who had first come to New London, the one who filled my heart with such hope and promise, the one who had walked with me along the ocean front and made me feel I could be cherished and loved like any other woman.

"What is this request?" I asked, sitting back in the seat. He leaned forward hopefully.

"Hire some detectives to find out what happened to Corinne and Christopher. Where have they gone? What are they doing? And . . . and . . ."

"And if they have had any deformed children?" I asked coldly. He nodded.

"Please," he begged, leaning as far forward as he could in his wheelchair.

So many nights I had lain awake thinking about Christopher and Corinne, trying to harden my heart against them, but in a small corner that perhaps even God didn't see, loving them still. "You told her she was dead that day she revealed her love for Christopher. Resurrecting her now will bring only pain and agony."

"I know, but I can't face the fact that I will go to my death not knowing the full extent of what . . . of what

I've begun. Please grant me this. I beseech you. I promise never to ask anything else of you, to make no demands, to sign over anything you want, whatever," he said. The tears rolled from his eyes, a symptom of his condition. He often cried at the slightest provocation, but the doctor told me he was often not aware of it himself.

To me he looked pitiful.

Suddenly, a feeling of utter defeat came over me as I looked at the broken, twisted man in the wheelchair. For the first time, I realized that something of mine had been damaged. Once I had had a strong, powerful husband, a man respected and feared in the community and business world. Despite what our relationship had been, I was still Olivia Foxworth, wife of Malcolm Foxworth, a leader of men. Now I had a pathetic invalid, merely a shadow of his former self.

In a real sense, Corinne and Christopher had done this to us. Where were they now? How well had they fared? Did the God who could wreak such havoc and vengeance upon the House of Foxworth follow them too?

"Very well," I said. "I will do so immediately."

"Oh, thank you, Olivia. God bless you."

"It's time for you to go back to your room and rest," I told him.

"Yes, yes. Whatever you say, Olivia." He turned about, making a pathetic effort to wheel himself away. I called for the nurse and she pushed him to his room. All the while he kept mumbling, "Thank you, Olivia. Thank you."

I sent for John Amos immediately.

"I want you to go into Charlottesville," I said as soon

as he came into the library, "and hire the best detectives you can find to trace the whereabouts of Corinne and Christopher. I want to know all about them, every little detail that can be discovered."

John scowled.

"What is the reason for this?" he asked. Then he saw the anger rise in my face. "Of course, if it's what you want."

"It's what I want," I said distinctly.

He nodded quickly. "I'll go immediately."

A little more than a month later, we received our first detailed report. John Amos brought the detective into the library. Malcolm was still in his room. I wasn't going to tell him anything until I learned it first myself.

The detective was a homely little man who looked more like a bank teller. Later I was to learn that that was an advantage for him. No one took any notice of him. His name was Cruthers and he had poor-fitting thick-lensed glasses that continually slipped down the bridge of his nose as he spoke. I was impatient with him, but I forced myself to listen.

"They live under the name of Dollanganger," he began. "That's why it took me a while to track them down."

"I'm not interested in the details of your struggle, Mr. Cruthers. Just give me the facts you have learned," I demanded sternly.

"Yes, Mrs. Foxworth. Christopher Dollanganger is working as a public relations executive for a large firm located in Gladstone, Pennsylvania. From what I could gather, he is very well liked," he added.

"Public relations?" I said.

"Of course, after you and Malcolm pulled out your

financial support of Christopher, he could not continue in medical school," John Amos said, and smiled. Cruthers stared at John.

"Go on with your report, Mr. Cruthers," I commanded.

"Mrs. Dollanganger is considered an attractive and good wife and mother."

"Mother?" I said quickly.

"They presently have a son, a boy almost two. The boy's name is Christopher."

"What have you learned about him?" I asked softly. My heart beating quickly in anticipation.

"A beautiful child," he said. "I saw him. Golden hair, blue eyes. Seemingly a bright boy."

"It can't be," I said. I sat back. "These are not the same people. Perhaps these two are a different Christopher and Corinne. Yes," I said, convinced of the possibility. "You've traced the wrong couple."

"Oh, but pardon me, Mrs. Foxworth, no. No, there's no doubt about who they are. I had pictures, don't forget. I've seen them both close up. They are your Christopher and Corinne."

"They are not mine," I insisted. He looked to John Amos and then stood there silently. "What else have you learned about them?" I asked.

"Well now, Mrs. Dollanganger is pregnant again," he said tentatively.

"Pregnant?" I looked to John Amos. There was a wry smile on his face again. He nodded. "This time the child will be different," I whispered.

"What's that, Mrs. Foxworth?" Cruthers asked.

"Nothing. I want you to stay with this and report here the day Mrs. Dollanganger gives birth. I want to know all about the new child. Do you understand?"

"Yes, I do, Mrs. Foxworth. I'll stay on it. She's due soon."

"Good," I said. "You shall receive a check in the mail tomorrow." I gestured for John Amos to show the detective out.

For a while I simply sat there digesting the information. Then I rose and started for Malcolm's door. I paused just before opening it.

No, I thought. Not yet. Not until we know about the new child.

19

The End of the Line

THE DAYS, THE MONTHS, THE YEARS PASSED, TRICKLING like grains of sand through an infinite hourglass. I found relief only in prayer and work. Cruthers had made two more appearances at Foxworth Hall, the first to announce the birth of a healthy girl named Cathy; the second, eight years later, to make an even more startling announcement—the birth of twins, a boy and a girl, once again healthy and perfect. It seemed Christopher and Corinne's family were all bright and beautiful; in fact, Mr. Cruthers reported, they were known in their town as the Dresden dolls, because of their beautiful blond hair, their blue eyes, their flawless complexions.

I never told Malcolm about Mr. Cruthers's visits. His stroke had aged him quickly, although he seemed to have reached a point from which he would degenerate no further.

Of course, his temperament changed. In the beginning, when he first had his stroke and his heart attack, there was still some fight left in him; he hadn't accepted his condition as permanent then. But when he sat in his wheelchair now, there wasn't that impatience, that stiff, demanding posture that revealed the battle continuing within him. The defiance that had once resided in his blue eyes gradually departed. His eyes dimmed like candles in the night, their once bright flames growing smaller and smaller as they lost the energy that had once fueled them.

And the shadows began to move in around him. Often I would find him content to sit in the darkest corner of his room or of the foyer. This man, who had once moved with such energy and power that he appeared to manufacture his own light, now sat draped in darkness. Slowly, with painstaking determination, the shadows of Foxworth Hall were claiming him.

Although his speech had improved to the point where he was easily understood by anyone, he began to refrain from conversation. His nurses, and he had nearly a dozen different ones over the years, learned to read his gestures and knew what he wanted when he waved his hand or jerked his head. The only times his voice rose was when he joined John Amos and me in our daily prayers.

I knew that his effort to survive and bear the pain and indignity of age and sickness came from his great desire to see and believe in his own redemption. We asked God to make good use of us, and we pleaded for His forgiveness.

I moved back and forth from the religious world to the business world, each time fully submerging myself in the work and the demands each required, for as long as I was occupied, I was comfortable and secure. I grew to despise those quiet moments when I was afforded some relaxation. Relaxation meant confronting my memories. Those memories hovered about me, buzzing in the back of my mind like a circle of mad insects, looking for an opportunity to pierce my fortress of relative peace. Old voices echoed; shadows and ghosts slipped along corridors, resurrected by the sight of one of Mal's or Joel's old toys, of the piano, now forever silenced in the parlor, of Corinne's old room.

I tried to avoid whole sections of the house, staying away from the north wing. I kept the door to the Swan Room closed and I kept the door to Malcolm's trophy room closed. I had pieces of furniture, trunks, pictures, and articles of clothing taken up to the attic. I did all that I could to hold back the past, to dam it up behind a protective wall of distance and time; but it had its ways of slipping through.

Memories and time took their toll on me as well. Once again my life was painted gray, as it had been before I came to Foxworth Hall, as I had feared it always would be. But I no longer feared gray, I had become one with it. It was the only color I wore, it was the color of my hair, the color of my eyes, the color of my hopes, the color of my life.

This was who I was; this was who I had become. Prayer and work had hardened me until I was a statue of myself. But I was convinced that this was what God wanted; this was what God had designed.

A letter, a pink, perfumed letter, changed all that. One afternoon, as I was sorting through my mail, I came upon a pale rose envelope so startling among the white formal business letters. It was addressed to Mr. and Mrs. Malcolm Neal Foxworth. I recognized the handwriting immediately. It still had the girlish swirls, but now the letters were oddly shaky. I sat for minutes, staring at the unopened envelope. What could Corinne want from us now? Hadn't she done enough? And yet, and yet my heart jumped for joy when I recognized that girlish handwriting. How I missed the life and love she had brought to Foxworth Hall. The only warmth in my life had fled along with Corinne and Christopher. Did she miss us as much as we missed her? I had to find out. With trembling fingers I opened the envelope.

In my hand the letter felt as soft and warm as if it were made of her very flesh. My own pounding pulse drummed through my veins until I felt it at the tips of my fingers. As I began to read, I heard her voice and saw her blue eyes pleading.

Dear Father and Mother,

I know how strange it must be for you to receive a letter from me after all these years. Unfortunately, the first letter I write to you must be one filled with tragic news. My Christopher, our Christopher, beautiful, gentle Christopher, who I know you loved despite everything, is dead.

Yes, dead. He was killed by a drunken driver. And on his thirty-fifth birthday!

But there is good news too. We have been blessed with four beautiful children, all with golden hair and blue eyes, with wonderfully perfect features, bright and lovely children, children you would be proud to call your grandchildren. We have a son, Christopher, fourteen; a daughter, Cathy, twelve; and twins, Cory and Carrie, four. How Christopher loved them so, and how they loved him.

And Christopher was doing so well. He couldn't go on to become a doctor. It was a terrible sacrifice, but one he was willing to make in the name of love. It was painful to watch him put aside his medical studies and take up another profession so that we could live and raise our family in comfort and security. But I blame no one, no one; and neither did he. He never stopped loving you and talking about all that you did for him. You must believe I am saying that because it is true. Please, please, believe me. You surely remember him and how he was and know that he would be that way even to the day he died.

I am writing to you now because Christopher's death has left us on the verge of destitution. I am selling everything of value just to keep us alive, fed, and clothed. I know that it was my own fault that I was never serious enough to develop any skills which could be put to practical use now. I take full responsibility for that. Mother certainly provided me with enough of a model, but I could never hope to have her strength and fortitude.

I beg you now to consider our plight and look upon us with forgiving eyes. I know much has to be done to win back your love, but I am willing to do anything, anything, to win that love back. Please think about permitting us to return to Foxworth Hall so that my children can grow up knowing the good things and the happy things. Please rescue us.

I promise we will be perfect; we will obey your every command. My children are well-mannered and intelligent and will understand anything that is required of them. We ask only for the chance to try.

Please have mercy on us and remind yourselves that my children are Foxworths, even though we thought it best to take on the name Dollanganger, a Foxworth ancestor.

I wait eagerly for your reply. I am a woman broken and lost and terribly afraid.

Love,
Corinne

There actually were teardrops at the bottom of the sheet. I didn't know if they were mine or hers. Christopher dead! No matter how much I felt they had been wrong, that their love was sinful, I never would have wished this upon them. God, indeed, was vengeful. I tried to stand, but the room seemed to be whirling around me, shadows and ghosts weaving in and out, their terrible maws laughing, mocking me. What had I done? What had I done? Had God misunderstood my prayers? I couldn't bear to think that. There had to be some other explanation. My mind frantically searched until it found John Amos. He would know, he would know what to do.

"God has delivered a message," he intoned, crumpling the delicate pink letter in his bony hand.

"A message, John Amos? What kind of a god would do this to Christopher?"

"A god who abhors sin. And it was you, Olivia, who confessed how vile the sin actually was. God is restoring order to His universe. And He has now presented you with an opportunity to help Him. Those children are the devil's spawn, born of an unholy union abominable in the eyes of God."

"What do you mean, John Amos? What does God expect of me now?"

He gazed heavenward, as if silently communicating with the Lord. His arms stretched out. He seemed to embrace an invisible power. Then, clenching his hands into fists, he grasped that power and struck his chest. "Let Corinne and her children come," he declared. "But hide those children away from the world forever. End the lineage of sin now. Do not let them remain in the world to infect others."

I left John Amos and spent the rest of the day alone in my room, praying to God for guidance. For though I understood John Amos's interpretation, I could not accept it. God forgive me, I still loved Corinne; but what had she done to me? She had forced me to become the captor of her children. She had forced me to be a vengeful instrument of the Lord. Forced me to be that cold gray woman I so longed not to be. I wanted to be a grandmother, I wanted children to love and dote on, who would look up to me with love in their eyes. And what had she presented me with? The devil's spawn. Now every time their faces gazed into mine, I would see the devil; every time their hands touched me, I would be touched by the devil; every time their voices called me, I would be called by the devil. I envisioned their sweet faces, their silky blond hair, their bright blue eyes. Oh, I would have to steel myself not to love them. For the devil always favored those he sent to do his work with charms and beguilements. I would have to turn myself into a gray stone fortress lest those charms pierce my heart and claim me for the devil's work.

That night, the last drops of love drained from my heart, and I became only the instrument of the Lord. I dreamt that night of a dollhouse, a dollhouse filled with such sin that it emanated its own hellfires. The voice of God spoke to me. Olivia, it boomed, I have put you on earth to end that fire. I poured water over that fire, but still it burned. I tried to blow out that fire with my own breath, but it still burned. Then I built a glass enclosure around it, and slowly, slowly that fire was stifled until it was burning only embers.

The next morning I resolved to carry out John Amos's plan. I knew then and there I must confront Malcolm. He was sitting in his wheelchair gazing out the parlor window at the bright summer flowers that mocked the perpetual winter that lived in Foxworth Hall.

"Corinne is coming home," I announced.

"Corinne?" he whispered. "Corinne?"

"Yes, Malcolm, yesterday I received a letter from her. Christopher was killed in a car accident, and Corinne begged us to take her back. And we shall." I had struggled many hours with the decision about what to tell Malcolm, and had decided that he must never know of the existence of Corinne's children. Malcolm loved Corinne so, as he had loved his mother before her, as he had loved Alicia, I knew that once he knew there were children, especially girls, his heart would be captured once again. No, I must take matters into my own hands this time; John Amos was the only one whom I could trust. It would be easy to hide the children from Malcolm. I would hide them in the north wing, just as he had hidden Alicia, their true grandmother. He was so frail, and I knew he would be so taken with Corinne's return, he'd never suspect anything.

"I am going to go now and write Corinne a letter, welcoming her back to Foxworth Hall."

Malcolm still had not turned his face from the window. I walked over and rested a hand on his thin, stooped shoulder. I felt him trembling, and peered around to see the tears coursing down his cheeks.

Dear Corinne,

You are welcome to return to Foxworth Hall. However, I have not shown your father your letter. If he knew you had children with Christopher, nothing, nothing would persuade him to take you back. With the help of John Amos, he has found in the Lord a refuge from his pain, and he could never accept children born of an unholy, incestuous union.

You don't know that your father suffered a severe stroke and heart attack on the day you left. Your actions reduced this strong and vibrant man to a frail shell of his former self.

However, I have considered your plight, and prayed for guidance. This is my decision: You may bring your children to Foxworth Hall, but your father must never know of their existence. The doctors tell me Malcolm does not have much longer to live. Until the Lord calls him to His bosom, your children will stay up in the north wing, shut away from his view and his knowledge. I will see to it that they are clothed and fed.

I will expect you to redeem yourself and try to make compensation for the pain you have caused me and your father.

You must understand that it is up to you to prepare your children, and to make certain they remain hidden and under control. If they are disobedient, or in any way reveal themselves, you will have to leave Foxworth Hall as penniless as you arrived.

Inform me immediately of your decision.

Trusting in God,
Your Mother

20

Eyes That See

ON A NIGHT MUCH LIKE THE NIGHT WHEN I FIRST ARRIVED at Foxworth Hall years and years ago, they came. I had instructed Corinne to take the late train, so her arrival would be cloaked under darkness. It would be three o'clock in the morning when the train pulled into the empty depot, which stood alone by the railroad tracks, a solitary platform in the black night. I was sure that her sleepy brood of four children would think that they had been left far from civilization, surrounded only by fields and meadows and the dark purple mountains hovering against the horizon like lurking giants of the night.

I would not send a car for them. Even though it was a long walk from the depot, I could not take the chance of having anyone, servant or outsider, know of the existence of Corinne's children. They would stumble along the dark, deserted road. Every tree, every shadow, every sound, would frighten them. Their hearts would beat in dread.

Suddenly Foxworth Hall would loom before them, like a witch's castle in the fairy tales their mother surely would have read them. Its dark windows would look like dead eyes and its enormous roof like an ink stain against the sky. There would be nothing inviting in its appearance. All of them would gaze up at it, silent with their own fears, their little hearts pounding.

I wanted to be alone when Corinne and her children arrived. I wanted them to see no one but me. This was my moment, and I insisted, despite my obedience to John Amos's plans and despite his protests, that he retire to his room for the evening.

I had put Malcolm to bed around ten o'clock.

"Please, Olivia," he'd begged. "I know this is the night Corinne is coming, and I'd like to be up to welcome her."

Love shone in his eyes, and I could see that in all these years his doting on Corinne had not died. Oh, yes, I was right not to have told him of the existence of the children. He would have fallen under their spell, as he always fell under the spell of beauty.

"Malcolm, Corinne will certainly be exhausted when she arrives. And if you stay up so late, so will you. This way, you will be well rested and be able to greet her in the morning with full enthusiasm."

Now the only thing left for me to do was wait. I had already prepared the room in the north wing for their arrival. I had cleaned and dusted and moved the two double beds myself, for I couldn't allow a servant to suspect even a breath of my plan. As I'd moved the beds around, I came upon Alicia's hairbrush, still filled with strands of hair. Over the years the fine golden strands had matted into a dusty, musty web. I set the brush on the bureau without removing a single thread. Now Alicia's grandchildren would live here, just as she had. And I knew, just knew, that her granddaughters would use that brush. Oh, yes, they'd be the sort who made sure to brush their hair one hundred, or even five hundred strokes a day.

I awaited their arrival for hours, pacing the long, dark corridors of Foxworth Hall. From time to time I would go to the window next to the servants' entrance and gaze out into the night. A light snow had begun to fall. As I was pacing back and forth, back and forth, suddenly I heard a branch snap, and I ran again to the window. There they were, like thieves in the night, four bundled children and their cloaked mother. I opened the door and motioned them inside. Without a word I herded them all up the steep and narrow back staircase. Corinne knew she was forbidden to speak. She knew that one whisper, one clumsy move, would reverberate through the long, empty halls of her childhood home and alert the servants.

I led them directly to the far room in the north wing. I yanked open the door and nudged them into the room, like a gentle jailer might usher a condemned man into his last cell. When they were all inside, I quietly shut the door.

Then I turned on the lamp. Before me were four beautiful children. The boy, almost a man, was an exact replica of Christopher, the same blond hair, the same blue eyes, the same sweet, intelligent expression on his face. Oh, how I longed to embrace him. But I held back, reminding myself of all I knew, of all that had transpired. The girl was the spit and image of her mother at that age, and a flood of memories threatened to engulf me and drown my hard resolve. I quickly looked away from her and examined the twins. Two cherubs stared up at me with big, frightened blue eyes. As I stared down at them, they moved closer to each other, as if trying to merge into one being.

"Just as you said, Corinne, your children are beautiful. But," I added, "are you sure they are intelligent? Do they have some invisible afflictions not apparent to the eyes?"

"None," Corinne cried. "My children are perfect, as you can plainly see, physically and mentally!"

She glared at me and began to undress the girl twin, who was nodding at her feet. Cooperatively, the older girl began to undress the boy twin as Christopher's lookalike lifted one of the big suitcases onto the bed. He opened it and took out two pairs of small yellow pajamas with feet.

Corinne lifted the twins into one of the beds and pressed kisses on their flushed cheeks, her hand trembling as she brushed back the curls that graced their foreheads, and pulled the covers up to their chins. "Good night, my darlings," she whispered.

I could not believe that their mother was going to allow two teenagers of the opposite sex, to share the other bed. Oh, how quickly all John Amos had predicted was being revealed! I scowled at Corinne. "Your two older children cannot sleep in one bed."

She looked surprised. "They're only children," she flared at me. "Mother, you haven't changed one bit, have you? You still have a nasty, suspicious mind! Christopher and Cathy are innocent."

"Innocent?" I snapped back. "That is exactly what your father and I always presumed about you and your half uncle!"

Corinne blanched. "If you think like that, then give

them separate rooms and separate beds! Lord knows this house has enough of them!"

"That is impossible," I said as icily as I could. "This is the only bedroom with its own adjoining bath, and where my husband won't hear them walking overhead, or flushing the toilet. If they are separated, and scattered about all over upstairs, he will hear their voices, or their noise, or the servants will. Now, I have given this arrangement a great deal of thought. This is the only safe room. Put the two girls in one bed, and the two boys in the other," I commanded.

Corinne refused to look at me, but slumped over to the bed and carried the boy twin to the empty bed. The two older children glared at me as I continued to lay down the rules they were to abide by in this room.

After I finished, Corinne drew the two other children to her. Her hands stroked their hair and backs. "It's all right," I heard her whisper. "Trust me." Then she turned to me for an instant and her face twisted with the most ferocious look I had ever seen on her. "Mother, have some pity and compassion for my children. They are your flesh and blood too. Keep that in your mind." As she continued to list their virtues and accomplishments, I closed my ears. For they were not of my flesh and blood, nor was she. And much as I had loved her, for the sake of my eternal soul I could no longer afford to do so. I was tempted by her pleas, by her children's sweetness, but I hardened my heart.

When Corinne saw that her words were not succeeding in softening my resolve, she turned back to her children and bid them good night.

I waited at the door as Corinne slowly parted from her children. Finally I pulled her arm, and just before I closed the door behind us, I looked back at the children. The twins were sound asleep. The two older ones stood side by side, the boy holding the girl's hand, just as Christopher had held Corinne's. I saw him look into her eyes, and saw him smile, a smile that sent a cold chill up my spine. For it was a smile I had seen before, it was the smile of Christopher for Corinne, the smile I had been too blind to see. But now my eyes were opened.

I locked the door behind me.

From bestselling author
V.C. Andrews,
comes the second book
in the exciting *Logan* series.

V.C. ANDREWS®

Heart Song

COMING MID-MAY 1997
FROM POCKET STAR BOOKS

1253

The Phenomenal
V.C. ANDREWS®

- ☐ FLOWERS IN THE ATTIC.....72941-1/$6.99
- ☐ PETALS ON THE WIND.....72947-0/$6.99
- ☐ IF THERE BE THORNS.....72945-4/$6.99
- ☐ MY SWEET AUDRINA.....72946-2/$6.99
- ☐ SEEDS OF YESTERDAY.....72948-9/$6.99
- ☐ HEAVEN.....72944-6/$6.99
- ☐ DARK ANGEL.....72939-X/$6.99
- ☐ GARDEN OF SHADOWS.....72942-X/$6.99
- ☐ FALLEN HEARTS.....72940-3/$6.99
- ☐ GATES OF PARADISE.....72943-8/$6.99
- ☐ WEB OF DREAMS.....72949-7/$6.99
- ☐ DAWN.....67068-9/$6.99
- ☐ SECRETS OF THE MORNING.....69512-6/$6.99
- ☐ TWILIGHT'S CHILD.....69514-2/$6.99
- ☐ MIDNIGHT WHISPERS.....69516-9/$6.99
- ☐ DARKEST HOUR.....75932-9/$6.99
- ☐ RUBY.....75934-5/$6.99
- ☐ PEARL IN THE MIST.....75936-1/$6.99
- ☐ ALL THAT GLITTERS.....87319-9/$6.99
- ☐ HIDDEN JEWEL.....87320-2/$6.99
- ☐ TARNISHED GOLD.....87321-0/$6.99
- ☐ MELODY.....53471-8/$7.50

And Look For **Heart Song**
Coming in mid-May 1997

Simon & Schuster Mail Order
200 Old Tappan Rd., Old Tappan, N.J. 07675
Please send me the books I have checked above. I am enclosing $_____(please add $0.75 to cover the postage and handling for each order. Please add appropriate sales tax). Send check or money order–no cash or C.O.D.'s please. Allow up to six weeks for delivery. For purchase over $10.00 you may use VISA: card number, expiration date and customer signature must be included.

Name ____________________
Address ____________________
City ____________________ State/Zip __________
VISA Card # ____________________ Exp.Date __________
Signature ____________________ 752-19

From bestselling author V.C. Andrews,
comes the first book in the exciting
new *Logan* series.

V.C. ANDREWS®

Melody

Melody is the story of a West Virginian girl abandoned with her estranged family in Cape Cod after the death of her father. There she discovers the truth behind the lies and secrets of the Logan family.

Available from Pocket Star Books

1200-01

The Eagerly Awaited Prequel to the Captivating Landry Series!

V.C. ANDREWS®

Her high school graduation just days away, Gabriel is blissfully happy, despite the ever-widening rift between her Mama and her conniving, whiskey-drinking Daddy. Then rich cannery owner Octavious Tate surprises her near a secluded pond and shatters her sweet innocence, forever...

Tarnished Gold

Available from Pocket Books

1172-01